CIVIC CENTER

ALSO BY DENNIS MCFARLAND

Letter from Point Clear
Prince Edward
Singing Boy
A Face at the Window
School for the Blind
The Music Room

NOSTALGIA

NOSTALGIA

Dennis McFarland

PANTHEON BOOKS   NEW YORK

Copyright © 2013 by Dennis McFarland

All rights reserved. Published in the United States by Pantheon Books, a division of Random House, Inc., New York, and in Canada by Random House of Canada Limited, Toronto.

Pantheon Books and colophon are registered trademarks of Random House, Inc.

Library of Congress Cataloging-in-Publication Data
McFarland, Dennis.
Nostalgia / Dennis McFarland.
    pages cm
  ISBN 978-0-307-90834-6
  1. Soldiers—Fiction. 2. Disabled veterans—Fiction. 3. United States—History—Civil War, 1861–1865—Fiction. I. Title.
    PS3563.C3629N67 2013   813'.54—dc23   2013003361

www.pantheonbooks.com

Jacket art: Civil War lithograph by Kurz & Allison (detail).
Everett Collection / SuperStock
Jacket design by Peter Mendelsund

Printed in the United States of America
First Edition
2 4 6 8 9 7 5 3 1

For M., K., & S., with love & gratitude

from Ancient Greek νοσταλγία (*nostalgia*),

from νόστος (*nostos*, return home) + ἄλγος (*algos*, pain)

NOSTALGIA

The Dream of the Forest

S|ummerfield Hayes—erstwhile private in the Fortieth New York Volunteers, Army of the Potomac—rests alongside a silent muddy creek and resolves not to fall asleep. Injured; abandoned in the Wilderness, left to dodge snipers and stragglers from both sides of the contest; forsaken to the unlikely prospect of outlasting the ruin of his shrapnel wounds and the slow-falling curtain of starvation and exposure—he knows himself lost in every sense of the word, adrift in body and mind. He wonders if his lifelong urge to run, the itch of a trapped animal, has in this flight been fulfilled at last. He looks up for a moment at the stone arch of a bridge that spans the creek; he closes his eyes and studies its afterimage on the back of his eyelids, a graceful curve, silver against dark red. He touches the crown of his head, a dull soreness there and a patch of caked blood. He moves his fingers to his forehead and a lump beneath the skin above his right eye, a boyhood scar that makes him recall his life at home with his sister. No breeze stirs the trees, the stillness of the forest alien, collusive. The pain in his leg and spine grows sharp, which conjures his mother's face, more nightmarish than comforting, pressed against glass, underwater. He diverts his mind the only way he knows how: some limping drive to survive has managed to find the sole scrap of peace within him—a dot on his map of horrors, a memory, a day some few weeks ago in April, an afternoon of sunshine, a ball game.

He'd joined the Fortieth (known as the Mozart Regiment) early in 1864, when the regiment was on furlough in New York, and—along with more than a hundred new recruits—returned with them in February to the army's winter quarters near Brandy Station. Yet another spring was approaching, and the great general who aimed to deliver at last a victory to Mr. Lincoln had decided to wait out the rains before pushing forward. A handful of men in Hayes's new company, those who read newspapers and had heard Hayes's name before, were soon after him to marshal for them a regimental nine. The regiment's many New Yorkers fancied themselves not only best suited but also morally obligated to bring some gravity to the loose infantile pottering that had previously transpired—raucous ragtag bouts of town ball, amalgams of Knickerbockers this and Massachusetts that, even the occasional one-a-cat. Boredom raged through the camp like a fever; with each passing day, engaging the enemy felt more abstract and elusive; sick to death of rain, mildew, mud, and diarrhea, the soldiers meant to fill the time with something new and better, lift their spirits, and, once a team was established, extend a challenge to the other regiments in the brigade. Hayes suggested that the way to start was to arrange a match within the regiment—he proposed bachelors versus married men—from which the best nine would be culled, deriving a second nine in reserve. Somebody approached the sergeant, who approached the lieutenant, who approached the captain, who approached (with beer, it was rumored) the colonel. The colonel granted permission for the match so long as two conditions were met: all fatigue duty should be carried out regularly and impeccably before, during, and after said match; and he, the colonel, should serve as umpire, with all the attending conventional courtesies (more beer, it was understood).

Hayes knew himself to be lucky, observing that other fresh fish like himself had received no particular welcome of any kind at Brandy Station—save the daily misery of drilling in the muck, sleeping in the cold, and the ubiquitous threat of contagion—and many were received with suspicion, as unfit substitutes or bounty jumpers. He was especially glad to have been procured for the special purpose of getting up a match and overseeing practices, because his sister Sarah's letters from Hicks Street lacked any grasp of the course he'd chosen. Why, she wanted to know, repeatedly, had he found it compulsory to forsake her; forsake his mates at his club, who'd so generously embraced and promoted him; forsake his plans for school, when his name had never been drawn in any draft lottery? And what was to become of her, with Summerfield her only living family this side of the Atlantic, should, God forbid, he not return? Did he not think it a sufficient loss, in the span of only a few years, their having been orphaned?

These were harder questions—or at least required longer, more thoughtful answers—than those of the infantry boys in Virginia, who wanted to know how the Eckford Club of Brooklyn had fared last season (a reduced number of games, only ten, but all wins, and the championship for the second year in a row). And had Hayes ever the chance to know the great Jim Creighton, inventor of the sinister speedball and dew-drop? (Tempted to lie, Hayes told the truth: he knew somebody who'd known Creighton.)

A sad story, somebody said, that Creighton boy, dying so young.

Tragic, said another. The boy's heart stopped for no clear reason.

Ironic, said a third, dying young like that without ever setting foot on a battlefield.

The soldiers, many of whom had survived against great odds, and who'd shown valor at Kelly's Ford and Mine Run, proved diffident when it came to volunteering for a legitimate base ball team. But of course everyone already knew who the best players were, and all that was needed was some legitimate nominating, followed by a bit of legitimate coaxing. The chaplain, a sanguine bespectacled fellow from Yonkers, manufactured five very fine, if lively, base balls by cutting strips of rubber from old overshoes, boiling the strips till they grew gummy and could be formed into small spheres, then wrapping these with yarn and covering them with horsehide. Soldiers whittled a number of bats from a variety of woods and in a variety of lengths and shapes. They found no entirely suitable plot of ground, though the patch they settled on was acceptable but for an alarming downward dip in the center field. The seat of a wooden chair, with legs and back removed, was employed as the home base, and haversacks, filled with sawdust, served as the three others. The practices comprised as much argument as they did physical exercise, and Hayes, young, new, and untested in battle, found himself at the awkward post of arbiter. Some insisted that certain foul flies, judging how far afield they landed, must surely be ruled as outs. Others complained about the dubious delivery of the opposing pitcher. Base runners failed to touch bases, or not. And some of the more senior members (mostly from the married nine, who elected to call themselves the Twighoppers) had to be cured of the old habit of soaking, for they'd played town ball growing up and still very much relished plunking a runner with the ball. A hulking teamster from Bushwick, named Vesey, who could wallop just about anything tossed his way, claimed exemption during practices from having to run round the bases when he'd obviously launched a crusher.

The appointed day of the match started dark and rainy, causing among some men grumbling, among others a dejected silence. But as if heaven meant to offer a small solace in a world of mangling and unnatural death, the skies cleared a half-hour before match time. Birdsong and the awakened scents of the forest charged the air. Since the army had recently begun sending officers' furniture to the rear (apparently headquarters was at least *contemplating* battle), it took some effort to secure for the colonel a lolling chair; once found, the chair was placed near the home base, where the colonel, in a fine mood and freshly groomed in his frock coat, situated himself with a lap desk and a pipe. First he assigned one of the sleepy drummers the task of keeping Banjo, Company D's stray foxhound, off the field of play. Then he presided over the toss of a coin, which determined that the Bachelors should go first to the bat. Vesey—who'd insisted on going first in the order and who wielded a great pudding stirrer of an instrument nearly four feet long—swung at the first ball, missed, glared at the Twighoppers' pitcher, and the match was under way. Vesey swung at the second ball and missed, likewise the third, and, quick as that, went out on strikes. Amid a mix of applause, cheers, and laughter, he returned head down to his mates, pausing briefly to draw his forearm over his whiskers.

Hayes, kneeling nearby in the dirt and sunshine, watched him, a large and able competitor, utterly surprised by defeat. The big man's trousers, altogether too tight on him, fell short around his ankles, too short even to blouse inside his socks, and Hayes smiled, his heart full of a warmth he might have called love of the game.

Shyness had prevented him from making it known, but this April afternoon was Hayes's birthday. He'd turned nineteen years.

BENEATH THE BRIDGE, he has fallen asleep despite his resolve, but not for long, never for long. The noise of his dreaming, as usual, awakens him, and as usual, he begins to tear at his clothes in an effort to expose his injuries. Soon he is naked, his trousers crumpled at his ankles, and he twists round and contorts, trying to explore with his hands the two wounds, one high in the middle of his back, the other along the back of his left thigh—each the bad work of shrapnel. He can achieve no position that allows him to see the wounds, though they recurrently burn like the heat of a hundred needles and sometimes soak his clothes with blood. If he could only see them, he might breathe easier, confirming by sight they're not mortal. He draws back on his trousers and shirt but leaves off with any buttons or buckles, for his hands have started again to shake, violently, the most irksome of his strange physical alterations.

His hearing has returned almost fully, though the fierce ringing in his ears remains. A high-pitched sizzling whir, it revives in him a sickening regret and sometimes vibrates his skull. He has noticed a soreness at the crown of his head, and when he touches the spot, he feels what's left there of a scab; he has no recollection of what caused this particular injury, but thankfully it appears to be healing.

When he is able to sleep, he most often has the old dream-come-true, which he first had about a week before the brigades began to cross the Rapidan: he'd startled awake in his tent one warm night near the end of April, crying out and rousing his bunkmate, Leggett, for in the dream his comrades had abandoned him on the battlefield. Now when the nightmare comes, it comes with the mechanics of memory, and he generally continues to doze till he is awakened by the popping dream-din of musketry, the gut-thunder of artillery, or, by far the worst, the grim fire-yelps of men dying. For a few seconds, the scent of gunpowder lingers in his nostrils, or the sweet coppery stench of charred flesh, and he begins again to tear at his clothes.

He rests in rocky soil beneath a bridge; this much he knows. The stone arch overhead spans a creek of about twenty paces in width. He doesn't know the name of the creek. From the sunlight that slides through the pines on the opposite bank and agitates on the brown water, he judges the time of day to be around six in the evening. Regarding his whereabouts, he knows only that he is most likely somewhere between Culpeper and Washington City. In his bread bag are some leftover rations—two worm castles, some sugar and pickled cabbage, the stub of a candle, and a strip of dry lucifers; in his knapsack, the book sent to him by his sister, her letters, his Christian Commission Testament, and a varnished, inscribed base ball. He figures he has averaged eight to ten miles a day, slipping footsore along streams, crouching through woods and fields, venturing onto roads only after dark. Though he has done no wrong, he must play the fugitive; though he himself was the one deserted, he is certain to be taken for a deserter and has no paper to prove otherwise. Even if he were to try joining another regiment, he might be arrested, perhaps quickly tried and executed. He has heard that the streets of Washington teem with soldiers of every stripe and condition, and he thinks that there he might escape scrutiny while he arranges, somehow, a return to Brooklyn.

His bunkmate, Truman Leggett—a garrulous and morbid man of thirty who possessed the minimum number of teeth necessary to pass the army's physical examination—was keen on telling terrible stories. Around a campfire, Leggett would recount how he'd once come to the rescue of a neighbor woman whose house cat had crawled into a wall and given birth to kittens. The mother cat had abandoned the kittens, which cried at all hours of the night. Leggett took down some molding boards to gain access to the litter, and when he reached into an unseen cranny of the wall to remove the kittens, what he withdrew was a wretched furry thing with five heads, twelve legs, and a single tail, five kittens fused by nature into one grotesque beast. "Like something out of a Greek myth," said Leggett, wide-eyed in the firelight. "Had to put the poor thing out of its misery." Then he reported in careful detail his slaying of the kittens, his crushing one head at a time with a mallet. Another of his favorites was an account of a deserter's execution, which he'd witnessed in a different regiment earlier in the war. This tale he could draw out at great length, and Hayes observed that Leggett generally added an item or two with each retelling. The deserter, brought to the place of his death in an open wagon, followed behind another cart that bore his coffin. The troops, assembled to witness the execution, watched in silence as the gloomy cortege passed— musicians and clergymen, as well as the twelve soldiers who composed the firing party. Whatever shape the man's desertion had taken—an unchecked impulse to go home, Leggett said—he was clearly sorry for it and begged the forgiveness of the troops and Almighty God. The captain covered the man's eyes with a handkerchief, and the firing party took its position six paces away. The deserter, suddenly too weak to stand, sat down on the coffin. The order was given to fire. "They shot him clear to pieces," said Leggett. "He perched for a spell without moving there on the edge of the box, then he quaked a little and slid to the ground." Unfortunately, the poor fellow was still alive, and reserves had to be summoned to finish the job. Afterward, the troops were required to file by the bloody corpse and take a good long look. Leggett supplied a vivid description of the man's several wounds, with special attention given the shots that penetrated his face and brain.

Now as the sun sets behind the trees, and the woods and the water grow slowly darker, Hayes recalls Leggett's explaining how the firing party's arms were prepared—one of them contained a blank cartridge, so that afterward no soldier could say without a doubt that he had fired the shot that killed the man. And he recalls Leggett saying of the deserter, "I never in my lifetime saw a man more forlorn."

He resolves to sleep a bit more and then use the darkness for making tracks. He takes a few bites of hardtack from his haversack and a swig from his canteen. Like his less material but boundless remorse—and like the sure belief that everywhere and always he is being watched—hunger has become a constant companion. It is a modest hollow spasm in his stomach, never sated, only soothed, and he has learned not to mind it, this signal that not all his organs have failed. As he closes his eyes, he hears a faint boom and roll of artillery, a sound he has heard off and on throughout his flight, but now, as each time before, he's unable to determine whether this deep rumble occurs in the real distant fields and woods of Virginia or only inside his head.

Forlorn is the word that ushers him back to sleep. This time he does not dream of his comrades deserting him in the Wilderness but of his sister, who stands turned away from him as he fastens the covered button on her lace collar; he can barely hear the whisper of her breathing, barely smell the minty scent of her hair. When he awakens next, someone has built a fire near his feet. He is drenched with sweat, and as he pulls on the sleeve of his shirt to wipe his face, no less a figure than Brigadier General J. H. Hobart Ward, commander of Hayes's brigade, limps heavily into the orange glow, red-eyed and stinking of bourbon. He nods sadly and looks down at Hayes with compassion. "Was it the tree limbs, son?" he asks, stroking his droopy mustache. "Is that what did you in?" Hayes is as moved by the general's wordplay as by his show of empathy, but before he can reply, he awakens again—this time truly—into absolute silence and bathed in the light of a clear half-moon. He raises himself up and watches for a moment the creek, sable and gleaming now, coursing eerily by without so much as a tinkle. Stars nestle cold and sharp in the black boughs overhead. In the woods at his back, crickets chirp, and there is the odd anonymous click of movement among last years' fallen leaves and twigs. He quickly shifts a few feet to one side, into the dark shadow cast by the bridge, for the feeling that he is stalked, observed by unseen eyes, sends a chill up his spine. He thinks how he would welcome the once-vexing clamor of a city now, the clanging of horsecars, the blasts of ferry whistles. Soon a rustling in the woods, small but menacing, seems to be edging toward him, and he draws his only weapon, a bowie knife that belonged to Billy Swift, the Bachelors' half-pint second baseman. He swivels on his haunches and waits, ready to face the bloodsucker that means to collect thirty dollars for collaring a deserter.

A stirring in the dry leaves, then only silence.

After a long while, he stretches out again on the dirt, knife in hand, and drifts yet again to sleep. When he opens his eyes, perhaps only a minute later, he thinks he must be dreaming, for staring back at him an arm's length away, stands a red chicken. He tries to speak to it—his lips form the words *Well, hello, cock-a-doodle-doo*—but no actual sound emerges. Still, as if the chicken has heard, it blinks its yellow eyes in the moonlight, shudders, and walks right up to him, offering itself for his continued survival.

IN THE SPRING OF 1861, little more than a week before the first shots were fired at Fort Sumter, Hayes's mother and father perished in an extraordinary accident far away from home, during a visit to Ireland. Some weeks earlier, they'd sailed on a steamer from New York to Queenstown and then trained up to Dublin to visit Mr. Hayes's only living relation, his mother's unmarried sister, Margaret. Two days before they were to leave Dublin and start their journey back to America, they were riding in an omnibus that stopped to discharge a passenger on a considerable incline, next to a bridge and alongside a canal. When the omnibus began to slide backward down the incline, the driver lost control of the horses, and in a matter of seconds the thing had crashed through a wooden railing and fallen, horses and all, into the lock chamber of the canal. All ten passengers, trapped inside the omnibus, drowned. The Hayeses had planned to be away no more than six weeks and meant to be back on Hicks Street in time for Summerfield's sixteenth birthday in April. Because of the events at Fort Sumter, news of the tragic accident in Dublin arrived in Brooklyn amid what the local papers were calling "war excitement."

Now, near dawn, when Hayes's wounds pain him most severely—always, mysteriously, the two of them in concert—his mother's face rises up in his mind, flanked by her pale, white hands, pressed watery and wavering against the window of the omnibus. He imagines that as she clawed the glass her thoughts flew to him and Sarah. She'd not wished to leave home with war looming, but Mr. Hayes had prevailed, taking a view similar to some of the rebels themselves, that no war of any significance was on the horizon. He'd heard that the former senator from South Carolina had vowed in the rebel congress to drink all the blood that might result from secession. It was very like Mr. Hayes to be wrong and even to cite foolish supporters for his arguments. It was also like him to prevail upon Mrs. Hayes in any number of ways that went against her own wishes. It was *not* like him—in taking the view he did of the impending war—to be optimistic. Summerfield understood, even at his young age, that this departure in his father's usual outlook was a convenience and born of a definite pessimism concerning things in Dublin: Mr. Hayes declared that if they did not make the journey, Aunt Maggie might die, and he would forever regret not having seen her. Aunt Maggie was not ill. She enjoyed a reputation for being strong as an ox. But of course it was inarguable that she might die, for anyone might. The real outcome of the journey, his own death along with that of the mother of his children, surpassed even Mr. Hayes's gloomy expectations. Sarah, eighteen years old at the time, was devastated and blamed their father for the tragedy, then, and even to this day.

"He forced Mommy to go," she'd said to Summerfield one warm afternoon in May, in the parlor at Hicks Street. Summerfield had been out playing ball after his classes; a careless batsman, overly excited at hitting the ball, had flung the bat wildly and struck Summerfield just above the right eye, giving rise to an alarming purple knot. As Sarah went on bitterly about their father in the parlor, she dabbed a cold wet cloth gently over her brother's forehead.

With little conviction, Summerfield suggested that Mrs. Hayes might simply have refused to go.

Sarah explained that their mother had been as clever as she was beautiful and that she usually managed to find paths to her own desires, circumventing their father's requirements, often without his knowledge. But in this one thing, she'd found no path, and she'd paid for it with her life. "She gave him the illusion of always having his way," said Sarah, "because she knew it brought him pleasure."

"But after all," said Summerfield, with even less conviction than before, "he couldn't have known what was going to happen."

"Hold still," said Sarah. "Of course he couldn't know. But he would have his way no matter what." She poured fresh water from a pitcher into the bowl on her mother's nearby gaming table, wrung out the cloth, dipped it again into the water, folded it into a small square, and softly laid it over her brother's brow. "It's a pleasure of weak men, Summerfield," she said, "always going around imposing their will on women."

"And I guess it must be a pleasure of strong women," said Summerfield, "always going around imposing their will on men."

Sarah made no reply to this remark, but he thought he saw a smile cross her face, faintly, before she said, "There, at least I've got the dirt off it." She made a few finishing dabs with the cloth and added, "I'll say this for you, Summerfield Hayes—you certainly did inherit his black eyebrows. Very handsome, even with nasty lumps. You look as though you might be growing a horn. If that's not gone down by this time tomorrow, I think we'd best send for Dr. Tilbrook."

He was glad to have these opinions of Sarah's concerning their parents, for what she'd said deciphered for him a paradox: he'd always had a sense that while his mother deferred to his father in practically everything, there was something weak about him and strong about her. He'd thought this odd sense might be tied to finances—Mr. Hayes, a dance instructor at a nearby studio opposite the City Hall, had little money of his own, while Mrs. Hayes came from a good deal of wealth—but Sarah's ideas were a better explanation. The notion of his mother contriving her own happiness surreptitiously, so as not to disquiet Mr. Hayes's vanity, made Summerfield think of the biblical wisdom that it is more blessed to give than to receive. He supposed it would apply even when what one gave was the illusion of something.

The knot caused by the blow to his head shrank in due course but never went away entirely. Though it was barely visible, he could feel the small lump with his fingers; he invariably recalled that afternoon in the parlor, and he believed that day was the start of a change in his connection to his sister. Throughout their growing up, her manner toward him had been typical of an older sister to a younger brother, what was often described as "maternal." With the shocking loss of their parents, that manner might have hardened, yet Summerfield felt, that afternoon in the parlor, a move toward parity. In company, she was not an outspoken girl, and she would have been mortified to be overheard speaking so frankly about their dead father. If, in front of others, she spoke only lovingly and praising of Mr. Hayes,

Summerfield did not consider her a hypocrite. He recognized that there were different versions of truth and that some versions would do only for the two of them, together, alone. As she began to make a habit of taking him into her confidence—which happened to coincide with the passing of his boyhood—his feelings for her naturally began to change, from the clear thing they had always been to something else, less clear and altogether unsettling.

As he pauses at the edge of a pasture in the dim gray light before dawn, he touches his fingers to the spot above his right eye, which has the curious power to unite him to Hicks Street and Sarah. He has walked most of the night, on a road for a while, though the moonlight made him especially wary. Once, in the deadly quiet of the night, a single gunshot somewhere in the distance sent him scurrying into a ditch. For the last two or three hours he has again followed a stream, generally northeast, which has brought him at last to this open field. His heart pounds inside his chest, partly due to exertion, partly to his ongoing certainty of being tracked. As he waits here and gazes over the pasture, he knows that, at some gap behind, another waits, in the dark of the woods. His wounds burn and throb, and he believes they are again leaking blood. He longs to rest but knows he must cross the clearing before dawn. The half-moon, near the horizon, pours its pale milk over the pasture at a sharp angle, and the occasional lone tree, despite the brightening sky, casts an unearthly long shadow over the ground. An abandoned breastwork cuts through one end of the pasture, resembling a piece of frayed rope laid down not far from the smooth ribbon of the stream. Around the periphery he sees the wrecked remains of wooden fences, the bulk of the rails stripped and used for an earlier encampment's firewood. He adjusts the straps on his bread bag and his knapsack so that they put less pressure on the wound in his back, then sets out, thinking about his sister as he goes, recalling the afternoon in the parlor, wondering if his decision to enlist in the army mustn't surely have reminded her of their father—a journey, a separation, insisted upon. If so, she did not give him any illusion of bowing to his will. She had opposed him unreservedly and was still aggrieved.

Halfway across the clearing, he recalls the single letter from their parents, in their father's hand, posted from Ireland shortly after their arrival there: their quarters on the steamer had been cramped but bearable; the ship was equipped with, of all things, a barber's saloon.

Once he gains the woods at the other side, he removes his gear and collapses to the ground, where he turns to face the field. He sees no one there, but he expects the stalker will wait until he himself sleeps, as he surely must, to take up the slack. He opens his knapsack and frees the chicken, which scrambles frantically away but in a crazy circle that carries it back very close to the spot where it was freed. From his bread bag, he takes a corner of hardtack and crumbles it into his palm; the chicken cautiously edges nearer and stands close to his outstretched hand; it gazes off in another direction entirely, and when, after a moment, it pecks a crumb from Hayes's palm, it does so as an apparent whim. Soon, in like fashion, the chicken has eaten all the crumbs, and Hayes shoos it away. Again the bird bustles madly in a wide arc that returns it close to Hayes's side, where it twitches its head one way and another and occasionally picks at something near its feet. Of course Hayes had thought to kill and eat the chicken, but he felt sick when he imagined slaughtering and preparing it. And besides, how could he possibly risk a fire and roasting meat, giving away his location by both sight and smell?

He lies back on the ground, thinking perhaps he has a fever. He resolves not to cry out or even to moan, though the pain of his wounds threatens to take his breath away. After a few moments, he props himself onto his elbows and sees a figure coming toward him across the field—the silhouette of a man, arms lifted in the air in a gesture of surrender. Hayes finds the bowie knife and moves swiftly farther into the dark skirt of the woods, slipping behind the trunk of a pine and pressing his cheek against its craggy bark. His mother's face rises up in his mind—oddly, his dread and physical agony mix to make a feeling very much like longing—and he hears the *screak* of her fingernails on the glass of the omnibus window.

THE YOUNGSTERS IN the drum corps never got enough sleep, required as they were to be on call at all hours, day and night. During the second half of the third inning—the teams tied at eleven runs apiece—the young drummer assigned by the colonel to keep Banjo away from the playing field nodded off. He leaned against a barrel, his mouth slightly ajar, and his cap had slid down covering most of his face. With one man out in the inning, a batter for the Twighoppers struck a ball straight into the ground a few paces from the home base, where it lay spinning in place, and before anyone in the field could reach it, Banjo bounded forward, gripped the ball in her maw, and sprinted into the outfield, where she commenced to run in great loops, chased by a gathering number of players and spectators. A merry chaos prevailed for two or three minutes till the foxhound lit out for the trees and disappeared into the piney forest with her prize.

The captain of Hayes's company dispatched a detail of six soldiers to track the dog and retrieve the ball, and meanwhile the batter for the Twighoppers was granted the first base and the match resumed. Soon a rumble of voices and laughter started up among the troops near the first base; like an ocean wave it spread along the margins of the field, growing louder as it went and wholly distracting the players. From his lolling chair, the colonel—who apparently had seen no reason why the reward of beer should be delayed until the conclusion of the match—cast a lost and dangerous-looking glare slowly round the lines, then stood at last, drew his pepperbox, and fired into the air. Having thus silenced the proceedings, he raised his voice to the general public and roared: "What the devil is so bloody funny?"

After some seconds, a young private was pushed forward by his comrades into the open, where he stood startled to find himself so uncomfortably near the colonel. He straightened himself up and saluted, to which the colonel responded, "Well, Private, let's have it!"

"Well . . . , sir," he said, haltingly, "it's just that . . ." He raised one hand, pointed toward the woods, and said, "It's just that somebody said that bitch, Banjo . . . somebody said the bitch'd absquatulated with one of the chaplain's balls."

The colonel, pistol still in hand, studied the soldier for a moment, unblinking. "'Absquatulated with one of the chaplain's balls'?" he said impatiently.

"Yes, sir," said the private.

The colonel's grimace faded as he began to grasp the joke. Then at last he lowered his head and started to quake with silent laughter, prompting a renewed uproar from the troops.

Once things had settled down and play resumed again, still with one out in the inning and the runner on the first base, the Bachelors' second baseman, Billy Swift—aptly named; the kind of scrappy fielder who hurled himself at every ball that came near him—would astound the spectators. When Coulter, the Twighoppers' brawny catcher, shot a rocket into the air between the first and second bases, Swift not only found the ball and brought it down on the fly—leaping nearly his own height off the field—but managed to tag the runner trying to advance, thus turning the Twighoppers out of the inning in abrupt and astonishing fashion.

As the troops still cheered Swift's antics, a half-dozen soldiers emerged from the pines in the distance, one of them waving the dog-stolen ball triumphantly over his head, and the troops' ovation swelled. The foxhound trotted contrite behind the group of soldiers. At that same moment a cloud blotted out the sun. A strong wind swept across the whole place, bending the younger pines at the edge of the forest. Then the sun returned, blinding and hot.

Camp near Brandy Station
Saturday evening, April 30

Dearest Sister,

No official word has come down but I believe we are soon to move. These last few days our drills & target practice have increased three-fold & there is a universal stirring in the air. It has been nearly two weeks since all sutlers & citizens were ordered to vamoose & every day wagons of "inessential" goods & property are being sent back to Alexandria. Sometimes I imagine our low hill as seen from a bird in the sky & I think we resemble a busy colony of ants. Our river is all that separates us from General Lee's army. They are dug in & unassailable on the other side, so we must trust our commanders to find a means of eluding them & coming at them another way. I write to you now for I am uncertain of when time

& circumstances will allow another letter. I want to let you know that my long weeks of waiting to "see the elephant" are nearing an end. Though I anticipate future misery, I feel sure of my survival. Truman says "them's the famous last words of a fresh fish" & well they might be, but if death comes for me down here in this wasted land they call Virginia, it will most definitely take me by surprise. I know what store you set by dreams, so I tell you that my dreams of battle are decidedly unhappy, but in them I am <u>alive</u>.

The rumors you have heard in Brooklyn about our rations are unfounded. We have beef & pork, tea & coffee, bread & potatoes, sugar & molasses. I understand the food has not always been this ample or good, but now there is no cause for complaint. Please tell Mrs. B to set her mind at ease in this regard—she'll be glad to hear we even have plenty of soap. We are having less rain & more sun & wildflowers have begun sprouting everywhere. Less agreeable is the "weather" that looms over the men in the form of their contrary opinions about our officers. Every day brings a new argument with soldiers squaring off on one side or another of this or that colonel or general. They are like children fighting over the faults & merits of their family elders, a disposition that has redoubled as we draw closer to crossing the river. Likewise, from what I hear, our commanders often do not think much of one another, though Gen. Grant seems to enjoy the admiration of more than most. The last time he came over here from his hdqrs I was farther away from him than our house is from City Hall, but I could sure hear the bands playing across the way.

Besides my usual duties, I have been busy with base ball & writing letters for my comrades. You would be astounded by how many of our boys can not read or write. Many did not advance beyond the fourth grade. What is most satisfying is how grateful they are for my services with the pen & it is surely little enough to give. Thank you for the book, dear Sarah. One of our surgeons happened by my tent of an afternoon when I was sitting on my rubber blanket reading. He commended me for studying what he took to be my Bible & when I showed him otherwise he declared himself, like you, a great fan of Dickens. His name is Speck, though he is quite a large man & entirely visible I assure you. Also like you, he does not much care for Hawthorne. He said of <u>The Scarlet Letter</u> that it is gloomy beyond toleration. Some of my mates tease me about being a bookworm &

say they are confounded to find in me such a mix of base ball & books. They also say I will soon regret having a thing so heavy as an English novel to carry in my knapsack. These same ones then entreat me to read to them from it when we are idle. I am nearly finished with the first part & it is both a pleasure & a comfort.

The company I take with Mr. Dickens is the nearest I can come here to having your own. Let me say that I think of you every day & pray for your safety & happiness every night. I so much want you to understand me, Sarah, not for my own sake, but for yours, should I be wrong about my survival & the worst should happen. Can you not see how impossible it was for me to go on playing base ball in Brooklyn, knowing all the while the main cause for the opportunity, that so many in our club had already put on a different uniform, in the service of Uncle Sam? As for college & the law, will they not still be there for me when I return? I am truly sorry for your loneliness & do blame myself for it though I think I am trying to do right. I am thankful for your letters even with their scoldings. My hope is that you will forgive me & that in time you will find less in me that needs forgiving.

Thank you too for including the clipping from the <u>Eagle,</u> Rev. T.C.'s sketch of his visit with Mr. D in England. I cannot say it shed a lot of light, as you pointed out, but I enjoyed reading it all the same. We are not familiar with Mrs. Hamilton, though I trust your assessment of her & look forward to seeing for myself. I am glad you have been to the academy for I know how music has the power to cheer you. Is the panorama all it is purported to be? I am skeptical of such grand projects but gazing out across our winter quarters from Cole's Hill I think it does sometimes resemble a vast painting in motion.

I have had a compliment from the colonel. He said that if the army of the Potomac had a base ball officer, I would be a major general. He added that word had reached his ear that I was the worst poker player in the regiment, which is true. The captain came to my defense then, saying that I could reload a musket as fast as any man in the company.

A fellow from Maine has taught me the game of backgammon, which is about the best sport I have ever had sitting still. Be prepared, dear Sarah, for I shall force you to learn it. You will be amused to know that I have tried to grow whiskers, which has provided a topic of much mirth around camp. We had a chance to take an image last week & I have enclosed the results for you here, at the risk of a certain impression of vanity.

As I have already said, I am not sure when I shall write again, though it is my plan to describe my battle experience to you in detail. Thank you for the dried berries, which arrived in time for my birthday. There is a general here called Hays but he spells it without the "e." No relation, I reckon.

As always your loving brother,
Summerfield

WHEN HE WAS a boy he discovered that he could shut his eyes and see on the back of his eyelids a ghostly version of what he had just been looking at. Now, from behind the pine tree (around which he has wrapped one arm), he stares at the figure that approaches, a black featureless specter caught against a mist that hovers over the barren field. But when he shuts his eyes, he sees no ghostly version of the thing. He thinks maybe the thing itself is ghostly enough, and when he opens his eyes again it has vanished. Slowly he pulls himself up, bracing against the bark of the pine, still wielding the knife, and squinting into the ever-brightening emptiness of the pasture. A wild instinct impels him to turn and look into the woods at his back, but these are as silent and unpeopled as the field; their divergent vertical stripes exhale the musty coolness of a church. He returns his gaze to the pasture and sees only that the trench and the toppled wooden crosses of the breastwork appear to have grown darker, likewise the stream and the wrecked posts and railings, yet the long shadows cast by the solitary trees are fading. Now he collapses to the ground and presses the wound in his back hard against the tree, meaning to staunch its bleeding. He wonders why God has judged him so harshly and sought to punish him so severely. The silver blade of the knife gleams in his lap, a tool, a promise, a quick end to his plight. As he moves a hand to touch it, his fingers tremble, and then both his hands flutter as before, uncontrolled, like little sovereign wings attached to his wrists.

He makes of them fists that he rams to the ground on either side of his legs, grinding his knuckles one way and the other, leaving marks in the soil that look like gray roses. After a moment smoke begins to rise out of the roses' styles, prompting him to leap frightened to his feet. Again he sees the figure approaching in the pasture, the silhouette of a man, waving his arms in an attitude of surrender. This time, leaving the knife on the ground, he runs toward it in a rage. The thing freezes for an instant, and next it twirls in some unworldly way, its shape complex and unidentifiable. Then, as it retreats, he sees the bright white tail bobbing, only a buck come out to forage at dawn.

He feels something beneath his foot and bends to find the rim of a tin pot protruding from the earth. Buried alongside it, a piece of bone. Suddenly aware that he is exposed, unprotected in the midst of the field, he crouches and zigzags quickly back to the trees. Once the cool dark cloak of the forest has enfolded him, he stands with his back to the pasture and notes that he is free of pain, and sleepy. He moves deeper into the trees and finds a spot beneath some young dogwoods, where he rakes together a mound of pine straw for a mattress. As he sits down and arranges his gear around him, he observes that the chicken, so reluctant to depart, is now nowhere to be seen. He lies back and rests his head on the straw, looking up through the bright green leaves of the dogwoods to the darker pine boughs and odd-shaped patches of silver sky. He closes his eyes and sees these same patches wafting like black jetsam in a sea of milk. *Handsome,* Sarah whispers in his ear, *even with nasty lumps.* And, sighing, shaking her head, *Oh, Summerfield Hayes . . .*

Here is what he has never written to his sister in any letter nor admitted in any form to anyone: in the months leading up to his enlistment, he'd dreamed of her, and they were the wrong kind of dreams. He didn't so much fear his own snarled feelings as he feared what he imagined hers might be. His could be the dark secret he aged out of, or erased with experience and time, or carried with him if necessary to the grave. But should she return his feelings in this corrupted way, he could see nothing in their future but grief. She'd stayed tepid toward the attentions of no fewer than three of his club mates. Now and again, alone with her and shaken to his toes, he thought he saw in her eyes the spark of an unspoken sentiment, affecting and regrettable. Surely, he thought, a war was strong enough a blast to put things right.

ROSAMEL, the Frenchman from Company H who would play the center field for the Bachelors, had stopped by Hayes's tent the day before the match. He spoke nearly perfect English, with a charming accent, and could usually be counted on for a smile. But today—a day that had started out sunny and soon gave way to storm clouds and rain—he seemed troubled. Hayes bid him to come into the hut, out of the rain.

Nearby, his sack coat draped over his head, Truman Leggett had set up a tripod and built a fire for heating coffee. Because of the rain, the fire produced more than the usual amount of smoke, which rose in fitful puffs straight up into the air. As Hayes set aside his book, Rosamel (like Leggett, a man of about thirty) sat cross-legged next to him on the pine-strewn floor. He wore a coal-black mustache, the right side of which he routinely worried with the tip of his tongue, a habit, Hayes had observed, that sometimes made him seem pensive, at other times insane. Now he removed the last vestige of a former, more dashing uniform, a soiled and tattered red fez, which he held, with both hands, crown down, in his lap.

He spoke softly and went straight to the point: "I have come to make to you a confession," he said.

Hayes nodded, knitting his own brow to match the apparent gravity of what was to follow.

"I have made myself a member of the unmarried man's side," Rosamel continued, "but I have done so with . . ." He paused here, carefully choosing his next words. "With some convenient evasions," he added at last.

"Well, I chose you for the team," said Hayes. "You didn't make yourself a member."

"That is true," said Rosamel, "you are right. My part was to declare myself unmarried when that is the case only in a practical sense.

A year before the war, my wife fell in love with another man. We have lived apart since then and for three years additional. We have no . . ." Again he paused, thinking. "We have no connection of any sort, and I do not anticipate any in the future."

"But you're still legally married," said Hayes.

"Yes, in our church, you see, it is, do you have this word . . . *indissoluble?*"

Again Hayes nodded. After a moment, he said, "This is what you came to confess?"

Rosamel signaled his consent by dropping his head to his chest and passing the sweatband of the fez between his fingers so that the hat went in a circular motion.

Hayes judged the Frenchman's concern trivial as it applied to the match, but he thought, for the sake of Rosamel's pride, he should honor the seriousness with which he'd brought it. At last he said, "Well, if you like, I can take this to the captain to consider. But in my judgment, you made the right choice. As you have said, you're no longer married in any practical sense, and practically is how we would best proceed."

"Very good," said Rosamel, visibly relieved. "I think no need to disturb the captain. Of course I imagined you would understand me." He set aside the fez and reached for Hayes's book, whose leather cover was the same shade of red; he lifted the book from the ground, felt the weight of it, and turned it to read the words on the spine. "This is about the French Revolution, yes?" he asked.

"It's set during that period, yes," said Hayes. "Have you read it?"

"No," he answered, "but of course I have heard of it."

"Do you mind if I ask," said Hayes, "how you were employed in New York, before the war?"

Rosamel held the book in his hands for another moment; as he set it down, he said, softly, "I was a schoolteacher."

"Oh," said Hayes, "my sister's a schoolteacher. In Brooklyn."

Rosamel smiled and then quickly darkened his expression again, returning to the former subject. "You see," he said, "I could not determine where I truly belonged."

With that, he stood, put his fez back on, left the hut, and walked away in the rain. Hayes moved outside, came alongside Leggett, and watched the Frenchman retreat unsteadily down a slope rutted by rain.

"What an odd and interesting fellow," said Hayes.

"French," said Leggett, as if that explained everything. He squatted, poked his fire with a stick of wood, and then let his gaze join Hayes's, trained on Rosamel's back. "Not too many of 'em left," he said after a moment. "Oh, I imagine since he was first mustered in, he seen near about three-quarters of his outfit slaughtered."

HE WAKES with a start, flat on his back, jolted by gunshot and the clang of a minié ball against something metal. He draws up his knees and covers his ears with his hands, but the lingering noise—the unbroken hiss of a snake, the fierce whirring in his ears that makes the bones of his face shudder—comes from within him. Though he has slept only briefly, the air has grown hot, even in the shade of the woods, and what he first takes to be sweat inside his shirt and trousers is, of course, blood, blood saturating the crevices of his groin, blooming like a grotesque flower between his shoulder blades, pressed beneath his ribs and spine. This sopping ordeal, he thinks, is an apt expression of his disappointment at having awakened into the same ravaged and ravaging world from which he cannot escape, even asleep. He has dreamed of Rosamel, the Frenchman who stopped by the hut one rainy afternoon in April, so very long ago, a schoolteacher whose wife fell in love with another man: Rosamel was digging a grave for a fallen soldier, who lay facedown in the rain and mud near the mound of dirt Rosamel heaped up. Rosamel worked waist-deep inside the grave, his red fez cocked at an angle on his head. As he arced the spade into the air over one shoulder, a barrage of gunfire exploded from the nearby trees, and a ball struck the metal blade, *ping!*

Now Hayes wipes his eyes, gathers his gear, stands, and moves away toward the stream. The pain in his thigh feels worse, and as he limps through the trees, his woolen trousers, wet with blood, cling to his skin. The scent of pinesap that permeates the warm air is nauseating, and he tells himself he must eat, but first he must do something

about the state of his clothes. A short way upstream, he spies an escarpment, crosshatched by roots, in the bank; about shoulder-deep, with
a narrow dirt floor next to the water, it will provide some privacy. He
climbs down to the spot and bends to remove his shoes. He untucks
the trousers from his socks. He struggles with the buttons on the trousers but finds that if he takes long, deep breaths, one after another, he
can steady his hands. He teeters as he starts to remove the trousers
but leans against the roots of the escarpment for support. Carefully he
peels the fabric of his shirt away from his skin; he reaches one hand
up to remove his forage hat so that he can pull the shirt over his head,
but he is surprised that he has no hat. He stands still for a moment,
recalling a feeling of sun on the top of his bare head; he has not had a
hat since the beginning. Lost and deserted without so much as a hat,
he thinks, and the thought makes him feel like crying. He notes, too,
that despite his sticking to the woods for the most part, and traveling
by road at night, his arms are two distinct colors now, marked by a
line above his elbows—his forearms darker for having been exposed
to the sun. His right arm is splotched with bruises from wrist to shoulder, but—like the soreness at the crown of his head—he cannot recall
what inflicted these fading injuries.

Once he has taken everything off, he stoops naked at the edge of
the stream and immerses the shirt, the trousers, and the socks, agitating them one by one in the cool water. He steels himself for the sickening sight of blood in the water, but in a magical way, the stream spares
him, absorbing and diffusing the blood instantly, without a trace. He
hangs the wet clothes over the roots in the side of the bank and then
finds his canteen and fills it. Afterward, he walks into the water, placing his feet down gingerly on the mucky bottom. At midstream, the
water is cold and reaches as high as his chest. He recalls what Dr.
Speck once told him about the need to keep wounds clean, and he
thinks perhaps the stream will do his injuries some good. He shuts
his eyes, bends his knees, and puts his head under. He turns upstream
so that the mild current beats against his face. Underwater, the noise
inside his ears seems louder, but he decides to play the boyhood game
of seeing how long he can stay down. After quite a long time, he starts
to panic, not because he runs out of breath, but because it strikes him

that he could stay under indefinitely, as if he no longer requires air at all. He surfaces and begins to wade out. He notices that a blue jay has lit on the bank just above his clothes, stands there stock-still, and appears to be watching him with interest. A thought forms in his mind: *I am already dead . . . this isn't real.*

Then, as he moves nearer and the bird flies away, another thought: *If it is a dream, it means to continue.*

He sees a roundish rock on the ground, about the size of a base ball, which he lifts and palms in his right hand. As a boy, he'd adopted the great Jim Creighton's practice of tossing an iron ball the same size as a base ball, to build strength in his arm. Now he backs up against the escarpment and looks across the stream for a suitable target; he picks a knot on the wide trunk of an oak, then runs forward to the water's edge and releases, only inches from the ground, a stiff-armed underhand toss that rises to the mark, a perfect strike. The resonant thud the rock sounds against the oak is recklessly loud, however, and makes him uneasy. Next he finds a stick, breaks it over his knee to a proper length, and then tosses smaller rocks into the air and bats them into the stream. He continues diverting himself this way until he is overcome with a sense that he's being watched, a naked fool in the woods. Again he hears—from somewhere far away or from inside his head—the rolling boom of artillery. As he turns to his clothes draped over the roots of the escarpment, he sees, directly beneath his trousers, something shiny resting in the dirt—the open-face pocket watch, entirely forgotten, that had come to him from across the Atlantic among his father's things. He lifts it from the ground and turns it over in his hand. The crystal is cracked, the gold bezel nicked in several spots. The fob is missing, and the hands have stopped at ten minutes past nine o'clock. He twists the crown, but when he holds the watch to his ear, he hears no movement. He decides to open the case and find a patch of sunlight in which to lay it—perhaps it will work again once it has dried out. As he reaches into his knapsack and pulls out the bowie knife for this purpose, he notices, for the first time, that there are initials carved into the knife's handle: F.R.

Silently, he mouths the name *Felix Rosamel*. The knife had belonged to Rosamel, not to Billy Swift, as he'd thought before. Rosamel gave him the knife, not Billy. The knife could not have belonged to Billy, could not have been given to him by Billy . . .

He is unable to complete the thought. It is as if a door in his mind slammed shut.

With the blade of the knife, he opens the watchcase, then blows on it and places it on the bank in a trembling scrap of sunlight. He puts his wet clothes and his shoes back on. As he climbs the bank, a wind rustles the trees overhead, and some dry pine needles sail down, light on the water, and are carried away. He cannot wait for the watch to dry, so he retrieves it, closes the case, and drops it into his bread bag. He adjusts the straps on the bag and knapsack and begins to move upstream, dogged now by a word that seems to nip at his heels with every step. *Nursemaid,* a word that Rosamel figures into somehow, a defiant, threatened Rosamel.

He trudges ahead, a dutiful creature, putting one foot in front of the other, though a dull ache pervades his body, starting and renewing with each step in the soles of his feet, rising through his legs and into his spine. Soon the ache changes to numbness, though he can still feel his heart inside his chest as he goes. The wet clothes cling to his skin disagreeably, and worse, he recalls Leggett's warning about wet socks causing blisters. Now and again, he believes he hears the gait of another traveler, taking a path parallel to his, but this no longer concerns him. He can no longer feel the concern. Dimly, in his mind's eye, he sees himself somewhere in the past, before he entered the dream of the forest, naked on the ground, trying to inspect his wounds. *I said leave him,* says a voice within the whirring inside his ears. And *Take his weapon.*

SARAH CAME INTO the library in a kind of flurry, with Mrs. Bannister trailing close behind. Summerfield—lounging in the window seat with its many pillows and its view, through a film of lace, of Hicks Street—had been reading; but now, at dusk, his book lay in the slope of his lap, closed, though his index finger still held the page. His primary experience of the women's arrival in the room was auditory, the noise of the door, a rustling of skirts. It did not strike him as significant enough an event to pull him from his rapt observation, through the curtains, of a small pink pig rooting about the iron railings of the opposite dooryard.

"Sarah, *please,*" he heard Mrs. Bannister cry, with even more than her usual amount of exasperation, exasperation being Mrs. Bannister's primary response to life and the world.

"Summerfield," said Sarah, sternly. "Mrs. B and I want a word with you."

His head rested against the wall at his back, and now he allowed it to drop at an angle in the general direction of her voice, a languid gesture that apparently gave her pause. Her dress was brown, he noted, like the woodwork in the room, and she clutched a white cloth of some kind at her waist, as if she'd come into the library prepared to wipe up a mess. Her hair was pulled into one of the beaded nets she was fond of sewing, and in the library's twilight, he thought she might have emerged from an old painting. She attempted a smile but could not quite bring it off. "I can see that you're feeling dreamy," she said to him at last, "but I need you to give me your real attention."

He widened his eyes to indicate compliance.

"I cannot imagine what you've said to Mrs. B," she continued, "but whatever it was, she has misconstrued it to mean that after Christmas you plan to join the army."

"He only told me he was *thinking* of it," piped in Mrs. Bannister. "And he told me in confidence . . . a thing I doubt I'll ever have again after this."

"Well?" said Sarah.

Now he sat up straight and dropped his feet to the floor. He moved to the hearth, where he found the poker and stirred the fire. With his back to the room, he said, "It's time we should light the lamps, don't you think?"

"I can see perfectly well, Summerfield," said Sarah. "And there's nothing wrong with my hearing either."

In the window seat, Summerfield's thinking had gone something like this: he'd reviewed the faces of some of the members of the Eckford Club, particularly the style of whiskers each wore (those who wore whiskers); he'd batted around some of the more curious combinations of their names, Beach and Reach, Wood and Mills; he'd reflected that since he would soon be leaving Brooklyn, it would not be necessary this December to purchase a subscription for the skating pond, though rumor had it that the skating pond, under new management, was much improved, and Sarah would probably not wish to skate without him, but it would be easy enough for her to accompany any number of friends as their guest; he'd spied the pig across the way and imagined it first in short pants and a vest, sliding around the icy oval of the Dime Pond, then stripped of its hide, blood red and hanging from its back legs in the window of the butcher shop on State Street. As soon as Sarah declared that she and Mrs. Bannister wanted a word with him, he was sure of her subject. Two days earlier, when he'd mentioned his intentions to Mrs. B, he figured she wouldn't be able to keep to herself what he'd said. He had used her for precisely this purpose, for the contrivance felt more palatable than his having to approach Sarah directly. When he'd envisioned himself going to her straight, he couldn't find the right opening words and dreaded her reaction. She would be hurt and frightened. While the strategy of using Mrs. B would provoke a confrontation by Sarah, unpleasant enough, it relieved him of the burden of initiating the subject. He knew it was a coward's way, but the idea, once it occurred to him, gained ground and refused to retreat. The irony of the situation didn't escape him—he saw himself adequately brave to go to war but shrank from disappointing his sister.

Now he put down the poker, turned to face her, and found her standing unnecessarily erect, a few feet away. She did not blink.

"I see," she said after a moment. "Then it's true."

"Sarah," said Mrs. Bannister, from behind. "Why don't I bring you up your knitting? Summerfield, go on and light the lamps, dear. Sit here, the two of you, by the fire. I'll tell Jane to serve coffee in here."

"Believe it or not, Mrs. B," said Sarah, not taking her eyes off Summerfield, "there are some things that cannot be fixed by coffee and knitting." Then, to him: "We had a plan. You would stay out of school awhile longer, continue clerking for the shipwrights, play with the club. Then on to college."

He shrugged, but felt shabby for it. "Sarah," he said, "sometimes plans change. There's a war."

"Oh, *war*," she said. "What we have, as you well know, Summerfield, is an ocean of blood . . . already a full ocean of it. Do you really think it indispensable that you add your own little drop?"

"I don't know—"

"Because, Summerfield," she added, undeterred, "your own little drop will make very little difference to the ocean. I beg you to think what a difference it will make to us . . . to me."

"I have, Sarah."

"You have what?"

"I have considered."

She turned away and moved to the window, putting her back to him. "I was prepared to be hurt by your not considering me," she said, softly. "Now I see how it feels to have been considered and set aside."

"Sarah—"

She turned again, struck, apparently, by a new idea. "Are the admission sums from the Union Grounds not given to the Sanitary Commission?" she asked. "Is that not a sufficient contribution?"

"No, Sarah," he answered. "It's not enough. I need to do this."

"But why do you need to do it?"

"Because I just do."

Her eyes lingered on him another moment, blankly, and then she gave him a look he would not easily shake: she tilted her head ever so slightly and seemed to say, *Who are you?*

Since it was a question for which he had no ready answer, she dropped her shoulders and then sailed past Mrs. Bannister and out of the room.

He found himself biting his lower lip, recalling the demoralization at the end of a lost match—there was the awful finality of it, the impossibility of its reversal, but also the palliative of there being another match soon.

"Give her some time," said Mrs. Bannister. "She'll need a good deal of time, I suspect. Go on and light the lamps, Summerfield. I'll tell Jane to bring up some coffee for you."

He thanked her, and she left the room, closing the door behind her.

He passed the evening alone. The lamplighter came by and lit the lamps in Hicks Street. Soon a gentle snow began to fall outside, the first of the season. When he stepped to the window to look for the young pig he'd seen before, there was no sign of it. He kept up the fire himself, drank coffee, and read the newspaper, which included an amusing story about Ben Franklin and a prank he once played on his mother to test her "instinct of natural affection." (After an absence of many years, Franklin had traveled to her house in Boston, to see, though he was much changed, if she would recognize him; not only did she not recognize him, she didn't much care for him and tried, over the course of the evening he spent among her boarders, to turn him out into the street—during a snowstorm.) The newspaper also contained a notice from the Kings County Board of Supervisors, who were now prepared to pay an additional three hundred dollars bounty to volunteer recruits, over and above that offered by the United States and the state of New York.

Later on, Mrs. Bannister returned to the library and told Summerfield that Sarah wouldn't be coming down for supper; she reiterated her earlier conclusions about the need for time and asked his forgiveness for being such an old blatherskite. He told her, truthfully, there was nothing to forgive.

He had his supper in the library, on a tray. He lit his father's pipe but smoked only a fraction of a bowl, for honestly he didn't like it. The snowfall continued as it had begun, never growing any heavier, and it melted rather than collected in the street. At last he decided to extinguish the lights and retire.

Just as he was about to draw the drapes over the lace curtains and put the room in darkness, the library door opened slowly, and in crept his sister, dressed in a nightgown and bonnet and wearing a capelike sweater. A fair amount of light came through the window from the nearby streetlamp, and they stood for a few seconds looking at each other. The golden lamplight, filtered through the lace curtains, fell in cobwebby patterns across her face. She smiled, but sadly, and though he remained still, inwardly he experienced the kind of shakiness that used to attend helping a girl into a carriage and not knowing exactly where to put his hands. Sarah glanced toward the windows and said, "It's snowing."

Before the hearth were two wing chairs, once occupied for long hours by their mother and father on winter evenings. The chairs were covered in leather the yellowish-brown color of the butterscotch candy their mother had loved. With his open hand, Summerfield now indicated the one on the left, customarily taken by their mother, and Sarah sat down, drew her legs up under her, and wrapped the sweater tighter around her shoulders.

Summerfield found a woolen blanket in the window seat, which he brought to her, and she thanked him for it. He took the other chair, and they each stared into the embers of the fire, silent for a good long while.

At last she said, "You've been smoking Papa's pipe again."

"Yes," he said.

"I wish you wouldn't."

"I know."

A little later, he said, "How did you know you would find me still here?"

"I suspected as much," she said. "The lights in my room brightened."

Some time ago, the house had been piped for gas, but not properly, and when one dimmed the lamps in the library or the parlor, those in the bedrooms upstairs grew brighter.

"Ah," said Summerfield, "of course."

Another long silence ensued, after which she said, "You knew Mrs. B would tell me."

"Yes," he said.

"It was your way of letting me know without telling me yourself."

"Yes."

"Summerfield," she said, "don't think I've accepted it. I haven't. I'm only no longer reeling."

"Right," he said.

After another long moment, she sighed deeply and said, "Oh, how I do miss Mommy."

"I know," he said. "So do I."

"Yes, but not quite as I do," she said. "Not quite as I do."

"You could be home looking after your sister and playing base ball," said Speck, the surgeon. "I can't figure why you would risk everything out here in this godforsaken place."

As Hayes went about his own suddenly urgent chores, making ready at last to move out, the surgeon sat on the folding stool he'd brought along with him, his gaze oscillating between Hayes's small industry and the great commotion down the hillside as far as the eye could see. It was half past five o'clock in the afternoon. The previous night, a storm of rain and wind had swept over the camp, leaving everything with a fresh-washed look. This was followed by a day of bright sunshine, and now the blue light overhead had begun changing to lavender; a ladder of flat gray clouds, above the scalloped line of the treetops, climbed the southwestern sky. Mule wagons from Brandy Station were still being unloaded and reloaded at this late hour, and the myriad of campfires, very like stars, blinked over the countryside as horses and soldiers milled and hustled among them. The smoke from Speck's cigar lingered around his own head and occasionally he fanned it away, not deliberately, but by the gesticulations of his hands. A handsome man of about forty, with kindly gray eyes and light brown wavy hair, he wore side-whiskers and a mustache of darkest brown. He'd just returned from his second visit to the sinks in only half an hour, bitterly complaining of a case of the flux. Hayes, kneeling on the ground nearby, was busy rolling his own half of a tent, and Leggett's half, into two separate woolen blankets. A few yards away at the fire and chatting with Billy Swift (who'd brought some tobacco to trade for coffee), Leggett was cooking the several days' rations they'd been told to prepare for the imminent march. Actual orders remained altogether hazier than the many more specific rumors that swarmed about, but at least one thing was clear—they would not be sleeping that night on Cole's Hill.

His eyes fixed on his work, and entirely abstracted, Hayes said, "What about the evils of slavery? The preservation of the Union?"

Because Speck stayed silent, Hayes did eventually look up at the surgeon and found the man looking back at him skeptically. Hayes supposed his lukewarm remark didn't merit a reply, but then the surgeon said, "It's 1864, son. Those answers are spent by now and gasping for breath." He drew on the cigar and expelled a plume of smoke upward. "You don't belong among these . . . ," he began, but checked himself. "What are you doing here, son?" he asked. "Tell me the truth."

Hayes went back to work. "Couldn't you ask that question of any man, sir?" he said. "Including yourself?"

"No," said the surgeon. "Two minutes spent with most of them reveals their purpose clearly enough. Glory, spelled out in capital letters . . . esprit de corps, idleness, lack of imagination . . . various forms of enchantment . . . even bloodlust, I'm sorry to say. Or, as in my case, duty, tinged with a desire for personal advancement. But you, Hayes, you're different. I can't read you."

"Well," said Hayes, after a moment, "perhaps I can't read myself, Dr. Speck."

"Yes, that occurred to me," he said. He looked away down the hillside again and took a long draw on the cigar. "I've seen you play ball," he added, thoughtfully. "Both here and, once last summer, at the Union Grounds. There's no ambiguity there, Hayes. You're entirely at home. As self-possessed as a man twice your age. Tell me, how did you end up with that club of mechanics, anyway?"

Hayes explained that he'd wanted to postpone college for a spell, he'd taken a clerking job at a shipwrights', where he'd met a couple of the Eckford men (a chippy, a caulker), and one thing led to another.

"And you've found they accept you as one of their own?" asked the surgeon.

"Well, sir, I *am* one of their own," said Hayes. "We're a club."

"Yes, yes, but you know what I mean. Do you not find it difficult . . . the social navigation?"

"What, because they come from Williamsburgh and Greenpoint and work at the docks?" said Hayes.

"Yes," said Speck. "Are you not something of a black sheep?"

"I've come in for some teasing now and then," said Hayes, "but it's all in fun. We each put on the same ball suit before a match. And once the play begins, we're boys again, with the cares and concerns of boys. What I find . . . people generally see you about as different as you see yourself."

Speck regarded him with a quizzical look for a moment, then smiled and said, "I'm sure you're right, Hayes. I do hope you had the good sense to lay all this stuff out in the sun today, before you started packing."

"Yes, sir," said Hayes. "Well, maybe not all, but most . . . the tents and the blankets at least."

Now Speck turned down the corners of his mouth and shook his head. "Hayes," he said, gravely. "Have you thought about what it will mean to point your weapon into the face of another man?"

"Yes, sir, I have."

"And . . . ?"

"I hope my courage won't fail me."

The surgeon nodded and returned his gaze down the hill toward Leggett and Billy Swift and the campfire. He clenched the cigar between his teeth and placed his hands on his knees. After a moment, he removed the cigar and called out to Leggett. "Soldier! You don't need to use that damned frying pan for *everything*. Get yourself a good green stick and toast that, directly over the fire."

Both Leggett and Billy Swift stared at the surgeon for a moment, squinting, and then Leggett shrugged his shoulders and went about his business, unaltered. Billy Swift laughed, struck Leggett playfully upside the head, and then called out to the surgeon, "Frying's the only cooking he knows how to do, Major! He'd fry up your molasses cookies if you let him!" Billy Swift—noting his failure to amuse the surgeon and construing it apparently as a signal to take his leave—said something brief and final to Leggett, then waved to Hayes and sauntered away down the hillside.

"Why do they oppose all modification?" said Speck, softly, to Hayes.

Hayes, still squatting, held one spare pair of socks to his nose, then another, to determine which was the less offensive. He hadn't thought Speck sought a real answer to the question, so he was surprised when the surgeon said, "Well, Hayes, what do you think?"

Hayes saw that the surgeon hadn't diverted his gaze from Leggett's fire. "With respect, sir," he said, "I'd say most everybody here has already undergone a fair amount of modification."

Now Speck looked down at him, piercingly, and Hayes feared he'd spoken too frankly.

But the doctor nodded after a moment, his gray eyes watering, and then looked away, back at Leggett. "Is that man your company cook?" he asked.

"No, sir," said Hayes. "He's only my—"

"Get your rations from the company cook," said the surgeon.

"Yes, sir."

Speck stood, brushing ashes down the front of his shirt. "Well," he said, "I'd best go collect my sword and the rest of my sweltering gear."

Hayes noticed that the surgeon was sweating. "Sir," said Hayes, standing and squaring his shoulders, about to salute, but Speck reached for his hand. The surgeon held him thus with his right hand, tossed the butt of the cigar to the ground, and put his left on Hayes's shoulder. He glanced at Hayes's cartridge box, resting atop one of the rolled blankets. "Have you ever seen the wound these damned balls inflict in a man?" he asked. "The ragged tear an iron fragment cuts into a man's flesh? The shattered bone?"

"No, sir," said Hayes.

"Of course you haven't," he said, "not yet, but you will."

He released Hayes, took up his folding stool, and made to go. Three or four feet away, he stopped, turned, and looked again into Hayes's eyes. "Everything's about to change," he said. "By sunrise tomorrow nothing will be the same. Of course I'm bound to be sticking with my own regiment. I don't know when I shall see you again."

"No, sir," said Hayes.

"I trust you'll understand me if I say I hope I don't see you anytime soon."

"Yes, sir."

"Good luck to you, Hayes. God be with you."

"Thank you, sir."

Once again the surgeon made to leave but returned to Hayes, and when next he spoke, it was with a confidential tone. "If you *are* wounded, son," he said, "above all else, try to keep it clean. And if you should find yourself in a hospital, resist all drugs as best you can. Fresh air, clean water, sunlight, these will always be the best medicines."

"Yes, sir," said Hayes. "Thank you, sir."

Now the man started down the hill slowly, walking slump-shouldered, as if he were headed toward a punishment. Then, abruptly, he turned back in the direction of the sinks and quickened his pace.

In another minute, Leggett was at Hayes's side. He pushed his hat off his forehead and said, "What did Major Sawbones want with you?"

"I'm not sure," answered Hayes, continuing to look down the path of the surgeon's departure. "He'd like for you to stop *frying* everything in sight."

Leggett laughed through his nose. "And I'd like to cross the Niagara Falls on a tightrope, but chances are that's not gonna happen. I'd say he's taken quite a fancy to you, anyways. Likable fellow that you are."

"He was in a dark enough mood, I guess," said Hayes.

"Ahh," said Leggett, nodding slowly, "you'll be running into plenty of that I reckon. As the sun sets tonight, I expect there'll be no shortage of dark moods."

He squatted and began rooting through a pile of equipment on the ground, muttering something about needing his "good knife." When he'd found it, he stood and pulled out a shirttail for the purpose of wiping the blade. "What I heard just now from Swift," he said, "our whole corps is to march downriver to Ely's Ford tonight. That'll put us a stone's throw from Chancellorsville . . . not a place I ever meant to revisit, I can tell you that. I just hope to heaven we don't end up back in the Wilderness." Now he quickly looked down at what Hayes had been about and pointed his finger at the scattered gear. "Bare essentials, Hayes," he said, "bare essentials. Remember: after a few miles, five pounds feels like ten, and so forth. When we're under way, fill your canteen every chance you get. It's gonna be a warm night.

And don't wash your feet till we get to where we're going. Wet feet, wet socks, sure blisters."

"How far's Ely's Ford?" asked Hayes.

"Far enough to make you wish it was closer," said Leggett. He turned back toward the campfire and his cooking. As he started to move away, he said, "I'll tell you another thing. If them boys over there light up that bonfire they been building, they'll get a hidin' from the captain. Seems some paleface is always burning up his digs and showing Johnny we're on the move."

Hayes stayed still for another minute, surveying the busy scene that stretched before him and thinking of the last letter he'd written to Sarah. In it, he'd described the encampment as an anthill and as a great panoramic painting in motion. A few hours from now—laden with knapsack, tent, blanket, gun, and ammunition—he would stand shoulder to shoulder with the men in his company, not far from this same spot, waiting his turn to fall in and move out. Across the knolls and gaps of darkness, musket barrels and bayonets would catch the sparse light from a sliver of a moon, a trembling necklace of upright and parallel lines, a fantastic flying fence in a dream, not of this world.

The air in the woods has grown heavy and stifling, the leaf- and needle-strewn ground boggy, the undergrowth thicker, the terrain undulating. Overhead, dark clouds, bloated and close, threaten to let loose a torrent. He has already heard rumbles of thunder, both ahead and behind. Mosquitoes dance about his head and arms, gnats whiz straight into his eyes and ears, and every other minute there's a stick on the ground that resembles a snake and gives him a start. He can no longer tell what time of day it is. Hours earlier, the stream he'd been following turned westward, and so he left it, striking out in what his best lights told him was northeast. He means to stop soon and sleep, though he has no shelter from the coming downpour. He figures he'll burrow in under the densest brush he can find. Anyway, the combination of his sweating and the heaviness of the air has kept his clothes still wet. A blunt mallet pounds inside his head, and his old friend, hunger, grumbles below. He has very little left in his bread bag now, and he must make it last.

Ahead, he sees a clearing of some sort, an opening in the treetops where the gloomy light pours down onto a tract of blackened earth. As he draws closer, astonishment swells inside him, choking his breath—it is a swamp, the same swamp he has already encountered some hours ago, a scum-covered expanse out of which dead trees rise, their trunks swollen at the waterline. He stops some yards away, throws down his gear, and sits cross-legged on the ground, defeated; he pulls his shirt up over his head like a hood, a paltry protection from the gnats and mosquitoes. Now he admits to himself what has been a smoldering fear, kept at bay these last several hours since leaving the stream: he is lost, utterly. How can he have traveled in a great circle? The sky offers no help. Strangely, he finds himself thinking of how he'll explain himself once back home in Brooklyn—what will he tell Sarah and his club mates?—and he envisions a headline above a story in the *Eagle,* SHORTEST MILITARY CAREER IN HISTORY. The absurdity of this concern, at this moment, makes him laugh, and once he has started, he feels he cannot stop, which frightens him into an abrupt silence, a silence that seems to expand outward from him in broader and broader circles until it fills the entire forest. He lowers his shirt from his head. Even the insects have deserted him. No bird sings. No breeze whispers in the pines. *The war has ended,* he thinks, *this is the stillness of peace.* And, *No, it's only a dream of death.* Next a flash of white light and a peal of thunder that make him bring his arms to his head, followed by what at first sounds like wind approaching but quickly becomes rain, pelting, quickening the world. The dead stuff of the forest floor quivers, the underbrush quakes, the brown-green swamp appears to boil.

He rolls onto his belly and creeps beneath the surrounding brush. Even in the face of his shame, Sarah won't quite suppress her temptation to gloat. He'll buckle pathetically under the interrogations of every man he meets. He'll not be thought creditable, his story, the truth, taken as pretext. Certainly he'll not be welcomed back by the Eckford Club. He'll withdraw to an upstairs room, lower the shades, Ishmael of Hicks Street.

Now he lays the haversack flat over his head, gripping its straps with his hands close to his ears. He feels the eyes of another traveler, nearby, watching him, but he cannot stir up the necessary pains to worry. The boys of the regiment, a receding but still-loved assembly, fight another battle toward Richmond, he thinks—perhaps the same rain falls on them—and as this thought forms in his mind, a hundred or more of them (somebody's darlings) fall to their death . . . as he himself lives on, lost in the woods, fatuous to the core, and frets about his homecoming to Brooklyn.

The rain on the bag sounds something like musketry. A shot of lightning. A long cannonade of thunder. Razors in his wounds. He sees himself from the high branch of a tree, drenched, prostrate, for-gotten by God; and his mother, underwater, presses her face against the omnibus glass, long tresses of her hair, unpinned, serpentine, rise and fall about her head. The battle-ring in his ears merges with the din of the rain, and as he drifts into—what?—vacancy, all affairs empty, all cares worthless, it's as if the storm and the whole silken pageant of May has moved inside his skull, home there, not wild but infinite, obliterating.

He falls asleep and, in sleep, immediately returns to the burning Wilderness. The woods—sentient, willful, a tight network of limbs and vines—push back at him and breathe smoke into his eyes, scorch-ing his face and hands, as he struggles to advance. Now and again he catches a glimpse of fire through the tangle, and as he proceeds, inch by inch, men and boys emerge from the thicket, some charred, some bleeding from the head, all panic-stricken and weeping, all making as best they can for the rear. He recognizes them only by their sort— youngsters from the drum corps, various officers, teamsters, horseless cavalrymen, an assortment of Negro servants in rags—and yet as each one passes, meeting his eye, he thinks, *I know him.* It is a dilemma, this knowing but not being able to name, and somehow it mirrors another: he can tell that a great clamor of battle, battle cries, and wails of the wounded surrounds him, and yet he hears almost nothing; the grim drama unfolds in silence but for a repeated plucking of a single string that emanates from above the trees. The figures moving to the rear, transformed by the certainty of his *knowing* them, begin to pass straight through him as they go, each depleting him further in the passing; likewise, one quietly divests him of his haversack, another his canteen, another his bread bag and weapon. The plucking of the string, growing steadily louder, becomes a high-pitched whir that settles across the membranes inside his ears. Soon he comes face-to-face with a wall of flames, so hot it singes his eyelashes. Out of the fire a team of horses canters, pulling a caisson on which rides the commander of the brigade, hatless and drunk, the sixteen buttons of his frock coat blazing. The caisson, also bound for the rear, passes in silence, to one side, and as it goes the general lifts his head in a wobbly way and looks directly at him. *Summerfield!* he cries, silently. *Wake up!* Then the brigadier general—a hero at Gettysburg, now reduced to a seedy role in a private's dream—draws a pistol and aims it at Summerfield's heart. Frozen in the moment of his death, Summerfield thinks, *Killing me he kills himself.* The sizzle-string inside his ears abates, and next he is falling down the well of dying, borne by two adolescent angels whom he identifies as those that once hung on to the posts at the foot of his boyhood bed. Of surprisingly limited intelligence, they speak to his mind in the form of three single musical quavers, which enter him with tiny trembling tails through the pupil of his right eye.

Cool

   Quill

      Abiding

When he awakens warm and sodden and quite stationary, belly down on the ground, he thinks at first that he is at the bottom of a well. But of course he has only resumed the waking dream of the forest (lost, now he recalls), and he wonders at how soundly he has slept. The rain has stopped, but there is still the sad noise of its dripping from the trees. He rolls onto his back and sits up, groping in the darkness for his canteen, but he finds only sticks, leaves, and his own shoes. He gets onto his hands and knees and pats the wet ground in a widening circle, blindly, frantically, ever harder and in vain. At last he strikes an object of some weight, his book, Dickens—soaked, cast aside as rubbish—the solitary thing the thief has left him. This is real, not a dream. He is wide awake. He has been robbed as he slept. Sarah's letters gone, his Testament gone, he possesses nothing that would identify him. He feels himself starting to shake, the tremor in his hands spreading upward into his arms and down his trunk, and so he topples onto one side and hugs his knees to his chest. The acrid scents of gunpowder and something fouler, sweeter, seep up through the rain-drenched straw beneath him.

IN THE FIRST HALF of the sixth inning—the match still tied, now at fifteen runs—Vesey went to the bat again and sent a splendid grounder to the left field, bringing in all three of the runs the Bachelors would add to their score before yielding to the Twighoppers.

When Birdsall, the Twighoppers' second baseman, took the bat, he watched a total of nineteen pitches before finding one he deemed suitable, then landed himself on the first base with a grounder muffed by the Bachelors' short stop. Next came Fowler for the Twighoppers, who watched twenty pitches before swinging the bat the first time and watching another seventeen before finally going out on strikes. Hayes, who'd stationed himself with the Bachelors (since that was his own personal category), discerned a mounting grumble among the spectators and decided to pay the Twighoppers a visit.

He requested a time-out from the colonel and approached Coulter, their catcher, most experienced player, and unofficial leader—the likely instigator of this strategy of "patience" at the home base, intended to tire the opposing pitcher. He spoke privately with Coulter, cupping a hand to the side of his mouth. The catcher, who stood head and shoulders above him in height, was required to bend down in order to hear properly. As he spoke, Hayes was aware of their two sharp and disparate shadows on the ground at their feet. "The colonel is getting tight," he said to Coulter. "If we ask him to start calling strikes on batsmen who don't swing at fair pitches, he'll do it. But he's not likely to do it with much accuracy. Can I impose on you to speak a word of caution to your boys?"

Coulter, head bowed, took a moment to absorb what Hayes had said. At last he pressed his lips together and nodded slowly, indicating that he understood Hayes's implications. "I'll speak to 'em straightaway," he said.

"Good man," said Hayes, swatting him on the upper arm, and when the next Twighopper came to the bat, decorum had been restored.

Vesey, in the right field, handled the next hit, putting the runner out with a powerful throw to the first base, and then Coulter himself came to the bat. Perhaps having mended his ways with too much zeal, he swung at the first errant toss from the pitcher and missed. He watched the next two, then poked a missile so high and deep into the center field that a brief hush fell over the grounds, followed by an outburst of cheers. Rosamel, at that position for the Bachelors and judging the hit correctly, had turned and run like a deer toward the farther reaches of the field, headlong down the slope there, and entirely disappearing (along with the ball) from view. Both Birdsall and Coulter crossed the home base for the Twighoppers, amid cheers, and then Rosamel reappeared, charging forward in a state of high spirits and waving the ball madly over his head, signifying that he'd made the catch.

Immediately, cries of "Judgment!" went up both from players and spectators as the Bachelors abandoned their positions and rallied around Rosamel, patting the Frenchman on the back. Amid the uproar, the colonel rose from his chair and again fired his pistol into the air, silencing even the birds in the trees. He holstered his weapon and began taking off his frock coat, an enterprise of momentous struggle. He turned a shockingly red face toward Hayes, who went quickly to his aid.

"I could see no more of what happened than anyone else," he said to Hayes, who helped him out of the coat and laid it across an arm of the chair. "How am I to make a judgment? What possible basis is there?"

Somebody called out "Judgment!" again, which emboldened others, and soon there was another full chorus in swing.

"With respect, sir," said Hayes, "you might consult Rosamel in the matter."

"Rosamel?" said the colonel. "Who in blazes is Rosamel?"

"The man who claims to have caught the ball, sir."

In a matter of seconds, Hayes produced Rosamel, who, questioned by the colonel, swore upon his honor that he'd caught the ball on the fly, adding, with a shrug of his shoulders, "I know it is very incredible."

"Rosamel's an honest man, sir," said Hayes. "He wouldn't lie."

Now the colonel held up his hands to quiet the crowd. Once he had everyone's attention, he said, "Rosamel is an honest man. He wouldn't lie. Judgment is three outs, inning over, score—"

He turned again to Hayes, who whispered the score.

"Bachelors eighteen runs, Twighoppers fifteen!"

A few forage hats went flying into the air. The burly Coulter was seen kicking the dirt before taking his position behind the home base. When Hayes returned to his spot near the Bachelors' bench, Billy Swift came over, sporting a long blade of switchgrass between his teeth; he squatted next to Hayes and put an arm around his shoulders. "The colonel's gettin' tight," he said.

"I know," said Hayes.

"Grand, ain't it?" said Billy, grinning out over the field, up at the blue sky, and back at the spectators. "Positively grand."

THEY LEFT the midday service at Holy Trinity and walked the short distance to Hicks Street in silence. Then, intoxicated by the cloudless sky, bracing air, and abundance of sunshine; the exhilarating music and ceremony they'd just witnessed in church; the houses along the way, dressed in wreaths and garlands of evergreens; and the good cheer evident on the faces of everyone they met—he failed to check himself. "What a brilliant Christmas!" he cried, and she immediately removed her hand from his arm.

In casting a pall over the season, she'd established a tacit understanding that such expressions of joy would unbalance the crisp civility (mixed with private preoccupation) she was managing to maintain toward him. The previous two Christmases without their parents had been sad affairs fraught with a variety of failed experiments, from which, he'd hoped, the third might benefit. But of course the announcement of his intention to enlist in the army squashed any possibility of that. Mrs. B, with the help of her sister Jane, carried on in spirited fashion, overspending both time and money for what Summerfield secretly dubbed "compensating oysters"—an emblem for the many preparations meant to brighten Sarah's unyielding mood. He himself had arranged a small tree and some mistletoe on the gaming table in the parlor, where they'd placed their Christmas boxes. But all such gestures ran more than one risk: they might offend the vigil she was keeping in honor of his imminent betrayal; or, though intended to gladden the heart, they might rekindle instead the loss of their mother, who'd observed the holiday with grace and ingenuity. He supposed his thoughtless exclamation in the street might even have done both.

She lifted her chin an inch and touched her gloved hand to the knot at the hollow of her neck that held her bonnet in place. "Yes, isn't it," she said.

In the next minute they arrived at the house, and he was on the fourth or fifth step before he saw that she hadn't followed him up. He turned and found her standing at the foot of the stoop, apparently lost in thought. He went back down to her and stopped on the bottom step, where he offered his hand. He'd interrupted her reverie, but she surprised him now by smiling up at him sadly—maybe penitently?— as she placed her hand in his. On the landing, she paused again. "I want you to know that I'm aware of the absolute horror I've been," she said.

"You haven't been a—"

"Of course I have," she said. "Just now, you were struck by the beautiful day, while I was thinking how impossible it felt to have to go inside and face Mrs. B's feast. Of all the ungrateful . . . honestly, I can't even think of a word to call myself. And you, Summerfield . . . you would like to have had people in today . . . or go to the festival at the pond . . . or to the theater, and I—"

"But I only suggested those things in case *you* might like to do them," he said.

"Right, but I didn't, did I? I've been nothing but selfish, disagreeable, and tiresome."

He leaned against the railing and crossed his arms. "It's Dr. Littlejohn's sermon that's provoked this," he said.

"It most certainly is not," she said. "I hardly listened to Dr. Littlejohn's sermon. I'm afraid my thoughts were quite elsewhere."

"Well, then you should be ashamed of yourself," he said. "You were brought up better than that."

"I am ashamed," she said, "but not about Dr. Littlejohn's sermon. I go to church to sing and pray and take the sacraments, not to be lectured."

Suddenly the door opened, and Jane, obviously upset, stuck her head outside. "Summerfield, Sarah," she said, "I heard your voices. My poor sister's taken terribly ill."

Inside the dark hallway, festooned holly twined around the frame of the great mirror, and the aromas of Mrs. B's cooking rose from the kitchen below. Sarah quickly shed her bonnet and cape and stood her parasol in an urn by the door. "Where is she now?" she asked Jane.

Jane, younger than Mrs. B by four years, smaller in every way and as thin as Mrs. B was portly, had the pale and shrinking manner of someone who'd spent her life in another's shadow. She leaned in close to Sarah now and whispered as if she were betraying a confidence. "She's upstairs . . . in bed . . . with a pan at her side. Really very ill."

"How is she ill, Jane?" asked Summerfield.

She looked at him a little stunned—an unexpected burden had fallen her way, which she doubted her ability to shoulder—and tears clouded her eyes. "She's sure it was her sampling of the oysters that did it," she said. "She had me throw the rest of 'em out. A terrible waste, too, costly as they—"

"All right," said Sarah, "I'm going up to her."

"Oh, no," said Jane, taking Sarah's arm, "she won't like you to. She was very plain on that point. The last thing she wants is to spoil anybody's Christmas."

"Well, I'm going up all the same," said Sarah. At the base of the stairs, she turned to Summerfield. "You might need to fetch the doctor . . . but let me go see her first."

"I've already got everything laid out for you in the dining room," protested Jane.

"That's fine, Jane," said Sarah. "That's lovely, but first come with me, and let's see what's what."

Summerfield stood in the chilly hall and watched the two women climb the stairs and disappear around the bend at the top. Disappointed, he stayed there a minute longer and listened to their footsteps on the second flight and then on the third. Sarah's reversal of feelings had arrived, late but happily, on the stoop outside—he'd barely begun to enjoy it—only to be usurped by the exigencies of the sickroom. He went into the parlor, where he took a chair close to the fire and loosened his tie a half inch. He dreaded having to call Dr. Tilbrook away from home today. He thought of his clever "compensating oysters"— how peculiar that the delicacies intended to brighten matters had darkened them instead. As he imagined himself going to fetch the doctor, he experienced an urge to *run*, a strong physical impulse that had visited him now and again ever since he was a boy. It felt sometimes as if an animal inhabited his body and wanted letting out—an excess of energy he'd learned to use to an advantage (with inconsistent results), charging up to the line and releasing the base ball from his hand.

Now he got out of the chair and stirred about the parlor. He moved to the gaming table and lit the dozen or so little candles on the tree, then pushed back the doors to the dining room, bright with sunlight, where Jane had set the Christmas table: two place settings on either side at the end nearer the windows; their mother's best dishes, silver, and candlesticks; at the table's center a crystal vase of white chrysanthemums and a decanter of red wine; on the sideboard, a small turkey with a ring of sausages round it, white bread, pickles, applesauce, onions, and celery. He imagined there would be potatoes and some sort of soup yet to come, hot from the kitchen, and, later, dessert. He poured some of the wine into one of the goblets and took it with him to the window. He looked down into Jane's fallow garden, then lifted the goblet to his lips, and at that moment, a bird slammed into the glass, so startling him and causing him to recoil he spilled wine down the front of his white shirt.

He was doing his best with a napkin from the table when Sarah appeared in the wide doorway and stood looking at him.

"A bird smashed into the window," he said, blotting the front of his shirt.

"A bird?" she said, distressed and gliding quickly to the window. She peered down into the garden. "What sort of bird? Was it hurt?"

"Have you no sympathy for me?" he said. "I've spoiled my Sunday shirt."

She moved to him and took the napkin from his hands. "I would have heaps of sympathy for you if you'd smashed your head against the window," she said. "Now go and change, and I'll get things ready."

"What about Mrs. B?" he said.

"I think she's in no danger, though I did have the feeling she would rather die than send for Dr. Tilbrook on Christmas. I persuaded Jane to stay with her."

"How did you do that?"

"I told her we were perfectly capable of serving ourselves," she said, taking a clean napkin from a drawer in the sideboard. She turned to the table and began fussing with the chrysanthemums, straightening a stem or two, and added, "I told her we were no longer children."

A few minutes later, when he returned to the dining room in a fresh shirt, she'd added to the sideboard a soup tureen and dishes of lima beans, potato balls, grapes, and raisins, as well as Mrs. B's tipsy cake on a glass stand. She said her brief time with Mrs. B had caused her to lose her appetite but that she would sit with him and have half a glass of wine while he ate. Thus the Christmas meal passed quietly but pleasantly enough, and he rediscovered a thing he'd known before: that the familiar wild energy he'd felt earlier could be tamed with overeating. Midmeal, the bell rang, producing in them disparate reactions—his intrigued, hers anxious—but when he went to the door, no one stood on the stoop. Looking into the street, he saw a band of young hooligans, down a ways toward Remsen, going about pulling bell knobs for a prank.

With effusive apologies, Jane interrupted them twice, once to tend the fire in the parlor and again to bring up the coffee from the kitchen, each time reassuring them that she meant to return *instantly* to her sister's bedside, not to worry. They had coffee and cake by the fire in the parlor and opened their Christmas boxes. Hers from him contained two white handkerchiefs he'd bought on Montague Street, which she claimed to "adore." His from her contained a silver watch with a fob chain.

"But we agreed not to spend more than ten dollars," he said, dangling the beautiful shiny thing by the fob.

"It was Papa's," she said. "I only had it cleaned and repaired. All this time it was among the things at Mr. Brisling's offices."

He turned the crown, then held the watch to his ear—the ticking, how it mimicked something alive, made him feel light-headed.

"By the way," she said, "Mr. Brisling wants us to stop in after the New Year. Something to do with selling one of Mommy's properties in Flatbush. I do look forward to the day when we can execute these sorts of things on our own."

He understood her allusion: he would one day be a lawyer himself, provided of course he survived to study the law.

They were sitting at opposite ends of the green sofa. The candles on the little tree had melted down. The sun had left the windows in the dining room, and the parlor had grown dimmer. When he looked at her, she held his gaze in some meaningful way. At last she said, "You've had to grow up very fast, haven't you, Summerfield? Too fast, I fear."

"If it's true of me," he said, "then surely it's true of you as well."

"But I was born grown up," she said, laughing. "I don't recall myself as much of a little girl, ever. Do you?"

"No, not really," he said. "You always seemed impossibly old to me. You would forever be older than I, so whatever age you were . . . it always seemed unattainable to me."

"But you," she said. "You were such an amusing mixture of mischief and good manners . . . such a boy. Always on the move. Never still for long—until you discovered books, of course. Even then, reading, you would squirm around as if you needed tying down. Or your foot would be twitching, or you'd be drumming with your fingers."

"You were very observant," he said, not entirely happy with the path of her conversation. Their mother had been inclined to such wistful reminiscing, and he'd never quite dodged the intimation, when she did it, that she'd preferred him the way she remembered him, the way he *used* to be.

Sarah leaned forward and took the new handkerchiefs from the table, folded them neatly, and laid them in her lap. "There's a boy at the school," she said, "Harmon Fellows, twelve years old. His father was killed last month in Virginia, a place called Payne's Farm. He was absent from school for a week, and when he returned to the classroom, oh, how he'd aged! No longer a little boy at all."

"I'm sorry," he said.

"You see," she said, "I worry that when boys have to grow up too fast . . . they can get confused about their feelings."

Now he reached for his cup, though it was empty. He turned it once in its saucer and then rubbed his hand on the leg of his trousers. "I don't know what you mean," he said.

"I see a great confusion in his eyes," she said. "He's caught in a condition that's neither here nor there . . . not the boy he was, certainly not yet a man . . . and I can see that he's no longer at home inside his skin."

She paused, gazed into the fire for a moment, and then looked at him again. "He's carrying an unhappy truth inside himself," she said. "And one has the feeling he wants, above all else, to escape it."

She stopped there in what seemed a purposeful way, and he allowed a few seconds to pass in silence. Unable to find his bearings with any confidence, he said, "Well, that would make sense, I suppose."

She only looked at him but didn't say anything more. Over the course of the past two weeks, as he'd accustomed himself to her cool withdrawal, he'd thought that if he'd meant to drive a wedge between them, he'd done so by announcing his intentions—the actual war was hardly required. But this, now, whatever it was, lacked the clarity of the wedge.

Thankfully, a new idea came into his head, and to his rescue. He said, "Your Mr. Gilfinian tells me he's petitioning the school board for increases for all his female teachers."

He might have sworn she blushed then, but he couldn't be sure, and at that moment, Jane reappeared at the doors to the dining room, cupping something in her hands and weeping. "I found it outside the door, in the garden," she said, in a child's voice. "Its little heart was still beating, still beating when I first brought it inside."

Sarah—quickly up and putting her arm around the woman, leading her through the dining room, toward the hall and the stairs to the kitchen—glanced back at him once, as if to express regret, and then she was gone. The candles on the dining room table were still lit; their flames, having bent as the women moved through the room, now stood straight again. He heard Jane's voice faintly from the kitchen stairs. "The poor thing died in my hands," she said. "It died in my own hands."

He had meant to propose a toast to the memory of their parents, and so he went to the dining table, poured an inch of wine into his goblet, and said aloud, "To Mommy and Papa."

He emptied the glass and poured another inch. "To Papa and Mommy," he said, and emptied the glass again.

Now he returned to the parlor and paused near the middle of the carpet, just behind the sofa. The handkerchiefs he'd given Sarah were good ones, he told himself, but he wished he'd thought of something more original. He wished they'd not seemed so like a boy's present to his mother. He wished he could rid himself of the impression that she was growing unnecessarily complicated, that her every word and gesture carried veiled meanings.

She'd asked him to join her yesterday for the Christmas exercises at her school, and since she'd declined every holiday invitation and extended only this one, he'd arranged to leave the office early. The schoolchildren, delightful to the last, gave recitations and sang carols and enjoyed cakes, lemonade, and lady apples. It was sometime during these activities that Mr. Gilfinian, the school's principal, a clean-shaven energetic man of about thirty, took Summerfield aside and said he wanted him to know that he was petitioning the school board for wage increases for all seven of his female teachers. While he spoke to Summerfield, he appeared to keep one eye on Sarah across the room and from time to time nodded in her direction, as if to imply that he was a champion on her behalf in particular. Summerfield assured the man that his efforts would be appreciated and refrained from saying that Sarah depended very little upon her teacher's wages, for even with an increase they wouldn't support a housemaid.

Among the children, a rumor had somehow got started that he, Summerfield, was Sarah's betrothed. No fewer than five little girls approached him, flushed and giddy, and asked if he was Miss Hayes's "fiancé," a word that apparently bewitched them, its charm undiminished by his negative answer. He began to think that the persistent flow of them was caused by a belief that, with enough repetition of the word, his answer would change. The young boys, for their part, seemed only able to stare at him from a distance and to avert their eyes whenever he happened to catch them at it.

Afterward, on the walk home, Sarah had thanked him for coming but otherwise kept her thoughts to herself. He told her about the little girls and the rumor, which did manage to make her laugh, briefly, though she couldn't account for it—she said she'd informed the children in advance that it was her brother who would be visiting. He mentioned the boys, too, how they'd stared, and she explained that she'd also told the children that her brother played base ball for one of the city's most famous clubs.

"But I should think that would have made them want to meet me all the more," he'd said.

She stopped and placed a hand on each of his arms, as if she meant to instruct him. "Summerfield," she'd said, giving him a most serious look, "don't you see? It put you beyond their reach."

He was still standing near the middle of the carpet in the parlor— recalling that moment with his sister in the street, virtually transported there—when he felt the first wave of nausea go bucking through him. He steadied himself with one hand to the back of the sofa and yanked at his tie with the other.

Now the pace of the evening was to escalate, though with an inverse prolonging effect. He would view much of it as through the bottom of a glass bottle. A remarkably cheerful Dr. Tilbrook would make an appearance after all, at *his* bedside. Some sort of vile aromatic bitters would be administered. And somehow, as if by an unprecedented miracle, night would fall.

In his room, Sarah and Dr. Tilbrook would agree about the inferiority of the gas they were lately being delivered—it burned faster and provided a poorer light. In hushed tones meant to spare him, he would hear them speak about a small fortune's worth of perfectly good oysters, thrown out, when all along it had been the sausages. Doubled over in agony and heaving, he would strike his head against the rim of a pan, and he would think of a small gray bird crashing with a thump against a windowpane.

And then, he would open his eyes and see her face as she sat smiling beside him on the bed, holding a cold cloth to his brow. He would think she'd changed her dress, but perhaps she'd only put on an apron over what she'd worn all day. The light in the room would seem an odd mix of gold and pale white. She would catch him glancing at the window and say that, yes, indeed, Christmas Eve's full moon seemed even brighter a day later, tonight, on Christmas. At his first attempt to speak, his lips would feel as if they were glued shut, but with some effort he would ask his question: "In church today," he would say, "what did you pray for?"

Her smile would not fade even slightly. "For more than one thing," she would say.

"But was there a dominant thing?"

"Oh, I think you know."

"Yes, but I want to hear you say it."

"All right," she would say. "I prayed that you might still change your mind. There, I've said it. Now try to sleep."

LATE IN THE AFTERNOON, Leggett returned to the tent in an even fouler mood than before. Agitated and unhappy about their having to sleep in the Wilderness, he'd left the tent an hour earlier to go scouting and see what he could learn; Hayes surmised from the looks of him that either he'd learned nothing or what he'd learned had failed to please him. The long march, which had taken its toll on everybody, seemed to have shrunken Leggett, and he appeared to Hayes bonier, with sharp angles and a permanent scowl. Now he tore about noisily rearranging everything Hayes had already arranged, sweating, slinging gear this way and that, and swearing under his breath. Hayes sat on the ground nearby, barefoot and opposite St. Clair, the fellow from Maine with the backgammon set, who'd stopped by for a few games. St. Clair had beat him in every game but one, yet Hayes felt proud, for in that one, he'd executed a near-perfect backgame and taken St. Clair for four points. With a knifelike glower, Leggett dismissed them both as frivolous and stupid, and soon St. Clair leaned across the board and whispered to Hayes, "I think I'd best be on my way."

Last night, they'd left camp between eleven and midnight, a great raucous migration through darkness. As rumored, the Second Corps was to march down into the fork of land between the Rappahannock and the Rapidan, toward Richardsville, and from there on to Ely's Ford. They went in two columns of two divisions each, splitting the corps in half and advancing along two separate routes, one more southerly than the other. For the first few hours—afforded little light from the stars and a sliver of moon—they could see nothing of their surroundings; in generally fine spirits, happy to be on the move at last, the men brightened the night with laughter and song. But as time wore on, their heavy packs grew heavier, and the march grew quieter. At first light, Hayes saw violets along the edges of the road and the shredded blankets and overcoats discarded by soldiers desperately wanting to reduce their burden. At sunrise, the two columns united near Richardsville, where they slowed to a snail's pace, moving onward to the Rapidan and the ford.

The day, which started out soft and cool, quickly became hot, more like summer than spring. Once the forward units reached the river and began to cross the canvas pontoon bridge laid by the engineers, what had been a march became a long standing-still wait. Hayes spotted the foxhound Banjo weaving her way through the lines, begging for a scrap. Things picked up a bit midmorning, when the engineers completed their wooden bridge, but it would still be early afternoon before the whole corps got to the other side. When Hayes's company finally reached the river, Hayes followed Leggett's lead and waded straight through the waist-deep water, holding his gear over his head.

Also prompted by Leggett, he filled his canteen. On the opposite bank, they passed through a narrow gulley and then had to climb a steep bluff before they reached a table of flatland thick with trees and scrub. Through the woods, on hard-packed paths of mud, they continued to Chancellorsville. Hayes noticed Leggett peering around—into the thicket at his left, then at his right, then up at the overhanging limbs—like a child, awed, moving through a cathedral. When at last they reached their destination, the men, weary and wretched from the long grueling march, were happy to be done for the day. But Leggett threw his gear angrily to the ground. "So here's where I've ended up after all," he said to Hayes. "Back where I was a year ago. A place I swore I'd never return to." He removed his hat, wiped his brow with the back of his hand, and looked at Hayes as if Hayes were responsible. "We've come this far," he said. "There's plenty of daylight left. Why don't we keep going till we're out of these godforsaken woods?" And leaving Hayes to pitch the tent and arrange their camp, Leggett had stalked off, determined to find out the reasoning behind the decision to stop in the Wilderness.

Now Hayes watched St. Clair disappear into the trees with his backgammon set under his arm. Leggett continued to knock things about, grumbling softly, and Hayes decided to keep quiet. He knew Leggett would soon settle down and say what he'd learned. It wasn't Leggett's nature to go for long without talking. The sun had sunk fully behind the trees now, thankfully, since it had been oppressive. All around, birds were raising a din, an objection, Hayes imagined, to having their forest invaded by nearly thirty thousand men in blue. Leggett found his canteen and took a long drink. At last he looked at Hayes as if he recognized him and still counted him as a friend. "We're waiting for the damned cracker line to catch up," he said. "The general don't want us to get too far ahead of the supply wagons. Now I ask you, Hayes: what good is supplies if we end up butchered by rebels out here in these gnarly infernal woods?"

Leggett lay down on the ground, eyes open, gazing straight upward. "You're an educated man, Hayes," he said, after a moment. "So tell me. If you had to go into town, say, and there was a vicious dog along the road that attacked you and tore up your leg . . . would you take that same road into town the next time? Or would you find a different way to go? That's my question."

"Assuming there was another route to take," said Hayes, "yes, I would go a different way."

"That's all I'm saying," said Leggett. "That's all I'm saying."

"But isn't the cavalry forward?" asked Hayes.

"Sure, they're forward, some of them," answered Leggett. "But they can't be forward in every direction, can they? And besides, a good many of them have been sent back to protect the cracker line. Do you know what the problem with generals is? They always think and act like they know more than they do know. They're always making assumptions about the enemy, and they might be right, and they might be wrong."

"Well, I guess they have to make decisions," Hayes said. "Regardless of what they know or don't know."

"I understand that," Leggett said. "It's hard to sit up tall on a horse with a saber on your belt and a plume in your cap and just scratch your head and shrug your shoulders. But there's another problem that's less comprehensible."

"What's that?"

"How slow they are to learn from experience," said Leggett. He pulled his cap down over his face. "Very slow to learn from their mistakes," he added.

Later on, long after dark and after they'd eaten, Billy Swift stopped by and, a few minutes after that, Rosamel. They had only a small fire, since the night was unpleasantly warm. Somewhere off in the distance, they could hear music—Swift told them a group of contrabands was putting on an amusement—and, farther away still, the occasional pop of a picket's gun. Their own muskets were stacked in a pyramid near the tent. Once Rosamel had taken a corner of Hayes's blanket and sat down with the three other men—and, like the three others, removed his shoes—Billy Swift said, "Rosamel, you're not cutting your usual dashing figure. I don't think I've ever see you looking so bedraggled."

"I have never been so . . . what is this word?"

"*Débraillé*, I think," said Hayes.

"Ah, yes, I have never been so bedraggled," said Rosamel, taking off his red fez and holding it in his lap. "And I cannot feel my feet. They are numb."

"You're lucky," said Swift. "I wish my feet was numb."

"I wish they didn't stink quite so much," said Hayes. "Maybe you ought to think about washing them every now and then."

"I washed them this afternoon," said Swift, pulling one foot up to his nose and sniffing.

This antic from the half-pint Swift made Hayes think of a monkey. "Swift," he said, "I'm kidding."

Swift found a pinecone on the ground and threw it across the fire at Hayes, who caught it with one hand right in front of his face. Hayes considered throwing it back but only tossed it into the fire.

"I do not like this forest," said Rosamel, "this Wilderness. It is inhabited with the remains of dead men. There are bones . . . pieces of rotting uniforms . . . even the skeletons of horses."

"Leggett doesn't much care for it either," said Hayes, glancing at Leggett, who only continued staring into the fire.

"I noticed he was awful quiet," said Swift. "Uncharacteristic, I'd say. Do you reckon he's feeling his age, after marching twenty-odd miles?"

Leggett looked at Billy Swift as if he'd not noticed him till now. He scrutinized the boy for a few seconds, then said, "And I reckon I prefer the company of my thoughts and memories to the likes of you."

"Oh, come on, Leggett," said Swift, undeterred, not in the least offended. "I don't recollect any previous time when we weren't compatible with your thoughts and memories. I'd say they've been our good friends."

Leggett appeared to consider what Billy Swift had said, for it was undoubtedly true. "Well, if you don't mind," said Leggett, "I'll just keep them to myself tonight."

"It is this forest," said Rosamel. "It makes a man pensive."

"Tell us about the fellow who was shot dead sitting on the fence rail," said Swift, but Leggett only cast him another scrutinizing glare.

Evidently determined to get some kind of rise out of Leggett, Swift said, "Tell us the long long story about the private who set off the bomb the rebels had buried—"

Just then, they heard hushed laughter from the surrounding darkness, and Swift fell silent. Another foursome of soldiers emerged into the firelight, and one of the young privates sent a skull from the tip of his bayonet clattering across the ground into their circle, right toward Hayes. "Take a look, boys," said the soldier who'd loosed it, "that's where we're headed tomorrow."

The thing quickly came to rest with its black eye sockets aimed straight up at Hayes, who'd never before seen a bare human skull; startled, he rolled backward off the blanket, and Leggett, on his feet in a flash, relieved the offending private of his weapon, casting it to the ground, and planted a hard fist to the young man's gut. Doubling over and losing his hat, the soldier rammed his bare head into Leggett, knocking him off his feet, and then the two of them were at each other on the ground. In an instant all were involved, disengaging Leggett and the other soldier, whose companions retrieved his weapon and hat and soon led him away into the darkness.

Throughout the brief skirmish, no words had been exchanged. Also without a word, Leggett collected himself, put on his shoes, retrieved the skull from the ground, and moved off into the woods clutching it to his chest.

The three others stood staring in the direction where Leggett had disappeared. After a moment, Rosamel said, "There's a bad egg."

"I didn't think it cause to lose his temper, though," said Billy Swift. "Leggett's just plain played-out, like the rest of us." He turned to Hayes. "I don't guess you've got any help-me-to-sleep in your canteen."

"No," said Hayes. "Just water."

"Well, I'll be off then. I expect the bugles'll be blasting at the first sign of light."

Rosamel left with Swift, and Hayes began rolling up the blankets from the ground. A minute later, Swift was back, alone. "Hayes," he said, "it's not likely we'll be having any more base ball for a long while. And we never got so far as to offering a challenge to another regiment.

So I was wondering, if you don't mind my asking . . . would you have put me in the first nine?"

Hayes smiled as he shook the straw and grit from one of the blankets. "What do you think, Billy?" he said.

"I think yes."

"You think right."

Swift grinned. "Thanks an awful lot, Hayes," he said. "And good luck to you."

Hayes watched him go, a strangely unsettling sight: as Billy Swift walked away with a cheerful spring in his step, the darkness closed abruptly around him.

When Leggett returned three minutes later, Hayes saw that the man's hands were black with soil.

"I buried it," said Leggett. "Best I could with only my hands for a spade."

Hayes nodded. "Let's settle in," he said. "The fire's almost out."

They'd spread pine boughs on the floor of the tent, but the night didn't cool off much, and they lay with their heads outside. When Hayes closed his eyes, he saw the clear image of the troops before him on the road—what he'd seen for hours on end throughout the day—a sea of caps and hats bobbing up and down. The fire died, and the dark was absolute, not even a star penetrated the tangled canopy above. Leggett remained quiet, though Hayes, who'd learned every nuance of the other man's breathing, knew he was awake. If it was introspection that kept him quiet, Hayes thought it might be an opportunity to broach a long-deferred topic. "Leggett," he said softly, after a while, "why do you never write or receive any letters?"

Hayes suspected that Leggett might lack the skills of reading and writing and thought the man's pride may have prevented him from asking any favors along those lines. Additionally, despite all the tales Leggett had shared around innumerable campfires, they were remarkably absent of familial characters and events. Hayes knew that he'd grown up on a farm near Whitehall, but little else.

"Don't have nobody to write to," said Leggett. "My only brother's dead near two years now, killed at Oak Grove. My pa died long before the war ever started, and my ma married a man at the ironworks who took her back to England with him. She wrote us a letter or two, but then there was an end to it. She was in love with the man before Pa died, so I guess she had some shame about it . . . Reckon she wanted to forget us and everything that happened."

He stopped there, rolled onto his side, putting his back to Hayes. He said nothing more then, and given Leggett's melancholy mood, Hayes decided not to press.

After a good long silence, Leggett said, "But sometimes, in my mind, I write a letter to my sweet Jinny."

"Jinny?" said Hayes.

"You'd be surprised to learn a man like me was ever married, but I was. For two happy years and seven happy months. We lived on the farm, made a good life for ourselves. Jinny wanted a baby, and so did I, but it took a long time and then, four months in, she lost it. I always thought she was strong . . . a small thing, for sure, but strong. But she lost it, with a good deal of pain and anguish, and three days afterward she caught the purple fever. You never saw such suffering. Two weeks of hell on earth, and when she finally passed, it felt like a blessing. I loved her more than anything, more than anything I'll ever love again. Sometimes I write to her in my thoughts, tell her about what's going on, how much I miss her. Do a fair amount of complaining in general. Nights like this, right before a battle . . . I always find myself wishing everything had turned out different."

Hayes didn't know what to say. He supposed this story—grim in its own sad surprising way—was the foundation of all Leggett's others. Before he could form any words, Leggett said, "Now how about leaving me alone and letting me get some sleep."

A bird had started up somewhere off in the trees—three persistent chirrups, repeated over and over. Hayes waited a few minutes more, and then said, "What's that bird, Leggett?"

"It's a damned whip-poor-will," answered Leggett. "I sure wish he'd shut up, too."

Hayes drifted off thinking he'd never felt this tired, never felt this exhausted in his entire life, not even the time he'd tossed more than three hundred pitches in a match. He fell asleep but not very deeply, and right away he dreamed a dream he'd had about a week before, of being abandoned by his comrades on the field of battle. He lay on the ground exactly where he'd just fallen asleep, unable to move as the woods around him filled with smoke and gunfire. The men in his company and hundreds of total strangers went by him on horse-back and on foot, one snatching away the tent, another his musket, his knife, his bread bag. When one of the figures snatched the blanket from beneath him, he started awake.

He heard the comforting sound of Leggett's snoring and soon drifted into a deeper, more peaceful sleep. Sometime later he was awakened by a kind of warm pressure against his left arm. Leggett had moved close and rested his brow against Hayes's shoulder. The man seemed to be having difficulty breathing, and Hayes felt some current of fear pass from Leggett into himself. The prospect of his first seeing the elephant had remained fairly abstract—in looming overly long it had lacked durability—but now, encountering Leggett in the middle of the night, somehow impaired, Hayes's heart suddenly filled with dread, and quickened. He stirred, but before he could say any-thing, Leggett pressed his head harder against his shoulder. "I've got toothache," Leggett whispered. "I'm going out of my mind."

By the time the bugles roused them at dawn, they'd searched the neighboring tents and found a lamp to use, then found and waked a dentist nearly a mile away through the woods; the dentist had found an additional lamp and a tooth key, extracted the bad tooth, and sent them on their way; and Leggett's jaw had swollen to the size of a base ball. But they'd not had much sleep.

The woods at dawn, enveloped in fog, were pleasantly cool yet all the more eerie. Familiar scents of coffee and tobacco wafted through the trees, and in the early hours before the troops struck camp and began to assemble for the day's march, Hayes was inundated with cus-tomers eager for his letter writing. Leggett busied himself with pack-ing and assured Hayes that he preferred the aftermath of soreness and swelling in his face to the torture that had been its cause.

Their advance west out the Catharpin Road was bewildering and chaotic. The cavalry, instead of leading the infantry, stayed back with the wagons. Thus the infantry columns, forced to splay and detour around the hundreds of horses and wagons that clogged the road, inched forward in knotted factions and great confusion. The fog burned away early, and soon after the men were under way, the sun beat down upon them relentlessly. Despite all this—and despite the unsettling effect of advancing without a cavalry escort—Leggett put a hand on Hayes's shoulder and said how glad he was to be on a course that would get them, at last, out of the forest.

Then, inexplicably, less than three hours along, they stopped.

The men, jammed close together, began milling about in the heat.

Hayes asked Leggett why he thought they'd halted.

"Don't know," Leggett said, reaching for his canteen. "I guess they can't decide which way to take us. But if they make us wait here, we'll know we're in trouble."

"How so?" asked Hayes.

Leggett passed him the canteen. Hayes had his own, of course, but it was Leggett's way of being friendly. "Sometimes waiting's a strategy," said Leggett. "But more often than not, it's what you do when you don't know what to do next."

Hayes reached into his vest pocket, took out his watch, and saw that he'd lost the fob. The watch slipped from his palm, hit the ground, and skittered, vanishing amid the feet in the crush of soldiers. Hayes squatted and found it easily enough, but already somebody had stepped on it unawares. Through the broken crystal the hands read ten minutes past nine o'clock; he held it to his ear but heard no ticking.

They would stay there, stuck on the narrow road among the pines, for what would seem an interminably long time as the woods around them continued to heat up. Hayes was sure he could smell pinesap and another, burnt odor he couldn't name. Soon, he got Leggett settled in a patch of deep shade off the road and persuaded him to hold his canteen against his swollen jaw. Leggett lay on his side, his knapsack for a pillow, and gazed meditatively at a single white mushroom that sprouted nearby from the dry brown leaves and needles covering the ground. There was, Hayes thought, something oddly mesmerizing about the perfect little mushroom, an innocence about it amid the gruff army, the stomping and yelling and grumbling, the dust clouds left by the horses, the pyramids of stacked firearms. Their brigade—stalled right near the intersection with the Brock Road, at a place called Todd's Tavern—was near the midpoint of the corps, which stretched a couple of miles ahead and behind. After a while, they heard sounds of combat, from faraway north, and out the Catharpin Road as well, to the west. Leggett rose onto his haunches, pointed west, and said, "You hear that, Hayes? That's artillery. It's started. Here it comes . . . and we didn't get out of the damned Wilderness."

WHILE THE BRIGHT FOG OBSCURES, it also reveals. He limps waywardly through brush and first stumbles upon his haversack, discarded by the thief who robbed him while he slept; though it's entirely empty, it is like finding a friend; he pulls the strap over his head and then puts the Dickens novel inside. Less than a minute later, he sees a base ball lying on a bed of leaves. He lifts it from the ground—amber colored, it has been varnished, inscribed with the words 25 APRIL 1864, BACHELORS 24, TWIGHOPPERS 21. This, too, is like a friend, and now, as he moves on, he feels less lonely. The book, the haversack, and the base ball together have restored him a sense of identity, though they have done nothing to restore his sense of direction. For hours (he supposes it's hours) he wanders the damp and misty woods, which are varied only by the occasional ravine. He has blisters on his feet from walking in wet socks, but he thinks the burning sensation they provide with every step helps to keep him alive. His other, more serious wounds, in his thigh and back, have negotiated new terms with his body: they have agreed to bleed less and to swap their sporadic needlelike sting for a duller persistent ache, and in return they have acquired an odor, something like rotting oysters. This change seems a harbinger of others. Along the way, he soon notices that the maddening whir inside his ears sounds more like an undying wind or possibly rainfall on leaves, altogether less strident. Soon, as he rambles, perhaps in circles, he becomes increasingly aware of a kind of nagging absence, and he understands that it's his fellow traveler with the hidden eyes, always watching, now gone. Soon the hollow spasms in his belly migrate into the back of his head, an odd place to experience hunger, unnerving and almost painful. He thinks of these spasms as "brain-pangs" and believes they are compromising his ability to concentrate. Again and again, he must exert an extreme effort of will in order to recall his goal—to get to Washington City and not be killed as a deserter on the way; to get from there to Brooklyn, Hicks Street, and his sister, Sarah.

In time the fog evaporates, and he can see, through the trees, the brighter world of another barren field. He moves in that direction; the field appears to have been recently burned; its openness frightens him, and so he stays within the screen of the woods as he follows its borders. Slowly (for he does everything slowly now) he walks the entire periphery of the field, returning to the spot where he first saw it, and again he struggles to recall his goal. He knows enough to understand that his aim is not to circumnavigate barren plots of land, and so he turns back into the woods, deliberately walking away from the field. Because he is sweating, he stops to open his haversack and take out his canteen but recalls that he has no canteen, no water.

Now water becomes his goal. Moving very slowly, he keeps an eye out for berry bushes and any leaves that might hold rainwater.

Sometime later, he stands in a dark hollow, bending down the tender branches of a young tree so he might lick rainwater from its leaves, when he notices that the fog has returned to the woods. This alarms him, for it seems that he has lost part of the day—this is the morning fog of a different day. Perhaps he has even lost whole days, and, if so, how many? The fright lodges in his stomach, where it convulses, and soon he is on his hands and knees, vomiting a yellow fluid dotted with dark red berries, berries he can't recall having eaten. He puts his hand to his forehead and feels a knot there beneath the skin; he cannot account for it, though he knows he once knew its origin, and it has the odd power to bring Hicks Street and his sister to mind. He shuts his eyes, tight, and wills her to stand before him, to be there when he opens his eyes.

He opens his eyes and sees only a puddle of vomit on the ground, gluey and grotesque. This, he thinks, is patent evidence of God's having deserted him absolutely. Was that why his comrades deserted him on the field of battle, because they somehow discerned that God had deserted him already? *I've no time to be playing nursemaid,* said the officer on the horse, and the horse balked as he tried to turn it. But what officer? The words were spoken to Rosamel, the Frenchman, the Zu-Zu with the fez. *Leave him. Take his weapon.* He knows these were the words spoken and that they were spoken to Rosamel, and he hears them now as he heard them then, not with his ears, but only in his thoughts. He'd had to read the officer's lips, for he'd lost his hearing the previous day. All through the night, he'd tried to stay awake, knowing that if he fell asleep the bugles wouldn't wake him.

When he gets to his feet, his hands are shaking, and so he thrusts them into the pockets of his trousers. After only a few steps, he has to sit down, for his legs wobble beneath him. Once he's on the ground again, he finds that even sitting requires more strength than he has, and so he lies flat on his back. Again he closes his eyes.

While he sleeps, time passes, but how much time?

He awakens to more fog, but doesn't know if it is the same fog as before or that of a different day. The air is unpleasantly warm and moist. He can smell the foul odor of his wounds. His arms are covered with bug bites, two dozen or more, tiny red welts. He has no food or drink. His tongue is swollen inside his mouth. He props himself onto his elbows and looks down a path through the brush, where he can see, in a small clearing only ten or twelve paces away, the wheels of a limber with a field gun. He sits up straight and wipes his eyes. The limber is attached to a caisson, and leaning against the caisson, smoking a cigar (as it happens, the source of all the fog), stands Brigadier General Ward. The general wears a sad smile beneath his enormous droopy mustache, and when he notices that Hayes is awake, he says, "It was the tree limbs, wasn't it, son? That, and little Billy Boy." He waves his hand back and forth in front of his face, fanning away flies.

Hayes, who feels as if he might cry, nods and tries to say *Yes, sir,* but no sound comes from him, and in any case, he's not sure what it is he's concurring with. Now he shakes his head, as if to negate the previous assent, and the general laughs. He takes a long draw on the cigar, tilts back his head, and exhales a plume of smoke toward the sky. "You're delirious, son," he says. "But look on the bright side: now you don't have to kill yourself."

Again he shuts his eyes, holds them shut while counting his breaths, and when he reaches the number twenty, he opens them.

It's nighttime and astoundingly hot. He rests on a bed of pine needles, his bread bag for a pillow, though (because of the book inside it) a very firm pillow. He feels entirely too weak to stand, but he knows he must. Through the trees, the light of a full moon lays a lace cloth over the forest floor. It occurs to him he might abrogate his conviction that God has deserted him and pray for help. He manages to get onto his knees. He imagines himself a little boy, in church. He bows his head, praying silently, moving his lips. "O Merciful God, and Heavenly Father, who hast taught us in thy Holy Word that thou dost not willingly afflict or grieve the children of men; Look with pity, we beseech thee, upon the sorrows of thy servant . . ."

He pauses here to consider if this is a true depiction of himself. Is he God's servant? He thinks not, though he has tried to practice kindness, with the recent exceptions of thrusting his bayonet into the belly of a young redheaded boy; and crushing with the stock of his musket the nose of an old man; and firing his weapon blindly into a smoke-filled thicket, killing an unknown number of faceless men. With those exceptions he has tried to practice charity, even when selfish fantasies may have led him (if only mentally) down creaking staircases and into rooms where he didn't belong. No, not God's servant, but perhaps an unconfident applicant for the position . . .

"In thy wisdom thou hast seen fit to visit him with trouble, and to bring distress upon him. Remember him, O Lord, in mercy; sanctify thy fatherly correction to him; endue his soul with patience under his affliction, and with resignation to thy blessed will; comfort him with a sense of thy goodness; lift up thy countenance upon him, and give him peace; through Jesus Christ our Lord. Amen."

Because the prayer seemed to go by quickly, he prays it again and again, and soon he grows light-headed, a not-disagreeable feeling that flushes down into his limbs.

And next he is standing on his feet and walking.

He drifts without any certain direction through a tangled maze of unvaried character. Light-headedness gives way to a sharp heat

behind his eyes, his feet turn strangely cold, and then he hears it—
the unmistakable plash of water. He follows the sound to its source,
a lovely little stream cascading over a crown of rocks and roots into
a perfectly round black pool; over the surface of the pool, the moon
has knit a quivering net of silver-white ropes. He drops his bag to the
ground, removes his shoes and socks, and walks into the chest-deep
water. Its coolness has the odd effect of both reviving him and drain-
ing him of something vital. He immerses himself, and as he crouches,
fully submerged, the water holds him, as if it's alive, purposive. He
senses its invitation—he could give himself to it and become himself the life of the water. But he stands, sending a radiating quake
of moonlit rings over the surface of the pool. He makes a cup of his
hands and drinks, greedily at first, and then long and slow.

Still at the middle of the pool, he looks up and sees, across the other
side, an ancient dead tree, rising out of the ground like a great obelisk,
broken off at a height of about thirty feet. Washed in moonlight, its
wide trunk—mottled, scabrous, papery—is pocked by dark impressions that resemble human features. And its many craggy arms, of
various lengths and girths, all point in the same direction. Never was
there a clearer signpost.

He retrieves his bag, shoes, and socks from the bank and crosses
to the other side. Once he has put his shoes back on, he sets out again
through the woods on the indicated course. He feels no pain in his
body, only extreme fatigue, and a new fragility that makes him think
of spiderwebs in the backyard garden at Hicks Street. After a while,
he comes to an expanse of pastureland that stretches flat and far away
to a range of low hills at the horizon; atop the hills is a black clump
of trees that looks like a giant panther resting on its haunches, surveying its dominion; deep with grasses and white wildflowers that catch
the moon, the pasture is bisected by two gleaming parallel lines. Any
reluctance he might have felt about the openness of the field is coun-
termanded by the lure of these magical-looking lines; he starts toward
them, even as he doubts his strength to get that far. He is still drenched
through and through from the stream and the pool, and the skin on
his arms appears to glisten in the night air. With every step he grows

weaker, and when he turns for a moment to look at the woods from which he has emerged, he's perplexed by the shallow swale he has left in the weeds—he feels himself too insignificant to disturb even the grasses. The parallel lines ahead of him dim and move farther apart, and soon they themselves appear to be crossed by what look like the pickets of a fence.

He is not to reach them.

Only a few steps away, he collapses, rolling onto his back, the word *railroad* chugging through his mind. He pulls the strap of his haversack over his head and chastises himself for failing to fill his canteen at the stream; then he recalls that he had no canteen to fill. He knows he is dying, and he thinks he no longer has to worry about how he'll be received in Brooklyn. He won't be received at all, not even his body, for there's nothing by which it might be identified. Sarah's letters would have made him known to the stranger who finds him, or the little Testament with his name, regiment, and home address, but these are stolen from him. He recalls the useless varnished base ball with its inscription, the score of a match on a certain date. He recalls the useless words, in his sister's hand, on the flyleaf of the book: "April '64—To my brother, with all my love, Sarah."

A wave of anger breaks through him, but he cannot ride it, for it hurts too much, roiling the liquid centers of his wounds.

The full moon pours down a frigid light.

Now he glimpses the cluster of stars in the gray dome straight up above him, small and luminous and faintly green. With what little consciousness he has left, he concentrates on these, and he sees that they are actually tiny holes in the sky, leaking a mix of gases into the world, meant not for the living, but only for the dying.

He breathes it in. It invades every corner of his body, sorting out and stilling every organ.

Shame and repentance, he thinks. *The sure consequences of rashness and want of thought* . . . And at last she arrives, Sarah, mild, like ash, but only for the briefest moment, to kiss him, and then she is gone.

He touches his fingers to his lips.

He tries to speak—he wants to hear the sound of his own voice once more before he dies, but he can't even manage a whisper. Most surprisingly, he finds himself addressing his father: "Papa, I tried to do right, didn't I?"

It is only a thought, a query, made of air.

He closes his eyes and crosses his feet at the ankles.

He folds his hands over his heart and allows himself to accept this gift, a peaceful death.

BY THE END of the eighth inning, the Twighoppers had narrowed the Bachelors' advantage to two runs, and the score in the match stood at 23 to 21. The afternoon had grown steadily warmer, and the sun came into the field at such an angle that many of the spectators were forced to shield their eyes—which created an effect, Hayes noticed, of their saluting. In the frequent breezes, the earth, long sodden and now baked hard, sometimes gave off a modest stirring of dust. The only clouds in the sky resembled bolls of cotton, and occasionally one cast a round shadow that crossed the field like the stamp of a phenomenon creeping beneath the ground.

At the onset of the ninth, the Bachelors' first two batsmen produced no fruit. Then Vesey—the day's hero, responsible for nearly half the Bachelors' runs—went to the bat. In the heat, he'd rolled the cuffs of his already too-short trousers to the knee, and had they not been so overly tight, they would have resembled sky-blue pantaloons. He didn't find the first toss to his liking; swung at the second and missed; then drove the third high into the center field, depriving the ball of its cover along the way, which fell like a bird shot from the air, near where the Twighoppers' pitcher stood. The ball dropped and rolled some distance past the man in the center field, and by the time he'd retrieved it and fired it to the short stop, Vesey was rounding the third base. Any soldier not already on his feet soon was, for clearly the short stop's throw to Coulter would get to the home base about the same moment as Vesey. Five or six paces from Coulter, Vesey did an extraordinary and shocking thing—he dove headlong, both feet leaving the ground, one arm stretched out before him, and landed belly down with his fingers touching the base. Coulter, disconcerted by Vesey's surprise tactic, dropped the ball, and a roar of laughter went up from the crowd. Soldiers shoved one another play-fully, in disbelief. And before the racket began to abate, new convul-sions erupted from them: as Vesey had got onto his hands and knees in an effort to stand, the seat of his trousers parted, from crotch to waist—an event rendered all the more entertaining by the fact that, like nearly all the soldiers, he wore no drawers.

Some minutes later, when the players changed sides, the low rumble of fun among the spectators took on a ragged cadence that soon gave birth to a chant: *Hayes Hayes Hayes Hayes Hayes Hayes Hayes* . . .

Hayes stood and tried to wave the crowd into submission, but they would have none of it. Aware that the match was in its final chapter, they wanted to see him in the game.

The colonel signaled for Hayes to come forward for a word. He greeted Hayes with arched eyebrows and a kind of knowing smile that Hayes thought altogether odd.

"The purpose of this demonstration is clear," said the colonel, against the background of the unrelenting chant. "I'm of the feel-ing that, whenever possible, clarity should be rewarded. Don't you agree?"

Hayes, who could see that the colonel's stein had exerted a philo-sophical influence, said, "I appreciate your feeling, Colonel. But with respect, I believe in this case clarity might compete with fairness. If I was to come into the match, I should've pitched for each side equally."

"But it's my understanding that you're unmarried."

"Yes, sir."

"Then you couldn't come into the match for the married side, could you? I wonder if you mightn't have an inflated view of your ability, Hayes. Are you really so superior to everybody else?"

Hayes hesitated, weighing the choices the colonel had given him: dishonesty or cheek.

"Well?" said the colonel.

Hayes clasped his hands at the base of his spine and shifted his weight from one foot to the other; the persistent chanting of the crowd felt like a physical pressure. "Colonel," he said at last, "it's less a ques-tion of ability than experience."

"I'm keen to see this superior experience," said the colonel. "It seems the spectators are, too. Please deign to accommodate us and take your position."

He had no alternative but to move to the middle of the field and accept the base ball from the pitcher—this executed amid torrents of cheering.

He reckoned the best strategy would be the quickest strategy. With three pitches, he sent the first batsman down on strikes.

Exuberant cheers from the crowd, head-shaking from the poor batsman.

Likewise, the second man went out on strikes, swinging in vain at three in a row.

More cheers, more head-shaking.

The third Twighopper at the bat watched a pitch, then swung and missed at the next three, and thus Hayes finished the inning with ten pitches.

He was besieged by soldiers, much backslapping, and shouts of victory. The regimental band began to play, and when Hayes emerged from the knot of comrades, he saw the colonel struggling up from his chair and looking one way and another, as if he hadn't quite grasped that the match was over.

Suddenly somebody grabbed Hayes from the side and pulled him into a bone-crushing embrace: Vesey, the big man from Bushwick, a sack coat tied by the arms around his middle to hide the split trousers, and tears in his eyes.

A CLATTERING OF WHEELS, a ringing of wheels. He passes in and out of awareness, on his back, shaken to the teeth, rocked by the quaking conveyance beneath him. Darkness. A stench, like being downwind to the sinks at Brandy Station.

Stars overhead, razor sharp, flute the sky.

Men, asleep, pressed up against him, and always the deep rattle of wheels below. A mammoth world, beyond understanding. A raging world, hurtling him through the night.

A train.

Not dead.

He is a little boy. They have been somewhere to visit some people who live on a farm, friends of his mother. A pasture, dotted with white flowers. It's a long carriage ride home, and he falls asleep. Warm night air. He wakes, pressed against his father, rocked by the quaking conveyance beneath him. A clattering of wheels. In and out of awareness. He's being carried up the steps of a house. Darkness and light. Through doors, down passages, carried. A lamp, swinging. Laid in a bed. Undressed, washed, dressed again. Covered. Unkissed.

Alive.

A mammoth world, beyond understanding.

TWO

Mr. X

He only seemed to contrast his present cheerfulness and felicity with the dire endurance that was over,'" reads the big old man with the deep delicate voice, quite near Hayes's bedside. Hayes lets his eyes close and tries to concentrate, not on the words but on the sound, which, like everything, is both strange and familiar. He imagines he has made a long journey, inside some sort of box; now and again, due to a certain tilt, a certain jolt, a lid fell open, allowing him a glimpse of what was about, but only a glimpse, quickly overwhelmed by darkness. His strongest feeling is that of having been *brought* to this place, deposited without his consent or collaboration, like cargo. In the bed, he strives not to move a muscle—the dubitable hope of the cornered animal, that there might be safety in stillness.

In the large room, the old man's voice hums pleasantly beneath a babel of human exchanges (the full range of the choir, basses and tenors, altos and sopranos); a jangle of small metal objects; the scraping of furniture and shuffling of many feet over a wooden floor; occasional groans of pain; occasional groans of frustration; and, from outdoors, the ringing of a bell (deeper than a cowbell, higher than a church bell), sporadic, as if blown by wind. The sea of sound has a calamitous character (and like a sea ebbs and flows), and sailing over it all, somewhere a woman sings a hymn of inexhaustible verses, in a voice of penetrating shrillness, off pitch, altogether alarming. Still, what Hayes finds most grim within the clamor are the odd pockets of silence, which seem to signal failure, bewilderment, disappointment, horror, despair. For a moment he experiences a rocking sensation, as if he rests on the deck of a boat, but it's a phantom thing, a scrap of memory lingering in his limbs.

He parts his eyelids carefully, and from his flat position, close to the floor—his neck banked only slightly forward by a pillow—he can see a good portion of the room: a network of white-painted rafters, a whitewash of sunlight in the vault of the roof, a lantern on a long chain. Dark pictures hang in frames above gas burners on the narrow walls between the many windows—a church, perhaps, serving as a hospital ward, though certainly not with the smells of church but rather those belonging to illness, human suffering, dying flesh, and other odors, too, vaguely chemical. Great diaphanous swags of white netting fall from the rafters, festooning the place with a celebratory air; a warm foul-smelling breeze wafts through the windows, sets everything in motion, sickening light, dizzying shadow. A brown rat trots across the rafter directly overhead, stops, looks down at Hayes, scurries on, and vanishes into the eaves.

"'He embraced her, solemnly commended her to Heaven,'" Hayes hears and lowers his gaze to the gray-haired, gray-bearded man, dressed in a wine-colored suit and sitting in a wooden chair, his head bent over a red-covered book. Large, big-headed, and hunched over, he makes Hayes think of a buffalo. A dark and polished cane with a plain silver handle leans against the man's chair. A crumpled knapsack lies at his feet. Hayes detects a tired hoarseness in the man's voice and an accent that seems a blend of more than one region; sees that he is quite flushed, the rims around his eyes dark pink; and tries to recall how he knows him, at least to some degree, already. (The man cannot be a surgeon, for in that role he wouldn't read to Hayes from a novel, nor would he wear a wine-colored suit.) Back of him, along some sort of central artery, a parade of travelers flows—several women of various ages, most of them plain-looking in hoopless black or brown dresses, unadorned in every way; many scrappy-looking soldiers, busy but slow-moving, all bewhiskered, all unkempt, one or two with a broom, another with a pan of bloody rags; a skinny black woman toting a stack of cream-colored blankets; two Catholic nuns; a pale, richly suited man with a birdcage; a bonneted old woman peddling milk; three black-garbed, thin-lipped preachers clutching Bibles; a Negro boy with a yellow, floppy-eared dog; and a number of wounded men, in a diversity of dress and half dress, some with canes, some with crutches. Of this last sort, one now and again pauses to whisper a word into the old man's ear or merely to stroke his hair—one young patient with a bandaged head even stops to kiss the old man's brow. These mild, apparently commonplace intrusions he suffers unruffled, as an ox suffers gnats. To Hayes, it all feels like a lot of clutter, much too rich a brew, and he's aware that there's a significant blank space inside his mind: a large white leaf of paper devoid of everything but a few suggestive scribbles (a train, a moon, stars, a river, a steamboat, a stretcher, a lovely young woman), lacking substance and shading. He thinks of a white tablecloth in the dining room at Hicks Street, specks of orange pollen at its middle where a vase of flowers has been removed. He's aware, too, that beneath these mental impressions of blank paper and white tablecloths—which now seem tightly drawn, tightly laid—some horrible sadness waits. But he is pleased to observe that his strategy of holding utterly still has had a calming effect throughout his body. His injuries cause him no pain. The persistent whirring inside his ears has abated to a soft, intermittent rasping sound. His hands are stable, at rest. He thinks that if someone were to supply him with a pad and pencil now, he would be able to write his name. Though he would of course decline to do so—might even pretend to lack the ability—he relishes the idea of having the option.

"'Doctor Manette was very cheerful at the little supper,'" reads the old man. "'They were only three at table, and Miss Pross made the third.'" He stops abruptly, lifts his gray head, and looks at Hayes long and hard, as if the stir of Hayes's thinking has caused the interruption. To Hayes there's something familiar in this, too, a notion that the old man is supersensible to his thoughts. The man smiles kindly, admiringly (though there is surely little to admire), reaches out a soft warm hand, and pats Hayes on the knee.

Just then one of the scruffy characters with a broom appears behind the old man; working the handle in a scouring fashion, he passes, from right to left, limping, in and out of Hayes's line of vision. The broom makes a grating noise, and somehow Hayes knows that sand has been scattered on the floor as a means of cleaning without water. Though he won't turn his head to look, he understands, when the man speaks, that he addresses the patient in the adjacent bed. "I see you dogging me with them sunken eyes," says the man. "I expect I'll have that bedsheet for you tomorrow."

From his chair, the old man speaks into the pages of the book: "But that's what you told him yesterday. And the day before that. Must the poor creature be always made to lie in a puddle?"

Again Hayes doesn't turn to look, but he judges, from the abrupt halt of the grating noise, that the man with the broom has stopped in his tracks. Now he reappears, leaning in close to the old man's ear. With a challenging, saccharine tone, he says, "Well, why don't you take yourself over to the linen room and see what you can find that I can't? Or better still, I have no doubt but that you could go out and *buy* him some if you like." Now he straightens up, gives a conspirative nod to the end of his broom handle, and moves along.

The old man only laughs and looks again at Hayes. Again he smiles, this time wearily, and says softly, "Mr. Babb doesn't like me. He thinks I'm wealthy—which is beyond funny—and it makes him angry that I choose to visit the hospital when he would give his eye-teeth, if he had any, to be excused."

His gaze rests for a moment longer on Hayes's face, as if he hopes against hope for a reply, but then he lowers his eyes again to the book, removes a fan from the pocket of his coat, opens it, and fans himself as he continues reading: "'He regretted that Charles was not there; was more than half disposed to object to the loving little plot that kept him away; and drank to him affectionately.'"

He stops again and says to the man in the next bed, "I *will* find you a clean sheet, Leo, even if I have to go to my rooms and take it off my own bed."

Now he lowers his voice and speaks to Hayes: "It really is appalling the kind of incompetent rabble that can rise to power in a hospital. I've seen the likes of Mr. Babb kill a patient, dosing him with the ammonia nitrate meant for use as a foot wash. I almost thought it intentional." He shuts his eyes and shakes his head, apparently outraged, but he seems to check himself, willing himself back from that former atrocity to the more agreeable business at hand. He smiles at Hayes apologetically.

"From the looks of it," he says, "this novel's been left out in the rain. The covers are swollen and the pages wavy." He lifts the book to his nose. "Smells like wet rope, gone sour." He laughs softly to himself and adds, "But otherwise first-rate."

He coughs and clears his throat with some effort. Then reads: "'So, the time came for him to bid Lucie good night, and they separated. But, in the stillness of the third hour of the morning, Lucie came downstairs again, and stole into his room; not free from unshaped fears, beforehand. All things, however, were in their places; all was quiet; and he lay asleep, his white hair picturesque on the untroubled pillow . . .'"

HAYES HAS SLEPT AGAIN, and when he wakes, sweating inside a tent of gauze, he feels as if an animal inhabits his body and wants letting out—that excess of energy known to him since boyhood. He recalls the first time he felt it, an evening long ago when his father made him wait inside an office while he conducted a class in the adjacent studio. That night, a question began to form inside him (made not of words, but flesh and bone), a question whose answer, he would discover, was base ball. Even now, he imagines that if by some magical means he could be transported into the midst of a match, all would be right with the world again, order and reason restored. As it is, he must content himself with the memory of an afternoon near Brandy Station, when scores of soldiers threw their forage hats into the air, and their yells, echoing in the nearby woods, had nothing to do with killing or dying.

The old man who read to him earlier has gone, along with the chair he occupied. He can see through the netting that the gas burners on the walls of the ward have all been turned down low. The place is quiet but for the occasional sound of a man snoring, or another coughing, or sighing, or softly moaning. The many visitors have left.

Two or three male attendants roam the ward quietly, but the female nurses have retired to wherever they go at night. Hayes is certain that the female nurses will return in the early morning, though he cannot account for how he knows it. He seems to know a great deal he can't account for. An aroma of tobacco pervades the air, masking but not dispelling the other smells—what he now thinks of collectively as "rot." These are the hospital odors, but through the open windows wafts another foul smell, and Hayes knows, inexplicably, that it comes from a nearby stagnant canal, an open sewer. He knows, without raising his head from the pillow, that at the middle of the ward, he will find a night watcher, who sits at a table smoking a pipe and reading a magazine by the light of a shaded lamp. If Hayes leaves his bed and goes to visit the sinks, he must pass this table, and the man will peer at him briefly, without a hint of interest, without a word or a nod. Hayes knows the exact location of the water closet, at the end of the ward opposite the dining room. The ward itself is a long narrow pavilion with beds arranged in two rows along either wall. Hayes's bed (iron, with lengthwise wooden slats) has a number, which, by association, is Hayes's own number, 33. He knows that this ward is one of many like it, and that the hospital—located not far from wharves and a railroad depot—comprises dozens of buildings connected at their midpoints by covered passageways. He knows that among the buildings are a kitchen, a bakery, a post office, stables, a laundry, and a chapel. He knows that close to the stables and the chapel is the deadhouse.

He was wounded in battle; abandoned by his company in the field; left to find his own way home. He endured a long and perilous journey, keeping to brush and streambeds for fear of being shot, either as an enemy or as a deserter. It seemed to him at first that he hadn't survived, that he'd died, and that these new shadowy confines and ghostly drapes and shapes constituted the afterlife. Now he understands that he was rescued, brought by rail and boat and stretcher to a military hospital in Washington City, where he has been for a few days already. He was stripped and bathed and put into some kind of white bed-shirt with long sleeves and brown stains on the cuffs. He has been questioned and examined by two different officers in charge, as well as one very austere woman. He remains unable to speak, and when he has been given the opportunity to write his name, his hands shook so severely, both pad and pencil went flying. A tag, pinned to his chest, reads UNKNOWN. A pink card is clipped to the end of his bed, indicating by its color (he has gathered) what food he is to be served—soup, bread and butter, boiled potatoes, tea with milk. The other patients have two cards clipped to their beds, a colored one and a white one, which Hayes believes records the patient's diagnosis. If he's correct, he supposes it means he has not yet been diagnosed. He does not recall his wounds being dressed, but he imagines they have been seen to, for he suffers less pain than before. He walks with a slight limp—due to a persistent soreness in his thigh—though he can get by without the cane or crutches many others require. Exhausted by his ordeal, he sleeps day and night. When he is awake, he frets (itself another inducement to sleep). Apparently, he is being allowed to convalesce here, but not everyone has been kind to him, and he senses duplicity behind the smiles of those who have. He possesses no documentary proof of his impromptu discharge in the Wilderness. He has avoided the eyes of most of his fellow patients, for he believes they regard him as suspect. Some of them are horribly wounded—clearly dying—others quite low with disease. Still others linger in the wards because they lack the wherewithal to get home and have nowhere else to go. Since the sick and wounded arrive from Virginia by the hundreds every day, the beds in the wards have been moved closer together, to accommodate folding cots with canvas covers. Hayes believes there are those who would have him out of his hospital bed and stood before a firing squad. His single design for protecting himself is simple: for as long as possible, he will conceal his identity. This strategy—based on the notion that no one will proceed against him if they don't know his name—is less than infallible. But as it dovetails with his inability to speak or hold a pencil, it is also the only strategy he can think of.

Now he resolves to remember everything he knows, not to forget the particulars of his situation. Earlier, when the old gentleman read to him from the novel, Hayes's mind drifted into a dreamy state, in which he experienced things as if for the first time (thus the strange-but-familiar feeling). Perhaps, he thinks, this state might seem happier—"Where ignorance is bliss, 'tis folly to be wise"—but it is unsafe. Through the netting, he sees a tall black stovepipe running up into the vault of the roof. Across the way, two Union flags fall from poles that jut at an angle from brackets mounted to the window frames. He sees the lamp hanging from the ceiling, extinguished now as always; its brass parts glow in the lowered gas lamps, and soot dulls its chimney. This, he decides, will be his anchor. Any time he feels himself drifting, he'll look to the lamp, and it will bring him back to himself.

To Hayes's right, the young man in the next bed begins to hum a tune, softly. He is not much older than Hayes, freckled, with reddish-brown side-whiskers, and called by the name of Casper. Like most of the patients on the ward, he rarely takes off his bummer's cap, and Hayes, who arrived without one, envies the comfort he imagines it gives him. Casper's left arm has been amputated just below the elbow, and the stump, swaddled in yards of bandaging, he has adopted as an infant child. He holds it with his right hand and rocks it and now and again sings to it; if people speak too loudly near his bed, he sometimes hushes them, gently admonishing them not to wake the dear, sleeping stump. Hayes admires Casper's resourcefulness and good cheer. The soft tune he hums makes Hayes think of his own mother. (The young Summerfield stands in the hallway outside the slightly open door to her room, where, braiding his sister's hair, she holds some pins between her lips and hums a wistful melody.) Hayes closes his eyes and listens to Casper's lullaby, but soon he becomes aware of a small commotion to his left. The patient on that side of him—Leo, the poor man who has been shot through the bladder and leaks into his bedding—is outstretching his arm across the space between their beds. Hayes finds the part in the netting and takes from the man a small looking glass. Leo, entirely silent as always, seems satisfied and withdraws his arm, back into his own gauzy tent.

Hayes peers briefly into the glass (where he finds gazing back at him a pair of surprisingly ancient-looking eyes), and he tries to think why Leo would pass him the mirror in the middle of the night. He cannot imagine what the man's intention might be. But the next morning, when he finds Leo's bed empty and watches as a surly attendant strips its sodden sheets, he'll construe the incident of the looking glass as the feeble and brokenhearted impulse of a middle-aged soldier with no one to bid good-bye.

WHEN HE WAS very young, perhaps four or five, his father took him one evening (for reasons he was never told or, if told, never understood) to his Brooklyn dance studio, where Mr. Hayes was to conduct a gentlemen's class at eight o'clock. They'd set out on foot for the studio around seven, and as it was October, dusk had already cloaked the houses along Hicks Street. A bright yellow moon rose over the river, which meant that the fascinating new streetlamps, powered by gas piped beneath the ground, would not be lit tonight, a disappointment. Mr. Hayes said something about the "crisp" air, a remark Summerfield connected to the clopping of horses in the streets. He'd never before visited his father's studio—which was located on the upper level of a two-story building opposite the City Hall—and he was immediately taken with the large room's golden floor and enormous windows with arches at the top. Most odd, Mr. Hayes had brought along a pic-nic supper in a hamper, and after the ordeal of lighting the many tallow candles of the studio's two chandeliers, they retired to a small connected room that served as an office. Here an oil lamp was lit, and they ate slices of cold meat, apples, and asparagus at the corner of a dark imposing desk. There was lemon cheesecake for dessert, but just before they got to it, someone arrived at the office door—a dashing and jolly man, who, when introduced to Summerfield, clicked his heels together and saluted like a soldier: Mr. Houseberry (funny name), who played piano for the gentlemen's class. Mr. Hayes offered his piece of cheesecake to Mr. Houseberry, who made a negligible protest, sat down on a stool next to them, and ate it, exclaiming again and again, "What a treat! What a treat!"

When he was done, Mr. Houseberry pulled a handkerchief from inside his coat and began to wipe his mouth and whiskers. While still executing this thorough clean-up, he said gravely, "So, Mr. Hayes, tell me, where do you think this ugly slave business will end? This secession business, this Compromise business, where is it all going to end?"

Mr. Hayes glanced at Summerfield and drew his lips into a thin line. He shook his head sadly and sighed. "I honestly don't know," he said at last.

"Well, I think it'll surely end in war," said Mr. Houseberry and returned the handkerchief to its place inside the coat. Summerfield couldn't tell—not from the man's face, not from his tone—if war pleased or displeased him.

"I hope not," said Mr. Hayes. "Or if it does, I pray it comes quickly and ends quickly, long before Summerfield's of age."

"That's the bind, isn't it?" said Mr. Houseberry. "That's the pickle. Efforts to avoid only serve to delay. And then we'll be in for the ruin of the long-smoldering fire."

Mr. Hayes stood and took a step or two toward the doorway. Using his weary voice, which generally indicated it was time to move on, he said, "I hope you're wrong, John."

"About what?" said Mr. Houseberry, turning on his stool.

"About everything," said Mr. Hayes, holding open the door. "About everything."

After Mr. Houseberry retreated to the studio, Summerfield soon heard a succession of scales from the piano, a rapid report, staccato style, that sounded as if the notes were being fired from a gun. Mr. Hayes changed out of his street shoes into a pair of peculiar red dancing slippers and white silk socks, which he claimed made it easy for students to observe the movements of his feet. Then he looked thoughtfully at Summerfield, and as if to explain his sacrifice of the cheesecake, he said, "I'm afraid I don't pay Mr. Houseberry enough."

He lowered the lamp and got Summerfield settled on a bench with a soft cushion and a shawl. He told him he didn't need to fall asleep, but that he should rest there until the class was over. He bent down and indicated by tapping a finger to his own cheek that Summerfield should kiss him, a request so rare it made Summerfield timid. "Well, come on," said Mr. Hayes, tapping his finger again, and Summerfield craned his neck and pressed his mouth against his father's face just above the line of his whiskers. The kiss left a salty flavor on his lips, which he explored cautiously with the tip of his tongue. "You won't be afraid, will you?" said Mr. Hayes, and Summerfield shook his head. It was true, he would not be afraid.

A short windowless hallway without lamp or candle connected the office to the studio. When Mr. Hayes left, he closed the doors at either end, and Summerfield could then barely hear the sound of the piano. The walls of the tiny office were paneled with dark wood, which glowed in the low lamplight, reddish and beautiful. Soon Mr. Houseberry stopped playing scales and began what might have been a church song—it progressed in the orderly style of a church song—and though the music sounded soft through the walls, Summerfield knew it was probably loud in the studio. Briefly he wondered what "of age" might mean; it sounded to him like another way of saying "very old," but he couldn't make sense of things, and he wasn't even sure if he'd heard correctly. He rolled onto his side and noticed that the fabric on the cushion of the bench where he lay had a pattern of bees; his eyes were quite close to the bees, and he discovered that by fluttering his eyelids he could make the bees appear to dance. Soon, one of the bees, bored with dancing, flew away down into the kneehole of the enormous desk; Summerfield, following it there, found a very pleasant pond surrounded by willow trees, where his mother and his sister, waiting inside a white gazebo, greeted him affectionately.

When he awakened, he could see nothing but unrecognizable shapes, darker within a darkness that smelled of lamp oil. He sat up and felt his feet touch a solid floor. Nearby he could make out the brass crescent shape of a doorknob. From far away, he could hear music playing, a piano, something fast and merry, which grew louder once he'd got the door open, louder still as he groped his way down a black hall (floor squeaking beneath his feet) and found a second knob. The next door, heavy and perhaps swollen, required all his strength just to draw it open enough so that he could press himself sideways through, and he ended up for a moment with his back to the place he'd entered. When he turned, he faced a spectacle stranger than any dream: at the farther end of the room—which was hot and smelled of wool and tobacco—many black-suited men danced together as couples, whirling in a frenzied manner, laughing as they went round in a circle;

behind them, four great arched windows rose up to the ceiling, black storybook mountains. As the piano grew steadily louder, the notes faster and faster, a heavy man slipped and crashed to the floor, causing, like cascading dominoes, a mad pileup, roars of laughter, and a sudden end to the music. Then, strangest of all, he heard his father, crying out from the midst of the ruckus, "And that, gentlemen, is the ball . . . room . . . polka!"

Summerfield, who had moved slowly forward and stopped beneath the first of the chandeliers, now felt wax drip onto the sleeve of his jacket. He looked down, and when next he looked up, one white face from the jumble of men, one pair of eyes, had found him and stared back at him with a startled-dead expression.

He turned and ran to the door behind him, wriggled through, pushed it shut, and stood in the now-soothing dark. After another moment, he thought, *Papa, Papa's studio, dancing class, cushion with bees.* As he moved on, sliding his right shoulder along the wall, these thoughts, like stones in a stream, brought him back to himself.

But when he gained the bench inside the office and lay down again, he couldn't seem to rest, couldn't even keep his eyes closed for more than a second or two. Lying on his back, he held his hand up a few inches over his face; he could barely see his fingers, but as always, there were four, and a thumb.

What a surprising word, *thumb,* not at all like something that bled when pricked by a thorn.

From beyond the windowless hallway and closed doors, faintly the music started again, slow at first, but gradually faster and faster. He cupped his hands over his ears and squeezed his eyes shut, but of course this did not entirely deliver him from a world in which anything at all might happen, in which men were capable of absolutely anything. He was brought back to himself, but not entirely. He was unafraid again, but not entirely. Mostly, he felt too tight inside his body—too large for the confines of his skin—and a strong wild urge to run.

"BOY, WAKE UP!" the woman cries, and when he opens his eyes he sees, dressed all in black and leaning over him, the shrew everyone calls Matron. Her steel-gray hair, parted with razor sharpness straight down the middle, is pulled tightly into a knot at the back of her head. Overly thin, she appears always to tremble, and there's something wrong with her eyes—they are inflamed and protrude from their sockets. "Tell us your name, boy!" she shouts, as if her face were not inches from Hayes's own.

Now she stands erect, a posture from which she can look more thoroughly down at him. "Your *name*," she says as the attendant Babb moves with his pronounced limp beside her. Together they stare at Hayes, Babb's mouth pressed tight and turned southward at the corners. Hayes hears from outdoors what sounds like a boat whistle, and the familiar bell that seems to ring when the wind blows. Matron lifts her chin and restores her head to its customary drawn-back position, a bearing Hayes thinks the likely result of her having found too much in life from which to recoil. "Well then," she says at last, "I think he can do without any breakfast. Perhaps it will help him to find his tongue."

Babb, scrutinizing Hayes, nods and says, "Yes, ma'am. But do you think he can hear you?"

Matron moves to the foot of the bed. "Mr. Babb," she says, "please pass me that looking glass from that table. It shouldn't be there."

Babb hands her the mirror. "He hears me," she says. "He knows perfectly well what I'm asking him. Only he will not try to answer."

"He's lost his voice," says the freckled man, Casper, from the bed to Hayes's right.

"Perhaps so," says Matron, "perhaps not. But I have little patience for boys who won't make any effort. No breakfast today, Mr. Babb."

As they start to move away, Matron pauses and says, "And Mr. Babb, will you *please* get this other bed stripped, double-quick. And don't make me ask you twice."

Babb, stopped, calls to her, and she turns around. "I'll strip the bed," he says. "But since it's women's work, not suitable for a veteran soldier, and a convalescent one at that . . . and since you're in no position to be giving me orders . . . I'd thank you not to take that tone."

"Yes, yes, my apologies, Mr. Babb, I didn't mean to offend," says Matron quickly, and continues on her way.

Hayes rolls his head to the side and watches as Babb removes the soiled, wet linens from Leo's now-empty bed. Once Babb has every-thing wadded into a tight ball, he stops a colored boy passing by in the aisle and thrusts it onto the boy's chest. "Take these to the laundry double-quick," he says sternly to the boy. "And don't make me ask you twice neither."

Hayes hears Casper laughing softly and ventures a glance his way. Casper looks at Hayes—they share the amusing moment provided by Babb, but something else, too: Casper whispers, "You *can* hear every-thing, can't you?"

Hayes averts his eyes to the ceiling.

Several minutes pass, in which he senses the ward growing more crowded, busier, noisier, reacquiring its daytime circus atmosphere. Soon Casper is humming softly to his stump again, and Hayes stares up at the lamp on its chain. He will not allow himself to drift, will not lose the details of his situation. It is morning. On the opposite side of the ward, a steward moves from window to window, drawing the blinds. Perhaps at this same moment, Hayes thinks, a young woman in Brooklyn raises a window shade in a house on Hicks Street; she has only recently awakened and still wears her nightclothes. She stands at the window, looking into the garden, where the cherry trees are in bloom; she hopes to have a word from her brother today, for it has been a worrisome long time. Hayes stares at the lamp, which—in an agitation of the warming air—moves a half inch to one side and back to center. Or perhaps the young woman doesn't think about her brother at all. Perhaps she still sleeps, only sleeps. Perhaps she has dreamed of his dying and wakes in distress. Or maybe her dreams were all pleasant, full of cherry blossoms and butterflies, and she wishes she could return to them, for on waking, she recalls how angry she is at her brother for deserting her.

"Well, it looks to be Christmas in the month of May," says Casper to no one in particular. "And here comes Santa Claus."

Hayes lifts his head from the pillow and sees, a dozen beds away, the old gentleman in the wine-colored suit; he has removed his floppy gray hat, which hangs on its drawstring behind his neck; he appears freshly bathed and groomed and carries a slate-colored knapsack strapped over his shoulder, from which—as he makes his way up the ward's central aisle, moving from bed to bed—he distributes to the patients writing pads and pencils. When at last he reaches the empty bed to Hayes's left, he stops, drops his bag to the floor, and sits at the foot of the mattress. Hayes notices the two little gold acorns attached to the drawstring of the man's hat and he detects a sweet lemon-scented soap, one he thinks his sister, Sarah, sometimes uses. After a moment, the man turns and looks at Hayes, who only returns his eyes to the ceiling. The man heaves a great sigh, a perfect mix of sadness and resignation, then stands and moves around to the other side of Hayes's bed, between Hayes and Casper. He reaches into the bag and gives to Casper a small homemade writing pad and a pencil, for which Casper thanks him, smiling shyly.

"You don't usually visit us in the morning," says Casper.

"I decided not to work today," says the man. "It's going to be too hot, I think."

Hayes's hands, resting on his belly, already start to quiver—in his case, the gift of pencil and pad seems diagnostic, instructive, pointed. But the man removes from the bag a small red apple, which Hayes accepts, more awed than grateful. Evidently pleased with this reaction, the man leans in and kisses Hayes just above his right eye, where, years earlier, he'd been struck by a base ball bat, the blow that left the small, permanent lump beneath the skin. And then, without further ado, the old man moves on.

Hayes immediately becomes aware of Casper's studying him from across the short distance between their beds. When Hayes returns his gaze, Casper whispers, "How about a nibble? Just a nibble . . . promise not to take more."

Hayes passes him the apple, and Casper holds it between his thumb and middle finger, turning it one way and another, admiringly, tosses it into the air, and catches it. He takes a bite and closes his eyes, savoring the flavor, chewing slowly, then passes it back to Hayes with a sad, reverent expression that makes Hayes think of the Holy Eucharist. Hayes samples the apple—the first he has had since leaving Brooklyn—but to his disappointment, he finds he has no appetite, and he gives it back to Casper to finish.

A minute later, Babb appears at Casper's bed with a pan of water and a sack of lint and bandages. "Matron wants me to change that dressing," he says to Casper, "so hurry up and finish your little snack."

"If the dressing needs changing," says Casper, "I want Walt to change it."

"Well, Walt ain't gonna change it, 'cause Walt ain't no nurse, ain't no medical steward, ain't no doctor, and ain't been properly trained to do nothing in no hospital."

"He's dressed more wounds and changed more dressings than you could count," says Casper. "And if he did a poor job of it, it would still be better than what I'd get from the likes of you."

Babb gives Casper a sidelong glance, as if he has never been more insulted. He leaves the pan and the bandages on the table and limps away without a word.

He returns, with Matron, within the minute.

"Mr. Mallet," says Matron to Casper, "there's confusion enough in this hospital concerning assignment of duties among the staff. But one or two things are clear. I will not tolerate patients dictating—"

"I want Walt to do it," says Casper.

Matron attempts to close her eyes, though it appears to Hayes—who has a perfect view of her—that this is a feat she can only partially accomplish. Breathing quite deliberately, she seems to be tapping some inner reservoir of patience. At last she says, "The gentleman to whom you refer is not a member of my staff. Nor is he a member of any staff. Now will you cooperate, or will you force me to summon the wardmaster, though I am entirely loath to?"

Casper, who has been holding his bandaged stump protectively throughout the exchange, now lifts it to his lips, gives it a kiss, and strokes it a few times, reassuringly. Without looking up, he says, "We want our Walt to do it."

"But I've already explained to you," says Matron. "That's not possible. Mr. Babb will change your dressing."

Casper glances for a moment at Babb, who wears a snide expression, half grin, half grimace. "Then I reckon we'll make do with what we've already got," says Casper.

"That's not possible either," says Matron. "The surgeon has asked that it be changed today. And I have assigned the task to Mr. Babb."

At that moment, the old man in the wine-colored suit appears at the foot of Casper's bed, and Hayes notes that his arrival causes Matron to fairly swoon; all at once, he understands that this is surely the "gentleman" in question, "our Walt."

"May I be of assistance?" the man says to Matron.

"No, sir, you may not," says she. "As it happens, you're the very cause of our trouble. This is precisely the kind of nonconformity your peculiar attentions arouse in our patients."

The man turns up his palms. "What have *I* done?" he asks.

"Mr. Mallet refuses to have his dressing changed," says Matron, "unless it is changed by a certain genius who haunts our hospital night and day. He simply will not budge, and I suppose that now I'll have to inconvenience the wardmaster or Dr. Dinkle when——"

"Oh," says the gray-haired man, smiling, "then I can be of assistance after all. I've only just left Dr. Bliss, not two doors from here. I'll fetch him immediately."

This news seems to disconcert Matron further—"This is no matter for the surgeon in chief!" she cries—but the man is gone before she can stop him. She turns to Babb and says, "Let's not stand idle, Mr. Babb, when we've a hospital of very sick men to see to. Get number thirty-two ready, as I'm sure we'll have an occupant for it before lunch."

"You mean, 'Please, get number thirty-two ready,'" says Babb.

"Yes, Mr. Babb," says Matron, exasperated, "of course I mean *please.*"

They both move away and disappear into the flow of persons trafficking the ward's central aisle. Hayes notices that the air has grown uncomfortably warm and that the breeze coming through the nearby window would be more welcome if it did not carry with it the essence of the canal. He wonders if there might be a parade of some sort outdoors, for beneath the general clamor of street noise, he believes he hears the cadence of marching feet. He thinks it is a kind of parade passing at the end of his bed as well, but somehow it lacks any clear aim or harmony—certainly it lacks music, save the terrible hymn-singing woman who now and again appears and assaults the ear. For a moment, he amuses himself with the thought of Matron's depriving him of his breakfast—what little incentive, that!—and soon feels himself dozing off. Then, in no time at all, there are people near the bed again: Matron; "our Walt"; and an imposing man in surgeon's regalia, with a high forehead, a clean-shaven chin, and muttonchop whiskers, undoubtedly Dr. Bliss.

"Here's how I see it," Casper is saying to the three others. "This is mine, what there is left of it." He pauses here to pat his stump affectionately. "I might not get much say in most affairs," he says. "That's okay, that's a soldier's life. But by God, I can decide who gets to touch my wee babe. Give me that much at least."

Hayes notices that the gray-bearded man is smiling and even casts his smile for a second Hayes's way, as if he's very pleased with how Casper has made his case. Dr. Bliss, who has been provided a chair between the beds, turns and looks up at Matron. "And you have an objection?" he asks her.

Matron appears nonplussed that he should pose the question. "Well, yes, sir," she says, "I do. A very strong objection. What if every patient wants a particular person for one thing and another?"

"Then you've had many such requests?" asks the surgeon.

"No, sir," says Matron, "I have not, but there's a principle at stake, isn't there?"

"And what principle is that?"

"Well . . . the principle that . . . that some decisions belong to some and not to others."

"I should think the principle at stake would go something like this," says the surgeon. "That these men, who have given so much, and who complain so little, might not be denied wishes that are entirely within our powers to grant."

Matron, silent, dumbfounded, swallows deeply. Hayes observes that she has turned quite pale. Dr. Bliss rises from his chair and lays his hand on Casper's shoulder. "Have you much pain?" he asks him.

"Not with a little morphine," says Casper.

"Good," says the surgeon, then turns and gives an affirming nod to "our Walt," as if to say, *Carry on.* To Matron, he says, "Now please come with me, Matron. I want to consult with you in another matter." As they move away together, the surgeon's voice gradually fades as he continues: "And I want to know if you've had your walk outside today? I don't at all like your pallor. I can't overemphasize to you the importance of fresh air."

Once they're gone, the gray-haired man takes the surgeon's chair, leans his cane against the bedside table, and begins to laugh. He falls into a fit of coughing, and when he has gained his composure, says, "As if she didn't already sufficiently hate me."

Casper holds out his stump to the man, who begins—with what Hayes deems a good deal of poise—to unravel the bandage. Hayes rolls onto his side, putting his back to the business, for he has seen as much of it as he wants to see; somehow the idea of redressing the site of the amputation excites his own wounds. He sees that the mattress has been removed from Leo's bed. Probably, he thinks, Babb has taken it outside to air. He hears Walt softly talking to Casper as he works: ". . . his given name's Doctor, named for a certain Dr. Willard who delivered him as a baby . . . in Albany . . . which means, after the required medical training, he became Dr. Doctor Bliss. Well, don't look at me like that, my boy, I'm not making this up . . . I'm only reporting the truth as I know it. Dr. Doctor Willard Bliss. A fine man . . . an accomplished musician, too. Has an excellent singing voice, I'm told . . ."

Hayes closes one eye (the one nearer the pillow) and covers the other with his hand; he spreads two fingers and looks out, through the little triangle thus formed, at the river of visitors and nurses and preachers and attendants that passes at his feet—his aimless parade. Soon, something from the river spills into his triangle: a tall skinny man in a long gown staggers barefoot and florid into the space between the two beds. Apparently the victim of a head wound, he wears a turban of bandaging and glares down at Hayes with a look of bewilderment and fury. He is clean shaven, and his face and arms and legs appear to have been scalded with boiling water. "Pus in the blood, pus in the blood," he mutters. "Quick-step, quick-step, chicken guts and skillygallee." Now he throws himself onto the floor, face-down, whispering, "Killed a black snake six feet long . . . blowed a blanket up next to the stove . . ."

And then, after another moment, he is quiet.

Hayes leans over the side of the mattress enough to see that the man, prone and completely still, is peering with one eye down through a knothole in the wooden floor.

Next, a young woman comes along who looks strikingly like Sarah—same hair color, similar mouth—and says to Hayes, "I hope you don't mind if Major Cross stays here awhile. He can sometimes get loud, but he's harmless. You're the boy that doesn't talk. I'm Anne. You don't remember me, but I washed you the night you first arrived."

She smiles and looks again at the man on the floor. She cups one hand to the side of her mouth and whispers in a confidential tone: "He's not really a major, of course, but he insists everyone call him that, so we indulge him."

"A regular turkey shoot," says Major Cross, softly.

"I don't know why," says the young woman, "but that hole in the floor's the only thing that seems to bring him any peace. At first Matron wouldn't have it, but Walt there spoke to the wardmaster about it, and he instructed Matron to leave the poor man be . . . let him have his knothole for heaven's sake." She laughs and adds, "All the day long, if he likes."

Hayes removes his fingers from over his eyes. The young woman folds her hands at her waist and smiles again. "I wonder what in the world he thinks he sees down there," she says.

THE PROSPECT OF oyster soup initially repelled him, for, mistakenly, he thought it was oysters that had made him sick at Christmas. Then he recalled that sausages had been the culprits, not oysters. The soup is good and feels good going down. The man seems to derive enormous pleasure from feeding him, and so Hayes suppresses a puerile inkling of pride and doesn't object. He notices the cuffs of the man's coat, worn shiny and almost black at the rims. He accepts a sip of water from a white ceramic mug, and the man smiles in his kindly way, placing both the mug and the soup plate on the bedside table. He is not, as it turns out, an old man but merely gray. Though plenty talkative himself, he doesn't seem to mind that Hayes speaks none at all.

Indeed, he appears to enjoy practicing a kind of clairvoyance, often guessing with uncanny accuracy not only Hayes's thoughts but the exact moment that he is hungry, thirsty, too warm, not warm enough, in pain, or needing to visit the toilet. Though he frequently busies himself elsewhere while he is on the ward, he often leaves his hat and cane at Hayes's bedside, indicating his inevitable return. Today he was at the hospital the entire morning, left for the afternoon, and returned in the evening. At suppertime, Hayes went to the dining room and sat at a table for a few minutes but was unable to eat anything. When the man showed up at his bed sometime later, he said, "I think you must be hungry," and soon came back with the plate of oyster soup. Now he says, "I'll read to you and Casper for a while, but please feel free to doze off. Great literature serves purposes besides those for which it was written."

He stands and turns up the gas lamp behind the table a bit, though there is still a lot of light coming in through the windows. *Dusk*, thinks Hayes, but suddenly the word does not seem quite right. *Dust*, he thinks. *Outdoors, dust has fallen. No . . . "Can Honour's voice provoke the silent dusk?"*

Once the man has sat back down, he says, "I must say this is the hardest chair my backside has ever graced." Now he opens the book, clears his throat, and reads: " 'The marriage-day was shining brightly, and they were ready outside the closed door of the Doctor's room, where he was speaking with Charles Darnay. They were ready to go to church; the beautiful bride . . .' "

" *. . . provoke the silent dust?"* thinks Hayes.

He awakens—how long afterward, he cannot judge—to a conversation conducted in hushed tones at the foot of his bed. He is careful to keep his eyes closed and not to stir in any other way. "All over Virginia," says a man whose voice he believes to be that of Dr. Bliss, "boys lay dead and nameless. If they didn't take the grim precaution of pinning notes to their coats, or if no letters or Bibles or photographs are found on their persons, we can't know who they are. We put them into unmarked graves—you *know* this, Walt. Now they cannot speak, cannot tell us their names. And here, this one can, but won't."

"Sunstroke, I suppose," says another, whom Hayes recognizes as the gray-haired man. "Exposure, I imagine."

"More likely nostalgia, I'd say."

"Nostalgia?"

"Hmm," says the surgeon. "I've seen it worse than this. Nowadays, they're mostly put in the asylum . . . which is better, I guess, than their wandering the streets or the countryside."

"I don't think him crazy," says the other man.

"Perhaps not. But I don't know how long I can justify the use of his bed."

"Not all wounds bleed."

"No."

"Whatever his ordeal—and who among them hasn't had his ordeal?—it's obviously left him very low. When his strength comes back, so will his wits and his voice, that's my theory. Can't we indulge nature's process, even though it seems . . . well, slow and inconvenient?"

"There's a grand order," says the surgeon, with laughter in his voice. "Indulge nature's process. You're very modern, Walt. In your own way you express the cutting edge of science. Now, tell me—how's your own head?"

"Sometimes a good deal of pressure but little else. A persistent sore throat, I regret to say."

"You need to take yourself out of here, out of the hospitals, and soon."

"I think I'll be all right."

"Shall I be forced to order you out?"

"Maybe you shall, maybe you shall."

After a moment, the surgeon moves away, his silence a begrudging, and most likely temporary, compliance in both matters discussed.

Now, though Hayes keeps his eyes shut, he feels the warmth of the gray gentleman's gaze. He hears a chair being pulled alongside the bed and the man's resettling in. He expects soon to hear more of Dickens, but instead, a long silence ensues—so long that he opens his eyes at last, sensing that the silence was designed for that result. The ward is darkened outside a pool of dim light that falls from the nearby lamp. Casper sleeps soundly in the next bed; the gauzy tent, a mosquito curtain, has been lowered around him. "I think you must be an athlete," says the man, very softly, and smiling. "To me, you look like an athlete."

Hayes sees that the man does in fact hold the book open in his lap, and when next he speaks, his eyes rest on the pages as if he is reading. But what he says is not from Dickens: "I'm sure that whatever you've been through, whatever the story that landed you here, you've been very brave, for I see it in your face. I also see you've been badly harmed. I saw it in the faces of countless young men when I was in Falmouth, and I see it in yours. But I think you're hurt in a particular way. You strike me in your silence as someone who waked from a terrible dream, then looked down and saw the scar it had left on you. Nod to me now if you understand me, my boy, for I don't plan to speak to you quite this way again after this."

Hayes nods, or his head nods of its own will, he cannot be sure which. "Good," says the man. "If you already inspire in me love, it's for a reason. I mean to be your friend, and as a friend to set you straight when you're selling yourself short in your own mind, to correct your error in regard to yourself. I do it because of your clear deservingness. Don't let anyone persuade you that you've done wrong. You differ from these others only in your silence being more complete, and your injuries less plainspoken. But I can wait for you to break your silence . . . at least for as long as my own waning health will allow. I'll tell you something I've discovered about myself. I'm as touched by a man's troubles as by his charms. Think about it—while the latter might affect my heart to race forward, as if to meet a lost friend, the former makes my heart beat steadily . . . and me to relax and wait for him to come to me in his own time."

As the man spoke, he never raised his eyes from the book, but now he looks up briefly, and back down at the pages. "Let's see," he says, "here we are. 'Worn out by anxious watching, Mr. Lorry fell asleep at his post. On the tenth morning of his suspense, he was startled by the shining of the sun into the room where a heavy slumber had overtaken him when it was dark night. He rubbed his eyes and roused himself; but he doubted, when he had done so, whether he was not still asleep . . .'"

THEIR DIVISION, along with the rest of the Second Corps, remained stalled on the Catharpin Road for the rest of the morning. The sweltering heat, the rising and ebbing racket of musketry and artillery in the distances, and Leggett's ever-souring humor made it seem to Hayes an eternity. Stationed on a stump in the shade not far from where Leggett lay, Hayes was enlisted by half a dozen soldiers to write more letters, among them one for Vesey, the big man from Bushwick who'd played in the right field for the Bachelors. Vesey, tearful and shy-seeming, confessed in the letter to his mother that he'd once stolen two dollars from her brother William. (He explained to Hayes that his uncle had stayed with them for a while in Bushwick but now lived somewhere in Indiana.) He begged his mother's forgiveness, asked that she repay the money from his wages when she could spare it, and that she try to remember him for the constancy of his love rather than for his waywardness in matters of money. After he'd thanked Hayes for the letter and shook his hand, he said with a resigned air, "You see, I've a bad weakness for cards and dice." As the man walked away, Hayes saw that the split in his trousers (incurred by his leap for the home base, itself a kind of gamble) had been stitched up but that he limped a bit now, favoring his right foot.

When at last the order came for them to move, it further aggravated Leggett, for rather than continuing west, they were to reverse direction and then turn and march north instead, up the Brock Road. Leggett slapped his cap to his knee and said to Hayes, "Now let's see. We done marched east, south, and west . . . I guess north's all that's left." He stepped out into the sunlight, put his cap on his head, and spat blood onto the dust in the road. He turned back to Hayes and said, "They got us going in circles, son."

If it had been pandemonium near sunrise, with the infantry columns splintering and shouldering their way around the cavalry and supply wagons clogging the road—now, turning twenty thousand soldiers and funneling them into the windy Brock Road was a brand-new kind of bedlam. The officers scuttled back and forth on their mounts trying to forge some semblance of disposition, but dust and hopelessness rose all around. Hayes thought he caught a glimpse of the corps commander, conferring with other officers near the intersection of the two roads, and when he turned to consult Leggett in the matter, he found by his side, instead, a boy he didn't know. Pointing with his chin, Hayes said, "Do you think that's . . . do you happen to know . . . is that General Hancock over there?"

The boy looked at Hayes as if he didn't understand the question. Small and pale and anxious-looking, he sniffed the air and said, "Can you smell that? I think the woods is on fire." Hayes assured him that some of the men had built fires for heating coffee, but the boy only looked as if he might cry and backed away. A moment afterward, it seemed to Hayes that the young blue-clad stranger had evaporated into the sea of blue-clad soldiers surrounding them.

A few paces forward, Hayes spotted Leggett and elbowed his way through the throng of men between them. When Leggett saw him, he gave him a chilling blank stare. Hayes said, "I think I just saw General Hancock, turning his steed into the other road."

"Could've been his twin brother, I suppose," said Leggett, darkly, hoisting his musket sling over his shoulder.

Leggett appeared more peaked than ever—the swollen jaw put his face askew, and the eye on that side stayed half shut. "Well, anyway," said Hayes. "I'm pretty sure it was him."

"Did he look soo-perb?" asked Leggett, a reference to the major general's nickname.

Hayes, who thought Leggett was being unnecessarily difficult, squatted to retie his laces. When he stood again, Leggett put an arm around him. Hayes recalled their wandering through woods the night before, in search of a dentist or a doctor—and how their lantern had made the thicket shadows swing side to side. "Well," said Leggett, "if it can't be Julius Caesar leadin' us, I reckon Hancock's the next best thing. I'd just trust the situation a whole lot more if he wasn't acting under somebody else's orders."

It was Leggett's view that Hancock should have replaced Meade at the head of the Army of the Potomac, Hancock being far and away the more qualified officer. Because of Leggett's status as a veteran, Hayes seldom doubted his judgments in such matters. Indeed, Leggett's high opinion of General Hancock was mostly what had made Hayes so excited to catch a glimpse of the man. It occurred to him to remind Leggett that Meade himself was likely under orders from the general in chief, whom Leggett consummately admired, but he decided to let it drop; he was already feeling agitated, and he feared Leggett might offer another of his pessimistic rebuttals.

Leggett released Hayes and asked for the time.

"Somebody stepped on my watch," answered Hayes. "It's stuck at ten past nine."

Leggett squinted up at the cloudless sky. "Close to noon's my guess," he said.

Their brigade, led by General Hobart Ward, was second in line to go. Once again they had to maneuver around the supply trains, and artillery clogged the narrow route as well, but soon they were advancing at a fairly good pace. In his feet and legs, Hayes felt the previous day's long march, combined with last night's lack of sleep. He wondered if Leggett, older by more than a decade and sore in the mouth besides, wasn't suffering an even worse strain. Soon they were drenched with sweat, and any singing and joking among the men died away, leaving only the drumming of shoes on the hard-baked road, the clatter of gear, the cloudy rasp of labored breath, and the pop of gunfire in the woods to their left. So far, no officer of any rank had disclosed to the men their mission. They were moving away from the artillery they'd heard earlier to the west, while to the north, they'd heard only what sounded like skirmishes. But as they continued the advance up the Brock Road, with its encroaching brush and vines, the battle din ahead of them steadily escalated. After an hour or so, the road began to fill with smoke—at first white like a mist, then thicker and grayer—and the order came down the columns to increase the pace to double-quick. Leggett, who was two men in front of Hayes, looked back for a moment, and then moved to his right and began to trot ahead, disappearing toward the front.

A few minutes later, Hayes found him waiting at the edge of the road. Quite winded, Leggett fell in alongside Hayes, and said, "There's a corner up ahead a ways. There's a Sixth Corps division already up there"—he paused to take a gulp of air—"General Getty's. We got to get up there and help hold it. Otherwise we'll be cut off from the rest of the army."

Hayes couldn't think how any kind of battle could be staged inside these narrow roads; likewise, he couldn't imagine how any army could fight its way through the dense woods that surrounded them. Even if there were paths through the tall switch and tangled grapevines— which there didn't appear to be—how could any sort of lines be maintained? "Is it a clearing up there?" he asked Leggett. "Something like a field?"

"None's I know of," said Leggett.

"Well, then where are we to fight?"

Leggett looked straight ahead. "What do you think I've been talking about for the last two days?" he said. He turned his head just slightly toward the woods on Hayes's side and nodded. "We're gonna fight in there."

Now Leggett dropped back and fell in directly behind Hayes, and in a moment, Hayes heard him say, under his breath, "Like a bunch of savages."

After a while Hayes found that his body took charge of the marching. What had hurt him before stopped hurting. He no longer had to will himself forward, which left his mind free to drift. He examined his fear and found it building and darkening, like the smoke in the road. He found further that, like the feeling at the start of an important match, it was mixed with exhilaration. The difference was in the proportions: at the start of a match, one part fear to five parts exhilaration; now, exactly opposite. He wondered if he shouldn't have written a letter like Vesey's, unburdening himself should he not survive and asking for pardon. Vesey's sin had an enviable clarity about it, the bluntness of an Old Testament commandment. Hayes's—an unnatural regard for one's sister, and consequentially deserting her—was a bit more complicated. Never mind that Vesey's sin induced a shake of the head, and his a shrinking back in horror. And where, in that murkier picture, was the counterpart to money, which could be repaid? Where the recognizable weakness, a bent for gambling? He supposed there was an eve-of-battle letter that might be composed (with careful omissions), proclaiming love, hoping for sympathy, but he'd already done that, Saturday last. He had nothing to add. If death waited for him in those brambles, he would meet it with the satisfaction—despite his depraved nature—of having done right.

A bit farther along the road, he found himself asking, *But what if I'm patently wrong in everything I think?*

What if an hour from now he was to meet a horrible gory end, his last feelings soaked in remorse and terror? It was May, springtime. He'd just turned nineteen, had never crossed the Atlantic, never been with a woman. If he'd made different choices, he might now be playing ball at the Union Grounds, cheered by adoring spectators. The "problem" might well have withered away of its own accord. People grew out of things. After all, he'd once been agonizingly fond of his rocking horse. And what *would* it be like to look into another man's eyes and kill him? To witness one's comrades killed? The most blood he'd ever seen had been at winter quarters, when the commissary boys slaughtered cattle. Still, he believed himself to have a strong constitution, for no experience had ever instructed him otherwise. He'd lost both his parents at a tender age, and he hadn't wilted. He knew what it meant to persist, to fight hard and give one's all in quest of a victory. He would survive—and, if lucky, survive reasonably intact.

Some minutes before their pace started to slow, a bullet now and again zinged overhead, clipping the tree limbs above the road and raining down leaves and pine needles. The gunfire in the woods to the left grew louder, closer, denser, the smoke in the road thicker.

And then they stalled again.

They could hear a lot of shouting to the front but too far away to make out any words. Some of the men, dog tired, began to squat in the road while some few others collapsed to the ground and went instantly to sleep. Still others retreated into the brush to their right to relieve themselves. Many took advantage of the break to eat something. All around, men fell into conversations, but there seemed to be a general tacit understanding that these be carried on softly.

Farther away to the north they could hear the rolling thunder of artillery, evidence of a much greater clash than any skirmishes in the thicket. Hayes knelt on one knee, facing the western woods, and began fussing with his cartridge belt. He felt an almost panicky need to run an inspection on himself. The canteen, the haversack, the bayonet, the ramrod—touching these things with his hands was a bit like doing a sum and had the same occupying effect on his mind. If he'd learned anything in the army so far, it was how to endure long stretches of idleness, though he'd never before idled on a road in the woods with minié balls occasionally flying overhead. He turned in Leggett's direction, but Leggett had vanished.

Instead, he saw Billy Swift running in a crouched posture toward him from the rear. Swift squatted next to him and said, "What in blazes are we doing now?"

Hayes shrugged. "More waiting, I guess," he said.

Swift took a swig from his canteen. Gazing into the woods before them, he said, "Can you tell if it's coming closer?"

Hayes shook his head. "Sometimes it sounds closer, sometimes it sounds farther away."

Swift closed his eyes as if to listen more keenly. After a moment, he said, "Ever noticed how gunfire stops the birds from singing?" he said.

"It has a similar effect on me," said Hayes.

Swift looked at him with a sad expression. "I reckon I ought to be feeling afraid, but I don't."

"Don't worry," said Hayes. "I'm plenty afraid for both of us."

Swift didn't smile at this remark but only looked down at the ground; he picked up a small clod of dirt from the road and threw it into the brush; he glanced back at Hayes and then at the ground again. At last Hayes said, "What?"

Swift let out a sigh. "You know I look up to you, Hayes," he said. "I never expected to . . . well, you know, be on talking terms with the likes of you. Now, I want you to be square with me about something."

Hayes nodded.

"How good am I?" asked Swift. "Your honest opinion. Don't spare my feelings."

It took Hayes a moment to understand what Swift was asking. "You're good, Billy," he said.

"But how good?"

"Real good."

"But what I'm trying to ask . . . am I good enough to play for a legitimate club? I don't mean next week, naturally . . . but say a year or two from now."

"I don't see why not," said Hayes. "You just have to be willing to make certain sacrifices and spend most of your leisure hours—"

"I am, I am!" said Swift. "I am willing. Hayes, do you think there's a chance . . . assuming we both make it out of here . . . there's a chance you might—"

At that moment, the chaplain appeared at the edge of the road with Banjo, the stray foxhound, at his heels. "I've been looking for you," said the chaplain to Hayes and knelt next to him and Swift.

He removed his spectacles, which had fogged up in the heat, and began clearing them on the cuff of his coat.

Swift gave the dog a few pats on the head and then poured some water from his canteen into the cup of his hand, which she lapped up eagerly.

The chaplain replaced his eyeglasses and started rooting around inside his bread bag. Banjo, intent on getting her nose in as well, had to be pushed away two or three times.

"I'm delighted to have found you," said the chaplain, again to Hayes. "I was afraid . . . as we're about to be engaged . . . I wouldn't have the opportunity."

After another moment he pulled out a base ball.

"I thought you might like to have this," he said, passing it to Hayes. "I varnished it, you see, so the inscription won't wear off."

WELL INTO THE MIDDLE of the afternoon they felled and hauled trees, cleared as best they could the brush nearest the west side of the road, and threw themselves body and soul into fashioning a line of impressive earthworks. The very important corner, not half a mile north, was with the Orange Plank Road, the route of the rebel offensive. By four o'clock, three of Getty's brigades and two of Hancock's were dug in, with the rest of the Second Corps still coming up from the south. If the Confederates hoped to take the corner or any part of the Brock Road near it, they'd better be praying for a miracle.

Pressed up against Leggett in the trench, Hayes must have dozed off, for suddenly he was sitting before a fire in the library at Hicks Street, and his sister, Sarah, was asking him please to cut her the *thinnest* possible slice of marble cake. He heard the jingling of a small bell, like that on a shop door, and then Leggett's voice: "That's cannon!" he said. "And it sounds like its firing from our side!"

Hayes opened his eyes and found Leggett looking straight at him, his face only inches away. "I think we're attacking," he said. "Not defending. Now tell me why in the world did we break our backs making this damned ditch."

Leggett reached into his haversack and brought out an oblong cloth bag, gathered and tied at the top with string. "Here," he said, passing it to Hayes, "this is for you."

"Why, this is your coffee," said Hayes, feeling the weight of the thing, then bringing it to his nose and sniffing.

"That's right," said Leggett. "And it's got the sugar mixed into it already."

"Leggett," said Hayes, attempting to pass the bag back to him, "I've got plenty of my own."

Leggett pushed the bag back toward Hayes. "Take it, son," he said. "I want you to have it."

"But I don't want it," said Hayes, offering the bag again.

Now Leggett pushed the bag back at him with vigor, pressing it firmly into Hayes's chest. "Would you keep the damned coffee and be quiet about it," he whispered forcefully in Hayes's face, and Hayes saw that the man's eyes had clouded over with tears.

"Well, okay, then," he said. "I guess I'll keep it for you if you like."

"I *do* like," said Leggett.

"All right then," said Hayes.

"All right," said Leggett and then turned away and busied himself with untying and retying his shoes.

An interim of time transpired between this moment and the big thing that happened next, but Hayes would later recall only three vivid impressions: not very deep inside the woods, there was an explosion, and then an enormous cloud of blackest smoke rose up from the tops of the trees, swelling out five dark petals from its center even as it moved toward the Union line, and then they were enveloped in darkness; a human roar like nothing Hayes had ever heard descended on them slowly from their right, burgeoning down the earthworks like a locomotive coming into a station; and horses' hooves rained into the road behind them, so near Hayes's face (when he turned to look) he first took them for debris from some sort of rotating machine that had slipped its axle and was flinging out its dangerous inner parts.

Then the bellowed *Forward!* flew down the line, repeated rather like gunfire itself, and they were all leaving the earthworks—a blue wave breaking in a curl along a curve of shoreline—and charging into the woods.

The colonel—or was it only the captain?—barked something about Vermonters, and then it was brambles and switch and vines and a gnarly washboard of three ridges to cross. With each step deeper, the air grew hotter, the smoke thicker. In the troughs between the ridges, they sank ankle-deep into ribbons of swamp that threatened to suck the shoes off their feet. Hayes's ears and eyes felt as if they were on fire. When he called out for Leggett and received no reply, he tried his Christian name: "Truman!" he shouted, but all that came back was the heightening brattle of musketry and the screaming and yelling of other men. Soon the trees bore the multiple scars of bullets. The Wilderness—itself affronted, itself mangled and marred—swallowed the jagged lines of the army, and once inside its bowels, the men were less and less distinguishable to one another as friend or foe.

SARAH, seated on an ottoman near the grate, offered the boy another of Mrs. B's ginger biscuits, but he declined with an anguished look. It struck Summerfield that the poor boy would rather go hungry than further manage the weight of eating under the eyes of his teacher, with whom he was obviously, violently smitten. He'd got through the first round of tea painfully. He'd nearly dropped his cup when it startled him by rattling in its saucer. He'd brushed crumbs off his military-style vest, only to think better of it immediately, and then retrieved them one by one from the carpet and held them in the palm of his hand until Sarah indicated he should put them on the tea tray.

Summerfield had found the two of them in the parlor (and all the lamps already lit) when he arrived home a few minutes earlier. She'd never before had a pupil to the house. She'd introduced the boy, Harmon Fellows, said only that he was from the school, and passed Summerfield a cup of tea, though he wasn't accustomed to drinking tea at the end of his workday. Still, he welcomed it, along with the good fire in the grate, since the January afternoon had turned quite cold. He was trying to sort out the occasion as best he could, and he thought Sarah was conspicuously not helping, though she did seem to cast him a deeply meaningful look now and again. When he asked Harmon Fellows what he'd been up to at school, the boy only looked at him blankly, and so Sarah intervened to narrow the question: "Why don't you say what we did *today* at school?" she said.

The boy squinted and drew his mouth into a straight line. Summerfield noticed that his clothes, though good enough and all black, were too large for him and that his dark gold hair, parted on the side, glowed rather extremely in the gaslight. He judged him to be about twelve, yet—except when animated by any word or gesture from Sarah—he looked older than that around the eyes.

"Harmon Fellows," Sarah said, "you can't have forgotten our 'certain Persian of distinction.'"

"Oh, yes," said the boy. "We studied punctuation and read about a man who killed his dog."

"You, Harmon, read very well," said Sarah. She turned to Summerfield and added, pointedly, "A story about the effects of rashness."

"I see," said Summerfield. "And why did the man kill his dog . . . rashly, I suspect?"

Hesitating, Harmon looked at Sarah.

"Go on, Harmon, dear," she said. "It's very good practice for you. Just say what happened, in your own language."

"I thought it a bit juvenile," he said, suddenly world-weary.

"I know you did," said Sarah. "But my brother would like to hear nevertheless."

Summerfield saw wheels turning in the boy's head: in an effort to impress her, he'd run close to disappointing her instead. It further occurred to him—though it seemed unlikely—that maybe she'd invited the boy to the house so he, Summerfield, might witness first-hand the awkwardness of a schoolboy infatuation.

"It took place in Persia," Harmon said, now gazing into the fire. "A man badly wanted a son . . . so he'd have somebody to inherit his estate. He's very happy when a boy baby is born, but he's very anxious for him and will scurcely let the baby be taken out of his sight."

"*Scarcely*," said Sarah. "Not *scurcely*."

"Scarcely," said the boy. "Then one day his wife had to go out to the bath and left the baby with the man, and the man got called to the palace and had to leave the baby with the dog. No sooner was he gone than a snake came into the house, headed straight for the cradle. But the dog kills the snake before it can do any harm. And when the man came home, the dog went running out to greet him . . . all proud of himself for saving the baby's life. But the man sees blood on the dog and thinks the dog has eaten the baby, so he picks up a stick and kills the dog. The end."

"That's not quite the very end, is it?" said Sarah.

Harmon looked at her with a knitted brow, his eyes misting over. "Well, he goes inside the house and sees the baby's all right . . . sees the dead snake on the floor . . . and understands what he's done."

"He 'smote his breast with grief,'" said Sarah.

"That's right," said Harmon.

"So," said Summerfield, "the moral of the story is 'Don't be rash,' as I suspected."

"To be precise," said Sarah, "'Shame and repentance are the sure consequences of rashness and want of thought.'"

Summerfield stood and moved from the sofa to the mantel. He thought he might light his father's pipe to see how much it would annoy her. Since the New Year (and as his determination to join the army steeped in her thinking), she'd splintered into more than one person:

sometimes taciturn, inscrutable, possibly feeling peeved at him; sometimes warm, attentive in the old way, possibly having forgiven him;
and sometimes, oddest of all, entirely preoccupied, but pleasantly, as
if he weren't the slightest part of her thoughts. He never knew, arriving home, which of these he would find, and sometimes he found all
three in the course of a night, varying hour to hour. Now, apparently,
in the person of young Harmon Fellows, she'd meant to bring home
the lesson from school, so her errant brother also might be educated.

He thought there was something desperate and crude about the
strategy. She knew (because he'd told her) that a Union regiment, on
furlough in New York, had set up an enlistment office in Manhattan, which he intended to "stop by" before long. Now he turned from
the mantel and looked at her, placing the pipe in his mouth. She did
not look at him but perched regally on the ottoman, her eyes toward
the windows, her hair, her dress, her posture, everything just so. The
subtle change common to all her moods was that she took more pains
with her appearance lately; he couldn't have said what exactly were
the results—she was (just as their mother had been) never less than
beautiful; but he'd noticed that she rose earlier in the mornings, in
order, as far as he could tell, to spend more time before the dressing
mirror.

He returned the pipe to the mantel—it was hardly worth the effort
if she paid it no mind. "Well, in my opinion," he said, "the man was
most rash to leave the baby in the care of a dog."

"Oh," said the boy quickly, "it wasn't possible to disobey a royal
summons."

He looked at Sarah for her approval, which she delivered promptly,
with a nod and a smile.

Close to the grate, Summerfield felt too hot and so returned to the
sofa and sat down again. "Of course," he said. "That's how it is in
Persia. So what you're saying, Harmon, is that the man had no choice
but to go. And under the circumstances, he did what he thought best.
He did what he understood to be his duty."

"Yes, sir," answered the boy, "that's right."

"But Harmon," said Sarah. "What if the man hadn't been summoned by the king? What if he'd simply decided to go to the palace

because he *felt* it his duty? In other words, he wasn't required to go, but chose to go of his own free will. What would you think of him then?"

The boy furrowed his brow again and looked at her as if he was trying to read her thoughts and thereby discover the correct answer. At last his face brightened. "He wouldn't have done that," he said. "He loved the baby too much. He would have left the baby only if he was absolutely forced to."

"Very good, Harmon," she said. "Exactly right. So. If the man had a choice of staying or going, and chose to go of his own free will, then my brother would be correct—it would, indeed, be rash and wanting thought."

The boy now looked at Summerfield and nodded, as if hoping to find Summerfield pleased by this conclusion.

Summerfield reached for his teacup and finished what was in it. "Well," he said, now turning his gaze to Sarah, "it seems our little parlor doubles nicely as a classroom."

"God forbid learning should be confined to classrooms," said Sarah.

"Still," said Summerfield, "it's quite a long school day, only to be extended afterward."

"I believe Harmon enjoys school," said Sarah. "You may ask him yourself."

Summerfield laughed. "I don't suppose it would be quite fair, Harmon, for me to ask you how you enjoy school."

Again, the boy looked at him blankly.

"I mean," said Summerfield, "with your teacher right here next to you, you could hardly answer but one way."

The boy did not smile. He said, "I'm about done with school. Come Ash Wednesday, I'm to go to work."

Sarah cast Summerfield another of her deeply meaningful looks. "Work?" he said. "What sort of work?"

"In a factory," answered the boy. "In the Eastern District."

"What, making boot polish?"

Harmon didn't answer, for he was transfixed by Sarah's leaning forward to pour out more tea for herself. "Harmon," said Sarah, after a moment, "my brother asked if you'll be making boot polish?"

"No, sir," said the boy. "Rope."

"Oh, rope," said Summerfield. "But *must* you leave school to make rope?"

"Yes, sir," said the boy. "My father was slain in the war, you see. At Payne's Farm, in Virginia. And now I must go to work."

At last her purpose came clear in all its depth and breadth.

The coals shifted in the grate, falling with a whisper.

Now he recalled her mentioning the boy at Christmastime: forced to grow up too fast, changed, no longer a boy, not yet a man. He said, "I'm very sorry, my boy."

He ventured a glance in Sarah's direction, expecting perhaps to see something like triumph in her face, but found there instead a hint of misgiving. She slid a handkerchief from the sleeve of her dress, touched it lightly to her nose, and replaced it. Softly, he said to her, "Shall we ask Harmon to stay to supper?"

"His aunt's coming for him," she said. Now she pulled her silver watch on its long chain from her belt. "About now, in fact."

Things were to grow richer still, for when the aunt arrived, not more than five minutes later, she was of course wearing the mourning costume, with veil. She would go no farther than the frigid hall and politely declined Summerfield's proposal to accompany her and Harmon home, though it was nearly twilight.

Helping the boy with his cap and coat, Summerfield shuddered and said, "I bet we'll have skating soon." Then, more quietly, he offered the aunt his condolences.

She took his hand in her black glove. She was a tall woman, with a narrow face. "Thank you, Mr. Hayes," she said. "My brother was the whole world to me."

She released his hand, put her arm around Harmon's shoulders, and said, "We're all, all of us, heartbroken beyond words."

When they were gone from the stoop, and the doors closed, Sarah excused herself without delay and started up the stairs.

"You *used* those unfortunate people," he called to her back.

She stopped and turned. Her face in shadow, she looked down at him at the base of the stairs. "If you mean they were of use," she said, "then that's good news."

He felt himself trembling, and not entirely from cold. "You know that's not what I mean," he said. "It was guileful."

She only continued staring down at him, silent.

"And shabby," he added.

Now she put her back to him and continued as far as the bend in the stairs; then stopped again but didn't turn. To the curved wall before her, she said, "I'm not ashamed, Summerfield."

"Well, perhaps you should be," he said.

Now she turned to face him again. "I would exert whatever influence I can over you, by any means I can find."

"Clearly!"

He put his hand on the newel post. He was conscious of his breathing, and then, after a moment, conscious of hers.

When next she spoke, she lowered her voice and spoke with deliberate calm and a grain of tenderness. "If, some months from now," she said, "your name appears in a certain list in the newspaper . . . and I don't feel that I did all I possibly could to dissuade you . . . *then* I'll be ashamed."

She gathered the skirt of her dress in one hand, lifting it, and was quickly out of sight around the bend. He heard her footsteps on the landing overhead and then—like a question followed by an answer—the opening and closing of a door.

HAYES IMAGINES a long stop-and-go line of ambulances winding through the streets of Washington, for there seems no end to the fresh arrivals from Virginia—some brought on stretchers, some hobbling on crutches, others carried in the arms of their less seriously wounded comrades. About half of the bedside tables have been removed from the ward to make room for more beds and cots, which have been pushed yet closer together. Now each patient shares a table with another, and now the often-prostrate Major Cross is obliged to put his head under Hayes's bed in order to gain access to the cherished knothole in the floor. Hayes has noticed new signs of strain and fatigue in the faces of the doctors and nurses. Last night, a certain young steward, making his rounds of the ward in a state of drunkenness, tried to give Hayes Casper's dose of morphine. The already foul-tempered attendants, when they can be found, sulk and snap. Matron quivers and quails more than ever. The barber has pressed Hayes twice to consent to a "tidying up"; twice Hayes has refused; now the barber glares at Hayes as he passes his bed, and Hayes believes the barber has spoken ill of him to others. He believes he detects, among patients and staff alike, a growing resentment—that he is perceived to occupy a bed in the ward undeservedly. And he believes he detects, within the ward's usual foul stench, the sickeningly sweet smell of blood.

Jeffers, the new man in bed 32, suffers in the lungs, and when he speaks, his words come out like sawdust. Still, so far, he has spoken a good deal. When he encountered the mute and unresponsive Hayes, he turned his attention to the man in bed 31, who is dying of tetanus. Fairly soon Jeffers understood that this man, too, did not speak (lockjaw) and, furthermore, that his fixed smile was a symptom of disease and not of congeniality. Jeffers, a gaunt Philadelphian of about forty, now sits in his bed facing forward and addresses the air directly before him, an apt target, air being his main topic and concern. He is of the general opinion that there is too little of it available in the ward and that what little there is carries mephitic effluvia. Earlier this morning, he explained (to anyone who might care to know) that the hospital pavilions rest on cedar pilings a few feet off the ground, a design meant to improve ventilation. "Lucky for us," he said, bitterly. "Better admission to the fumes of the canal."

After lunch, Mrs. Duffy, the woman who daily sings in the wards, began strolling the aisle. At the present moment, she is worrying "Jerusalem the Golden" and, by Hayes's count, is on its thirteenth stanza. She performs without the aid of a hymnal, and despite the horrors she inflicts on the ear, Hayes can't help but admire the sheer magnitude of religious verse she has committed to memory. Equally impressive is the height of the woman's bonnet, which makes him think of an Indian cobra snake he once saw in a picture magazine. Now and again, Jeffers's labored exhalations in the next bed come with what sounds to Hayes like a small protest, a kind of jagged moan—and, as it happens, often coincides with one of Mrs. Duffy's particularly sour notes.

The ward is hot and noisy. Rain pounds the roof. A smaller number of the usual visitors roam about, some with dripping umbrellas. A carpenter with a ladder and a screwdriver is installing additional flag brackets to the window frames, increasing the number of Union flags on the ward, which now boasts six, with the promise of more to come. A new one hangs beside Hayes's bed, and when he goes to the toilet or the dining room, it brushes the top of his bare head. The flags add to the abundance of fabric in the place—with more beds have come more linens and mosquito curtains—and somehow, to Hayes, the flags, with their vivid colors, seem to make the ward hotter.

To his right, he can see that Casper is composing a letter, balancing a writing pad on his lap; presumably, judging from the words at the top of the page ("My dearest Joan"), to a sweetheart. A short distance away, near the stove, a half-dozen soldiers (one in a wheelchair) sit around the night watcher's table playing cards, but a mood of indignant silence seems to dominate their games. Nearby, a little tow-headed boy trips and falls amid the human traffic in the wide aisle, scuffs his knee on the rough floor, and begins to cry. His mother yanks him up by the arm and scolds him, making matters worse. Anne, the young nurse who looks like Hayes's sister, soon appears, stooping beside the boy and trying to console him.

A cloudburst now drums the roof, and Mrs. Duffy, forced to increase the volume of her singing, loses all semblance of intonation. To Hayes's left, Jeffers sighs and says, "A person would think it would cool the air, but all we get is steam."

Lightning flashes in the windows. A deep roll of thunder shakes the floor and walls. And as Mrs. Duffy is singing "'When in his strength I struggle, for very joy I leap; when in my sin I totter,'" the poor man in bed 31 goes into one of his spasms. There is a rush of nurses and attendants to the bedside as he begins to yelp and his body arches grotesquely upward, as if pulled and stretched by invisible wires.

In the midst of all this, an angry-looking captain, in some position of authority at the hospital, shows up at the foot of Hayes's bed. Hayes has seen him twice before and has already determined that the man means to do him harm. Aptly, he bears a striking resemblance to the mounted skunk who gave the order to abandon Hayes in the Wilderness.

"Please sit up, Private," says the man crossly.

The wound in Hayes's back stings as he manages to raise himself in the bed.

"State your name," says the captain.

Immediately Hayes feels his hands begin to shake. The captain moves around to the side of the bed and thrusts a pad and pencil into his lap.

"Then *write* your name," he says.

He looks on with disgust as Hayes grapples with the pad and pencil, unable even to adequately grip them. The pencil falls to the floor. The captain bends to retrieve it, then grasps Hayes's right hand. He roughly arranges Hayes's fingers on the pencil and places the point of it on the pad, as if, together, they will write Hayes's name. Hayes watches his own hand, under the captain's control, scrawl the word *deadbeat,* the crossing of the *t* executed with such force that the lead breaks.

The captain tears the leaf from the pad, wads it into a ball, tosses it onto Hayes's legs, and moves away. As he goes, Hayes hears him mutter, "I'll have you where you belong soon enough. Hospital rat."

Casper, who has witnessed the whole thing, shakes his head and says to Hayes, softly, "Pay him no mind . . . the stinking parlor soldier. We're not under his command. Besides, what makes him think you're a private? For all he knows, you're his superior officer. Jackanapes."

Suddenly the ward blazes bright white, and a knifelike clap of thunder barrels from one end to the other, causing much gasping, followed by a wave of laughter. Hayes stares for a moment at the lantern hanging from the ceiling, then eases himself down in his bed and covers his face with his pillow. He presses his hands hard over his ears.

In the darkness, the din of the ward eddies away like water into a drain, buried and barely audible. The noise inside Hayes's head—what he has come to think of as the sound of his brain—has continued to evolve; more grind than sizzle or whir, it is recognizable to him now as the rasp of a saw cutting through bone.

But this sound, too, withdraws as he trains his mind on the after-image of the lantern, which is suspended on the inside of the eyelids, blue-white against a complex of black rafters. He cannot quite make it hold still, but he finds that if he allows himself to follow its gentle heaves and surges (rather than resisting them), the feeling is something like being held fast, contained.

He can no longer deny a certain truth: that though his wounds still pain him from time to time, and though he still walks with a slight limp, he wears no bandages. He has watched the lovely Anne dressing Jeffers's wounds, front and back, but neither she, nor anyone else, has touched Hayes in this way. The only injuries assessed by any doctor are the pale bruises on his right arm, which were diagnosed as the effect of concentrated use of a musket, and the scab at the crown of his head, judged to be the vestige of his having been struck there with a blunt weapon, and further judged to be healing well. The ward surgeon has expressed a concern about Hayes's failure to eat adequately, but that is all. Somewhere near his feet lies a crumpled leaf of paper with the word *deadbeat* (malingerer) written on it. If his wounds are imaginary, then what of the pain? What of the bleeding? Imaginary too? And if everything's only a product of his mind, then perhaps he *is* a deserter. Perhaps he'll be court-martialed, right here in the hospital's administration building, taken out and stood against the wall of the guardhouse, executed. (One of the guns will be armed with a blank cartridge, so that no member of the firing party can say for sure that he was the one who killed Hayes.) Across the way, visitors to Washington City will watch the spectacle from the windows of the Smithsonian Castle. Mothers will cover the eyes of their children. Afterward, the entire population of the hospital will file by Hayes's body, heaped on the ground in the mud.

Beneath the pillow, he slowly relaxes his hands, letting in the hospital sounds gradually, and the drumming of rain and human voices bring him back to bed 33. He is not a deserter. He was himself deserted. There was an officer on a horse, a sergeant. With a rough jerk of the reins, the sergeant pulled the horse's head around in an abrupt turn. He spoke the words *Leave him* and *Take his weapon*.

What Hayes must do is find a way home, though he cannot think how he will purchase any car tickets without any money. Still, he understands that the first step to finding his way back to Brooklyn is finding a way out of the hospital. And before he can do that, he must find some clothes to wear.

Mrs. Duffy has stopped singing.

The man in bed 31 has stopped yelping.

Jeffers says, "Put me out to sea, that's what. God's sky and the sea air."

Hayes is thinking, *"My dearest Joan" might just as well be Casper's sister as his sweetheart,* when someone moves the pillow from his face.

It is Walt, leaning over him, frowning. "Are you all right, my boy?"

"That greenhorn captain came by to torment him," says Casper.

"What greenhorn captain?" says Walt, turning toward Casper. He places his hat on the table between the beds, where he also leans his cane and a soaked umbrella. Hayes notices a sprig of what looks like spearmint stuck in the buttonhole of the man's lapel.

"The blowhard," says Casper. "Somebody's favorite nephew."

"Don't believe I know him," says Walt and sits on the edge of Hayes's bed.

He takes a handkerchief from his jacket and begins to wipe his own cheeks and beard. "It's downright biblical outdoors," he says. "I've just navigated both a flood and an immense drove of cattle. A thousand of them, herded down the street by the most masculine drivers imaginable, whistling and singing. I might've been trampled to death . . . or drowned . . . or both. I hope you can see how much you boys mean to me."

He puts away the handkerchief and lifts his bag from the floor. "I've a few important errands," he says. "Three or four letters to write, et cetera, et cetera, a jar of pickles to deliver to an Irish lad named Paddy Sullivan. And then I'll be back."

"Pickles?" says Casper. "You never brought me any pickles."

"I don't recall your ever requesting any," says Walt, briefly rummaging inside the bag and then pulling the strap over his head. He turns to go but seizes on the wadded paper at Hayes's feet. "What's this?" he asks Casper, lifting it from the bed.

Casper shrugs one shoulder, the one with the intact arm. "The bugger made him write something," he says. "Guiding his hand, like, and then crumpled it up and tossed it there."

Walt opens the page and reads what's on it. He looks for a moment at Hayes, then folds the paper and puts it into the pocket of his coat.

"What's it say?" asks Casper.

"It says that a man's rank doesn't always correspond with his judgment or decency," answers Walt. He moves away, coughing as he goes.

He returns in the next moment. "What does he look like?" he asks Casper.

"Like the school-yard bully, all done up in army duds," says Casper. "Commander of the guard."

These last words, the captain's position, Casper has spoken in a grand exaggerated tone.

"Oh, *him*," says Walt, "oh, yes, he's to be avoided at all costs . . . impudent, insolent . . ."

He pauses for an additional moment, head bowed, apparently thinking, and then moves away.

A WHILE LATER, Walt stops at Hayes's bed, where he drops a bundle of clothes, tied up with string. "I thought it time you had something to wear," he says. "I did the best I could, but I don't promise a proper fit. There's very little left to choose from, you know."

He laughs—apparently at a stunned expression on Hayes's face—and then leaves again, mumbling something to himself about being off to the ice room and the water jar. As he goes, Hayes glimpses a surprisingly quick shift in the gray-haired man's mood, as if his cheeriness is worked up for the benefit of the sick and wounded soldiers, and in repose—or unwatched—he reverts to a comfortable sadness.

Hayes takes the clothes and limps to the bath-room at one end of the pavilion, where he changes into a clean shirt and drawers, trousers, and socks. The trousers are a bit tight in the waist and long in the leg, so he leaves the top button undone and rolls the cuffs. On a wall of the bath-room hangs a mirror not much bigger than a base ball. He steps back from it a few feet and moves side to side, bending his knees and going on tiptoe, trying to gain from these several round puzzle pieces an idea of how he looks.

When he returns to the bed, Anne waits for him with a basin, a sponge, and a block of soap. She pats the edge of the mattress.

"Don't you look lovely," she says. "Now sit here and let me wash your face for you."

He sits where she has indicated and allows himself to be washed, though it is not entirely agreeable being touched, he notes, even by someone as pleasing as Anne; he must will himself to hold still, for part of him wants to flinch. The brown soap smells like tallow candles; Anne herself, like lavender water.

Behind them, Jeffers cries out, "Abysmal!" and heaves a great sigh.

"Dr. Dinkle says the poor man won't last the night," whispers Anne, close to Hayes's ear. "Shot straight through the lungs. In the front and out the back. I feel so sorry for him I don't know what to do."

She tilts Hayes's head forward so she can wash the nape of his neck. When next he looks up, he sees Walt again, standing on the other side of Casper's bed and holding two drinking glasses filled with a red liquid. "Here," he says, "I've brought you ice water with cherry syrup. I imagined you might think it too hot today for tea."

As he moves around toward Hayes, he feigns a puzzled look. "And who is this handsome fellow?" he asks Anne. "I don't believe we've met."

He passes the glass into Hayes's hands.

"Oh, that's good," says Casper, between gulps.

"This is our mysterious Mr. X," says Anne. She wrings out the sponge in the basin and takes a small white towel from the pocket of her apron. As she dries Hayes's brow, she says, "He's just about my favorite patient—no wormy wounds to dress, no medicine to persuade down his throat. And he gives me no back talk."

Walt sits on Casper's bed, looking at Hayes. He says to Anne, "You remind me of the young woman who cooks my breakfast. Bighearted, but with a cool exacting edge. Likes everything just so. In quite a funk this morning over my being five minutes late."

"Now, Walt," says Anne. "Tell the truth. How late were we really?"

"Oh, I don't know," says Walt. "Maybe fifteen minutes, twenty at the most."

"Right," says Anne. "And how frequently are we fifteen or twenty minutes late?"

"You see what I mean," says Walt, softly, to Hayes. Then, to Anne, "If punctuality's not my strong suit, I'm sure I make up for it with other qualities. I've always been quite charming, for example, to the young lady's milk cow, Chloe."

"Chloe!" cries Anne, laughing. "That's my sister's name!"

"Your sister doesn't live in a pen just behind a small brick house near the Capitol, does she?" says Walt, and Anne laughs again and slaps him over the head with her towel.

At that moment Matron appears.

Walt lowers his face into his hands, whispering into his fingers, "Oh, dear."

"Miss Reynolds," says Matron. "Are you on your break? You look to me as though you're on your break."

"No, ma'am," says Anne, folding the towel and returning it to her apron. "I've just been bathing—"

"But this young man is perfectly capable of bathing himself," says Matron. "Do I need to remind you that we've never been so stretched as we are now?"

"No, ma'am."

"I think you must share with me your secret," Matron says. "Somehow, with so many suffering and dying all around me, I've not managed to find the time for socializing."

"No, ma'am," Anne repeats.

"And Miss Reynolds," says Matron, "what may I ask is the color of that dress you're wearing?"

Anne looks down at her dress. "It's lilac, ma'am," she answers.

"Lilac," says Matron. "Well, lilac may suit your altogether regrettable youthfulness, Miss Reynolds, but I don't see how you can think it a fitting shade for a military hospital. Please go and change at once."

"But, Matron, the ward surgeons have expressed a particular interest in—"

"Please, do not talk to me about surgeons," says Matron quickly. "What do surgeons know? That will be all. Go and change."

"Yes, ma'am," says Anne.

"And while you're at it, please tidy up your hair," Matron adds and then sails away, quaking as if carried by a breeze.

Hayes expects sniggering to follow her departure, but instead there's only silence, and then Anne lifts the basin from the bed.

Walt says, "Can you leave that?"

Anne looks at him, but he gives her nothing in the way of an explanation. After a moment, she says, "Okay . . . yes, I can leave it."

"And the towel, too?"

She replaces the basin, takes the towel from her apron, and lays it, still folded, alongside.

"Thank you, my dear girl," says Walt, solemnly.

After she has gone, Hayes notices that Casper, who has finished his drink, silently winces in pain as he leans over to place the glass on the table. Hayes, who has drunk less than half of his, passes it to Casper, whose face lights up. "Thanks," he says. "Good and strong, just how I like it."

"Now, Mr. X," says Walt, to Hayes. "There's something we must discuss. I'm reluctant to give advice regarding a man's personal appearance, though I do consider myself capable in some respects. With the considerable gifts God has given you, you can hardly go wrong, but . . . how can I put it? The whiskers, my boy. They're . . . inconclusive."

This remark causes Casper to laugh, though not, Hayes observes, unkindly.

Walt admonishes Casper with a shake of the head, then says to Hayes, "They suggest—in my opinion, awkwardly—a future you don't quite yet possess."

He pauses for a moment and looks penetratingly into Hayes's eyes. "What I mean to do," he says, "is offer you a shave."

Hayes is gazing directly into the man's abundant and scraggly beard. Not a lot of practice with the razor, he imagines.

"I know what you're thinking," says Walt. "You're thinking I lack the necessary experience."

This, too, causes Casper to laugh, and Walt gives him the same quick head-shaking as before.

"And who can blame you?" continues Walt, to Hayes. "But let me assure you, you won't be the first soldier I've shaved. I appear to have a natural ability, and it gives me a good deal of pleasure besides. You wouldn't deny me, would you, when a little passivity's all that's asked for?"

IF MATRON and the angry captain have been foils, meant to endear Hayes to the patronizing Anne, the affable Casper, and the kindly Walt—the drama of the ward a carefully contrived set piece, culminating in a razor—to Hayes, it has been persuasive. His willingness to play his appointed role feels to him like a sort of surrender, and if the gray-haired man slits his throat, at least there will be a quick end to the ongoing carnival of questions inside his head. He won't find his way back home, but perhaps he'll find peace. As he takes his seat in the oak chair at the end of the bed, he wonders: If he bleeds to death on the pavilion floor, will he truly have died? Or will the web-work of mosquito curtains draw up into the heavens, amid thunderous applause, and his comrades lift him by the arms? Will the sick, lame, and the dying walk again, missing limbs restored? Will the dead enter from the wings to take a bow?

Walt rolls Hayes's shirt collar away from his neck and, in that uncanny way he has of divining at least the flavor of Hayes's thoughts, puts on a British accent and whispers what are surely lines from a Shakespeare play: "'I must to the barber's, monsieur; for methinks I am marvelous hairy about the face.'"

The storms and the heat have cast a kind of numbing pall over the ward. Visitors have thinned out—even the relentless clergymen have withdrawn with their armloads of tracts—and the dominant sound is a low murmur made of subdued voices and rain on the roof. Before Walt begins, he puffs and coughs and then removes his own jacket and tie and lays them on Hayes's bed; he opens the collar of his shirt, revealing more than Hayes wants of the sweat-glistened mat of gray hair on his broad chest. Hayes dreads his touching him, the hot weight of his thick fingertips. He turns and faces forward as two women carrying teapots pass in front of him; they each look down, unsmiling, and appear to take in the scene, one of them with a particularly knowing glint in the eye. As they go, one whispers something to the other, and they both laugh.

Behind him, Hayes hears Jeffers's snoring, which sounds like the rasp of a surgeon's saw (the sound of Hayes's own brain). Walt is saying something to Casper, and though Hayes cannot make out any words other than *he* and *he* and *he*, he thinks the tone distinctly conspiratorial.

In the bed across the aisle, a boy not more than fifteen or sixteen, pretty enough to be a girl, sits propped up by pillows, with his eyes closed; he has no visible injuries, but his pallor's like ash. A woman, undoubtedly the boy's mother, sits in a chair by the bed, holding his hand. Hayes cannot see anything of her face. She has removed her bonnet, which hangs from one of the chair's finials. Something about the back of the woman's head and the angle of the bonnet (strings dangling) fills Hayes with sorrow and a kind of vague self-reproach. Now the boy in the bed suddenly opens his eyes and looks directly at Hayes, unblinking, a face so utterly blank it's frightening. The woman then turns in her chair, somehow knocking the bonnet to the floor: it is Hayes's own mother, smiling sadly at him from across the wide aisle. Hayes stiffens; a chill spreads through his limbs, even into the soles of his feet. The woman quickly puts her back to him, and then Walt is there, saying, "What is it, my boy? You look as if you've seen a ghost."

He takes one of Hayes's hands in his own and pats it repeatedly, as if to draw blood into it. "There now," he says. "You're not going to be like the sheep who keels over at being shorn, are you?"

In the next moment, he's brushing soap—slimy from having sat in the basin—over Hayes's cheeks and neck and chin. "We've no shortage of ghosts around here," he says. "Sometimes it seems that's mainly what we're about, ghost-making. Sometimes I think we've abandoned all other industries. Lately I've looked at my own face in a mirror—a certain time of night, at the end of a certain kind of day—and thought it was a ghost I saw. I'm surely not the man I was before. Which, in my case, is a good thing. I'm better now, if a bit shopworn."

He moves directly in front of Hayes and applies the brush to his mustache, then with his bare finger carefully wipes soap away from Hayes's lips. Somehow, the ease with which he does it renders it less objectionable than Hayes would have thought. "You see," he says, "just like ghosts, we're all, every one of us, in a state of suspension, aren't we? Especially the soldiers in the hospitals, of course. But you could say the same of the nation, couldn't you? Are we to live, or are we to die?"

He puts down the brush, and then Hayes feels the man's fingers rooting through his hair, exploring his scalp. "If only I had the skill to read your bumps!" says Walt. "I might at least know you in *that* fanciful way."

The woman across the aisle, the boy's mother, has discovered her fallen bonnet. When she bends to retrieve it, Hayes sees her face, the face of a total stranger.

Walt lays the small towel over Hayes's right shoulder. "What we want to do is get you out of here as soon as we can," he says, flashing a razor with a bone handle. "We don't want *you* turning into a ghost."

A soldier with an arm in a sling stops in the aisle and grins at Walt. "Where'd you get that fine-looking razor, Walt?" says the soldier.

"From Mr. Allen's in Pennsylvania Avenue," Walt answers. "He's a good friend of mine and gives me a special rate."

The soldier tugs gently on Walt's beard and says, "I didn't reckon you brought it from home."

Walt smacks the soldier's hand away from his beard, playfully, and the soldier moves on laughing. Now Walt's face grows serious; with his fingers against Hayes's temple, he pushes his head to one side, and soon Hayes feels and hears the scratch of the razor. He progresses slowly down the side of Hayes's cheek, but the short strokes of the razor are rapid. Regularly, he wipes the razor on the towel, which Hayes feels but cannot see. Hayes doesn't believe that Walt means to murder him, for he doesn't believe a quick end will be his fate. Long ago, he dreamed that his comrades would abandon him in the battlefield, and they did. But in the dream, he survived. In his heart of hearts, he believes his fortune's the tortuous test of survival.

Not far away, he sees a number of the hospital staff clustered around a bed, where no doubt a more critical procedure than shaving is under way. An air of holiness hangs there in that spot, while, in contrast, surrounding it, everyone and everything continue indifferently. A young medical cadet, one in the cluster observing, drops to the floor. Two attendants drag him by the arms, down to the end of the pavilion and the wardmaster's room, and this event, a small wrinkle in the plot, passes without the least commotion.

Walt, busy with the razor, makes little noises as he works, peeping like a bird. He has now reached the side of Hayes's neck, where the brisk short strokes go in many different directions rather than uniformly. Always, there is the pressure of his fingers, stretching the skin where the razor's applied. "You know," he says, "I'm really quite good at this. I do hope that whoever you are in the world, my friend, you've already discovered something you're especially good at. There's nothing so fortifying, I think, as that bright moment when you stumble into something you do really well. It always has about it a feeling of destiny."

He pulls Hayes's head toward himself and goes to work on the opposite cheek. "When I was about your age," he says, "I was a country schoolmaster." He wipes the razor on the towel and laughs. "*Not* something I was especially good at," he adds. "But I was earnest enough, I suppose, in my way. I did love the chance it gave me to spare the rod. That I enjoyed very much, sparing the rod. And playing base ball at recess."

A soldier in a wheelchair stops next to them and looks up at Walt with watery eyes. Both legs have been amputated, one a few inches above the knee, the other a few inches below. "Hello, Walt," he says, somehow smiling with the corners of his mouth turned downward.

"Oh," says Walt, "wait just a moment."

He balances the razor on Hayes's shoulder, reaches into the pocket of his baggy trousers, and produces a two-cent piece. "Your milk money, comrade. You see, I didn't forget."

Hayes notices that there's something indeterminate about the soldier's face—he might be an older man, young for his age, or a young man, old for his age. He accepts the coin, pockets it, and stretches his hands upward. Walt bends so the soldier can put his arms around his neck. As they release each other, the soldier kisses Walt on the temple and then rolls away.

"He was bringing in the wounded from the field, a few days ago, in the Wilderness," says Walt, taking up the razor again. "A rebel sharp-shooter seized on the occasion to shoot him in both legs."

He repositions Hayes's head and returns to his cheek, where he works silently for a minute. Then he says, "I did notice, by the way, how your eyes danced up at me with my mention of base ball. Ah, ha-ha, there they go again!" He moves Hayes's head back to the middle and tilts it up, exposing his neck. "I have in my possession your varnished memento, *Bachelors 24, Twighoppers 21*. And I'm aware from the inscription in your book, your soggy Dickens, that you have a sister. These are your clues, as it were. But I'm resisting the impulse to regard you as a riddle to be solved. I prefer to think of you as a slowly unfolding revelation. A rose in the garden. Now you must hold perfectly still . . . I'm about to undertake your Adam's apple."

Walt falls silent again, except for the occasional peep, and moves the razor, sometimes upward, sometimes downward, in strokes so delicate they almost tickle. After a moment, he says, "I don't know why I feel so disposed to tell you things about myself—except that there's a sweet quality to your silence that somehow invites confidences. It's been years since I've spoken to anyone of my schoolmastering days. All my life I've been enamored of men's voices, you see—the great thrill of the human voice, a man's breath made into meaning. What a thing! But my time in the hospitals has taught me to love silence—or, I should say, to love *silences*. Now would you kindly do *this* for me?"

He pulls his upper lip down over his teeth, stretching the skin beneath his mustache. Hayes follows suit and closes his eyes. "That's it, thank you," says Walt as he applies the razor above Hayes's mouth. "You know," he says, "I've worried more than once that on that glad day when the sound of you returns, I won't be sufficiently glad."

Hayes cannot think why he feels like crying, except that the words *a riddle to be solved* have lodged in his mind, and the rain has suddenly stopped falling on the roof, and it has made him think of the whispery lull right after an ocean wave breaks onto the shore.

"Almost done," says Walt. "Only the chin now."

Hayes peeks at him through his eyelashes. He appears to be concentrating quite hard; he peeps two or three times, holding the tip of his tongue firmly between his lips. In a moment, he presses his finger into the deep cleft of Hayes's chin, wiping soap away. "There's a barber's adventure," he says softly, "that handsome little fissure you have there."

Behind and above Walt, Major Cross's bright red face appears, his brow—what's visible of it below the bandages—tightly knitted together. "The maps are all wet," he says, irately, "wet, wet and shredded."

Walt, startled, turns and lays a hand on the man's forearm.

"No touching!" he cries, jerking back his arm. "You've let the maps get ruined."

"Sorry, Major," says Walt. "What about a horehound stick, would that suit you? I think I might have some licorice."

"Out of my way," says Major Cross, narrowing his eyes, and Walt moves back a step.

Major Cross doesn't budge but slowly begins to shake his head instead; his face appears to crumble, like that of a child whose feelings have been injured. "What shall we do?" he says. "What shall we do?" Then continuing to shake his head hopelessly, he moves into the narrow space between Hayes's bed and Jeffers's, lowers himself to the floor, and is soon prone. Hayes, who has turned around in the chair to watch, sees the man's head disappear beneath his bed.

When Hayes faces forward again, Walt is standing before him smiling. "You're a dead ringer for somebody I knew and loved not long ago," he says. "Same black hair, same gray eyes." He takes the towel from Hayes's shoulder. "You're all done," he says. "And a fine job if I do say so myself."

He produces a small mirror from his jacket pocket and passes it to Hayes. As Hayes holds the mirror up, Walt moves behind him and bends down, looking over Hayes's shoulder so he can see what Hayes sees. Though the sight of his barren face in the little oval causes in Hayes an unsettling mix of feelings—overwhelming and incomprehensible—he manages a nod and a grateful smile, which seems satisfying enough to Walt.

Hayes helps with the tidying up and then heads with the basin to the water closet to empty it. The towel has been rinsed and wrung in the basin, and as Hayes moves along the aisle he studies his whiskers floating in the soapy mixture—circles and arcs and black smudges among the bubbles—and something about the sight of them wafting to and fro causes his hands to start shaking. The certain knowledge that he's about to be at the center of a great noisy mess only makes matters worse, and then suddenly Babb stands before him. "I'll take that for you," says Babb and, just like that, relieves him of the basin.

Babb pauses for a moment and eyes Hayes head to toe. "Don't you look spiffy and slicked up," he says, unpleasantly, then turns and limps away with the basin.

Back at his bed, Hayes finds that Walt has pulled the chair alongside and taken a seat there. With Major Cross on the other side, Hayes must climb into bed from the end of it. As he does so, Casper hushes him and indicates Walt, who (Hayes sees now) sits with his cane at a slant between his legs, resting both hands on the handle, sound asleep. He has put his jacket back on and buttoned up his shirt, but left off his tie. While Hayes is looking at him, Walt's head tips an inch toward his chest, crushing and bending the end of his beard.

Casper sighs and adjusts the little pillow beneath his stub, which he pats affectionately, and then closes his own eyes.

Jeffers, whose cap has slid down over his face, covering his nose, moves his lips drily, says the single word *bellows* and then moves his lips again.

On the floor, Major Cross breathes with a steady peaceful rhythm, his bare feet, soles upward, one on top of the other.

Across the way, the young boy has turned onto his side and lies flat in his bed. The chair where his mother sat earlier is empty.

Down the aisle, the bed around which so many had gathered (and where the young cadet fainted) is also empty.

A few feet above Hayes, the Union flag appears to shudder, as if moved by an internal current, and then hangs slack again.

Far away, at one end of the pavilion, behind the closed door to the dining room, somebody drops a glass vessel. A feminine cry follows the muted jangle of glass, and it sounds oddly like an expression of pleasure.

Sunshine washes through the windows, igniting the strung-up mosquito curtains orange for a moment, and then dies away.

Outdoors, a cock crows, once, and then again.

Outdoors, the breeze-blown bell chimes, in three successive couplets.

Hayes worries with his tongue the smooth naked region above his upper lip. He looks at Walt, slumped in the nearby chair. He thinks of the happy thud an apple makes when it falls to the ground, and the satisfying resonant pop of a base ball well struck.

Owing to how his throat remains unslit, he thinks perhaps he'll allow himself to love the gray-bearded Walt, as the other men seem to. It occurs to him that he never loved his father until after his father had perished, and then it felt not entirely creditable, loving what's already lost.

Soon Sarah comes and sits beside him. She leans down to kiss his forehead and then, smiling, fixes an ivory comb that has come loose in her hair. She lays her white hand on his breast and, after a moment, begins to pat him there, in couplets, meant, he supposes, to imitate his heart.

Now that his body has got the rest it needed, Hayes sleeps lightly, as if he were back in the woods, lost and trying to find his way to Washington City. The ward, with its regular nocturnal disturbances, is not the place most conducive to sleeping, and his dreams generally take him to the battlefield, with its reports of musketry and din of grape and canister.

Late into the night, what wakes him the first time is the sound of nearby whispering. He lies on his stomach with one arm over his head; he can see out through a carrot-shaped opening formed by his upper arm and the pillow. There is the usual foul odor, the usual dull glow of the few gas lamps turned low, the usual fog of mosquito curtains. Babb, standing on the far side of Casper's bed, has just hushed Casper, and Casper, in a heated whisper, says, "That wasn't our agreement."

Babb answers, "Well, the agreement changed . . . It's getting harder to come by."

"You're a rotten devil," says Casper, and then sits up straighter in the bed, reaches around backward beneath his pillow, and pulls out a bill, which he passes to Babb. Holding the bill in one hand, Babb studies it for a moment, then pockets it.

Now he slowly opens his other hand near Casper's face.

"What's that?" says Casper.

"That's *it*," says Babb.

"Put it in some water."

"Ain't got no water."

"Then go get some."

"Don't have a mind to."

"What do you expect me to do then?"

"Lick it out of my hand."

"I'm not licking it out of your hand, you rotten, stinking—"

"Suit yourself," says Babb and turns away.

"Wait!" cries Casper, and Babb hushes him again.

"At least put it here in my own hand," whispers Casper.

"Don't have a mind to," says Babb, again holding his open palm close to Casper's face. "If you want it, lick it out."

Hayes can see in the low gaslight Casper's eyes glowing with tears.

"And be quick about it, too," Babb says, pressing the edge of his hand against Casper's lips.

With his one remaining hand, Casper tilts Babb's palm toward his mouth and begins to lick, at first tentatively, and then quite thoroughly, as Babb croons, "That's a good puppy . . ."

When Casper is done, he turns his head to the side and doesn't face forward again until Babb has gone, down the aisle to the middle of the pavilion and out of the ward. Then Casper heaves a deep sigh that ends in a soft moan. He adjusts the small pillow beneath his stub and gives it a few gentle pats. He lets his head fall back and expels another long sigh. One explosive sob escapes him, and he quickly flattens his hand over his mouth. After a moment, he takes a corner of the bedsheet and wipes his nose and eyes.

Hayes continues to watch him until Casper's breath becomes regular, and, still sitting up, he has apparently gone asleep.

Hayes soon allows his own eyes to close.

A loud wind wakes him the second time, a wind that turns out to be Jeffers, gasping for air, asleep, and rolling onto his side. Startled, Hayes raises himself onto his elbows, just in time to see Babb, now kneeling between the two beds, taking a wad of bills from under Jeffers's pillow. Babb turns and looks through the mosquito curtain directly at Hayes. His face, quite near Hayes's own, at first discloses alarm but quickly acquires the flat affect of a dead man. He lifts Hayes's mosquito curtain and drapes it over his own head, gathering and clutching it beneath his chin so that it looks like a woman's hood.

"Now, who you gonna tell?" he whispers sweetly, smiling. "You can't talk, can you? Can't even hold a pencil in your fingers."

He removes the curtain from around his face and lets it drop again. He shrugs his shoulders and says, through the gauze, "Besides . . . what use is it to *him* . . . where *he's* going?"

As Babb slips away, Hayes lowers his head onto his pillow.

A man nearby, and another farther away, are having what seem like antiphonal fits of coughing. The ward's walls and rafters throb amber and violet with the flickering lamps—somehow the very rhythm (thinks Hayes, eyes closing) of sleep.

Soon he climbs out of the bed and gets onto the floor, prone, with his head just under the edge of the iron frame and his right eye positioned over the knothole. It's darker down there than in the ward, but after a moment his eye adjusts to the gloom, and he can see Banjo, Company D's foxhound, scratching her muzzle with one of her hind feet. She looks up at him, comes over, and starts sniffing around the rim of the knothole and whimpering. Her whiskers touch his eyelash, and then he sees that it's a big brown rat, not a dog, and drawing back, he cracks his head against the wooden bed slats. He starts to slide away but stops when he hears somebody whispering his name beneath the floor. Carefully he crawls toward the hole again.

Hayes, Hayes, he hears. *They've took the goats, the rotten thieves. Quick, pull me out, Hayes.*

Hayes already knows it's Billy Swift down there with the rats, and when he peers through the knothole, he sees Billy standing directly below, reaching a trembling hand upward.

"Shhh," says Hayes, "nobody here knows my name."

Pull me out, Billy whispers, *quick,* but Hayes can't think how to do it. Smoke begins to swirl around the boy's face, and Hayes then sees, with horror, that Swift's feet and legs are on fire.

Now, grasping that he's having a nightmare, Hayes wills himself awake, only to find that in reality it's the hospital ward that's burning. The whole place is filled with smoke, and across the way mosquito curtains roll toward the rafters in bursts of orange flame.

He gets himself up and into the aisle, where he sees that some of the patients have already been evacuated, their beds already empty; other beds contain still-sleeping soldiers; and still others the black cylinders (tapered at the ends) of charred corpses. He tries to call out but cannot make his voice work. He sprints for the wardmaster's room, which he finds empty but for thick black smoke; he rushes through to the set of outer doors that exit the ward, and when he throws these open he awakens in his own bed, thrashing but restrained by two uniformed guards.

"Be *still!*" says the first, forcefully, and Hayes drops back against the iron bedstead, stupefied.

"Better," says the second, who reaches for Hayes's tag, reads what's on it, and releases it. "What's your name?"

Hayes is silent.

"If you won't say your name," says the first, "we'll just have to—"

At that moment, Matron appears, in a bonnet and a long nightgown. She looks at Hayes, wide-eyed, and says, "He's dressed."

"Yes, ma'am," says the first guard. "We stopped him at the doors. He was in a state, like somebody was after him."

"He was like a wildcat," says the second.

Hayes's mind is racing. He looks at Matron, like a ship's mast at the end of his bed, darkness behind her, and understands all at once that she herself is sick, that she suffers some sort of illness in the advanced stages.

And he believes with a sudden certainty that he is to die after all, that his sister, Sarah, will never see him alive again. He's consumed by guilt for having abandoned her and thinks his being deserted on the battlefield was God's scheme for evening the score.

Now he looks down at his clothes, which he doesn't recognize. If he could only see his wounds he might *know* if he is to live or die. He pushes himself up and starts to tear at his strange clothes, ripping open the shirt and the fly of the trousers. He feels many hands, pulling him one way and another, but he's strong and single-minded: he *will* see his wounds.

The guards struggle against him roughly—one claps him against the side of his head with something harder and heavier than any human hand—and Hayes then hears Matron's voice: "That will do!" she cries, and then, "Go . . . go . . . please . . . and leave us be."

"Now, see here," says one of the guards, indignantly, but Matron soothes and persuades both the soldiers—calling them "gentlemen," thanking them for their help, assuring them that she can manage now—and then they are gone.

Hayes, half naked, allows himself to be sorted out by the woman, who, to his complete amazement, soon has him in her arms, rocking him as if he were a child.

"There, there, my poor boy," she says, "get hold of yourself. I didn't know you were so terribly distraught. Everything's going to be all right, in time. Try to calm yourself, dear."

Hayes smells smoke and sees flames out of the corner of his right eye. He jerks his head in that direction, and Matron says, "What is it, my boy? What is it you think you see?"

And, after another moment, stroking the back of his head, she says, "It's nothing, my dear. Nothing at all. Don't be so very frightened. You're safe with us . . . safe and sound with us."

⟻ THREE ⟼

Smoke

Just as the land began to level off, they stumbled into a surprising pocket of clear air. For the last several minutes they'd been struggling, almost blindly, toward a continuous clap of musketry, which now suddenly ceased. In the abrupt quiet, a nearby soldier whistled the first phrase of "The Girl I Left Behind Me." Hayes saw a fragment of the ragged line of his squad zigzagging away into the thicket, and then Leggett, not more than six paces forward. "Truman!" he cried, and Leggett turned, met Hayes's eyes, quickly shook his head, and sighed, an assessment of the situation they found themselves in: the ground immediately beyond was littered with dead and wounded Union men. Half a dozen panicked soldiers brushed past Hayes, headed in the opposite direction (one jostling his shoulder), and then a solitary bullet zipped low through the trees and struck the barrel of his musket with a loud *ping!*, knocking it from his hands and onto the ground. He threw himself at it, prone, a reaction that likely saved his life, for in the next instant a fierce volley from an invisible enemy felled the still-standing soldiers on either side of him. The sound—unlike anything he'd ever heard, a mixture of concentrated gunfire, inhuman shrieks, and the dull drumroll of bodies hitting the ground—seemed to shake the earth. Arms outstretched, he gripped the weapon and squeezed his eyes shut. Amid the din rang a muffled chorus of *"Down down,"* and then he saw Leggett again, who now lay flat with his head thrust back, as if gazing at something high above and behind him in the trees.

Hayes wriggled forward as two undulant walls of blue-white smoke crept toward each other across the forest floor, closing in from either side. It occurred to him that he and his comrades had wandered astray and were now caught between the lines. The earth under his belly felt hot and damp and smelled of burnt pine. Beneath the battle-roar, which sprang from every direction and penetrated the soles of his feet, he could hear, from inside himself, the strangely poignant whisper of his own breathing.

Leggett had been shot in the mouth. Jets of blood pulsed into a brown mat of pine needles beneath his shoulders. Hayes, turning Leggett's head to one side, saw that the ball had exited the nape of his neck. Two broken amber-colored teeth lay in the rising pool of blood, glistening like gemstones. Hayes slid his hand beneath Leggett's neck and staunched the current—with the result that the tattered gaping cavity at the lower half of his face filled and began to overflow. Beneath the modest brim of his forage cap, which still hugged his brow, Leggett's eyes were as wide and vacant as a trout's. Ten seconds had passed since Hayes had spotted him and called his name, and now he was gone, utterly; the wet and ghastly thing Hayes cupped in his palm bore little that even suggested the man.

Hayes removed his hand, warm and sodden, brought it to his nostrils, and sniffed (rust, weak tea in a tin cup). He touched his lips to his palm (salt, a nickel on the tongue). He wiped his hand on his trousers, looked up to his right, and watched a trio of saplings twitch and quake as their gray bark was gashed and scarred, their new leaves sliced and splintered, by an unbroken tempest of bullets. From a bearing he now perceived as behind him, three or four commanders were shouting *Fire at will!* which, though it struck him as a kind of nonsense—exotic owls screeching in a jungle—did supply a feasible objective.

He unbuckled Leggett's belt and roughly freed it from beneath him, rolling the body one way and another as required. A short distance away, he saw a soldier burrowed in a shallow recess behind a clump of earth and rotting logs. Hayes crawled forward, dragging his weapon and Leggett's belt along the ground. The blare of combat, from both front and rear, was like the toothed jaws of a giant vise. He nestled in alongside the other soldier, whom he recognized as a private named Lynch, from West Cambridge, Massachusetts, and who turned out to be quite dead, though Hayes could not locate any wound. With a little adjusting, he put the man's broad back into service as a table on which to rest his musket. It was easy enough to discern the rebel line—some two hundred yards through the trees, the screen of smoke sparkled with repeating bursts of yellow fire—but he had no way of knowing who among his comrades might lie between that line and himself. He resolved to aim high enough to shoot over any such soldiers, and then he was loading, firing, reloading, and firing again, keeping careful count of his shots. He found he had to think his way through the series of loading steps only the first couple of times, and then he acquired the cold efficacy of an automaton.

A PRIVATE FROM another company, a round-faced boy Hayes knew only vaguely, landed next to him, wide-eyed and sweating. He looked at Hayes with wonder and shouted (for it was the only way to make oneself heard), "I've lost my squad. I don't know where I am. What should I do? I don't know what to do."

"Clahane," Hayes said, for he'd suddenly recalled the boy's name.

Stunned, he said, "Oh, you're Hayes, the ball player! I guess I best go find my squad. Trouble is, I don't know if they're forward or back."

"We've got ourselves between the lines," shouted Hayes. "If you go looking for them, you'll be shot. I'm surprised you got this far."

"Maybe I'm shot already," said the boy, knocking his fist hard against the side of his own head, as if to jolt himself from a trance. "Maybe I'm already dead."

He reached out a hand and pressed his fingers three times against Hayes's left cheek. Still, he didn't appear entirely convinced that Hayes was real. His gaze fell on the soldier whose back served as a fulcrum for Hayes's musket. "Who's that?" he said.

"Magnus Lynch," answered Hayes.

"Is he dead?" asked the boy, dreamily.

"Clahane," said Hayes, "stay here and dig in, like me. Fire your weapon."

"Fire my weapon," said Clahane, looking down curiously at his musket. "Yes, but are you sure that's the thing to do, Hayes?"

"We're engaged in battle," shouted Hayes. "You're supposed to fire your weapon."

Clahane craned his neck and looked out over the terrain directly before them. Hayes quickly put a hand on top of the boy's head and pressed him down.

"Do you suppose they're *all* dead?" said the boy.

"Fire your weapon," repeated Hayes.

"But what do I aim at?"

"Like this," answered Hayes and demonstrated the upward tilt of his barrel. "Watch what I do and follow."

Hayes led Clahane through the loading steps, which seemed to come back to the boy immediately, and soon, lying on his belly a musket's length away, he was grinning and firing, yelping delightedly with each blast. Hayes put his finger to his own lips to hush the boy—the colonel had instructed them that such squealing was secesh behavior and altogether unbecoming.

Hayes resumed firing and soon forgot about Clahane. Soon his right arm grew sore, and a blister formed in the tender flesh between his thumb and forefinger. Soon his weapon grew so hot that the powder would flash before he could load the ball, and so he began alternating his musket with the dead Magnus Lynch's. And when he'd exhausted his own ammunition, he opened a tin of Leggett's.

BECAUSE THE LIGHT in the woods faded, he knew that time was passing. In all the battle depictions he'd heard from veterans, he'd never known anyone to describe an engagement of such relentless ferocity and duration. He witnessed no wounded soldiers retreating or being carried to the rear by stretcher-bearers, no color guards, no visible colors ahead or behind. No rebels charged the Union line, and yet he sensed, at his back, some distance away, a chaotic ebb and flow of troops, fresh regiments arriving piecemeal as spent infantry withdrew.

One thing remained clear—to stand up meant certain death, and so Hayes stayed put and fired the two weapons sixty-seven times.

As he was loading the sixty-eighth, a bugle sounded somewhere off in the woods to his right, and the dozens of dead soldiers sprawled on the ground before him rose in unison onto all fours and begin to crawl forward. Hayes felt the skin on the back of his neck contract. He burst out laughing and turned to confer with Clahane about this extraordinary sight—but Clahane, hatless now, was stretched out flat and peaceful, his weapon beneath him, his cheek resting against the barrel. The boy might have been sleeping but for a bloody furrow that incised one side of his scalp and the fingers of blood that had flowed down from the wound and streaked his face.

Only a trick of the mind: when Hayes looked forward again, the dead soldiers were properly dead once more, and stationary. The forest itself, on the other hand, enlivened by gunfire, continued to pulse and shiver. A gray-green rain of shattered leaves wafted down from the canopy, a thing of simultaneous beauty and horror, and Hayes was struck by the coldness with which he observed it. Something deep within him had gone numb, and then, for a moment or two, he lost touch with all the certainties, small and large, that made him known to himself. It was a kind of blankness, for sure, the result of obliterative noise, but not entirely without character: nothing in the world mattered, nothing in life possessed any value, and all human endeavor was as foul and menacing as the scavenging of wild pigs in the street.

He looked at the barky vertical things that constituted what was called woods, and he couldn't think of the name for them—the word *book* came to mind, though he knew it to be wrong. He noted the scorch-marks on the back of Magnus Lynch's sack coat, and he felt a boyhood remorse at having ruined something good and the dread of being found out.

Then, as if these emotions had opened some sort of channel, he heard his sister speak his name, and the world was once again bizarre and recognizable. The shattered leaves rained down from *trees*. His country was at war with itself. He fought for the Army of the Potomac.

In the smoke and confusion his squad had wandered astray, and he'd got caught between the lines. Without his anchor (Leggett), he'd gone unmoored; it was the best he could do, to place himself in one spot like a piece of artillery and wage his singular offensive. But now he longed to find his own comrades, his own officers, and rest in the self-abandonment that came with following orders. He could go toward neither line without being taken for the enemy and shot, so he resolved to try a lateral move and see where that would take him.

As he gathered his gear, there came a lull in the fighting, and the deafening barrage slowly abated to the sporadic popping he associated with picket skirmishes. He thought it dusk now, but a dusk like none other, a failure of light that lacked the promise of darkness. He could hear the enormous thunder of combat farther away and then the deep rumble of more combat farther away still. What had seemed to him so convincingly the heart of the war was but a single lesion on the leprous body of a giant. He began to creep into the thicket. The sulfurous vapors that filled his lungs caused a hot tingle inside his chest. The ground before him sank gradually and then gradually rose beneath a bewilderment of vines and brush, strewn with bodies. Now and again, he crawled alongside a pair with limbs variously intermingled. Though he made no attempt to identify any of the fallen—indeed, he kept his eyes half closed most of the time—he did recognize the mangled corpse of his sergeant resting against the trunk of a tulip tree.

He gathered ammunition from the dead, as well as weapons, trussing with belts a bundle of muskets and dragging it along like a disabled companion. Woodsmoke mixed with gun smoke, and the dusky air grew hotter and darker still. He took a canteen from a dead comrade, drank from it, and poured the rest over his own head. He inched forward, sometimes through thorny brambles and patches of slime. His bundle of firearms got snagged repeatedly, and he found himself cultivating patience toward it, as he'd always tried to do with those who muffed balls on the playing field. For a little while he was back in New York, among his club mates after a match—music, speeches and laughter, chicken potpie and champagne.

HE REACHED THE CREST of an incline just as a young lieutenant colonel rode out of the smoke—lowering his head to clear a branch, teetering in the saddle—and stopped about ten yards away. Hayes couldn't think if he'd seen the man before, for so many of the young dark-haired officers looked alike. He watched as the man (obviously drunk) removed a flask from the pocket of his coat and took a long drink. He wiped his mustache with the back of his hand and then struggled so forcefully to screw the cap back on he broke the hinge and sent it spiraling to the ground. Rather than looking down after it, the man cast his gaze heavenward, as if to reprove a tiresome and trying God, and at that moment a bullet struck him in the left ear, knocking his hat into a nearby tangle of vines, where it lay cockeyed, suspended. He slumped violently forward, his face smacking the mane of the beautiful honey-colored mount, which danced two steps forward and back.

A second bullet struck the forehead of the horse, whose front legs buckled, catapulting the officer headfirst over the poll: a rag doll, an unseemly heap, buttressed by a sword. Third and fourth bullets struck the horse in the breast, and it shuddered and fitfully pivoted its hindquarters in an arc, so that when at last it collapsed, the full weight of its girth flattened the lieutenant colonel to the ground. The beast's long and final expiration sent dry leaves skittering toward Hayes, and then its lower lip sagged open, discharging a gluey braid of spittle.

Hayes crawled forward and uprighted the officer's flask before all the contents had spilled out. He found the cap, sniffed it, and screwed it on: bourbon, which he'd never cared for.

A BREEZE SWEPT THROUGH the woods, agitating the smoke, and the air went grayer, whiter, and grayer again. Hayes heard a *rat-a-tat* of drums, then a sound like heavy rain, rapidly approaching, and half a minute later he was being carried forward by a great wave of Union troops, Pennsylvania men from his own brigade, who were accompanied by a sudden onslaught of artillery some distance toward their right flank. Two veterans quickly lifted Hayes's bundle of guns (one shouted, "Well done!"), and soon the line dug in and a new inferno was under way.

Through the trees down to the right, Hayes could see vertical bars of paler light that indicated a clearing, most likely a road, where shells whistled and exploded above the roar of musketry. The man closest to Hayes, an older gentleman with gray whiskers, called out to him: "How'd you get so far out in front, son?"

"By accident!" shouted Hayes, and the older man laughed.

Hayes forgot to keep count of his shots, but he didn't mind. He thought of them now as countless, and he was sure he'd developed bruises up and down his right arm. The blister on his hand burst, and a new one formed alongside it.

They continued firing and advanced now and again in small increments, but every inch of gained ground cost them; men lay wounded all about, moaning or silent, half hidden in the underbrush. Hayes could tell that no significant progress was being made, and he thought the seemingly endless supply of Union soldiers worked almost to a disadvantage—the troops were jammed up against one another too close in the woods and resulted in an atmosphere of chaos. As the forest continued to grow darker and they drew ever closer to the opposing line, it became clear that the rebels occupied a higher ground. Even if the Union troops outnumbered them, as long as the Confederates had ammunition, they would hold their position. Each time they appeared to be weakening—and some small hope arose that a real advance might be made against them—they quickened with renewed vigor, always, always punctuated with the hideous rebel cry.

The gray-whiskered soldier who'd asked Hayes how he'd got so far out front took a bullet through the neck and bled to death in a matter of seconds. Careful to keep his head low, Hayes dragged the body a short ways to the rear where the dead were being piled. Many years ago, he'd watched longshoremen at the Atlantic Docks drag big sacks of grain down the gangplank of a barge and heave them onto wagons. Now, as he laid the gray-whiskered gentleman onto the heap, he recalled how he'd admired the muscle and workaday composure with which the longshoremen had toiled and how, for some time, he'd aspired to become a dockworker.

Soon after he returned to the line, an Irishman with a runny nose fell in next to him. His face bright red, he looked at Hayes, wiped his nose on the sleeve of his coat, and said, "Christ Jesus, I wish night would come!"

A minute later they advanced a few yards more, and the Irishman was cut down by a blast seemingly from very close range. Collapsing onto one knee, he shouted at Hayes, "Hey, what'd you do that for?"— evidently thinking that Hayes had struck him somehow and caused him to fall.

Hayes peered through the smoke and saw a dark mound straight in front, not a dozen paces away. Crouched, he ran forward and found there a little frayed old rebel in a droopy hat, who'd positioned him- self behind a blind of dead Union soldiers, set sideways like so many logs. The old man—skin and bones; barefoot in yellow-brown rags— yanked out his ramrod and pointed his musket at Hayes, but before he could get off a shot, Hayes kicked him with the sole of his shoe. The man went flat on his back, like a sheaf of straw, and Hayes came down hard with the stock of his musket, crushing his nose and rendering him apparently unconscious.

Hayes took the Confederate's weapon and began to scurry back to the line, when, from behind, he heard the screech of a banshee. He turned and saw the old man charging, blood pouring from his face; he leaped for Hayes, arms outflung, hands like claws, but midleap the old man was felled by a bullet to the chest.

Now Hayes knelt beside the wounded Irishman, who'd taken a ball in the knee and lay bleeding and ashy. The man braced him- self against Hayes, twisted round, and yelled at the old rebel's corpse, "That's for taking me drumstick, damn you!"

Hayes tore off the Irishman's trouser leg below the wound and made a tourniquet of the cloth. "Oh, Christ Jesus," said the man, rocking back, "how I wish night would come, how I wish night would come."

Hayes reached into his coat pocket and took out the flask of bour-bon. "Here," he said, passing it to the Irishman, "drink some of this."

"Good heavens, lad," said the man, staring at Hayes in awe. He tipped the flask to his lips and took a long drink. His eyes brimming with tears now, he said, "That'll lift me, sure."

Hayes was thinking about the old rebel who lay dead a few feet away in last year's fallen leaves. All afternoon the murderous force that had wreaked such havoc against the Union lines had remained entirely invisible, behind a tangle of forest and a wall of smoke. It was as if Hayes had earned his bruises and blisters firing his weapon at the *idea* of an enemy (though unquestionably an intractable one). Now, at last and for the first time, he'd come face-to-face with the foe, and the fearsome warrior—not even identifiably military, but elderly and indigent—weighed in at about ninety pounds. There had been a frac-tion of a second, just before he'd bashed the man's face, in which he'd thought to offer him a hand up from the ground. After all, but for the tattered CSA garb, he might have been the withered Methuselah who sat in the front-most pew Sundays at Trinity Church and snored and wheezed throughout the homily.

THE END OF THE FIGHTING, like nightfall, came abruptly. Hancock's troops were ordered to remain at the front, while General Getty's were allowed to retreat to the breastworks at the Brock Road. In the dark, the muddled army untangled and rearranged itself, and Hayes found his way to the edge (if not to the heart) of his regiment. Soon he lay on the ground among his comrades, so close to the enemy line he could hear the murmur of the rebels' conversations. From the nearby Orange Plank Road—where only an hour ago rolled the deafening thunder of artillery—he heard the rumble of wagons and the neighing and snorting of mules and horses. Underlying these sounds, the echo of the long afternoon's battle rang in his ears. The darkness, marked only by a smattering of small brushfires kindled by evening breezes, was nearly absolute. An enduring smell of smoke pervaded the air and made him recall winter nights on the Brooklyn skating ponds.

Across the heaving marshy terrain, countless soldiers lay clutching their arms. Now and again Hayes heard the muffled cries of the wounded, but for the most part these poor fellows went untended, for search lanterns drew rebel fire and renewed skirmishes. Not far away, a chaplain softly led some men in prayer. All around, there was the whisper of movement—a kind of lost and aimless shuffling that made Hayes think of the Second Corps as a great organism languishing battle-stunned on the forest floor, trying to sort itself out and catch its breath, restive and exhaling smoke. When, out of the night, he heard someone softly calling his name, he first imagined he'd fallen asleep and was dreaming.

Billy Swift, with Rosamel in tow, had sought him out, and the three greeted one another with astonished delight. Hayes remarked on the faces of the two others, how they were blackened with gunpowder, and Swift laughed and said that Hayes obviously hadn't had a chance to look in a mirror, for Hayes's face was as black as coal and all the blacker in the darkness. Swift and Rosamel got on the ground on either side of Hayes, pressing close against him, and Billy was soon resting his head on Hayes's shoulder. For some time the three lay without speaking, and it did seem to Hayes that there was not much that needed saying: they had each survived; nothing beyond that had been achieved; dawn would come, and it would all begin again.

At last—as if he were reporting an event from the afternoon in the Wilderness—Swift said, "Rosamel's wife ran off with another man."

"Yes, he told me," said Hayes, and they fell silent for another long interval.

Then Rosamel said, bleakly, *"Oui . . . ma Madeleine."*

Swift raised himself onto an elbow and spoke to Rosamel across Hayes's chest. "Why'd you let her go, Rosamel? That's what I don't understand. You should've locked her up."

"You say this because you have never had a woman," said Rosamel, keeping his head on the ground and speaking into the overhanging branches.

"Me, I would've shot the stinker," said Swift.

"She was not a stinker," said Rosamel.

"Rosamel," said Swift, "I meant the man she ran off with."

"Oh, yes," said Rosamel, "but you say that because you have never been to jail."

"You've been in jail?" asked Swift.

"*Oui*, in stupid Carcassonne."

"What for?"

"For three months."

"I mean, what did you do?"

"I don't wish to speak about it."

"Well, why did you bring it up then?"

Apparently, Rosamel had no ready answer for this last question, and Billy Swift lowered his head again onto Hayes's shoulder.

Then, after another long silence, Rosamel said, "What I did, I would do it again . . . but I would do it differently, to avoid the jail."

"We're keeping company with a common criminal, Hayes," said Swift. "What do you reckon Rosamel did to get into trouble with the law? I don't take him for the drunk-and-disorderly kind."

"Three months," said Hayes, "my guess is he stole something."

Now Rosamel propped himself onto an elbow, and Hayes saw that the man's cheek bore a gash.

"What happened to your face?" he asked him.

"It is of no matter," Rosamel answered. "Please continue."

"I imagine you stole something you thought was rightfully yours."

Rosamel only raised an eyebrow.

"Not worth much," said Hayes. "But it was important to you."

Rosamel now lay back down. After a moment, he said, "You are very wise, Hayes. It was a small clock, and I will say nothing more about it."

"How'd you do that, Hayes?" asked Swift. "How'd you know?"

Hayes shrugged. "It's just about the only crime I could think Rosamel capable of," he said.

Once more they fell into a long silence.

After a while, Billy Swift said, "Did you get something to eat, Hayes?"

"Couldn't muster any appetite," said Hayes. "But I drank a gallon of water."

"I sure wish I had something stronger," said Billy.

"I had a flask with some bourbon," said Hayes, "but I gave it to an Irishman I met from Pennsylvania."

"Now, what in the world did you do that for?" said Billy. "You might've saved it for me, Hayes. My grandpa was half Irish."

"He was wounded, Billy," said Hayes, solemnly, for—as it was the first reference to the day's combat—he felt perhaps he'd taken a liberty.

Swift said, "I overheard some fellows talking about somebody with your same name being killed, and I feared the worst, Hayes . . . that they were talking about you. Turned out they meant the commander of the other brigade."

"*Hays* with no *e*," said Hayes.

"No *e* and now no life," said Swift.

After yet another silence, Swift said softly, "I reckon old Leggett didn't make it either then."

Hayes shook his head.

"Was you with him?" asked Billy.

Hayes nodded and said, "Shot in the mouth."

"In the mouth?" said Swift, raising his own head for a moment and then lowering it down again.

Hayes nodded. "Came out the back of his neck," he said.

"Leggett . . . shot in the mouth," whispered Swift, and after another moment, Hayes realized that Swift was silently shaking with laughter.

"Yep," said Hayes, "right square in the mouth," and started to laugh, too.

"Leggett of all people," said Swift, beating his fists against Hayes's ribs, "the old gasbag."

Hayes shoved Swift away and doubled over on the ground. "I just took him to the dentist last night," he said, gulping for air. "With a toothache."

From the darkness, somebody hushed them, but this only threw Billy into new paroxysms.

Rosamel said, "What is wrong with you two boys? Are you crazy?"

This quieted them for a moment, but when Rosamel asked, "What is this . . . 'gasbag'?" they were in fits yet again.

At last Hayes composed himself and explained to Rosamel that Leggett—as Rosamel might have noticed—liked to tell stories, often long stories, and that sometimes it had been hard to get him to stop talking. When Hayes finished his explanation, Rosamel said, "But he was your friend."

"Yes," said Hayes. "He was my good friend."

Now they resumed their former positions, side by side on the ground, and soon they heard a faraway crackle of musketry, which quickly built to a climax and then subsided, very much like popping-corn in a pot.

"I was thinking," said Swift. "Instead of all this killing and dying, we could just have ourselves a match of base ball. Us against the rebs, and whoever wins wins the war."

"That would hardly be any kind of a contest," said Hayes. "I don't think Richmond would ever agree to it."

"I reckon you're right," said Swift. "But you have to admit it'd be a whole lot easier on the nerves."

Nobody said anything for a long time. Close by, a soldier was heard singing, "'Wild are the breezes tonight / But 'neath the roof, the hours as they fly / Are happy and calm and bright.'"

"I'm sure gonna miss him," said Swift, after a while.

"Me too," said Hayes.

"Me too," said Rosamel.

A while later, Swift said, "I'm aching all over."

"Me too," said Hayes.

"Me too," said Rosamel. "*All* over."

A while after that, Swift said, "Lord in heaven, Hayes, you stink."

"So do you," said Hayes.

After a pause, Swift whispered, "Rosamel stinks, too."

"I know," whispered Hayes.

After another pause, Swift added softly, "He stinks the worst of all of us."

HAYES DOZED OFF.

When he awakened minutes later, his right arm ached and tingled, the way it sometimes did after he'd pitched a long match. Rosamel and Swift slept on either side of him. Perhaps he'd dreamed of his sister, for now he felt sharp pangs of conscience over having disappointed her. These last years, since their parents had died, she had been for him a guide—if he behaved so as not to disappoint her, he would lead an exemplary life—and he'd done well. He could recall not a single instance in which he'd disappointed her but for this one enormous occasion of having left home to join the army.

Carefully he slid from between his two friends on the ground and stood up. He took a deep breath and gathered his gear, not making a sound. Then he turned and very slowly began to pick his way through the woods to find Leggett.

The ringing in his ears, the day's echo, had hardened into a low yellow hiss.

He suffered a hot throbbing sensation in the back of his left thigh and likewise high on his spine between the shoulders.

About thirty yards into the thicket, he saw a patch of fire on the ground, and as he moved toward it, flames leaped up a plait of dangling vines and ignited the dead tree above. A momentary beacon illuminated the dark Wilderness. Hayes stumbled into a newly dug trench and dropped to his knees a stone's throw from a heaped jumble of bodies. One pair of still-open eyes, glittered-up by the fire, found him, and he was a little boy again, back in his father's dance studio in Brooklyn, where the raucous behavior of black-suited men, falling upon one another like dominoes, had frightened him more meaningfully than he could ever explain.

Now a rabbit darted into the trench and froze, shaking violently as if from cold, stared at Hayes with black eyes aglow, and then scampered on out into the night. Hayes looked again at the mound of bodies and saw that at the very top two men's arms stuck straight up into the air, as if they were reaching for something in the overhanging trees. He looked down at his own hands, which had begun to tremble, and then he rose to his feet as the firelight died away.

Soon he climbed over a dead horse, cold cold the dew-dampened coat, and down into a shallow ravine.

He would find Leggett.

He passed through an undergrowth of bristling shrubs and a welter of strewn blankets, knapsacks, and the bodies of men, strangely leveled by the jungle and gloom, the dead, the wounded, the sleeping; passed through black shadows and listened to the sound of his own muffled steps; imagined himself marching along an unknown road, led by some instinct, as, in a different way, he'd felt led all day; thought of himself as a child of eight or nine, confident and in command, clucking his tongue and driving down Hicks Street a tandem of boys, good friends, reined and yoked with string.

A SHELL LANDED at the southern edge of the Plank Road and rolled into a hollow directly back of where Hayes lay against a rebel breastwork. For a fraction of a second, he took it for a rabbit scampering into the woods from the road. He watched the shell bump down the incline and knock against the trunk of a hazel bush. A dozen or more men buried their faces into the ground and covered their heads with their hands. Hayes, who did not bury his face or cover his head, thought it odd the way the canceling wail of musketry made certain single events seem to occur in silence. He'd noticed this strange effect earlier, as comrades dropped to the ground killed or wounded on either side of him—no separate audible sound marked their falling—and stranger still, he could draw no link between their falling and the continuous blare of the combat. The battle had begun, at dawn, in organized-enough fashion, but within minutes, the forest had sifted and strained the army just as it had done the day before: regiments broke apart and intermixed; here men clumped together, there a gap opened in the line. The early dreamy mists were quickly replaced by thick smoke, which no rays of sunlight could penetrate. For a long time, Hayes had seen no sign of any general or staff officer, though—without orders, often jubilant, and always chaotic—the troops had advanced and advanced again. Across log entrenchments built the night before by the rebels, they pushed deeper and deeper into the woods just below the road. Now they'd settled for a minute against the front side of a Confederate breastwork, and the return fire from the invisible rebels was clearly diminishing.

The shell, resting silently against the hazel bush, did not explode. One by one the men raised their heads and gazed about stunned and relieved. Happy still to be alive, a soldier stood and leaped over the entrenchment, and then they were advancing yet again, headlong into the thicket and yelping like coyotes. This was their ragged line of attack—one exuberant warrior acting on impulse, the rest following suit. (In like manner, a wounded soldier, dropping to the earth, had the power to ground all those around him.) A few yards farther in, Hayes understood that he and this hodgepodge of comrades had penetrated the Pennsylvania regiment and the marksmen who'd gone before them, and they were now at the very front: through the screen of smoke, he could see rebels for the first time, overcome and running away through the saplings like deer. Now the terrain grew swampy and the muck pulled off one of Hayes's shoes. When he dropped to retrieve it, the men around him hit the ground and rolled onto their bellies. To Hayes's surprise, Billy Swift suddenly fell hard against him, crying out that he was wounded and grabbing his leg and pressing his face into Hayes's ribs.

Hayes saw coffee gurgling out of a hole in Swift's canteen and streaming down his trouser leg. He laughed and shouted, "It's your canteen that's hit, Billy."

The other soldier lifted his head, brought his coffee-drenched fingers to his nose, sniffed them, and also laughed. "I'm not Billy," he shouted back, "I'm Albert." Loosing the canteen from his belt, he added, "Damned if I didn't take it for blood."

The men on either side of them were firing from where they lay. Hayes looked up beyond the smoke-enshrouded limbs of the scrub pines and spotted, low in the eastern sky to the rear, an eerie red disk that he identified, with some uncertainty, as the sun. He felt oddly undone by having taken the young soldier for Swift. He pulled his muddy shoe back on, but his hands had started to shake so badly that he struggled with the laces.

"Here, let me do it," said the other soldier.

As Hayes watched him tie the laces, he saw that tears streaked the soldier's cheeks.

When he finished, the soldier smiled sadly and leaned in and put his lips to Hayes's ear. "I'd thank you not to talk of this," he said.

Hayes thought at first he referred to the tears or the shoelacing or perhaps to Hayes's having called him Billy or to the fact that Hayes, who'd fallen in love with his own sister and fled an otherwise promising life, now found himself in a swampy jungle far from home and among men so keen to fire their weapons they sometimes failed to finish loading and then had to go pull a ramrod from the trunk of a tree.

But of course the soldier meant only the error that would make him the butt of a hundred campfire jokes, his having mistaken spilled coffee for blood.

THEY MIGHT HAVE ANTICIPATED support from the rear, but instead, and quite unexpectedly, a swell of Union troops slammed against them from north of the road on their right side, pushing them deeper into the woods to the left, creating a great crush, and altogether adding to the chaos. Soon Hayes lay in a trench pressed up against his new best friend of fifteen minutes' duration, a ruddy handsome Wisconsinite named Flowers, from one of General Wadsworth's brigades. Flowers had arrived next to Hayes ready to share his cache of cartridges (scavenged from the dead and wounded) and two extra muskets (likewise acquired); he explained to Hayes that by rotating the weapons they could avoid overheating them. Side by side, Hayes and Flowers fired against a new and clearly reinforced counterattack from the rebels. (Hayes would later learn that General Longstreet, Lee's "Old War Horse," had come to save the day for the Confederates.) No more was there any advancing but only a fierce stalemate in which the torrent of bullets surpassed both yesterday's fighting and that of the early morning. Union artillery had rolled into the road and was lofting shot and shell overhead, raining down leaves, sprays of pine, and even whole branches as they whistled through the treetops. Each time Flowers reloaded, he called out to Hayes his litany of complaints: How could a soldier be expected to find his way in this godforsaken labyrinth? Most of the time you couldn't even see the rednecks you were shooting at for all the damned smoke. Why, you were lucky enough if you could find a breath of air that didn't make you choke!

Leggett, thought Hayes, *Leggett with all his teeth and a formal education.*

"And please tell me what was the point of the endless hours of drills and exercises, perfecting our form?" shouted Flowers. "The skill of a straight line doesn't do a person much good in a place like this."

Flowers fired his weapon and began reloading.

"And what's the point of noble officers—illustrious generals and the like—if you can't find them and they can't find you? What use the willingness to toe the mark when orders can't be heard?"

He fired again, and again began reloading.

"What a damned muddle!" he shouted. "Look at you and me, Hayes. Here we are, jammed in together like two pickles in jar, and we don't even belong to the same corps!"

Just then a riderless horse lurched into the small clearing directly behind them, paused, and snorted. Flowers rose onto one knee and turned, then looked back at Hayes and grinned. At that moment a bullet tore a hole in his skull high above his left eye. The impact knocked him backward, startling the horse, which smashed into the trunk of a tree, righted itself, and disappeared into the thicket.

Another soldier scrambled alongside Flowers and started fussing with the dead man's belt. When he saw that Hayes was watching him, he glared at Hayes angrily and said, "I'm out of *caps*!"

AFTER FLOWERS, curious voids began to open in Hayes's ordeal: like a drowsy traveler in a carriage, he would now and again nod off, and then awaken farther along the way.

The fighting ebbed, and a hiatus ensued, though they could hear, from the distant rumble of combat elsewhere in the Wilderness, that the larger war persisted. South of the Orange Plank Road, for what had seemed hours, neither army had gained or yielded any ground, and for now, both were spent.

As best they could, they regrouped. Hayes found the Mozarters half a mile back toward the Brock Road. Some of the men made fires, brewed coffee, smoked, ate. Many slept.

They were supplied with fresh rounds of ammunition.

A hatless lieutenant rode through the woods, calling out, "Hello, anyone here from Frank's brigade? Hello, hello, anyone here from Colonel Frank's brigade?"

HAYES HELPED CARRY a wounded man on a blanket out to the Plank Road, where he was put into an ambulance. A good part of the man's jaw was blown away. Somebody offered him whiskey from a canteen, and when he tried to sip it, the whiskey flowed into the wound and made him howl with pain.

The road, pocked with chug-holes, was an endless stream of the dying, borne on stretchers and blankets, and smelled of manure.

Back in the woods, somebody said hello to Hayes, and weirdly, Hayes responded, "I'm not Billy, I'm Albert," for those words, turning over and over in his mind, had taken temporary possession of him.

There was no wind, and smoke lingered among the tree limbs.

HE SAT on the ground next to a man who reminded him of his father—he had his father's coloring and thick eyebrows and was about the age his father would have been if his father were still alive. The man had removed his shoes and held a block of soap in his hand. "What are you doing?" asked Hayes, and the man, smiling paternally, replied, "I'm rubbing soap on my stockings, see . . . it reduces blistering."

It turned out the man had Hayes's father's mellifluous voice as well. He offered the block of soap, and Hayes took off his own shoes and applied it to his own socks.

"You're Summerfield Hayes," said the man.

"Yes, sir," answered Hayes.

"My name's Phipps," said the man, and smiled again. "Oscar Phipps."

They shook hands, and Phipps said, "I'm very pleased to meet you. I should say, I'm very pleased we're each still alive, that I might meet you."

"Likewise," said Hayes.

"It's strange, isn't it, to concern ourselves with blisters, when our very lives are in doubt?"

"Yes, sir," said Hayes, "I guess it is."

"We exercise power where we can," said Phipps. "We can't save our own souls, but maybe we can keep our feet from blistering."

He smiled again. "Tell me, Hayes, how are you, son?"

Surprised by the question, then surprised again by his own frankness, Hayes answered, "I don't think I'm quite myself, Mr. Phipps."

"No," said Phipps, lowering his voice almost to a whisper, "I'm not either. I don't expect I'll ever be myself again."

He paused for a moment and slipped his shoes back on. Staring at his feet, he said, "And of course the question is—if we're not ourselves, then who are we?"

He looked at Hayes apologetically, then laughed softly, reached out, and patted him on the shoulder. "Sorry, my boy," he said. "That's pure fatigue talking. Pure fatigue. Pay me no mind."

It occurred to Hayes to tell the man he reminded him of his father, but the idea made him shy.

"I suppose we'll just have to leave our souls to God," added Phipps, lacing his shoes. "And meanwhile look after our feet."

Through the trees, somebody laughed, an unnerving sound, for it had a maniacal edge.

THE COLONEL ADDRESSED the regiment and told them (as far as Hayes could make out) that they should not lose heart, for he knew they were bound to win the contest.

A red-faced old man in a stovepipe hat sat on the ground near the colonel as he spoke. On the old man's knee perched a squirrel eating hardtack from his hand.

The colonel said it was Divine Providence that they should win, that he'd seen a sure sign of it in the skies over Brandy Station, two days before they'd left. In the afternoon, he said, it had been a battle over what weather should rule the heavens, fair or foul, blue or gray. It had been give-and-take for an hour or more, but at last the beautiful blue skies had blown the gray clear out.

A young soldier standing next to Hayes elbowed him in the arm, and when Hayes looked, the other soldier grinned and arched an eyebrow. Hayes smiled, but he wasn't sure what exactly the soldier had meant to convey.

Hayes said, "Who's the old man feeding the squirrel?"

The other soldier looked at him quizzically and asked, "Whereabouts?"

And when Hayes again faced the colonel's direction, he saw that the old man in the stovepipe hat had vanished.

SEARCHING IN VAIN for Swift, Hayes found Felix Rosamel, stretched out on the ground, wide-eyed and staring up into the tree limbs, worrying his mustache with the tip of his tongue and looking to Hayes quite insane. His face, splotched black with powder and spattered with mud, was absent of any light. His beret rested over his heart and was itself dark red and rather heart-shaped. Impassively, he told Hayes he'd not seen Billy all day.

As Hayes turned to go, Rosamel called him back. "The small clock," he said, "it belonged to my mother. It was to her a treasure. I will not say the details, but she owed money to a man and could not pay him and so he took from her the clock. He was a charlatan."

Hayes said he was sure Rosamel had done the right thing, the just thing, and Rosamel shook his head, as if to say that Hayes had failed to understand. From his place on the ground, he reached for Hayes's hand, and Hayes knelt beside him. Rosamel's eyelashes were caked with mud. He pulled Hayes close and said softly, "I introduced this horrible man to my mother."

THE PERVASIVE SMOKE, unstirred by any wind, hung in the pine boughs overhead, striped here and there by slanting bars of light.

The man named Coulter, who'd served as catcher for the opposing team in the regimental match at camp, ages and ages ago, said, "You know, Hayes, if you're gonna get lost in the woods, you can get lost just as well to the rear as to the front."

Hayes hadn't noticed before, but it appeared that Coulter had a kind of nervous tic and tended to blink his eyes rapidly and often.

Another man, with a swollen and purple upper lip, told a long story about being stung in the woods by a hornet. It was, he said, the hornet from the old saying "as mad as a hornet."

THERE WAS NO WIND, no breeze of any kind, and—despite the commotion in the woods and out on the road, despite the clattering of wheels and hooves and the groans of the wounded and dying, despite the restful scents of coffee, woodsmoke, and tobacco—a troubled stillness honeycombed the air, a silent wrathful thing that slept, but not deeply, and not for long.

SOMEBODY SAID it was that rebel muggins Longstreet who'd stopped them in their tracks, that Bobby Lee's Old War Horse was still coming along the Plank Road with more than thirty thousand troops, and his generals was off in those woods getting them all nice and arranged right now.

Bull, said another man, there wasn't but sixty thousand in the whole Army of Northern Virginia. Besides, Longstreet was apter to come up from the south, along the Brock Road.

Either way, said a third, they were in for an assault, weren't they?

A fourth man said the sooner the better for him, that this damned waiting made him feel all-overish. The sooner the better.

HAYES PLACED a folded handkerchief over the raw blisters on his hand and tied it with a piece of string. His bruised right arm ached, and no amount of swinging it in circles made any difference. Generally agitated, he couldn't seem to stay with any line of thinking for more than a few seconds. A river of anger heaved and churned inside him, but he could neither trace its source nor follow it to any destination.

He found a spot in the underbrush where he could be by himself and raked together a bed of dry leaves and sat down. He took off his cap and discovered that if he stared long enough at its blue clover-leaf insignia (indicating his corps and division) it began to resemble a flame, then a mouse with wings, then a tiny sea creature.

THEY WERE FLANKED by rebel troops that came up from the south, not along the Brock Road but through a ravine in the woods. Simultaneously assaulted anew from the front, they were caught in a vise and quickly began to lose all the terrain they'd earlier gained. So surprised were they by the rebels, there'd been no time to put out the campfires, which now set portions of the woods aflame. As Hayes's regiment defended against the frontal attack, they were barraged by fleeing Union troops to their left; they were ordered to turn to the crumbling flank, an endeavor that served only to further fragment them, and they too soon began to give way: like specters rising out of a dream of flames and smothering smoke and disorder and the panic of nowhere-to-turn, the rebels overwhelmed them.

Hayes did not join the tide of Union troops that were fleeing north toward the Plank Road; at the edge of a small clearing, he holed up with Oscar Phipps within the branches of a felled chinquapin tree, where he waited and watched. Again running low on ammunition, they held on to their arms, loaded and ready, but didn't fire, for fear of hitting their own comrades. A Union officer rode into the fray of retreating troops, waving his sword over his head and crying, to no effect whatsoever, "Rally, men, rally, for the love of God, rally!"

His mount, already wounded, pitched and staggered, and the officer himself was soon struck by a ball to the elbow. His sword went flashing to the ground, and the horse bolted with the injured officer back into the trees.

The clearing emptied for a moment, and then a rebel soldier—a redheaded ragamuffin with a blanket tied around his neck like a cape—emerged from the smoke, retrieved the sword, and began brandishing it, grinning, and strutting in a circle.

Oscar Phipps took aim.

The bullet struck the youngster in the chest, though he continued to stand and did not relinquish the sword; he placed his free hand over his heart and began to teeter slowly toward the chinquapin tree, narrowing his eyes and scrutinizing its branches; then, only three paces away, he dropped to the ground.

Phipps said, "God, forgive me," and then told Hayes to fix his bayonet. "The fighting's apt to get close now," he said.

They each fixed bayonets, and then Phipps said, "Let's go, before it's too late." He parted the branches and moved out, but Hayes grabbed his coattail and tried to tug him back.

"It's already too late," said Hayes, but Phipps pulled free and started to run across the clearing as it filled with a band of rebel soldiers.

A dozen men took aim at the retreating Phipps, but somebody yelled, "Wait, don't shoot him! Let's catch him!" and the band of rebels started toward Phipps and the thicket.

Later, reflecting on the moment, Hayes would imagine that he'd wanted to help Phipps and that creating a diversion seemed the best strategy; but (he would further reflect) such a rationale only meant to put a sane face on a monstrous act of animal rage. He leaped out of the branches and stood over the redheaded Confederate boy dead at his feet. "Gentlemen," he yelled, "mind this!"

The rebels, not ten yards away, stopped and turned. With one foot, Hayes rolled the dead soldier onto his back and then rammed the bayonet into the boy's belly. A hideous cry went up from the other men, and now they were after him.

Hayes bounded over the trunk of the fallen tree and was off, zigzagging like a hare as the tangled woods required. Soon he heard the crackle of muskets at his back, but he knew he would be a slippery target. Heaven had bestowed on him two exceptional talents: he could toss a base ball that most men found tricky to hit; and, by God, he could run.

ONE SPRING AFTERNOON, not long after he'd turned seven, he lay on the carpet in the library at Hicks Street, where his father was reading the newspaper. He'd come home tired from an interminable day at school and was in that after-school state of mind in which a boy, having been compelled to sit upright and think about one thing and another for many hours on end, wanted only to fling himself onto a flat surface and go mentally blank. The library's raised windows let in the various street noises of wheels and bells and hooves, as well as a pleasant rose-colored light made by sunshine bouncing off the brick house across the way. His father sat in one of the leather amber-colored wing chairs that faced the cold hearth. From his position on the floor back of the chairs, Summerfield could see his father's feet, crossed at the ankles in funny flowery embroidered slippers; his elbow, bare (as he'd rolled up his shirtsleeves) and resting on the arm of the chair; and, higher up, a corner of the newspaper. Now and again, his father would read to him an item he thought amusing (a Canadian man, dead at the ripe age of one hundred six, had left behind forty-three children and sixty-six grandchildren) or instructional (a nine-year-old boy, playing on the roof of his house, had plunged to his death), and Summerfield dreamily likened the flow of words to sand falling inside an hourglass. He enjoyed the sound of his father's voice and was especially interested in the way it changed whenever it found itself reading aloud—it deepened and grew whispery as it pronounced each word with unusual precision.

Now Mr. Hayes read to him a story that was both amusing and instructional. A crowd of boys, down around Schenck's wharf, were in the habit of tossing stones at the crew of a certain vessel docked nearby. Apparently they'd done it once too often, and the vessel's cook had at last fired a loaded gun into the crowd, injuring three. Immediately afterward, the vessel turned about and got under way but an industrious policeman from the First District, informed of what had happened, hopped the ferry, procured a rowboat on the New York side, hailed the vessel in the river, arrested the crew, and fetched them to the City Hall. The guilty cook said he was ordered by the mate to fire the gun and he'd meant only to scare the boys.

"'This is a curious way to scare them,'" read Mr. Hayes from the newspaper, "'and reminds us of the man who excused himself when charged with murder by saying that he had only knocked off the man's hat; but it so happened that the head was in the hat when he knocked it off.'

"Ha!" cried Mr. Hayes, and let loose a gale of deep reading-voice laughter.

Summerfield had closed his eyes, the better to absorb the details of the story. On hearing his father laugh, he opened his eyes and saw that Mr. Hayes had turned in the chair and was now craning his neck around the wing of it and looking at him. His father repeated the laugh, louder, as if to infect him with it, and at that moment Mrs. Hayes and Sarah entered from the hall wearing their cotton dresses of pale pink and pale green.

"What's all the fun in *here*?" asked Mrs. Hayes, not quite cheerfully, and then quickly added, "Summerfield Hayes, kindly get up off the floor before someone trips over you."

He rolled onto his hands and knees, unamused by the remark about the murdered man's head inside the hat, for his mind had got locked on the crowd of boys, fired upon at the wharf—he saw them break apart and scatter like bugs beneath an overturned rock. Some of them, injured, dropped to the planks. Some others likely crouched to tend the wounded. But surely others, maybe most, simply ran. Ran as hard and fast as their legs would carry them. Sprinted like mad from the foot of Joralemon Street. He felt a strong connection to these boys, at least as he imagined them—not for their tossing stones but for their running to save their own lives.

Twelve years later, in the woods of Virginia, the memory of that afternoon in the library with his family—and the newspaper story of the frightened and fleeing boys—returned to him as he darted through the tangled brush, dodging flames and hiding behind tree trunks, eluding the enraged men who meant to kill him.

OUT ON THE PLANK ROAD, a steady stream of blue-clad troops headed back toward the intersection with the Brock Road, the position from which they'd launched their first attack more than twenty-four hours earlier. All the ground gained by the morning's fierce fighting had been lost. They wove between wagons and ambulances and moved under the arcs of solid shot still being lobbed into the woods by Union artillery. Officers rode among the squads, exhorting them to turn, to rally, even striking the back of a soldier now and again with a sword—but the men were played-out. They'd not cast down their arms but still carried them on their shoulders. They were not in any state of panic but walked calmly. They stopped when ordered to by a mounted officer, but when he turned to admonish the next squad, they continued quietly on their way. They'd done all the fighting they meant to do, at least for now. Smoke billowed overhead, like low-lying clouds, lit silver here and there by the sun high in the sky. Meanwhile, the Confederate army, in good standing further to press their assault, mysteriously appeared to be stalling instead.

Hayes—winded but exhilarated by having escaped the band of rebels who'd chased him a mile through the forest—entered the flow. A man limping just in front of him fell; Hayes pulled him to the berm of the road and gave him a drink from his canteen. The man said, "Much obliged," and then lay back onto the ground and closed his eyes. "I just want a little sleep," he added softly.

"But you can't sleep here," said Hayes. "You'll be trampled."

The man rolled onto his side, drew his legs up to his belly, and folded his hands between his knees.

Hayes took the man's weapon, fixed the bayonet, and drove it into the ground next to him. He removed the man's forage cap and canteen and hung them on the stock as a signpost. When Hayes returned to the road, he fell in alongside an ambulance wagon, and after a moment or two he heard someone call, "Hayes, Hayes, it's you!"

One of the men sitting inside the ambulance was Oscar Phipps; he'd turned and now gazed down at Hayes over the side of the wagon. "Hayes, it's you!" he repeated.

"Mr. Phipps," cried Hayes. "Are you all right?"

"It's minor," answered Phipps. "A shell in the woods. I took some shrapnel to the knee. But I outran that bunch of rebel skunks, I tell you. Imagine that, Hayes, at my age. Sorry to have dashed off like that, but my idea was to draw them away from you, you see. At least I succeeded in doing that, as your presence here surely proves."

Phipps hung one arm over the side of the ambulance. "Take my hand, my boy," he said, "take my hand."

"Thank you, Mr. Phipps," said Hayes, grasping the man's hand.

Phipps smiled warmly and nodded. "If you don't survive to toss another match at the Union Grounds," he said, "it won't be because of me."

They moved along like that, hand in hand, for a good ways, and soon the same officers who'd commanded the men to rally were ordering them to the Brock Road, where they were already going anyway.

IN HIS LETTER to Sarah, Hayes had imagined the army (preparing to quit winter quarters) as viewed by a bird in the sky, and now, at the Brock Road, he again pictured it as a colony of ants—blue ants, and he wondered if such things actually existed in nature. He thought Leggett would be pleased that the breastworks, built and hastily abandoned the day before, would at last go into service, despite the ironic reason for it: demoralized and disarrayed, forced to retreat to where they'd started out, the Second Corps was in no condition to launch an assault, and so prepared to defend itself if assaulted.

Throughout the middle of the day, troops emerged from the woods and sought out their unit flags planted by color sergeants along the breastworks. Hundreds of stragglers, broken by the ferocity of the fighting, materialized from the rear. Officers moved up and down the road directing soldiers to their proper positions. The reorganized troops felled trees, clearing a swath out in front of the barricade, and stacked the timber against the works till it was as high as a man's chest. They sharpened branches and fashioned abatis pointed at the enemy.

The battle smoke faded, and bright sunshine engulfed them. They were supplied with fresh ammunition. Rumors (*General rumors*, thought Hayes, for each concerned a commander) shuttled through the ranks—General Longstreet, like General Jackson at Chancellorsville, had been accidentally wounded by his own troops, which accounted for the Confederates' stalling rather than pressing their advantage; the Union's own General Wadsworth had been killed; the long-awaited General Burnside was at last "going in on the right," whatever that meant; General Grant, unhappy with the corps' defensive position, had ordered a new attack for six o'clock. Heavy artillery rolled into the road—Hayes counted twelve pieces at the intersection with the Plank Road, close to where the Mozarters were situated. The captain encouraged Hayes's company (what of it had survived) to eat something, and to rest.

Hayes sat on a stump that was still sticky with sap and oiled his weapon. The cook, suitably named Fry, soon came along and offered him a piece of salt pork, which he declined, claiming, honestly, a lack of appetite.

"Grab a meal where you can," admonished Fry, narrowing his eyes. "Eat for the future, son, eat for the future."

The bright sun so bleached Fry's face it nearly obliterated his features, an effect Hayes found unsettling. Though he knew it to be irrational, he felt that the man forced the salt pork on him and that, in any case, his diet was none of Fry's business. His lack of hunger, should he have to explain it, was a small symptom of a larger wonder: unessential desires intermitted, he was stripped back to the bare imperatives of a warrior; his body, ruled by instinct, had sacrificed itself to the greater cause of killing; if breathing were not automatic, he wouldn't expend the energy to will it. He closed his eyes and managed to say, softly, "No."

Fry said, "Are you all right, Hayes?"

Now the man was probing him, to no useful end. Hayes wanted to say, *Leave me alone,* but instead he held his eyes shut and wished him away. He concentrated on the blood inside his own eyelids, a sunlit red-orange canvas on which he saw, in rapid succession, the red-liquid eruption from Leggett's shredded mouth; the red hole opened in Flowers's head by a ball above his eye; the flat belly of the red-haired boy, pierced by the blade of Hayes's bayonet (sucking sound going in, sucking sound coming out); and the phantom red-faced old man in the stovepipe hat, feeding hardtack to a squirrel. He heard Oscar Phipps's voice—*If we're not ourselves, then who are we?*—and Hayes was taken with the observation that a separate part of his brain replied to these presumably unwanted memories with a remarkable and confident neutrality. The reply from that quarter, quite numb, was what he'd already said to the company cook: *No.*

His weapon rested crosswise in his lap. He allowed himself to soak in the warmth of the sun, most evident on the bridge of his nose and on top of his hands. The Virginian May felt like June or July in New York. He was fully resigned to present conditions—had altered himself and *been* altered accordingly—yet, for a moment, the sun (combined with the leafy aroma of the slashed undergrowth nearby) filled him with longing for the ball grounds and the brilliant exercise in which, for the duration of a match, all of life's frustrating mysteries were suspended: men opposed each other in an ambience both predictable and accommodating to surprise; reached an outcome to which each, in his turn, had a say; and, at the end, triumphant or defeated, admired one another for the spirit of the play.

When Hayes opened his eyes, Fry had moved on.

He got himself up, gathered his gear, and moved forward to the front line, where he could see the continuing but dwindling trickle of blue-clad troops from the forest. There, among a regiment of men who called themselves Orange Blossoms, many of whom had curled up in the shade of the entrenchment wall and slept, Hayes placed himself near the brigade colors and waited and watched—waited and watched for what seemed hours. He examined the grimy faces of the soldiers as they stumbled and staggered and limped into the broad belt of the new clearing. Across the way, the sun dropped slowly closer to the treetops. Then, at last, Hayes saw Billy Swift emerge, alone, from the woods.

AFTER HAYES HAD LED Swift back to the regiment and got him a tin cup of hot coffee, the two found some shade and a patch of switchgrass and sat close to each other with their elbows on their knees. To Hayes, Swift looked as if he had aged a year or two—some light had gone from his eyes, which now appeared to remain only half open. An enormous black fly kept orbiting his head, buzzing now and again into his ears, and Swift swatted at it to no avail. When he complained, Hayes hushed him, carefully followed the fly for a moment, then reached out and grabbed it in midair, clenching it inside his fist. He squeezed it between his thumb and middle finger and dropped it into the grass.

Swift regarded him with awe, not smiling, as if Hayes was more curiosity than friend. "Where'd you learn to do that?" he said.

Hayes only shrugged, for it wasn't something he'd learned to do, nor to his recollection had he ever done it before.

They fell silent for some time, and after Swift finished the coffee, he chose a long blade of grass and inserted it between his front teeth. The two lay back, with their heads almost touching, and gazed up at the wagon-wheel branches of the pine tree above them. Swift sighed and said, "There's a cat up there in that tree."

"No," said Hayes. "Where?"

"Not a real cat," said Swift, "but look there at that biggest limb on the right-hand side."

Indeed, after a moment, Hayes discerned that bark and knotholes had conspired to etch the face of a cat on the underside of the branch, with needles for whiskers. "How about that?" he said, and Swift rolled onto his side and looked at him meaningfully.

"What?" said Hayes.

Swift pointed his thumb toward the woods at his back and said softly, "There's a spring about a hundred yards straight through there. I found it yesterday but didn't have time enough for more than a quick drink."

"A spring?"

Swift put his finger to his lips and whispered, "Hayes, it's a pool big enough for bathing. Wanna go absent without leave?"

SWIFT STOPPED SUDDENLY, turned, and put up his hand. When Hayes moved quietly to his side Swift whispered, "Looks like somebody else had the same idea."

Through the thicket, about ten yards forward, Hayes saw the small round pool—a modest recess in the earth filled with green water, sunlit through an opening in the canopy, with a smooth gray boulder forming a low wall at one end; opposite, a sort of sloping bank, covered with dry leaves, upon which were spread (like the cutout garb of a paper doll) the hat, uniform, and regalia of a brigadier general.

"If I'm not wrong," said Swift softly, "that's our own commander."

Hayes bent forward and rested his chin on Swift's shoulder. Indeed, knee-deep in the water and unadorned by anything other than a silver flask in one hand, stood Brigadier General J. H. Hobart Ward, of the corps' First Brigade; somehow, in nakedness, more stately—with his prominent brow and droopy whiskers, he looked like a statue in a Roman fountain. High on the boulder behind him, waited an aide, fully clothed and holding a bucket. Now the general nodded and dropped his chin to his chest, apparently the signal for the aide to empty the water from the bucket over his officer's head.

The general quaked like a wet dog and slung water from his hair. He took a long drink from the flask and passed it to the aide; then he climbed the low bank back to his uniform. The aide, joining him, produced a towel from a knapsack, and then, accomplished in silence, came the Homeric enterprise of dressing the general, the last turn of which—after the boots, the belt, the sash, the sword, the buttons, the hat, and another swig from the flask—was the lighting of a fresh cigar. The pale-blue smoke, a menagerie of snakes and dragons, warped up into the tree limbs.

Swift and Hayes waited silently and patiently for it to end, and fortunately, when it did, the general and his aide left the spring on a path that led away from their hiding spot in the thicket.

Hayes said, "Maybe we should get back, Billy."

For an answer, Swift took off running. Hayes quickly turned and looked in the direction from which they'd come and then followed. He stood his musket alongside Swift's, against a tree, and then put his back to the pool, shed his clothes, and piled them next to Swift's on the ground. When he was naked and turned toward the water, he saw Swift standing waist-deep in the pool and smiling at him.

"It's mossy at the edge there," said Swift, reaching toward him, "you better give me your hand."

Hayes offered his hand, only to be yanked sideways into the pool and pushed under. He spun free, surfaced, caught his breath, and went after Swift, who was scrambling toward the rock wall. Swift got only his hands on the boulder before Hayes grabbed him around the waist and tugged him back down. He locked Swift's head in one arm and splashed water into his face with his free hand. Swift dropped, slipping from Hayes's grip, found his footing, and butted Hayes in the stomach, knocking him backward. Hayes knelt on the bottom of the pool (a mix of clay and gravel), with only his head protruding, and said, "You're off your chump, Swift."

Swift grinned. "You think so?" he said. "Is that your honest opinion?"

Hayes noticed that Swift's eyes now appeared to be fully open, normal, not at half-mast as before. "Yes," said Hayes, "it is."

"Well, I won't argue with you. 'Cause you know what crazy thing I'm thinking right now? Right now, this minute, I'm thinking we could be in paradise instead of hell."

He looked away into the woods, took a deep breath, and sighed. He appeared to shudder and then said, "Where's the sun gone?"

"It's moved onto that rock," said Hayes.

Swift turned and looked at the boulder behind him. "That's inviting enough," he said.

As they moved toward the boulder, Hayes felt revived by the water—he was hungry and sleepy and full of affection for Billy—but he wasn't sure the change made him happy; he thought it might be dangerous to his survival. There was no pleasure to the pared mechanism of the warrior, but there was something about it that felt easier, safer. They lay next to each other on the warm rock, on their backs, in the sun. Hayes closed his eyes and had the odd sensation that he and Swift had boarded a conveyance of some sort, a magical boulder-carriage that might roll them out of the Wilderness.

After a minute, Swift said, "I reckon when you play for a genuine ball club there's no shortage of women after you."

This remark, combined with the giddy impression of motion, made Hayes laugh. "I reckon so," he said.

"If you don't mind a personal question, Hayes, I wonder if you ever . . . you know . . . what I'm trying to ask is . . . was there somebody special you left behind?"

Now the boulder tipped slightly to one side, and Hayes felt a mild wave of nausea. Sarah, having climbed on, knelt at his side with her minty scent and a cool wet cloth for his brow. The pool had revived him, he thought, and so revived, too, that particular thorny rose, the compelling ache. He noted with dreamy amusement an urge to cover himself.

Swift said, "Never mind, Hayes. I didn't mean to be curious."

"I left my sister behind," said Hayes. "But that's not the sort of 'someone special' you meant."

"I left my ma behind," said Swift. "And my little brother Valentine."

"Valentine?" said Hayes.

"Valentine Swift. Ain't that a good name? Eleven years old come this July. If there's anybody in the family gonna play serious ball, it's him. Quick as a fox, and he can already throw harder than me. Mark my word, Hayes—that's a name you'll be reading in the papers someday."

A strong breeze swept through the woods with a sound like a threshing machine, scattering Sarah and the thread of the conversation, and suddenly Hayes couldn't recall what Swift had last said. He opened his eyes just in time and long enough to see a whirl of gold-white papery leaves pass a few feet in the air above them.

After what seemed a long silence, Swift said, "Tell me, Hayes, what's your feelings about the afterlife?"

"Frankly, I haven't given it much thought," answered Hayes.

"My ma says we needn't fear the great change . . . that's what she calls dying, the great change. She says on the Day of Judgment we get resurrected. Our bodies get restored, but I'll be straight with you . . . after some of what I've seen these last two days, I'm not so certain."

It occurred to Hayes that Swift wanted some kind of reassurance and that the Christian thing to do would be to reassure him. But he suspected that any such attempt on his part would ring hollow. Hayes had always liked the idea of heaven, a place where God's will was pure and always done, not interfered with by human mischief, but the specifics of the thing—the dying and coming back to life, the rotting and the restoration, the sorting out of the sheep from the goats and so forth—it struck him as unlikely, or at least incomprehensible.

"I don't know, Billy," he said, "but I think we should get back now."

"Come on, five more minutes," said Swift. "I'm not even good and dry yet."

They were silent again for a few seconds. Hayes wanted to recall something from the recent past, having to do with goats—Sarah and goats . . . she'd taken his hand and held it as they looked together out a window—but he couldn't make the memory come to the surface.

Soon Swift said, sleepily, "I don't have nobody special either. I've never even been in love with a woman, not since I was a kid and got crushes on girls at school."

Hayes saw Sarah standing before the library windows at Hicks Street. Having just turned to face him, her eyes linger on him for a moment, blankly, and then she tilts her head to one side and gives him a chilling look that seems to say, *Who are you?*

Now he saw her at the bend in the stairs in the hallway, looking down at him. His hand rests on the newel post. *If, some months from now,* she says, *your name appears in a certain list in the newspaper . . . and I don't feel that I did all I possibly could to dissuade you . . . then I'll be ashamed.* She gathers the skirt of her dress in one hand, lifts it, and quickly moves out of sight. He listens for her footsteps on the landing overhead and for the opening and closing of her door. It's cold in the hallway, and he's alone with the sound of his own breathing.

"You know, Billy," said Hayes, after some time had passed, "I thought I saw you in the woods this morning . . . at the front. At the height of the fighting a fellow dropped in next to me, crying that he was shot. Turned out it was his canteen that had got hit. He felt the warm coffee running down his trousers and thought it was blood. I took him for you and called him by your name. He said, 'I'm not Billy, I'm Albert.' It was like when your heart skips a beat, only it was something that happened in my mind."

Swift said nothing.

"I've been seeing some things that aren't really there," Hayes continued. "Dead soldiers getting up and crawling and the like. I don't know what all. An old man in a stovepipe hat."

Swift remained silent, so at last Hayes said, "Do you think it's just . . . I don't know . . . the sort of thing that happens? Or do you think I should talk to the doctor?"

Swift still said nothing, and when Hayes raised his head to look at him, he saw that the boy had fallen sound asleep.

He decided to leave him be for a few minutes more, even though he was getting antsy about going back. He was glad Swift hadn't heard his mumbo jumbo about seeing things, for it felt like a lapse in judgment to have spoken about it, a moment of weakness. He looked down and saw a tiny circle of water resting in the palm of Swift's upturned hand, gleaming in the sun and throwing a star into Hayes's eyes. A white butterfly, perhaps attracted by the same spur of light, came along and lit on the ball of Swift's thumb. It lingered there for a few seconds and fluttered away. As if to answer the attention, the fingers on that hand twitched a little. Soon another breeze, gentler than before, quieter, stirred the warm air, and then Hayes heard a faraway clatter of musketry through the woods.

He sat up and shook Swift's shoulder. "Wake up, Billy. We need to get back."

Swift opened his eyes but otherwise didn't move.

"Can you hear that?" said Hayes.

Swift rubbed his eyes and listened for half a minute. "That's not us," he said. "It's too far away."

"Still," said Hayes, "it's time we got back."

Now Swift sat up but turned his face away. Softly, he said, "I'm not going back."

"What do you mean?"

"I'm going home."

"You can't do that, Billy."

"Why not?"

"Because you'll be taken for a deserter and shot, that's why. You fell asleep here. You're still dreaming."

Swift faced him now. "If you were a gambler," he said, "what would you reckon to be the better bet . . . me getting captured and shot as a deserter or me getting killed in there on that so-called battlefield . . . which ain't no battlefield at all? Now I've seen it, Hayes, I know it's not for me. I want to go home. I want to go back home and play base ball. I want to get earnest about it, like you. In a little while I want to come down to Brooklyn and watch you in a real match. Wouldn't that be—"

"But Billy," said Hayes, "if you desert you can't ever go home again."

Swift paused for a moment to absorb this. Then he said, "I've made up my mind. And I'd like to have your blessing."

"I can't do that, Billy."

"If you give me your blessing, I'll have the courage I need."

Hayes got up and went to where their clothes were piled on the ground. He retrieved Swift's trousers and threw them at him. As he stepped into his own, he said, "That's not a fair position to put me in."

Swift only stared at the blue trousers, which had landed at his feet. After another moment, he said, "No, you're right, it's not. Forget I asked you."

The two of them got dressed now without another word passing between them. Swift sat on the ground to lace his shoes. "When I signed up, I lied to them about my age," he said at last. "I'm only sixteen."

Hayes strapped on his belt. "Well, Billy, that wouldn't make any difference now," he said.

Swift rested his forearms on his knees for a moment. "We could go together," he said. "You could wait for me here, and I'll go get our knapsacks and all the food I can scare up."

Hayes moved to the nearby tree and retrieved both their weapons. He knelt beside Swift and said, "Look at me, Billy. You need to stop this talk. Now here, take your gun."

Swift took the gun from him. He shook his head. "I don't know what's got into me, Hayes," he said. "I thought a good bath in cold water was supposed to clear a person's head, not muddle it. I just got to feeling . . . well, never mind."

They stood. Hayes bent for the two forage hats on the ground, put one on his own head and then put the other on Swift's.

Swift came to attention and saluted him.

Before they left, they stooped together at the edge of the spring and filled their canteens. The sound of the fighting grew louder but stayed far away; perhaps, thought Hayes, it was General Burnside, "going in on the right," as rumored.

Not more than a yard or two into the thicket, Swift stumbled on a root and tumbled into the brush. He rolled onto his back, looked up at Hayes, and said, "I'd fallen asleep in the sun, that's all. I was still dreaming."

Hayes gave him a hand. The boy was light as a feather. No wonder he could hurl himself at grounders the way he did, without injury.

BACK AT THE FEDERAL LINE, Hayes fell asleep and dreamed of the lock chamber in Dublin where his parents met their death: In complete silence, the omnibus crashes into the canal with a great burst of silver bubbles, breaks apart from its team of horses, and slowly sinks away, a toy jewel box vanishing into black-green darkness; the half-dozen auburn horses plunge rapidly and then begin slowly to ascend, legs splayed and wafting, manes and tails like seaweed; a beautiful silent spectacle, the thing itself a poem on the subject of troubled sleep. Hayes, dressed in the uniform of the Union army, dives toward the sunken car, lodged aslant at the bottom of the chamber. He sees his sister's face behind one of its dark windows. She frowns and shakes her head. She places one hand flat against the glass and smiles, farewell. He means to break through with the stock of his musket, but he has lost his weapon and has run out of air besides. He rockets upward, and when he emerges, gasping, there is only the churning smoke of the Wilderness, and the surface of the water in flames.

From out of the smoke, he hears the colonel, softly crooning, "Steady, boys, steady, steady, steady now," and at first he thinks he's speaking to the frightened horses in the water, but it turns out the commander's trying to embolden a band of fleeing soldiers, Hayes's comrades, who are leaping over a wooden railing, retreating up the steep cobblestone incline, abandoning him.

He tries to call to them but can make no sound.

GENERAL GRANT DID ORDER a new attack for six o'clock, but the Confederates wouldn't wait that long. Shortly after four, with bugle blasts and a shrill chorus of the rebel yell, they charged into the

slashing before the Federal works. Behind the refortified entrenchment, the Second Corps infantry opened fire. From the intersection
of the Brock and Orange Plank Roads, Union artillery batteries
launched shell and case toward the woods and into the clearing.

Quickly the air grew hot, bristling with flying bark. Dark gray
smoke turned the sunny afternoon to an unnatural dusk.

For a good half hour, the Confederates threw line after line of
troops into the slashing. For a good half hour, line after line was
slaughtered.

Then the brush and razed saplings of the clearing caught fire.
A breeze from the woods blew the black pine-tar smoke back over
the entrenchment, blinding and choking the Federal soldiers. And
in a matter of minutes, the flames spread to the piled logs of the
breastworks.

The rebels seized the opportunity and hurled themselves at the
spot where fire had opened a break in the Union line.

FOR FIVE MINUTES OR MORE, Hayes and Swift were swept along by
the tide of Union troops suddenly fleeing for the rear. The intense heat
of the fire and rolling masses of black smoke bit into their eyes. The
crackle of musketry and the thunder of artillery (now turned toward
the breach) were deafening and confounding. Amid the pandemonium, jostled left and right, Hayes had lost his bearings. An aide to
General Hancock rushed through the throng on a mission to rally
the retreating infantry, his mount's neck bathed in white froth. Hayes
tugged at Swift's elbow, and Swift turned on him a completely bewildered face.

Then—not a dozen paces away, breaking through the smoke and
stirring up clouds of dust—a caisson roared by with the brigade commander, General Ward (lately seen naked at the spring), aboard. As
it passed with a rumble of hooves, the general met Hayes's eye—the
commander had lost his hat, and there was a strange wobbly affect
to his gaze. Hayes and Swift watched the caisson disappear into
the trees. They looked at each other, and Swift shouted, "He's wall-
papered! He's headed for the rear!"

Hayes cocked his head in the direction opposite from where the caisson had gone—toward the heat, toward the burgeoning wall of fire at the front—and said, "Let's go." They started to run and were presently caught in a wild river of troops from other brigades, hurrying to the breach in the Federal line. In another two minutes, they reached the spot where rebels were pouring over the barricade, and then it was fire and smoke, bayonets and swords, bloodcurdling screams, muskets for clubs, and shells exploding frighteningly near. The black smoke changed dusk to night. Hayes quickly lost Swift altogether, along with his sense of time and place. Apparently, he functioned best within an ebb and flow of awareness. It was something like having his eyes closed but seeing everything more sharply than usual. *Now* and *here*, yoked by a fitful hyphen, became an elusive blinking lamp: *now-here, nowhere, now-here, nowhere.*

Then of course there was the acrid stench of burnt hair, burnt flesh, burnt wool, burnt powder. Using his musket like a medieval pike, Hayes pressed a snaggletoothed boy to the smoking ground and straddled him. They locked eyes. An anonymous Union soldier reached in and slit the boy's throat with a bowie knife. In the next moment, Hayes was struck over the back of the head with something dull and heavy, and he fell face forward into a spray of blood.

HE AWAKENED, still alive, into a twilight of low-lying smoke and flames. The roar of combat persisted, though less feverishly. Flat on his belly beneath a close mantle of smoke, he had the impression that he lay somewhere in the slashing and that he had been dragged there and dropped. The back of his head was sore, and when he touched the spot, he felt a wet knot, tender to the touch. He'd lost his weapon, but on every side of him were dead soldiers and a number of guns. Here and there the smoke itself appeared to be on fire, pulsing orange, and braids of smoke rose continuously from the blackened earth. He crawled toward a musket, keeping his head close to the ground, the only way to breathe. Weapon in hand, he reached for his canteen, which felt hot, and managed a few swallows of warm water. He crawled farther, until he found a discarded blanket, then spread it out flat on the ground and gathered what other canteens he could from the nearby dead. He emptied the canteens onto the blanket. Now he rolled himself in the dampened blanket, covering even his head. He thought he heard, beneath the ongoing din of combat, men groaning in pain, and then suddenly he was trampled by a rush of soldiers, who tripped over him and kicked him—deliberately, he thought—as they passed.

Soon the musketry began to abate. Longer breaks opened between bursts of artillery. Gratefully cooled, he started to emerge from his woolen cocoon. He had no idea which way to go, but since he judged the troops who had trampled him to be rebels in retreat, he decided to head in the opposite direction. Blanket in one hand, gun in the other, he began to pull himself across the smoking ground. When he'd got only a yard or two—astonishingly, like something in a dream—he heard someone speak his name: "Hayes," said the voice, hoarsely, "Hayes."

He raised his head, choked on the smoke, lowered his head, and went into a fit of coughing. Tears flowed from his eyes. It was dark beneath the smoke, and he felt his heart thumping inside his chest. He wiped his face with a corner of the blanket.

Then he saw it, to his right, faceup in a shallow and smoking depression: a charred thing, its head nearest and cocked back, so that two white wet eyes glowed at him from beneath a blackened brow; singed and smoking along its tapering length, it spoke again. "Hayes," it said, more breath than substance. "Pull me out, Hayes."

It extended a raven hand to within Hayes's reach, and Hayes felt the earth give beneath him. The ground dropped a few inches, then tilted at an acute angle, so that he was left stranded on a high plane, looking down at the hand protruding from a smoking sleeve. The sensation was physically sickening—it came with an odor of hot metal and burnt sugar—and Hayes's tongue seemed to swell inside his mouth.

Billy Swift, scrappy second baseman from the Bronx County. Billy Swift, whose ma had told him he needn't fear the great change, for on the Day of Judgment we would be resurrected and restored.

"I couldn't make my legs work," said Swift. "I couldn't get out of the fire."

Hayes took hold of the boy's hand, which was surprisingly cool, but with only the slightest tug, the flesh pulled loose into Hayes's own hand, leaving a glistening claw of bone. Hayes threw the stuff to one side as Billy screamed and withdrew his arm. His body began to convulse. He was crying now, a jagged chirp that sounded oddly like laughter, and Hayes saw wisps of smoke escape the boy's open mouth. Yellow splinters of fire suddenly sprang up from the depression in which he lay, and just as Hayes went to throw the blanket over the flames, Swift's cartridge belt detonated, *pop pop pop pop pop pop pop*.

Hayes flattened himself to the ground and covered his head. When it was over, he pivoted round and crouched over Swift at the rim of the depression, keeping his head low beneath the layer of smoke. The boy lay still now, eyes closed, silent. Hayes didn't know how to touch him. He could see no way to touch him, but at last gently put his hand on the boy's stomach. Swift let out a broken, pathetic, high-pitched moan. Now Hayes saw, just below the boy's belt, a dark gaping wound. More than any other Hayes had seen so far, this was the wound Surgeon Speck had described to him at Brandy Station—the ball, flattened and distorted by its impact with human flesh, had bored through the body tearing muscle, splintering bone. Swift opened his eyes, which appeared to be submerged in a silver fluid, and looked at Hayes as if from a great distance, without recognition; mysteriously, he said, "We rode down the hill on a hand sleigh."

Hayes said, "When was that, Billy?"

Swift now gave Hayes a terrible pleading look. He moved his lips as if to speak but could form no audible words. He let his head fall to one side and gazed pointedly at the musket lying beside Hayes on the ground. With obvious and painful effort, he swallowed and tried again to speak. Hayes lowered his face closer to Swift's and heard the boy whisper, "I . . . beg . . . you."

Hayes glanced at the gun near his left knee. "I can't, Billy," he said. "Don't ask me to do that."

"I beg you," groaned Swift, and started again to weep.

Hayes felt his own hands go cold and numb. Looking down at the boy again, he saw that Swift's legs were badly burned, black, with patches of blue where the fabric of his trousers had survived. The charred leather of his shoes had bonded to his feet. The ball that had entered below the belt had likely smashed into his spine. The trough of his neck, beneath the blackened chin, was a dark orange color marked by watery blisters the size of walnuts, his right ear a crater and a crispy flap of skin. Where the flesh had come off his right hand, a wine-red mucus oozed from the torn wrist.

Swift closed his eyes again and whispered, "I . . . beg . . . you."

Under the circumstances, Hayes would need to lie down right alongside the boy. He would need to brace the weapon against his own shoulder while aiming it at Swift's temple.

Again Swift started to convulse, uttering a quaking series of grunts, and Hayes got himself arranged quickly. He loaded as if his own life depended upon it; rested the barrel on the rim of the depression; and fired a minié ball into the boy's brain.

He did not hear the shot, for at the exact same moment an errant shell exploded quite nearby, casting up a cataclysm of earth. Fragments smacked Hayes high in the middle of the back and along the backside of his left thigh. The pain was something like being struck by a base ball, but hotter. Far more stunning was the blast itself, which—apart from a persistent ringing in Hayes's ears—had annihilated all other sound. He could hear no further artillery, no musketry, no rebel yells, no groans from the wounded. Only a sudden silence, bathed in smoke.

In silence, he spread the blanket on the ground next to Swift. He rolled the boy onto it, then gathered it at two corners, and got himself onto all fours. In this manner he began to crawl toward what he hoped would be the Union barricade, dragging Swift behind. It was slow going, for the ground was riddled with the snarls of slashed saplings and underbrush; there were fires and stumps and dead or dying men to get around; and he needed to keep his head below the smoke.

BEHIND THE BROCK ROAD, he could stand and walk, and the thinning smoke only dimly obscured a golden sky beyond the black arms of the trees. He couldn't have said if the gold color signified sunrise or sunset, but the ambiguity was of no consequence—sufficient to call it twilight, the afterglow of combat, which he'd survived. He believed the only hope for Billy Swift was to take him to the field hospital, about two miles through the woods to the rear and, even hindered by his own wounds, he believed that if he proceeded slowly he could get that far. The great colony of blue ants, raided and scrambled once again, twitched and churned with more energy than ever; only now, as Hayes observed it, the elaborate spectacle of recovery unfolded in grotesque silence. Everywhere the injured lay about, and as Hayes moved along, dragging the blanket that bore Swift, some reached out a hand, while others only gazed with the vacant eyes of a hurt animal. A weeping steward knelt beside a captain, trying to stanch a bleeding wound in the man's shoulder. A stretcher-bearer tripped over a discarded haversack and rolled an unconscious soldier onto the ground. A shirtless private with his arm in a sling leaned against a log and read a tattered and bloodstained letter. Hayes was accosted by a corporal he didn't recognize, who barked some orders, pointing a finger down at Swift; Hayes nodded and saluted as if he'd understood and said, "Sir!" (It was queer to know himself to have spoken but only to feel his voice rather than to hear it.) The corporal placed his hands on Hayes's shoulders and peered into his eyes. Again he spoke, now with a look of concern, but the only words Hayes read from the man's lips were *regiment* and *dead*. Because it seemed to Hayes that the corporal wanted him to abandon his journey to the field hospital, he turned around and started back in the direction of the road. In the distance, beyond the still-smoking breastworks and the slashing, Hayes saw three pillars of fire rising up at the edge of the woods, whole trees ablaze from the base of the trunk to the topmost branches. He went only a few paces and stopped. He checked to make sure the corporal had moved on, then turned again and resumed his way to the hospital, a path clogged by ambulance wagons and scores of dead horses. He sought to load Swift into one of the wagons but was rudely rejected by a skittish member of the ambulance corps, and so he resolved to drag Swift into the woods to the side of the path and take a less populated course.

The forest grew darker and, most surprising, Hayes began to encounter the occasional civilian. A man with a white beard approached him, looked sadly down at Swift on the blanket, and seemed to make Hayes some kind of offer. Hayes only shook his head and moved on.

A while later, he saw another man rooting through the inside pockets of a dead soldier's jacket, and when the man noticed Hayes approaching, he ran away through the woods. A woman dressed all in black stood over the body of a slain rebel and appeared to be singing out of a hymnbook. (Hayes suspected the rebel soldier had been shot and had dragged himself there, hoping for a safe place to die.) Beside the woman stood the old red-faced man in the stovepipe hat Hayes had seen earlier in the day, and he was glad to know the man was real after all. Near this couple, a shredded blouse, soaked with blood, hung in a snarl of brambles.

It seemed to Hayes that he had traveled a long time, out of night, into day, and into night again, but he knew that—as the smoke of battle blurred these distinctions—he was bound to be confused. A single star fell from the now-lavender sky and lighted on the branch of a pine. The scent of roasted pork and coffee wafted through the woods, and Hayes thought that Swift, when he woke up, would be happy for that. He stopped and sat with his back against a tree, reached for his canteen but found it empty. A rabbit—the same one he'd seen in the trench the night before, when he'd gone to search for Leggett—limped into the dry leaves about a yard away from him. One of the rabbit's hind legs was torn and bloody; the poor animal crouched there for a moment, panting and trembling, and then hobbled away into the brush.

Hayes stood and took up the corners of the blanket, glad to note that Swift seemed to have grown lighter rather than heavier. Morphine, he thought, a good dose for Billy and maybe a little for himself. As he continued, the ringing in his ears, like a rapidly plucked and ever-tightening string, grew higher-pitched and provoked an ache behind his eyes. Just when he'd begun to worry about losing his way in the darkening woods, he saw through the trees a necklace of yellow lanterns, shifting and blinking like a swarm of fireflies; the pointed white gables of a myriad of tents; a green flag with the letter H.

FROM A DISTANCE, it might have been a circus or an Independence Day festival at the Military Garden, but still the sight of it sobered him.

He knew that Billy Swift would not wake up and was well beyond any need for opiates. He knew exactly what the corporal who'd accosted him on the road had said: *Private, get back to your* regiment . . . *that boy is dead.* He wandered toward the tents unable to think why he'd undertaken such a foolish enterprise, bringing Billy to the field hospital, and it felt to him only the latest mark of a flaw in his character that would doom him to a life of blunders and poor decisions.

He had to weave his way across a ground dense with wounded men, some writhing in agony. A nurse, transferring a man from an ambulance to a litter, looked at Hayes hopelessly. A steward wearing a white apron stepped in front of Hayes with a notebook strapped to a board. The man said something to Hayes and then bent to explore the pockets of Swift's blouse. He brought out a charred Christian Commission Testament, thumbed through the first few burnt-black pages, businesslike, and at last asked Hayes a question. Hayes wasn't sure if the man had asked for Swift's name and regiment or for Hayes's own. He said, "William Swift, Fortieth New York," and the man wrote it into his notebook. He pointed Hayes in a direction to the right side of the hospital tents, where there stood a great oak, older and taller than any tree Hayes had seen in the Wilderness. The steward waved his arms impatiently, as if Hayes should hurry, and then, as Hayes started to move, he tapped Hayes on the shoulder. The next thing the man said Hayes was able to read clearly, for, obviously exasperated, he spoke with emphasis: "You don't belong here, Private."

The path to the oak took Hayes near the crowd gathered round a surgeon's table beneath a tent flap, where a number of men held a number of lanterns. Hayes could see the bobbing straw hat of the surgeon, and as he passed by, the crowd suddenly unknotted to allow a patient to be carried away on a stretcher. The patient, still groggy from anesthesia, reached out a hand to Hayes, but the nurses bearing the stretcher didn't pause. It was Vesey, the big man from Bushwick, for whom Hayes had written a letter—could it be possible?—only the previous day. Hayes tried to catch up to them, but couldn't manage with Swift in tow, and he was afraid to leave Billy unattended. The look on Vesey's face—as he continued gazing back and reaching for Hayes—was one of urgent entreaty and surprise, as if Hayes were a long-lost friend who'd arrived just in the nick of time to save him from a disastrous misunderstanding: each of Vesey's legs had been amputated above the knee.

The oak stood at the center of a low rise that accommodated its massive roots. Nighttime had already settled beneath its branches. To the right of the wide trunk, three long rows of the dead had been laid out on the ground, some—wrapped tightly in charred-looking blankets—faceless, limbless, cylindrical shapes, tapered at each end. To the left stood a great heap of severed human arms, legs, feet, and hands, some blackened and already bloated. Hayes pulled Swift to the end of one of the rows to the right of the oak, pushed him onto half of the blanket, and covered him with the other half.

He could recall only fragments of any burial prayers, and so—unable to hear the sound of his own voice—he recited these as best he could, aware, as he spoke them into the darkness, that they lacked even a whisper of anything cogent: " 'Man, that is born of a woman, hath but a short time to live, and is full of misery. He cometh up, and is cut down, like a flower . . . he fleeth as it were a shadow . . . In the midst of life we are in death . . . of whom may we seek for succor, but of thee . . . Forasmuch as it hath pleased thee, Almighty God, in thy wise Providence, to take out of this world the soul of Billy Swift' . . ."

He stopped—or was stopped—as if he'd hit a rock wall. His mind went entirely astray—for an instant, he couldn't think what he was doing.

He shook himself and continued: " 'We brought nothing into this world, and it is certain we can carry nothing out. The Lord gave, and the Lord hath taken away' . . ."

Though he knew that "blessed be the Name of the Lord" immediately followed that last line, he couldn't make himself say it.

When he stood to go, his knees buckled beneath him.

And so he sat on the ground—vividly aware of the hill of limbs on one side, the rows of corpses on the other—and allowed himself to be mesmerized by a silhouette drama on a canvas wall a few yards away. The hospital tent glowed yellow from the light of lamps within, where a remarkable industry hummed. The surgeon worked rapidly, wielding a saw, his elbow like a rod on a locomotive; then the gentler motions of threading the needle (moistening the silk with saliva from his own mouth) and stitching the wound. Patients were removed from the table and new ones placed upon it at a dizzying rate. Hayes couldn't have said how long he sat on the ground and watched the shadow-play, but soon his own wounds began to sting sharply, his hands to shake, and then his mother's face rose up in his mind, pressed watery and wavering against the window of the omnibus. He imagined that as she clawed the glass her thoughts had flown to him and Sarah.

A medical officer, an assistant surgeon, pausing away from the tents for a cigar, approached with a lamp. He held it aloft, so that he could see Hayes and Hayes could see him.

"You've picked a morbid spot to meditate," Hayes understood him to say, and then the man asked for his name.

But when Hayes went to answer, he couldn't. The mechanisms of speech and sound, taken for granted and uncontemplated till now, had thoroughly left him.

FOUR

Under, and Stirring

ll afternoon Walt has been amusing a group of soldiers gathered around Casper's bed—first with Twenty Questions and
then with a succession of witty anecdotes. Though Hayes, in
his own bed, lies outside the circle, naturally he can hear every word,
every explosive round of laughter, every interruptive gibe, and he
would give just about anything for a little peace and quiet.

". . . when I visited Culpeper, February last," Walt's saying now, "a
true story, told me by a certain regimental surgeon. He was posted to
a field hospital in a little church, at the first Bull Run. It was July, of
course, and very hot, and he'd set up shop under a shade tree near the
road that led to the battlefield. His patient had taken a musket ball to
the arm, which had fractured the bone. The surgeon was in the midst
of applying a splint and an eight-yard bandage, when suddenly a vast
throng of soldiers came rushing down the road and shouting, 'The
rebs are after us, the rebs are after us!' "

Here Walt pauses to allow for the obligatory chortling and
sniggering.

"And the patient," he continues, "frightened near to death, is
instantly up from the table and hightailing it for the woods. As he
goes, the better part of the bandage comes undone, and the bemused
doctor's left standing under his shade tree watching him recede into

the distance . . . with this great long white streamer fluttering in his wake!"

A virtual tempest of laughter, altogether grander than the mildly entertaining story merits, and Hayes thinks perhaps his head will split.

Thankfully, it's milder weather today, a gray sky (what he can see of it out his window), but windy. The ward's many shades and flags and mosquito curtains flap unceasingly, and Hayes wishes he could somehow make everything *stop*—the shades, the flags, the curtains, the carnival of visitors and staff in the aisle, the dithering lamp on its long chain overhead. He needs to think, to sort out his situation, which seems to him direr since the previous night's episode involving Matron and two members of the guard. All day he has awaited the arrival of consequences, which have not materialized, unless one counts nuances—several small nicks in the usual grain of things. He's seen nothing of Matron all day. Anne, like Walt, seems to be avoiding him, and she wears the lilac-colored dress that Matron already forbade. Casper, quite inspired and pleased with himself, earlier led Hayes through a series of questions with numerical answers (which Hayes could indicate by holding up his fingers), intended to get at Hayes's identity. The ward surgeon, Dr. Dinkle, making his morning rounds, inspected Casper's dressing and ordered it changed, yet so far no one has shown up to do it—a concern to Hayes, since he believes he detects a foul odor emanating from Casper's bed. That same doctor passed Hayes without so much as a nod, even though Hayes had taken the pains to stand and salute. There are more patients on the ward than ever but noticeably fewer visitors. Mrs. Duffy, the hymn-singing woman—parking one pale hand on the footrail of Hayes's bed and repeatedly meeting his eye whenever she went especially flat—delivered with even more than her usual passion all eight verses of "Plunged in a Gulf of Dark Despair." And the chaplain—who, as he distributes the mail, usually has a sad smile for Hayes—stopped by after breakfast, bearing only the sadness without the smile, and pointedly left a copy of *Come to Jesus* on Hayes's table. Meanwhile, the mother across the way (earlier thought by Hayes to be the ghost of his own mother) has sat with her boy since dawn, holding his hand, though the boy has shown not one sign of life. And Jeffers, clearly dying in the bed on Hayes's left, no longer mutters to himself but only brays like a donkey, fighting for each inhalation, as now and again one of the young cadets, eager for experience, hovers over him.

These observations strike Hayes as pieces of a puzzle, and though he has tried and failed to make them compose a coherent picture, he believes they do suggest a certain shift of atmosphere, a certain shift in tone: Hayes—the hysterical soldier who, prompted apparently by hallucinations, ran amok and had to be tackled and restrained by the guard—has been a topic of wide conversation, and now everyone regards him with heightened curiosity and reticence. In some office of the hospital's administration building, his future is being repondered in light of last night's adventure.

In a more peaceful setting, he might anticipate the likely developments and prepare himself, perhaps even devise plans for eluding certain undesirable outcomes. But here, where nothing's ever still and there's never a moment's silence, it's like trying to pen a letter in a runaway carriage. Except for the double surprise of Matron's intervention and her sudden sympathy, he has not even been able to recall exactly how things ended the night before. He expects he fell asleep. Probably he was given a drug.

At last the group around Casper's bed disperses, but immediately, at Casper's urging, Walt is wearily dragging his chair near to Hayes, then sitting, smiling, and patting Hayes's knee. Walt looks more florid than usual and squints his eyes, as if he is enduring a pain inside his head; his bushy gray beard appears burdensome and unclean, an oat bag about his neck. Casper, who situates himself in his own bed so that he's angled toward Hayes, fluffs and rearranges the pillow that supports his stump. Hayes believes he sees a new flushed quality to Casper's cheeks as well, and that he seems unusually agitated. He recalls his own insight from the night before, that Matron herself was ill—which likely accounts for her absence today—and he thinks perhaps everybody on the ward will eventually succumb to one death or another. Now that he considers it, he understands that the hospital is a kind of mill, where the sick and wounded come either to die or to convalesce until they're returned to the front and killed—and that even the majority of those caring for the patients, subjected to a sea of contagions, won't survive. Before Hayes arrived at the hospital, he thought he'd died somewhere in Virginia, in a field of white wildflowers, beneath a canopy of gas-leaking stars. Then he was brought by train and boat to this place, where, exposed to surgical fevers and sewer emanations, he'll undoubtedly contract a fatal illness. He recalls a lost and round-faced boy in the Wilderness, knocking his fist against his own head and saying, *Maybe I'm already dead,* then touching Hayes to test whether or not Hayes was real. He recalls a shell rolling into a hollow, bumping against the trunk of a hazel bush but not exploding. He recalls awakening in a charred slashing where he'd been dumped after suffering what might have been a mortal blow to the back of the head. And he wonders if this mightn't be the dark-comedic form taken by the afterlife: one dies, one awakens in a new setting where one dies again, then awakens into yet another setting, and so on and so on, forever.

"Okay, my friend," Casper says, "just like we practiced now."

Casper wants to lead Hayes, for Walt's benefit, through the series of questions they earlier rehearsed, but Hayes, who only wants to be left alone, wearily shakes his head.

"Oh, where's the harm in it?" Casper pleads. "It's only Walt and me. You can trust us."

Walt gives Hayes an imploring look and another pat on the knee but says, "He doesn't have to do anything he doesn't want to do."

Hayes remembers being startled awake the night before by a heated exchange between Casper and the attendant Babb; Casper, unable to sleep, begging for morphine; Babb refusing because Casper had run out of money.

"Where's the harm in it?" Casper repeats, his eyes clouding over with tears.

Because it seems so important to Casper, and Hayes doesn't like to deny him—especially now that he believes Casper is dying, and dying without any extra morphine—he supposes he'll relent. As he nods and shrugs his shoulders, he feels a kind of despairing recklessness.

Quickly, Casper says to Walt, "Of course we're assuming Army of the Potomac." Then, to Hayes, "All right, Mr. X, tell us what corps you served in."

Hayes holds up two fingers.

"Second Corps, that would be General Hancock," says Casper and smiles at Walt. "And what division?"

Hayes holds up three fingers.

"Third Division," says Casper. "That would be . . . I don't recall, maybe General Mott. And what brigade, please?"

Hayes holds up one finger.

"Ha, you see!" cries Casper. "Second Corps, Third Division, First Brigade. What do you think of that?"

"Oh, that's very good, Casper," says Walt. "You've narrowed it to about two or three thousand possible names. Now all we have to do is request the necessary rosters, presumably from some office at the War Department . . . and providing they can be had, after several months of bureaucratic faineancy . . . we'll start reading the names aloud and Mr. X will nod to us when we hit the right one. Brilliant—and what fun!"

Walt chuckles softly, takes a handkerchief from his coat pocket, and wipes his eyes.

Casper is silent and only straightens himself in his bed and lowers his chin. After a moment, he says, "Why is there never any satisfaction to be found in this stinking place? I thought it was brilliant. I thought . . ."

The flag nearest them stirs and snaps in a sharp breeze coming through the window. Walt puts away his handkerchief, and then, shockingly, it becomes apparent that Casper is quietly weeping as he strokes his stump.

"My own boy!" Walt cries and is up and out of the chair. His cane falls noisily to the floor, and next he's cradling Casper's head in the crook of his arm. "I'm ever so sorry . . . I never meant to—"

Now he stops and lays a hand over Casper's brow. "My dear," he says, "you're positively *burning* with fever."

Dusk, yet too early to light the lamps. Poor Jeffers still struggles for each breath, but having lost more ground, he now makes only a sound of forced air, a repeated weak gasp followed by a sigh. The wind outside has died completely, and most of the visitors have departed for their suppers. Walt, too, has disappeared, though minutes earlier Hayes heard him tell Casper he would spend the night at the hospital if Casper wanted. At Casper's bedside, the corpulent and dour Dr. Dinkle, the ward surgeon, has tied a cloth over the bottom half of his own face to assuage the effect of the foul odor that arises from the unbound amputation wound. He is assisted by a diminutive man Hayes has never seen before, a Dr. Drum, clad in a black suit rather than a uniform and holding a white handkerchief to his mouth and nose. To Hayes's surprise, Matron has been summoned as well—evidently against her will—and stands on the opposite side of Casper's bed, ashen, perspiring, disconcerted. The two physicians, whose backs are to Hayes, confer in clinical tones with their heads tilted at each other, almost touching, the taller Dr. Dinkle bending toward the wound site and the small Dr. Drum standing straight.

"Altogether drier than desired," says Dr. Drum, "yet what secretion there is . . . watery, quite thin, do you see?"

"Yes, and mind the flaps," says Dr. Dinkle. "They were much better than that before."

"No sign of ligatures," says Dr. Drum.

"The last came away more than a week ago," says Dr. Dinkle. "And with no secondary hemorrhaging. He was properly healing . . . beautifully healing."

"Scorbutic diathesis the probable culprit," says Dr. Drum. "In my—"

"His diet's been the same as all the rest of his kind and condition," Matron pipes in, indignantly.

"Steady, Matron," says Dr. Dinkle, his own tone unaltered. "No one's blaming you."

"Though one would hope the abscesses on the boy's torso might not have gone undiscovered this long," says Dr. Drum.

"You see!" says Matron. "He *does* blame me! I don't know how in heaven's name I can be expected—"

"All right, Matron," says Dr. Dinkle. "Beef tea and brandy from now on. Brandy ten or twelve times a—"

"I should think as much as thirty ounces a day," says Dr. Drum.

"I was going to suggest about thirty-two," says Dr. Dinkle.

"Thirty-two ounces!" says Matron. "He'll be intoxicated."

"We're only trying to keep him alive, Matron," says Dr. Dinkle.

Hayes notices that Matron's hands shake, and now she squeezes them together at her waist in an effort to control them. Her bulging eyes leak tears, and beads of sweat dot her upper lip.

"It seems to me you might have thought of keeping him alive a bit sooner than this," she says. "You might have thought to check him yourselves for abscesses. Pyemia brought on by scorbutic diathesis, is it? Pyemia brought on by *amputation,* more likely. The only certainty I see here is the certainty of your uselessness to save *anyone* from *anything!*"

For a moment, Matron seems stunned by her own outburst, and then she turns to go, but Dr. Dinkle calls out to her, "Please be kind enough to bring some lint and cerate, Matron. And fetch me the dispensing steward. We're going to want opium."

She stops and appears to shudder from top to bottom. She inclines a trembling head a few inches forward, toward the doctors, and says, "Fetch your own lint. Fetch your own cerate. And fetch your own dispensing steward. Why, you put me in the mind of my own wretched father!"

She stalks away, into the flow of traffic in the wide aisle.

The two surgeons look at each other briefly and then turn back to the patient.

After a moment—as if Matron's flare-up and insubordination never occurred—Dr. Drum says, "And dilute sulfuric acid, don't you think?"

"Hmmm," says Dr. Dinkle. "I might prefer quinine."

Now Hayes sees Walt emerge from the aisle, holding a tumbler of amber-colored liquid. He assumes Matron's former position on the far side of Casper's bed. To Hayes, he looks broken in spirit, and when he speaks to the surgeons, his voice is childlike, hardly more than a whisper.

"I've found some punch," says Walt, and tries, unsuccessfully, to smile.

"Careful, careful," Dr. Dinkle says, presumably to Casper, for next Hayes hears Casper for the first time since the examination began: "Oh, yes," says Casper dreamily. "Let's have lots of punch."

TWICE WALT HAS DROPPED OFF to sleep, awakened, and resumed reading, as if no interim had transpired. Twice he has fallen into a fit of coughing, so severe the night watcher came over and urged him, to no avail, to go home. Deep under the sway of whatever mix of potions the surgeons have administered, Casper appears to sleep with eyes unclosed. For some time, he has gazed in silence at Walt as Walt reads from Hayes's book—attentive but uncomprehending, seemingly beyond desire or complaint. Even when Walt dozed off, Casper only continued watching him, apparently unchanged.

"'As they walked on in silence,'" Walt reads, "'he could not but see how used the people were to the spectacle of prisoners passing along the streets. The very children scarcely noticed him.'"

Hayes thinks the reading brings Walt comfort, though it surely brings none to the man's throat, which, judging by the weak rasp of his voice, has grown sore and dry. Hayes only half listens and has lost track of the narrative—his mind wanders and returns, only to wander again, usually to the past, often to Brooklyn. Some character has been arrested and is being escorted under guard through the streets. But which character? And which streets? London or Paris, he doesn't know for certain.

"'A few passers turned their heads,'" Walt reads, "'and a few shook their fingers at him as an aristocrat; otherwise, that a man in good clothes should be going to prison was no more remarkable than that a labourer in working clothes should be going to work.'"

WHEN SUMMERFIELD APPEARED at the kitchen door, Jane placed herself in between the two brown-and-white goats, taking them by their rope collars, and then all three looked at him with what seemed the same precise blend of thrill and trepidation. "They was standing by the front steps when Sarah came home from the school," Jane explained, "just like they was waiting for her. She said I might bring 'em in the garden and give 'em some oats and molasses. I had 'em tethered by the shed, but as it's so bitter cold I let 'em come inside for a spell."

It was just past four o'clock in the afternoon, a Friday. He'd walked all the way from the Fulton Landing and nearly frozen to death. Mrs. Bannister's supper aromas had greeted him in the chilly hall when he came in, and then a sound of bleating, so he'd gone down to the warm kitchen to inquire.

"But where did they come from?" he asked now. "Where do they belong?"

"No one knows," said Jane. "Like I said, they was just waiting at the front steps."

"Well," said Summerfield, moving forward and scratching one of the goats between its gray horns. "Be sure to keep a close eye on them, Jane. You know they can make a real mess of things."

"Oh, I will, I will," said Jane, "don't you worry."

"And don't think they can stay in the kitchen overnight, cold or no cold. They'll tear the place apart while we're sleeping."

"Oh, no, of course not," she said. "I've made a nice bed for 'em in the garden shed. I only brought 'em in for a little warmth and to keep me some company. I would never suppose they could sleep inside the house."

She leaned over and addressed the goats directly now, as if to disabuse them of any hopes they might have along these lines. "I surely wouldn't ever imagine we might keep 'em for our own either," she said. "I know they're only our temporary guests."

He asked about supper, and Jane told him there would be her sister's German chicken stew and biscuits and a berry pie.

Back upstairs, he hung his hat and coat in the hall and peeked into the parlor, where he found a good fire but no people. The light outside was already fading, and so he adjusted up the parlor's bracket lamps, then returned to the hall and climbed the stairs to the second floor. To his surprise, the door to his parents' room stood ajar.

"Oh, it's lovely," he heard Mrs. Bannister say, from inside.

When he stopped at the door, he saw candles glowing at their mother's dressing table, where Sarah sat with a shawl draped over her shoulders. Behind her stood Mrs. Bannister, both women admiring Sarah's image in the large mirror.

"It was one of her favorites," said Mrs. Bannister. "Her birthstone, you know."

Not wanting to startle the two women, he decided to clear his throat rather than rap on the door.

Sarah turned and looked at him from across the room. "Summerfield," she said, rising quickly, as if he'd caught them at something. "You're early, are you not?"

He pushed open the door and stepped inside. "What are you doing in here?" he asked.

Mrs. Bannister said, "Oh my, I'd no idea it was so late, I must see to supper," and glided past him and out of the room.

Sarah came to the door and closed it, then faced him, entirely composed if a bit flushed. The drapes in the room had been opened, the shades raised, and a good deal of soft gray light still entered from the tall windows. She wore a gold necklace with many dark red stones, which caught the candlelight from the dressing table. "You frightened Mrs. B," she said.

"How so?"

"You sounded as if you were scolding."

"I only asked what you were doing in here."

She returned to the dressing table, sat on the stool, and began putting away some things into the little drawers—combs and brushes and other pieces of jewelry. "Well," she said, "since you scared her away, you'll have to help me with this clasp."

He moved behind her. Beneath the cream-colored shawl, she wore a blue-plaid dress he'd seen often. The tortoiseshell combs in her hair were studded with pearls. "My fingers are cold," he said.

"Then tread lightly," she said.

He easily undid the closure, pulled the necklace from around her neck, and dropped it into her waiting palm. "What are these stones?" he asked.

"Garnets," she said. "Are you aware that tomorrow's her birthday?"

He turned away and looked at the wallpaper, a familiar but forgotten pattern of gold trellises and vines, sparrows and red blossoms. He moved to the round table near the middle of the room and sat in one of the chairs. A white cloth lay over the tabletop, which was otherwise clear. The dark green bed curtains were drawn. He recognized the room's old red-and-green carpet as the same one that had been used years earlier in the parlor. His father's embroidered smoking cap lay on the nearby chaise longue. At last he caught sight of Sarah, who sat watching him in the mirror.

She swiveled on the stool and looked at him with sympathy. "Summerfield," she said, "we can't make it into a museum. It's nearly three years. We have to sort it out eventually."

"I know we do," he said. "I just didn't expect . . . I was taken by surprise, that's all."

"You were surprised because you're home early," she said.

"It's awfully cold in here," he said.

"Yes, it is," she said, standing. "Let's go downstairs by the fire."

She blew out the candles and moved to the chaise longue, where she picked up the smoking cap. Just then he discovered that a drawer protruded a few inches from the table's edge. He drew back the cloth and opened the shallow drawer, where he saw a plain brown-covered book, which he took out and held up at an angle to catch the light from the windows. He opened it to the title page and read aloud: "*The Lover's Marriage Lighthouse: A Series of Sensible and Scientific Essays on the Subjects of Marriage and Free Divorce and on the Uses, Wants, and Supplies of the Spiritual, Intellectual, Affectional, and*—oh . . ."

He closed the book and started to return it to the drawer, but Sarah was already at his side, laughing and taking it from his hands. "'Intellectual, affectional, and *oh*'?" she said.

She opened the book, found the place where he'd left off, and continued, "*. . . Uses, Wants, and Supplies of the Spiritual, Intellectual, Affectional, and*—ha!—*Sexual Natures of Man and Woman, Being a Key to the Causes, Prevention, Remedies, and Cure of Mental and Physical Uncongenialities Pertaining to the Indissoluble Matrimonial*—why, Summerfield . . . you look as if you might swoon."

She closed the book and laid it inside the drawer. "Here," she said, smiling, and placed the smoking cap on his head. "We'd best have Mrs. B sort things out for us first on her own."

She left the room ahead of him, and as he followed her down the stairs, she said, "I was passing by their door on my way to the parlor, and it was as if something called to me from inside."

"A sense of duty?" he said.

"Oh, no, not that," she said. "It was more like an irresistible urge to snoop. By the way, Summerfield, we have goats now. Two goats in the garden."

He held open the parlor door for her. "Actually," he said, "they're in the kitchen. Jane thinks it's too cold for them outside."

"Oh, dear," said Sarah, taking a seat on the sofa. After a moment, she said, "Then you've seen them?"

He nodded, sitting at the opposite end of the sofa. He leaned forward, rested his elbows on his knees, and rubbed his hands together close to the grate. "They were bleating as I came into the house."

She laughed, and he asked her where they'd come from.

"I found them standing at the front stoop when I arrived home," she said. "It was as if they were anticipating my arrival. I must say they gave me the most soulful look when I said hello. And then they followed me right up the steps. I asked Jane to give them something to eat and to put them in the garden. I didn't know what else to do."

"You could have left them to find their way home," he said.

"You're right, of course, I could have," she said. "But you didn't see the way they looked at me, Summerfield . . . with those lovely little rectangular pupils in their eyes. It really was as if they fully expected me to take charge. 'We've lost our way,' they said. 'But you, nice lady, you'll know what to do.' I simply didn't have it in me to reject them. I suppose we'll have to put an announcement in the newspaper."

"I suppose."

"You look very handsome in Papa's hat."

"Thank you."

"So, tell me," she said, pulling the shawl tighter around her shoulders, "why *are* you home early?"

"You know," he said, "upstairs just now . . . I wasn't about to 'swoon,' as you put it."

"I shouldn't have teased you," she said. "It was bad form and I apologize." She started to get up, saying, "I think you've caught a chill—wouldn't you like coffee?"

"No, wait, Sarah, there's something I must tell you," he said, and she sat back down.

"All right," she said, and just like that her eyes filled with tears. She took from the sleeve of her dress one of the handkerchiefs he'd given her for Christmas and cautiously wiped the corners of her eyes.

All the way from the Fulton Landing he'd steeled himself in the cold, but it seemed that things at home had conspired to undo him, and now, seeing her busy with the handkerchief, he felt the last vestige of his resolve melt away. He said, "I can see you've already guessed what it is."

Now she looked up at him dry-eyed and changed, as if her natural self had quit the room and she'd left this brittle shell for him to deal with further. "Really, Summerfield," she said, "must you turn every-thing into a game?"

"That's not my intention," he said.

Impatiently, she said, "You're home early today because you left the shipwrights' after dinner and went somewhere to execute a bit of business. I regret that my clairvoyant powers aren't quite sufficient to provide every detail."

"I took the ferry to New York," he said.

"You took the ferry to New York," she said, without feeling. "And in New York you visited a certain office."

"Yes," he said. "I've enrolled with the Fortieth New York Infantry, on furlough and staying in the Park Barracks. They'll soon depart for Fort Schuyler, where I'm to join them."

"Fort Schuyler?" she said. "Where's that?"

"The Bronx."

"Oh, only the Bronx," she said. "Not very far."

"From there we'll go into camp at Brandy Station, in Virginia."

"You said soon. How soon?"

"A week."

"A week?" she said. "That *is* soon."

"Yes."

She stared for a moment at the fire. The lamps on the walls flickered. She looked down into her lap, carefully folded the handkerchief, and tucked it back into her sleeve. "Well," she said, and stood.

She did not look at him but only moved around the sofa and toward the hall.

"Sarah, please," he said, getting to his feet, but she'd already opened the door. He felt the cold air from the hall enter the room.

Halfway out, she paused. She returned to him, head down, still never meeting his eye. She put her arms around him and held him tight for a good long time, without a word. Then she released him and was gone. She closed the hall door behind her in such a way that it made no sound at all.

Once again, he would have his supper alone, on a tray, upstairs in the library. Once again, he would light his father's pipe and then put it away, disappointed that he didn't enjoy it more.

The next time he saw her was just before first light, when she anxiously awakened him and told him about the prowler in the garden. He got out of bed and went to the window, where he peered down— heard faintly the bleating of the goats but could see no prowler.

She moved to his side and then gasped as they spied a shadowy figure vanish behind the shed at the back of the garden. He raised the sash and called out, "Who's there?"

The bleating stopped. Sarah shuddered from cold, and he lowered the window.

They stood there next to each other in their nightclothes, in the near dark, and continued watching for another minute. To the east, Venus blazed and shimmered above the black housetops and barren trees.

Sarah took his hand and rested her head against his shoulder. "How can the world be so very cold?" she said softly.

"It's winter," he said. "Spring will come again."

"Ah, yes," she said. "Renewal. And with it, renewal of the war. Renewal of the killing and dying, renewal of heartbreak and grief."

Something stirred behind them, and when they turned, they saw

Jane and Mrs. B, with night bonnets and candlesticks, lurking in the open doorway like specters.

"They've took our goats," said Jane, shaking her head. "The rotten thieves took our goats."

"THE TRUTH HAS the great advantage of being true," his mother used to say, and now, in his dream, she has come to remind him. "However else it might be assailed," she says, looking down at him from the open window of a red omnibus, "this quality remains unchanged. Put your faith in the truth, Summerfield. At the end of the day, it may not save your life, but it will likely save your soul." There's the crack of a whip, and the omnibus rattles away, up a steep incline on a cobblestone road next to a canal. Then he hears the rebel yell, the maniacal whooping from the nearby trees, and he thinks, *We did, some of us, sometimes, enjoy the killing.* He cups his hands over his ears, but the yelling swells and swells till it wakes him.

The ward, bathed in moonlight, seems unnaturally quiet—he senses the absence of some formerly reliable noise—but perhaps it's only because of the dream-roar from which he just awakened. Walt, asleep, still sits in the chair between Hayes's bed and Casper's, leaning back with his head rolled to one side. His cane rests at an angle between his legs, its silver handle gleaming in the moonlight, which also falls over the muddy toes of his black Morocco boots. Hayes sees that across the way there's a new soldier in the bed where the devoted mother kept her vigil for days on end.

And now he sees, too, that Casper's bed is empty. He closes his eyes and thinks of Casper's happily tossing an apple into the air and catching it in his palm.

A moment later, he hears Casper hissing, "Don't you touch me," and then sees him being helped back to the bed by Babb and another attendant. Soon enough they have him arranged and the mosquito curtain draped neatly around the bed; without a word, they depart into the darkness at the end of the ward. Immediately Casper cradles his stump and launches a very loud, dry-mouthed serenade: "'Here's to the maid all dressed in blue, always tidy, always true . . .'"

Walt startles awake and gets up out of the chair as if an alarm bell has sounded, then quickly moves to Casper and starts to hush him through the mosquito curtain.

"'When she kisses, she kisses sweet,'" wails Casper, "'and makes things stand that have no feet.'"

Walt pulls back the gauzy curtain and puts his hand over Casper's mouth, laughing. "Shhhh, my boy," he says, and takes a cup from Casper's side of the table and helps him drink.

For the next minute or two, Walt talks softly to Casper, an almost-crooning sound, too low for Hayes to understand any words.

Soon the ward is quiet again.

Walt removes Casper's cap, sits next to him on the bed, and strokes Casper's freckled brow and hair. Hayes raises himself on his elbows for a moment and looks over: in the dim glow from the lowered lamps and the moonlight, the gray-bearded man might be a doting grandfather, soothing a sick boy back to sleep.

Walt notices Hayes, turns, and smiles sadly. He tilts his head to one side, as if Hayes has asked a question. He whispers, "Our sweet Casper's a bit corned."

After a pause, he loses the smile and adds, "Nobody . . . nobody survives pyemia."

Hayes lets his head sink back onto the pillow and ponders the network of shadows in the white-painted rafters overhead, something like a ship's rigging.

Oddly quiet, he thinks, and then, after a moment, he can almost feel the ward sway to and fro as it drifts gently out to sea.

Quiet, he thinks, *eerily quiet,* and then, *Jeffers.*

He rolls onto his side, facing the other bed. In the gloom and through the gauze of the two mosquito curtains, he can only barely discern the man's outline—perfectly still, and silent.

HE OPENS HIS EYES just in time to glimpse the cone as it descends over his nose and mouth—and then Dr. Drum with a bottle: a sweet pungent odor, a stinging sensation in his nose and throat. He jerks his head back and tries to sit up, but soldiers on either side of his bed press down hard on his arms and legs. An unmistakable voice—that of the angry captain—says, "Hold him!" and "You there . . . grasp his head." Someone pulls on his ears and yanks his neck forward, he hears Casper say, "Leave him be, you bunch of scoundrels," and then he's lying on the kitchen floor at Hicks Street. Most odd, there doesn't seem to be anything unusual about it, except that the floor is covered with a jumble of white bedsheets. Two goats—one with an impressive beard—look down at him, each smiling rather Christlike, which, though charming, doesn't quite dispel the feeling that he's in some kind of danger. A mosquito curtain drops into his face but is quickly taken away. He's vividly aware of his body in all its parts—indeed, for the first time ever, he understands that he *is* his body, and his body is himself and made of many parts. The sense of danger, he thinks, attaches to the fact that at the moment he's unable to move any of those parts, though the impulse to move clangs and pounds inside him like a steam engine. Someone says, "He's under," and he thinks, *Yes,* Under, *precisely.*

The goats move away, a disappointment he intends to bear with manly composure.

Despite his evident paralysis, there's a great deal of internal motion throughout his body and limbs—his blood, coursing so fiercely he fears it might break through the skin. He inhales, runs up to the line, and releases the base ball only inches from the ground, his knuckles nearly brushing the fragrant grass. He exhales. The batsman swings and sends the ball straight up, high into the air. All the men on the playing field are set in motion, one way and another, and it makes him think of music.

Sarah twirls her parasol and says, "Why, Summerfield, you're an athlete *and* a poet."

A cloud blots out the sun. A strong wind sweeps across the whole place, bending the young pines at the edge of the forest.

A brief interval of darkness, and then the sun returns, blinding and hot.

"He's stirring," a man says.

"Tell us who you are," says another.

Yes, he thinks, *Under, and Stirring.*

Gargantuan figures, like dark mountains, emerge from the light and hover over him. "Tell us who you are," one of the mountains echoes. "Tell us who you are."

He tries to say, "I'm Under, and Stirring," but cannot will his voice to make the necessary sounds.

His friend Casper says, "You bunch of scoundrels. What are you doing to him? Why can't you let him be? This is your work, jackanapes. You wouldn't last a day in the field. Your own men would see to that."

"Remove that man," says the angry captain. "Take him to the wardmaster's room."

"Ha!" cries Casper. "Court-martial me, why don't you? I'm dead already, you stinking parlor soldier."

Hayes has a terrible taste in his mouth, as if he has drunk lamp oil, and his throat feels sore and mucous. He coughs, which sparks a sharp ache in his head, which in turn sends a wave of nausea to his belly.

He closes his eyes, and the base ball comes down at last, uncaught, and thumps pleasantly somewhere off to the right side.

THE NEW MAN in Jeffers's bed might be Abraham Lincoln's double except that he has lost both his legs, each amputated above the knee. Hayes—who feels dizzy any time he moves his head even slightly—can't think when the man was substituted for Jeffers, or when Jeffers was moved to the deadhouse. He recalls, as if from a dream, Anne lifting the tag on the new man's shirt and saying, *Mr. R-a-u-g-h, do you say that*—*"rough"?* and the man replying, in a very deep voice, *Raw*.

Casper has not yet returned from the wardmaster's room, if indeed that's where he was taken, and Hayes worries he may never see him again, that he'll doze off, and when he awakens, a new man will have been substituted for Casper as well. He's not sure what time of day it is, but he thinks it's still morning, for the black-clad clergy (always most prevalent in the morning) have been lurking about with their tracts. A short while ago, an especially insensible example snaked up next to Private Raugh and read aloud to him a preachment that included a passage on the evils of dancing. Raugh, immobile and unresponsive throughout, has been sleeping ever afterward. So far, since Raugh's arrival on the ward, Hayes has heard the man utter only the one word, *raw.*

Hayes's head aches, his throat burns, and the nausea persists. He wants water but fears vomiting on the way to the water jar. He fears calling attention to himself in any way, which might provoke a reprise of Dr. Drum and the angry captain. When awake, he has pretended to be asleep and endeavored to keep still, the recent assault having put him back to the mind and manners of a cornered animal.

"It's mucus," says Dr. Drum, peering into the basin held by Anne, "only mucus and more mucus. Entirely to be expected."

Hayes rocks forward, heaves, retches, and vomits yet again.

After a pause, Anne (wearing the lovely forbidden lilac dress) looks into his eyes and says, "No more?"

Shot through with shame, he shakes his head.

"All done?" she says.

He nods, wishing he were dead.

She passes the basin to an attendant who waits behind her and takes a towel from her apron and wipes Hayes's mouth. "There," she says, in a heartening way. "You just lie back and rest now."

When the surgeon and the attendant move away, Hayes sees Walt at the foot of the bed, still wearing his hat and haversack and gazing down at him gravely. As Walt removes the bag, a meaningful look passes between him and Anne, something vaguely disapproving, and then Casper—once again in his own bed—cries, "Oh, God, I'm cold I'm cold I'm cold!"

"I'll fetch some blankets," Anne says to Walt, "but in the meantime that's brandy in the cup there. Persuade him to drink as much as you can."

Casper lets out a chattering drone as Walt quickly sheds his own coat and lays it over him. Walt then helps Casper take the brandy, cooing assurances and generally quieting the boy.

"Scoundrel," says Casper, his voice shaking, "scoundrel."

"Who's a scoundrel?" asks Walt.

"Commander of the guard. Ja-ja-jackanapes."

Walt casts Hayes an inquiring glance, then returns to helping Casper with the cup. "Here," he says, "drink some more of this, my boy, it'll warm you."

In another minute, Anne's back with blankets, and she and Walt get Casper tucked in. "They put him in the wardmaster's room and kept him a long time out of bed," says Anne. "And now his fever's up again."

"Who put him in the wardmaster's room?" asks Walt.

"Jackanapes ca-captain," says Casper. He joggles his head toward Hayes. "They e-e-etherized him."

Walt looks at Hayes, back at Casper, and finally at Anne. "I don't understand," he says.

Anne moves around the bed and stands close to him, taking his arm as if they are about to set out on a walk. "I must go," she says softly. "But early this morning—from what I've gathered—Dr. Drum etherized our friend here in bed thirty-two. It's ether that caused the nausea."

"But why etherize him?"

"Dr. Drum's test for detecting malingerers," says Anne. "If Mr. X were feigning dumbness, see, he'd likely speak as he was recovering from the anesthesia . . . before he had his wits about him."

"Ha-ha!" cries Casper. "He didn't say *nothing*!"

"But who *is* Dr. Drum?" asks Walt.

"A friend of the ward surgeon," says Anne. "Visiting from the Christian Street Hospital, in Philadelphia. Now I must go. You might bring Mr. X some tea when you have time."

After she has gone, Walt stands between the two beds for a moment, looking first at Casper, then at Hayes, as if they are the two horns of a dilemma. At last he takes his bag by the strap and says, "I shall return. I've got a host of errands. And then some banging to do on a certain drum."

Casper lets out an insane horselaugh, and when Walt hushes him, Casper covers his mouth with his one remaining hand. Walt starts to go but pauses and looks past Hayes at the new man sleeping in Jeffers's bed. "Why, he's the very spit of Abe Lincoln," he says.

When Walt has left, it seems to Hayes that the noise of the ward increases, and likewise the temperature. There's laughter and moaning and coughing and the rumble of a hundred conversations; a metallic rattle of unknown origin; the dull clank of the bell outdoors; the scuffle of wheels and boots and canes and crutches on the wooden floor.

Suddenly Major Cross shows up and stares down at Hayes with his scarlet face and gauze-white turban. "Dr. Drum means to take me with him to Philly-delphia," he says.

He leans forward and whispers in Hayes's ear: "Before it's over, I'm going to tie him to a chair and feed him last year's hay."

Then Major Cross is prone on the floor in the narrow slot between Hayes's bed and Raugh's. Hayes can no longer see any sign of the man, but now and again he hears his muttering and sighing.

When Casper speaks next, his voice is thoroughly calm. "There, there, little fellow," he says, consoling his stump. "Don't you worry . . . you'll be whole again soon enough."

CASPER AND RAUGH ARE undoubtedly drugged, for how else could they sleep amid such commotion? The din of the ward—when it approaches a peak, as now, in the middle of the afternoon—sounds to Hayes like combat, like musketry, and though he recognizes this as misapprehension, he cannot avert a powerful urge to take cover beneath the bed. He has learned the importance of fighting such urges. Succumbing to them can bring about harsh consequences: when he mistakenly thought the hospital had caught fire and tried to run out the doors and had to be restrained by guards, a forced etherization soon followed.

He wishes Walt would come back from his errands, for he feels safest when Walt is near. Even the man's cane or hat or umbrella, left at Hayes's bedside, has the power to soothe. Today Walt did not leave any of these, though he did promise to return. In the interim, the aftereffects of the ether have departed, except for a sore throat; the rekindling of his old symptoms (trembling hands, stinging shrapnel wounds); and a sharpened wariness (he minds the flow of traffic in the aisle with increased vigilance, surreptitiously, to avoid meeting the eye of any passerby).

A while ago, he took up *Come to Jesus,* which he found demoralizing and soon only pretended to read, resting the spine in his lap to stay the quaking pages. One sentence has lodged in his mind: "God requires purity of heart as well as of outward conduct, and he knows all our thoughts." The assertion offers nothing new in the way of theology—both its principles are familiar to him—yet, as it plays over and over in his head, Hayes sees that his experience of these conditions has changed. Purity of heart, once a worthy ideal, has become an unsportsmanlike precept, policed by surveillance, in a realm where ideas arise before they can be eluded. The state of being thoroughly known, once a solace, has become an invasion of privacy. The state of being never alone, once a comfort, has become the inescapable burden of never being *left* alone.

"... I forgot my glove in the wagon," mumbles Casper, in his sleep, and then Hayes looks up and sees that Walt and Dr. Bliss stand at the foot of Casper's bed.

"He had the shakes something terrible," says Walt.

Dr. Bliss moves to one side, pulls down the blanket from around Casper's neck, and lays a hand carefully on his brow. "I believe he's feeling more than warm enough now," he says.

Both the men step to the end of Hayes's bed. Hayes starts to get up to salute, but Dr. Bliss raises a hand and says, "Keep still, son."

Hayes, panicked and disgraced, is suddenly aware that some of the buttonholes on his shirt and on the fly of his trousers are torn. The surgeon slides a chair between the two beds and says, to Walt, "If you don't mind, I should like you to take a seat here and play the visitor."

"I don't need to *play* the visitor," says Walt. "I *am* the visitor. But as a visitor, I must say I find that chair uncommonly hard."

The surgeon lifts the blanket from Casper's bed, fashions it into a cushion, and places it on the chair. Walt thanks him, sits, and leans his cane against Hayes's table, huffing and puffing.

"And Walt," says Dr. Bliss, "I hate to ask ... but if you don't mind, kindly remove your hat."

"I had every intention of doing so," says Walt.

He takes off the saggy-brimmed hat and wearily lifts the strap to his haversack over his head. Struck again by the man's blending of youth and old age, Hayes believes Walt looks more played-out than he has yet seen him. Walt smiles, crinkling his eyes, then reaches forward and pats Hayes's head as if he were a puppy. "'Some feelings are to mortals given,'" he says, in an altered voice, "'with less of earth in them than heaven.'"

"That's the idea," says Dr. Bliss, moving around to the other side of the bed and leaning in close to Hayes. "Recite us some poetry, Walt. Cheer us up."

"'And if there be a human tear,'" Walt continues, "'From passion's dross refined and clear . . .'"

"May I see inside your mouth?" says Dr. Bliss, and Hayes opens his mouth. "Stick out your tongue, please," says the doctor. "Turn a bit toward the light."

"'A tear so limpid and so meek,'" continues Walt, "'It would not stain an angel's cheek—'"

Apparently satisfied with the looks of Hayes's throat, the surgeon takes out a pocket watch, places his fingers on Hayes's wrist, and times his pulse. Mortified, Hayes cannot make his hand stop quivering. Still touching Hayes's wrist, the doctor says, "Try to ease yourself, son. You've nothing to fear from us."

When the examination is finished and Dr. Bliss returns to the end of the bed, Walt looks at Hayes sadly and says, "'Tis that which pious fathers shed / Upon a duteous soldier's head.'"

"Shakespeare?" says Dr. Bliss.

"Walter Scott," answers Walt, "though I've bent him some to the occasion."

"Ah, here's one of our invited guests now," says the surgeon, as Dr. Drum arrives and stands next to him at the footrail.

Clean shaven and balding (the line of his steel-gray hair starting somewhere near the crown), Dr. Drum rises not quite to Dr. Bliss's shoulder.

"This gentleman," says Dr. Bliss to Hayes, "is Dr. Drum. I don't believe you've been properly introduced."

Hayes nods, but Drum only gazes at him blankly.

"I understand you administered ether to this young soldier today," says Dr. Bliss.

Drum, who appears cheerfully prepared for the interview, blinks his eyes and picks at a loose thread on the cuff of his black suit coat. "That is true," he says, aloof. "As requested to by your own Captain Gracie."

"Our own Captain Gracie?" says Dr. Bliss. "And why would a contract surgeon perform a procedure at the behest of a line officer? Is that how you do things in Philadelphia?"

Drum lifts his chin and smiles at Hayes with a kind of patronizing cordiality, as if Hayes were the source of a frivolous complaint. "Oh, I don't think we've done him any harm," he says.

"I didn't say you had," says Dr. Bliss. "Though I doubt you've done him any good. He's already wasting from lack of appetite."

"I secured the ward surgeon's authorization," says Drum. "And I believe we've gained some useful intelligence besides."

Dr. Bliss starts to answer, but utters only the word *intelligence*, when, at that moment, Dr. Dinkle and the angry captain arrive at the foot-rail. Walt takes Hayes's hand and gives him a reassuring wink as Dr. Bliss makes the necessary greetings and thanks the others for joining him. Then each of the men at the end of the bed turns his attention to Hayes in an auxiliary way, as if Hayes were a fire around which they've gathered to chat. Most disconcerting to Hayes, the light from the nearby window keeps coming and going—likely the effect of passing afternoon clouds—and the scene is bright one moment and dim the next. As he studies the men's faces, he believes he reads contrition in Dr. Dinkle's but clear defiance in the angry captain's.

"Here's the situation as I understand it," says Dr. Bliss. "Captain Gracie requested ether be administered to this patient, and Dr. Drum did so with the permission of Dr. Dinkle. But what I most fail to grasp is why the captain would make such an unusual request."

Obviously Dr. Bliss means to draw a response from the captain, but before the captain can speak, Drum says, "It's not a conspiracy, Major Bliss. The captain and I fell into conversation, over the course of which I told him something of my work at the Christian Street Hospital.

I happened to mention that we'd developed a good test for malinger-ers, and he told me he knew a likely candidate."

Dr. Bliss allows his gaze to dwell on Drum for a moment, apparently absorbing what he has been told, and then he turns to Dr. Dinkle. "In the future," he says, "I should like any such nonmedical procedure to be cleared with me."

"Naturally, sir," says Dr. Dinkle. "It was never my—"

"Nonmedical?" says Drum. "Why do you characterize it so?"

"Because it's designed to probe a disciplinary concern," says Dr. Bliss, "and not to cure illness."

"Oh, make no mistake," says Drum. "We've cured many a soldier this way of what 'ailed' him. The lame walk again, the deaf hear, and the dumb speak. Why, there's been more than one idler who—"

"All right, Dr. Drum," says Dr. Bliss, "I don't mean to debate you, certainly not here and not now. I am this hospital's surgeon in chief. I only aim to hone a point of protocol with my ward surgeons. Now, I thank you for your time."

"But this soldier has proved authentic," says Drum quickly, "the genuine article, red-hot nostalgia. I'm told he suffers delusions to boot. I'm keen to have him moved to my own hospital, where we're doing marvelous things on our own hook . . . marvelous things with a great range of nervous disorders and—"

"It *is* a reasonable course," says Dr. Dinkle, clasping Drum by the elbow—evidently intending to rein him in even while supporting his cause.

"I'll take it under consideration," says Dr. Bliss, with a conclusive tone.

Dr. Dinkle thanks Dr. Bliss and against some noticeable resistance escorts Dr. Drum away.

The captain, seeing the party break up without his having contributed, faces the surgeon in chief and stands very tall. "I wonder if it has occurred to you, Major Bliss, that you might be harboring a deserter."

The surgeon smiles impassively and says, "I wonder if it has occurred to you that you might be impugning a hero."

Hayes, neither a deserter nor a hero, suppresses an urge to laugh—

it suddenly strikes him as comical, his being fought over this way; likewise, in equal parts absurd and fitting, his name tag, which reads UNKNOWN.

"We want that bed," says the captain, narrowing his eyes at the surgeon. "I don't need to tell you what we've got landing at our doors daily . . . landing daily and by the hundreds."

"No, Captain Gracie," says Dr. Bliss, "you don't need to tell me."

"If you won't let him go to Philadelphia, at least there's the asylum. Surely—"

"Yes, Captain," says Dr. Bliss. "Thank you very much."

Thus dismissed, the captain pauses for a moment and takes a last look at Hayes. "This safety in silence is temporary," he says. "And not very safe. The commission will be coming back through in a few days. I reckon they'll do some sensible culling where it's called for. They'll have this one sorted out fast enough, one way or another."

"No doubt," says Dr. Bliss. "No doubt."

As soon as the captain is gone, Walt says, "*What* commission?"

"I'm sure you've seen them, not knowing what they were," answers the doctor. "A concoction of surgeons and line officers, touring the hospitals sporadically . . . altogether softheaded in my view. Routinely they send a score of patients back to the front before their wounds have sufficiently healed . . . or while they're still too sick to fight. And a good portion of my convalescent helpers as well."

"And you have no say in the matter?"

"Oh, yes, I have a say. Only I don't have final say."

Walt, who has released Hayes's hand, now takes out his handkerchief and wipes his own brow; he lets out a long sigh and shifts in his chair, agitated and indignant. "Do you not outrank that man, that insufferable Captain Gracie?"

"Of course I do, Walt," answers Dr. Bliss, "but rank isn't everything. One has to maintain relations. The men in these beds are patients *and* soldiers. I can't be drawn into constant squabbles over who's in charge of them."

"But you won't give our friend over to that nippent little Drum, will you, and let him be carted off to Philadelphia? And surely you won't send him to the asylum?"

Dr. Bliss pulls on his whiskers thoughtfully and looks at Hayes. "I'm not certain I can prevent it," he says. "He can't stay here indefinitely."

"But he won't stay indefinitely," says Walt. "After all, the war will end. If it's a case of not knowing what to do with him—which I believe it is—why can't we leave him be for now? If we don't yet have our answer, let's wait for it to come clear. Things often do, you know . . . come clear with ample time and tolerance."

"I'm beginning to see the nature of your attraction to this young man," says Dr. Bliss. "It's philosophical."

"Not at all," says Walt, and looks out the window. "He attracts me the same way they all do—which is to say, affectively. How can I fail to be attracted when my feelings are so thoroughly and permanently absorbed?"

He looks back at the doctor and says, "If it's merely the question of a bed, I can bring him to my own rooms and give him one."

"Now *that* would be irregular," says Dr. Bliss. "Look, Walt, I want you to go home, and I don't mean back to your rooms. I mean for you to get back to Brooklyn, at least for a few months. Otherwise, you're bound for a full collapse."

Walt closes his eyes for a moment and bows his head. "I'll not deny that I'm sleeping less than first-rate," he says softly. "And more and more I feel I must have an intermission. But I won't be going tonight. Nor tomorrow. Tomorrow's my birthday."

Bliss moves between the beds and puts a hand on Walt's shoulder. "Well, *he's* not going anywhere tonight or tomorrow either," he says. "I'll do what I can for him, Walt. A direct opposition's not always the best strategy. Have you never said yes and meant no?"

"Probably," says Walt, "once or twice." He laughs and adds, "But not nearly so often as I've said no and meant yes."

"I want you to go to your rooms," says the surgeon, after a moment. "Have yourself a good supper and bath and a good night's rest. Don't return to the hospital this evening."

"But evening's when I enjoy myself most," says Walt. "In the absence of Matron's incessant looming and casting me the evil eye."

"You needn't worry about Matron," says Dr. Bliss. "I've done for her what I'll have to do for you in the end—I've sent her home. I admire the woman's perseverance, but her illness has finally got the best of her . . . and begun to affect her mind."

"What, no more Matron?" says Walt. He looks at Hayes with mock dejection and adds, "Now I suppose I shall miss her."

For another moment, the two men seem to ponder Hayes—the surgeon with his hand still resting on Walt's shoulder, and Walt with cloudy eyes. At last Dr. Bliss says, "Don't you think you might write your name for us now, son? There's no physical reason why you shouldn't."

Walt bends, reaches into his bag, pulls out first a large orange and a pair of suspenders, both of which he lays aside, and then his scrapbook and a pencil. He offers these last two to Hayes, one in each hand.

Hayes, shocked to be addressed so suddenly, believes he can in fact write his name, and might do it, despite his ambivalence about revealing his identity. But as he looks at the scrapbook and the pencil, the two hands holding them are horribly charred, tumid with great watery blisters, and he shudders and draws his knees toward his chest. A burnt and sickening sweet smell invades his nostrils. He rolls onto his side and puts his back to the men.

"Did you see the blood leave his face?" he hears Walt say, somewhere behind him, far away. "He's terrified. Never mind, dear boy, never mind."

Hayes doesn't move, willing his limbs to stay frozen, despite a sharp sting of boots smacking his ribs. He fears his shrapnel wounds have started to bleed. Soon he hears Dr. Bliss ask, "Does that man in the next bed look like Lincoln?"

"The very spit," answers Walt. "The poor creature . . . He sleeps, only sleeps . . . and when he opens his eyes, they gleam with rage. He refuses my smallest gifts and won't even talk to me."

"Swap places with him," says Dr. Bliss. "Would you feel like chatting?"

Walt doesn't respond for a few seconds—Hayes imagines him doing mentally what the surgeon has suggested—and then he says, "No, I suppose I wouldn't."

There's a lull in the babel and clatter of the ward, and Hayes's breath starts to come more easily. He believes he hears out the darkening window a rumble of thunder, but he can never be sure he's not somehow still hearing the war.

He thinks, *I'm told he suffers delusions to boot,* and encounters a peculiar puzzlement over the word *boot.*

Back to the front, he thinks, an absurd yet fascinating phrase.

He thinks, *I mean for you to get back to Brooklyn,* and envisions himself seated alongside Walt in a railcar, Walt patting him on the knee, and saying with his curious compound of maternal maleness, "We're almost home, my dear."

"Now, Walt," says Dr. Bliss. "Here's a thorny question: should we wish for our young friend to gain back his speech, or wish for him not to?"

"Ah, yes," says Walt. "Down one road waits a Gracie, down the other a Drum. Scylla and Charybdis. I wonder . . . have you seen this thing before—what you call nostalgia—and coupled with loss of speech?"

"Twice before," answers the doctor. "Each suffered temporary loss of hearing as well . . . symptoms associated with a shell exploding close-by. But I've heard of others—soldiers released from Confederate prisons, for example—who'd simply gone mute in the face of unspeakable horror."

"Unspeakable horror?" says Walt. "If that's the case, I'm surprised you don't see more of them."

"We very well might," says the doctor, "if more of them survived."

"Oh, of course," says Walt, "they would have to survive, wouldn't they?"

After a long pause, Walt adds, "Maybe it's not so bad, losing the so-called art of speech. Most of life gives language the slip anyway, I find. Look at me: I rattle all day long and into the night and say only a fraction of what I feel, a fraction of what I know in my heart."

"Well," says Dr. Bliss, "maybe some men's fractions are better than other men's sums."

"Ha!" says Walt. "Let me assure you—for each of my fractions, there are worlds and worlds and worlds of uncertainties. It's almost enough to make me wish I'd been a doctor."

———

LONG AFTER DARK, a dozen or more new arrivals straggle into the
ward, ragged and muddy, bloody, staggering, pale, and desolate. The
female nurses fetch basins, blocks of soap, and fresh shirts, then set
about bathing the men from the waist up, after which the male nurses
and attendants take over, finish with the washing, and find them beds.
The ward surgeon and a number of stewards soon appear, and Hayes,
observing from a distance, notes the noise and fuss that arise from the
staff while the soldiers stay entirely quiet.

Casper—awakened, sweat-drenched, and yellowish—sits up and
starts rocking and raving: "My stomach hurts, my chest hurts, bring
my medicine, God help me, the virus eats me alive, I hurt and I'm
cold and I want my Joanie . . ."

Anne comes over with a basin and places it on the table. She hushes
Casper, helps him drink from his cup, and soon gets him settled back
onto his pillow. She starts to wash his face, but Casper takes hold of
her wrist. "Give me more of that punch," he says.

"You've had the limit for today," she says calmly, "but I'll have
more for you tomorrow."

"Then fetch me a pill."

"You've already had your pill, too."

"I need another!" he shouts.

Anne hushes him again and says, "Casper, you're hurting my arm."

"I'm sorry," he cries, releasing her wrist. A whimpering scolded
child, he adds, "Please forgive me. I never meant to hurt you. I never
meant to hurt anybody."

"Thank you," says Anne, "I forgive you. Now, I'll go and see Dr.
Dinkle about getting you more medicine . . . and more punch . . . if
you promise me you'll wait here quietly. Can you do that? Can you
wait here quietly?"

"Oh, yes," says Casper. "I promise. I'll wait. I won't make a peep."

"Good," says Anne and starts to move away with Casper's cup.

"But hurry!" he calls as she goes.

Now he rolls his head to the side and looks dazed, ashamed, and
glassy-eyed at Hayes. "I was dreaming about my old bloodhound

Scruggs," he says. "He was racing around and barking like mad, and I was trying to get him to keep still, but he was in too much of a fluster . . . all wet from the rain and yelping . . . determined to get me into a tussle with the landlord."

Anne returns in a minute and satisfies Casper's orders: another opium pill and more of the brandy punch. She gets him settled for the night and tidies the bedcovers, then turns her attentions businesslike to Hayes. She takes a clean towel from her apron, wets and wrings it in the basin, and as she bathes Hayes's face and arms, she works without her usual smile and without speaking. He inhales the scent of her lavender water. He hears music coming from the next ward, not far away, a melodeon, male and female voices, a plaintive folk hymn. Anne begins to hum along with the tune, and when Hayes looks up, he sees that her cheeks glow with tears. As he meets her eye she is not at all timid but radiates the quiet composure of a long-abiding friend. Silently, she tells him not to worry, it's late, she's tired and overwrought, but she'll be all right. Silently, he tells her he's never been one to take tears too sharply.

There was a time, back in Brooklyn, when his sister had tilted her head ever so slightly and given him a look that seemed to say, *Who are you?* Now Anne tilts her head similarly but looks at him with bone-deep empathy. Astonishing him, she scrapes with one bare knuckle the tears from her cheeks and rubs them onto his.

"War paint," she whispers, drawing a wet line straight down beneath each of his eyes.

Next she coaxes him forward so she can wash the nape of his neck. She remarks on how long his hair has grown, pulls down his shirt collar, and spreads it wide, then resumes bathing him, softly singing along with the music from the next ward, " 'I'll march to Canaan's land, I'll land on Canaan's shore, / Where pleasures never end, and troubles come no more. / Farewell, farewell, farewell, my loving friends, farewell.' "

WHEN THE MOSQUITO CURTAINS are lowered over the beds in the dim gaslight, they resemble broad tree trunks with pale-golden bark—

bark so tissuelike that Hayes, who lives inside one of the trees, can look through it into the dreamy orchard. During the night, he sees Walt, sitting close to Casper and writing in one of his scrapbooks as he so often does. Sometime later, Walt has gone, but Babb is kneeling by Raugh's bed and sliding his arms beneath Raugh's pillow. What Babb doesn't understand is that Raugh sleeps most of the day and lies awake, eyes closed, most of the night. One large powerful hand shoots out and clamps Babb by the neck. With supernatural strength, Raugh lifts him from the floor and thrusts him choking and gagging into a distant part of the orchard. Still later, Matron stops by, dressed for travel and looking, as they say, not quite right in the upper story. Gazing intently at Hayes, eyes bulging, she laughs softly and says, "I have Graves' disease, you see, and must go to my mother's house in Maryland." She slips something beneath Hayes's pillow, adding, "This might be useful to you," and disappears. Soon somebody climbs inside the tree with Hayes and snuggles next to him. Hayes, sitting up quickly, smells brandy and sickness, and then a hatless and tremulous Casper, sweating profusely, lays his head on Hayes's chest, his bandaged stump resting heavily against Hayes's belly. "You're the best chum a fellow could ever have, Mr. X," says Casper, loud, and Hayes hushes him.

"You share your apples and never criticize," continues Casper, more softly, "and I'm going to tell you a secret I wouldn't tell another body in all creation. I was glad when I got shot. I thought, *Good, now I can get fixed up and go home.* Even after the surgeon was done with his sawing, I told myself it was better to go home with one hand than to die with two. Put your arms around me, will you?"

Hayes holds Casper, despite the odor and the sweat, for what else can he do? In a matter of seconds Casper's breathing becomes even and regular. A good while later, he lets out a great sigh and grows markedly heavier.

"I'll tell you something else, too, Mr. X," he whispers. "I don't plan to kick up a dust when the time comes . . . but honestly, I'd prefer not to die."

———

THE YEAR BEFORE the Hayeses traveled to Ireland and perished in a Dublin canal, Mr. Hayes borrowed a boat from a physician friend and took the family rowing on a Sunday afternoon in July. Summerfield, fifteen and strong for his age, stationed himself at the rear rowing thwart and took up one pair of oars. Mr. Hayes, with the other pair, sat forward, behind him, and the two women placed themselves, with parasols, aft. It was a splendid afternoon of familial harmony and church bells, tall sails and whistles in the harbor, warm breezes and towering white clouds. Summerfield, inexperienced at rowing but naturally able, found the thrill of propulsion over the water—the direct link between muscle and motion—nearly dizzying. When they'd got a good ways upriver, not far from the bank, Mr. Hayes, worn out and winded, ordered Summerfield to stop, please, and to *breathe* for a minute.

As the boat began to drift, Summerfield gazed toward the river's edge and was shortly entranced by the interaction of shapes at the bank: one line of trees, low and dark near the water, appeared to move in counterpoint to another, bright upon a bluff, and above the higher line a tier of majestic clouds played a faster melody all its own. This visual suggestion of music made him think of the wonderful moment when a batsman knocks a ball into the field, igniting among the players a burst of movement. Without stopping to think, he pointed and cried, "Look!"

The others turned their heads and watched in silence for a few seconds. His father said, "What is it, Summerfield? I don't see anything."

His mother said, "Oh, yes, I see—there's a jolly fisherman just there in the shade . . . exactly like a painting."

"No," answered Summerfield, "not that. Look at the way everything moves."

Mrs. Hayes returned her eyes to the bank, bewildered, and Mr. Hayes patted Summerfield's shoulder and said, facetiously, "Yes, son, everything does move, doesn't it?"

Sarah, who'd never taken her gaze from the bank and left it there still, said, "He means the lovely way the trees and the clouds drift against one another, even as we drift in our little boat."

She turned and smiled at Summerfield. He said, "It made me think of base ball."

At his back, he heard his father's hearty laugh, but Sarah twirled her parasol gaily and said, "Of course . . . when the ball's struck and all the players scamper this way and that. Why, Summerfield, you're an athlete *and* a poet."

MIDDAY, Babb passes the end of the bed, and Hayes spies a necklace of purple bruises about the man's neck. This prompts him to reach beneath his pillow, where he finds a creased and oil-stained scrap of paper—on it, written in all capital letters:

CAPT. GRACIE

+

ABIGAIL COX, WARD K

As he folds the note and slips it into a pocket of his trousers, he catches Raugh watching him from the next bed with a terrible and familiar pleading look in his eyes. At first he experiences the alarm of being discovered at something secret, but then a chill goes down his spine; he feels his own heart race as his hands start to tremble. A compulsion to run so pervades him he quickly leaves the bed, but immediately, in the crowded aisle, he collides with Babb, who says, "Where *you* going? Oh, I forgot . . . you can't answer me, can you?"

At this close range Hayes can see among the bruises on Babb's neck the clear imprint of a thumb.

"Boo!" says Babb, laughs, and moves away.

Hayes returns to the bed and ventures a glance at Raugh, whose sunken eyes have resumed their usual ceiling-gazing. Hayes thinks the man's resemblance to Abe Lincoln superficial, a shared gauntness and cut of whiskers. Hayes sits on the bed with his back to Raugh and studies Casper, passed out drunk in the middle of the day. The boy's name is Casper Mallet, one of his arms has been amputated, and he's dying of a disease called pyemia, yet—these particulars aside—he is very much like Billy Swift, who did *not* give a bowie knife to Hayes before he was abandoned in the field, for Billy Swift at that time was already dead (though Hayes cannot quite recall how Swift died). The knife came from a likable Zu-Zu with a big black mustache and a red fez, Felix Rosamel, which accounted for the initials F.R. on the knife's handle. But what has become of the knife now? Hayes supposes it would have been taken from him by whoever brought him to the hospital. The lost and unaccounted-for knife—in his mind's eye, the size of a sword, humming and vibrating against a bank of iridescent clouds—seems suddenly crucial and dangerous: like a loose thread in a story, it will reappear, doubtless in the wrong hands, doubtless for the purpose of cutting his throat.

To shake off this grim vagary, he again stands and moves among the crowd in the central aisle. He finds his way to the bath-room and the small round mirror that hangs there on a wall. He puts his mouth inches from the mirror and watches his lips move as he tries to form the words *Summerfield Hayes*. He tries again and again, making no sound whatsoever but causing a worrisome mental sensation—the muscles that govern his lips and tongue seize control of the task, steer matters their own way, and soon have him mouthing gibberish, the independent little fluttering machine in the mirror (flashing two rows of teeth) comical and scary. He pulls himself away and leaves the bath-room, and as he threads through the aisle back to the bed, he wonders if he saw in the mirror a reflection of gibberish or if the repetition of the two words that constitute his name (so long unsounded, so long unheard) only struck him as gibberish.

The brass and sooty lamp on its chain works its magic. He stares at it long enough to calm himself, and soon even the brown rat that peers down from the rafter seems a friend. Before long Hayes feels sleepy. Not only is the hospital fare making people sick, there is likely some sort of sleeping potion in the water. He dozes off but only briefly, for he's shortly roused by an extraordinary hubbub throughout the ward, a kind of gentle uprising, reverential and happy in nature. He has dreamed of his sister—as they walked together beneath overarching and leaf-shedding oaks, she kept changing into the nurse Anne and then back again into herself—and now, when Hayes opens his eyes, the surgeon in chief stands at the foot of Raugh's bed with Captain

Gracie, two other members of the guard, and no less than the president of the United States, who holds in one hand a black stovepipe hat.
Hayes hears the surgeon say, "I thought you might like to meet your
long-lost brother," and Mr. Lincoln looks down at the sleeping Raugh
and smiles. As he smiles, the crevices in his face close together like the
ribs of a fan, rucking the pouched skin beneath the eyes, and the large
ears (like seashells) move upward a fraction of an inch. Hayes thinks it
the face of a man diligent yet bereaved and that he has come in from
bad weather—his tie's askew, his forelock drops low toward the bridge
of the nose, and a fob chain appears on the brink of spilling from its
vest pocket. After a moment, the president says, "Yes, I do believe I
see the resemblance."

He loses the smile and adds, "Of course, they are each my brother,
only this unlucky man *looks* the part."

After he says this, he chuckles drily, his gaze shifts to Hayes, and
then he inclines his head to allow Dr. Bliss to whisper something in his
ear. Though Hayes trusts in his heart of hearts that he's only dreaming, he starts to get to his feet, but the president says, "Stay as you are,"
bends forward, and reaches for his hand. He looks deeply into Hayes's
eyes, and Hayes senses a nearly whole presence pouring forward to
greet him, even with some never-shared part withheld. The great
man's hand is noticeably soft and cool. "I extend to you the gratitude
of our nation, son," he says, "and wish you a full and fast recovery."

As he releases his hand, Hayes notices a fever blister the size of a
half dime on Lincoln's lower lip and detects the scent of his breath,
which he likens to a mix of anise and oatmeal. When the entourage
moves on, Hayes catches sight of Raugh, now watching them go—
crushed and bitter Raugh, who'd only pretended to sleep throughout.

IN THE AFTERNOON, storm clouds darken the sky, and the air grows
heavy and hot, suffused with the stench from the canal. The unrest
incited by the president's surprise visit lingers long after his departure,
the ward noisier and more crowded than ever, and when rain begins
to pelt the roof, visitors who might otherwise have moved on continue
to mill about. The flags and mosquito curtains stir and flap in the

winds that erupt through the windows, and soon lightning and thunder add to the turmoil.

Casper wakes from his nap raving, Babb and a medical steward escort him away, and when he returns a few minutes later from wherever they took him, he's benumbed, and insists on getting into bed with Hayes. This of course is not allowed, and Casper, looking yellowish and dazed, sinks into a sulk. Immediately Hayes thinks of the little mirror in the bath-room, the "fluttering machine" there, and notes a shift in his feelings—though previously resigned to muteness, entirely acquiescent, now he would be pleased to explain to Casper that it's too hot in the ward today for sharing a bed.

When Walt shows up around three o'clock, he brings with him a friend, whom he introduces to Hayes and Casper as Mr. Burroughs. The two men divest themselves of wilted-looking hats and drenched umbrellas, and Burroughs takes the only chair as Walt sits on the end of Hayes's mattress. Walt tells them that his friend often guides him on walks in the Washington forests, and though Mr. Burroughs works for the Treasury Department, his heart and soul reside in "the wilds and the woodlands."

Burroughs—in his late twenties, handsome and slender, well dressed in business attire, clean shaven, with dark chin-length locks—impresses Hayes immediately as a cheering, helpful sort of man, and quite enamored of Walt. At Walt's urging, he is soon amusing them with his ability to imitate birdcalls. Casper, at first buoyed up, quickly appears to drift—which Hayes construes as an indication that whatever drug the steward dosed him with earlier has taken its full effect.

"Most assuredly the hermit thrush!" cries Walt now. "I would recognize it anywhere. I don't know how you do it, John."

"It's not as good as you think," says Burroughs, "but I continue to practice . . . continue to improve, I hope."

"I didn't see it before, John," says Walt, "but you and our Mr. X bear a striking resemblance, don't you think? You might be—"

"*Tweet, tweet, tweet, tweet,*" cries Casper, wagging his head side to side. "*Chirp, chirp, chirp!*"

Walt looks at him with mild irritation and sympathy. "Aha," he says, "that must be the Casper-bird," and Casper casts him a look of suspicion, as if he can't determine whether or not he has been insulted. Hayes finds himself wishing he could tell Walt about Casper's being carried from the ward earlier and drugged.

As lightning ignites the windows and a rumble of thunder rolls through the pavilion, shaking the floor and walls, Mrs. Duffy arrives in a high-starched bonnet to offer her imperious hymn-shrieking. Hayes flinches, squeezes his eyes shut for a moment, and stuffs his hands into his pockets. A great clatter of wagon wheels and horses rises up out in the street. Bells toll, near and far away, and a bugle sounds in the distance. Rain drums the roof, and it seems to Hayes that the scores of people in the ward fairly shout at one another to make themselves heard.

Just then Anne, obviously in a rush, stops by and places a crown made out of paper onto Walt's head. She leans in and kisses him on the knob of his cheek above his whiskers. She gives him a small jar and says, "For your birthday, dear Walt. My mother's own berry preserves, and they're for *you* so don't go giving them away."

Walt, quite red-faced, thanks her and then receives a kiss on the cheek from Burroughs as Anne departs. At that moment Captain Gracie passes by in the aisle and looks at Walt with such open contempt that Burroughs raises his eyebrows and says, "I don't think you'll be getting any birthday kiss from that man. A friend of yours?"

"He despises me," says Walt. "Thinks me a shirker and a coward. He would have me on a battlefield in Virginia, a soldier rather than a soldiers' missionary."

Burroughs laughs and says, "I can scarcely imagine anything more incongruous than you, Walt, killing people."

Hayes observes that Casper—who doesn't seem to have noticed Captain Gracie—stares at Walt and the paper crown with amused puzzlement. After a moment, as if to change the subject in his own mind, Casper extends his stump toward Burroughs and says, "Won't you give the wee babe a pat? We're generally shy with strangers, but we like your kindly eyes and your fancy cravat."

Burroughs pats the stump, smiling, and Casper pulls it back, crying, "Not so hard, it hurts!"

"I'm ever so sorry," says Burroughs and looks at Walt for guidance.

"John," says Walt, "why don't you show us another one, an easy one we can all do? What about the barred owl?"

Burroughs looks doubtful but smiles again, clears his throat, and croons, *"Hoo, hoo, hoo-hoo, hoo, hoo, hoo-hooooo."*

Walt mimics him, not nearly as convincing, and then says, "You try it, Casper."

Casper—who is gazing blankly at the small patch of floor between the beds and caressing his stump—says, "That Dr. Drum took Major Cross with him to Philadelphia. He means to electrify him. Why does my Joanie not come to see me?"

Softly, Walt says, "I'll write to her again, dear boy, this very day."

Casper raises his head briefly and then returns his eyes to the spot on the floor. He slowly allows his eyelids to drop. He whispers, "Will you tell her I'm sorry . . ." and, even while the others are still looking at him, dozes off.

After a moment, Burroughs turns to Walt and says, "His girl, I presume?"

"Fiancée," says Walt, "though I must say, she doesn't behave like one. Has so far sent him exactly one silly letter, mostly regarding itself—all about the letter paper, where she'd bought it and at what cost, and about the ink, which she'd made in her mama's own kitchen, from copperas and nutgalls. Went on at length about the coming of horsecars to Providence, Rhode Island, and then urged Casper 'to try not to be too dumpish.' I've written her myself and received no reply."

Walt pauses and brings his hands together below his lips—sadly, thoughtfully, as if he's about to pray. He raises his head and looks searchingly at Casper, then says to Burroughs, "I regret you didn't meet him before. Nobody asks my opinion, of course, but I think he's about as ruined by remedies as by infection. What you see here is the vestige of a charming and witty young fellow—now brandy-fuddled, now drug-addicted—but once resilient . . . and handsome, though you would hardly know it."

He sets aside his cane and lifts a bulging haversack from the floor; he places the jar of preserves inside and then takes out one of his scrapbooks, into which he scribbles a note. As he bends to put it away, and still leans forward, he says, "Look around you, John, and tell me what you truly think. Now we see that General Grant evidently believes we can supply him an infinite store of young men for slaughter . . . does the price of victory not grow too great?"

He sits up straight again and adds, "You know there's no keener advocate of union than me—I grasp, probably more than most, how democracy profits from a meshing of conflicts and contradictions . . . a play of cross-purposes. But shall we preserve it at a cost of five white corpses for each black slave freed? Ten for each? Twenty? Twenty-five? Where shall we draw the line?"

"I've heard he's a good deal drunk, Grant," says Burroughs, "though I doubt that distinguishes him among generals."

Hayes detects in Walt's face a hint of disappointment at Burroughs's response, which has sought to join sides with him while neglecting his question. Burroughs, apparently detecting the same, says, "The world's turned on its head nowadays, Walt—an effect that's been a long time coming."

"Oh, I don't mind that," says Walt, waving away Burroughs's notion with one hand. "I even like to think myself a modest contributor. But look to the future. Our youth and our nation are the same thing—what we do to them we do to it. Seeing them—and by extension it—dismembered, disemboweled, cut down and left to rot in the open air . . . buried in an unmarked grave . . . that's what troubles me."

Burroughs appears to be contriving an addendum to his previous remark when Walt turns to Hayes and says, "Won't you try the barred owl for us, my friend? I bet you could whistle it if you only tried. It would make me such a lovely birthday gift. Demonstrate it again, please, John."

Hayes quickly shakes his head, overwhelmed by the confounding clamor in the ward; thinking *infinite store,* he imagines himself liquefied and poured through Major Cross's knothole beneath the bed. When he turns his head to the side, the sunken-eyed Raugh, strangely awake, casts him a knowing smile, which he cannot interpret and which causes him to shudder. He thinks of his ornery and garrulous bunkmate, Truman Leggett, and how, at the end of the first day of fighting in the Wilderness, he'd sought him in the woods and sat next to him on the ground for hours, under starlight, and of how neither of them had said a word.

"Never mind, my boy," he hears Walt say now. "We don't mean to upset you."

The fetid smell of the canal wafts in through the nearest window, and Burroughs groans and covers his nose and mouth with a handkerchief. Walt looks at Hayes with eyes blurred by tears but immediately seems to shake himself.

"Do you know," he says, a bit too blithely, "we saw no fewer than three dead cats floating in the canal on our way over here? It's ghastly beyond words. We were nearly run over in the street half a dozen times, splattered with mud, and accosted by a crazy woman who took us for her father and brother. She delayed us considerably, and then we arrive to learn we've only just missed seeing Mr. Lincoln."

He turns to Burroughs and adds, "It's not fair, is it, my darling Bertie?"

"No, my sweet papa," answers Burroughs. "Not at all fair."

"That's what the crazy woman kept calling us," says Walt to Hayes, "darling Bertie and sweet papa."

He sighs and continues, "I suppose fate means to deprive me of ever meeting Mr. Lincoln . . . only to come near but never to meet. We nod to each other from opposite sides of a road, lock eyes across a grand portico, wave as he passes aboard a carriage . . . but alas, I expect we shall never exchange a word. A cosmic omission if you ask me."

Hayes peers again at Raugh, who is so clearly sound asleep it makes him think he only imagined the chilling smile. Beyond, a few beds away, a man with a grotesquely swollen face and protruding tongue weeps as he catches in a tin the river of saliva that flows from his mouth. Hayes wishes he could ask Walt what illness could cause such a hideous symptom.

"It's probably just as well," says Burroughs, pulling a watch from his vest pocket and checking the time. "With all your reverence, Walt, meeting him would likely be a letdown."

"How do you know my reverence mightn't be deepened?" asks Walt.

"First, I don't think that's possible," says Burroughs, laughing. "And second, I believe most of our heroes benefit from a polite distance."

"Yes, well, you also believe Shakespeare's plays were written by Francis Bacon."

"I believe no such thing," says Burroughs. "You confuse me with your friend O'Connor!"

"Oh, yes, yes, foolish me," says Walt. "Sorry."

"Walt, are you all right?"

"Obviously not," says Walt. "I imagine it's the bad air at my new accommodations, my moldy boardinghouse."

"Most unfortunate, your having to move," says Burroughs. "Sixth Street was altogether better for you . . . and farther from the canal. I say, what *is* that incessant caterwauling?"

"Why, that's the Songbird of the Washington City Hospitals," answers Walt. "Our treasure, Mrs. Duffy. The Source of All Things Annoying."

Walt now smiles at Hayes benevolently, as if he would remind him of their short sweet history, and with this smart appraisal of Mrs. Duffy, bind them together once and for all. The hammer-and-nails of the rain on the roof stops sharply, causing Hayes to catch his breath. A fresh and genuine desire hatches in his mind, fancifully assuming the mental image of a silver-blue fish that wriggles at the end of a line, spokes of sunlight flashing from its scales. He looks first at Burroughs, then at Walt, and says, "Is there any way you can make her shut up?"

⇥ FIVE ⇤

Letters

Dearest Sarah, these will likely be the last words you have from me, for I can see no road that takes me back to you alive. I confess that I am weak in mind & body. For a long time I have been a patient at a military hospital in Washington City. As foreseen, I survived the battlefield in the month of May, but I cannot discern God's design in my survival.

I regret the air of self-pity.

I cannot see God's design in my survival unless it is punishment. Now that the whitewashers have removed the oil lamp from over my bed—a measure, I believe, meant to undo me further—I have found this new device to be steadying in a similar way—mentally composing letters to you that will never be written down or sent. Sometimes, as now, as another dawn approaches & I'm unable to sleep, I think of you at home & long to see you.

I am quite wasted, from a persistent lack of appetite.

I consume a bare minimum of food & drink, for food & drink here—I am convinced—are the agents of poison & debilitating drugs. As a result, I am wasted, I fear, beyond easy recognition. In Virginia—oh, so long ago—Dr. Speck said that if I should find myself in a hospital, I should avoid drugs to the degree possible. I count among my modest achievements here that I have managed to avoid any that have not either been forced upon me or administered covertly.

My dear Sarah, these will likely be the last words you have from me, for I cannot see my way back to Hicks Street. Every day brings a new danger.

Down toward the wardmaster's room, somebody whispers with the night watcher at his small table. Clouds of tobacco smoke surround the two figures. Across the way, there is a flag with a crooked hem—on the wall above the window some sort of pastoral scene in a triangular frame, & a brown stain upon the plaster the size & shape of a horse's head.

In the Wilderness, I saw a horse, struck by a bullet—its front legs buckled, & its rider (a lieutenant colonel I didn't know) rolled headfirst over the poll. Leaves, propelled by the fallen animal's breath, skittered across the ground.

I have lost the ability to speak. Though my tongue is uninjured, there seems to be a defect in the nerves. I have spoken a single sentence since my arrival here, a question, & so shocking it was that Walt collapsed upon the floor—by my count, nearly three weeks ago, on the occasion of his birthday.

Walt stood—evidently thrilled & stunned to hear me speak—laughed heartily, & fainted dead away—in truth, not the effect of my speaking, but of the illness that provokes the doctors to urge him home. I regret to say that I've seen less of him since then, & each time he has come lately, looking pale & played-out, I wonder if it won't be the last. Due to overcrowding, the guard now turns away many visitors at the door. I cannot tell how they determine whom to allow in & whom to turn away.

Tents have been erected outdoors to accommodate the ever-mounting number of sick & wounded arriving from Virginia. If I could get myself transferred to a bed in one of these tents, an escape might be more manageable. The question is, Escape to what?

Walt's friend Burroughs has come by a couple of times on his own, bearing gifts from Walt for Casper & me. I find Burroughs a bit inscrutable (one of Papa's favorite words, do you remember?). While he's affable enough, I've come to think he exercises some supernatural control over my nerves—it was he who caused me to speak that first & only time, he who prevents me from speaking further now. How utterly cracked . . . supernatural control! If I do indeed end up in the asylum, it will be no wonder.

A commission of surgeons & officers has come through, determining the various fates of us in the beds. By their prescript, I'm to be removed to the Asylum for the Insane until I'm improved, though I've the distinct impression that people do not improve at the Asylum for the Insane. I've no idea how long it will be before this prescript is enforced, but I am hoping to gain back my power of speech—or at the very least my ability to hold a pencil . . . then make my case for returning to the front. I don't see why muteness should disqualify me. Except for my being wasted, a condition that could be remedied with generous portions of untainted food, I'm fit in every other way. Still, seeing how I'm perceived by the staff here, I suspect that even if I were to explain the real circumstances that brought me here—recount my being abandoned in the field on orders of a drunken sergeant—no one will believe me. As you can see, my dear Sarah, it's a muddle. I hope this letter finds you disposed favorably toward me in general. I must say I think it was unworthy of you to use our mother's feelings against me as you did those last days in Brooklyn.

HE HEARS a low rumble of laughter, turns his head to the side, and sees Raugh through the two layers of mosquito curtain. Raugh looks back at him, grinning, eyes wet and shiny in the dim light of near dawn.

"I'm defeated," says Raugh, softly, "defeated, see?"

He holds Hayes's undoubtedly baffled gaze for a moment and laughs again. He points toward the end of the bed and repeats, "De . . . feated."

The ward is sweltering and still, pervaded by tobacco smoke. Hayes cannot think what Raugh means—they are each of them in some way defeated, after all, and surely there's nothing amusing about it. He looks over at the man again, who eyes him as before and points toward the end of the bed.

"De . . . feated," he says, and Hayes, seeing the abrupt curve of

Raugh's stumps beneath the bedsheet, understands at last. He manages a smile, even as a wave of nausea heaves through him.

Raugh grins and nods, his eyes brimming with tears; he sighs and rights his head on the pillow, looking up into the rafters. "Poor Randall Abner Raugh," he whispers. "De-feeted at Spotsylvania Court House."

Here's a riddle you will like from our chaplain's little gazette: Why is the pupil of the eye to be pitied? Because it is continually under the lash!

Casper's raving has become so intolerable they keep him now in a drug-stupor night & day. The man down the way who sometimes wept as he endeavored to catch the river of saliva that poured from his mouth has been removed at last to the deadhouse. Most of his hair & teeth had fallen out. Three days before the man passed, Burroughs was here with Walt, & observing the sorry spectacle of the poor man with his tin cup, Burroughs said to Walt, You see, that's what comes of stubborn doctors & their heroic dosing. His remark seemed to carry a warning & indeed Walt replied, Don't worry, John, I'm not taking any calomel. Burroughs, quite disgusted, went on to say he knew for a fact that the Surgeon General had banned this drug last year & he, John, couldn't see why it was still allowed. I know nothing of the calomel or its uses, but I pray that none has been slipped into my food or water.

There is so much I have not told you—nothing of battle (I have spared you that), nothing of my improbable journey through the Virginia forest. I cannot tell where God is in all this. I fear that in our recklessness we have repelled Him.

Casper has been mumbling angrily in his sleep about a certain "Millerite." I wonder if you've heard of it? I wonder what it means?

My perceptions cannot entirely be trusted, but everything about the hospital— its sights & sounds & smells, its atmosphere—strikes me as a kind of limbo, somewhere between life & death.

I imagine it lacks the concrete of Heaven, too, if there should be anything like concrete there. I have been thinking of the "fire that does not consume," for frequently

I witness out of the corner of my eye flames & smoke, even when there are none actually there. I would think it a premonition of catastrophe, but somehow it feels to issue more from the past, not the future.

Captain Gracie smiles now when he passes the foot of my bed, a smile sweet with malice & secret knowledge. I believe he's unhappy with my impending transfer to the Asylum for the Insane & that he still contrives to see me court-martialed as a deserter. I believe that before all is said & done, he will succeed.

My wounds have been entirely neglected. It is clearer to me every day that the hospital is keeping me sick & if only I can escape it I'll regain my health & be fit to fight again.

They are only figments of my imagination, I know, I know, but still they terrify me when they appear. If you had asked me before the war whether or not I believed in ghosts, I would have said no. (Surely, if ghosts existed, our own parents would have returned to bid us farewell.) Always at the end of my bed, always at night, first Leggett, then Billy Swift. Of course I dare not cry out. I wonder if they mean to remind me that they are dead, for I do often forget. If they must appear, I wish they would appear friendlier. I believe we loved one another in the condensed way of comrades. I cannot think of any harm I did either of them.

. . . quite deteriorated, the drugs . . . the whirring in my ears has come back, put there by Burroughs, I think . . .

The happy thing about letters such as these is that I needn't weigh repercussions. No need to worry about increasing your concern, no need to spare you certain details.

A mute man can kill as competently as any other, perhaps even better—think how blind people hear more keenly than those with sight.

Among the advantages of the battlefield . . . here, I cannot tell friend from enemy even though they stand before me visible. My mind hurls possibilities & I'm helpless to distinguish what's true or false. What even is Walt? I cannot even discern the man's <u>category</u>!

At times I wonder: Have I concocted the story of the sergeant on his horse, fabricated "Leave him . . . I've no time to play nursemaid," fabricated "Take his weapon"? If so, was it not to cover the fact of my desertion? Desertion, after all, is what best explains my having no documentation of any discharge (no matter how informal it may have been). What I must admit to, finally, is the deeply flawed—no, I should say, depraved—nature of my character . . .

. . . deeply depraved character of my nature . . .

Yes, it's a depraved nature that brought me to this place & likewise drove me from Hicks Street, away from your love & companionship, drove me into the abyss of battle, & if I am indeed a deserter drove me to that as well. I find myself robbed, dear Sarah, of all . . .

. . . horrible, horrible nightmares . . . I dare not cry out . . .

My dear Sarah, these will likely be the last words you have from me. I shall be candid here, for nobody can read what has not been written down.

I cannot explain how it is that the urging in the pit of my stomach (hunger), combined with a certain hollowed-out feeling, keeps me settled on Earth. Otherwise I fear I might disappear.

It was a group of men, perhaps as many as a dozen. They asked all the usual questions. I believe I tore at my clothing in their presence, because of the sudden & profuse bleeding of my wounds. Now, when the bell rings outdoors, it's as if it rings inside my skull. The clank & clang of the trains, the sundry calls & whistles, the clattering of wheels & clopping of hooves are like a grand Death-chorus. The stench of the canal sanctifies the air in preparation for . . .

Evidently, what began as a steadying device no longer steadies. I love you, my dear one—no, I will not call you sister here, not now—I love you, with all my heart. You twirled your parasol at the front of the boat, smiled down at me as if you knew me better than any other person on Earth, knew me better than I knew myself. You said, Why, Summerfield, you're an athlete & a poet. The calamity in

Ireland, the loss of Mommy & Papa, only pushed us together closer than we were already.

Nobody can read what has not been written down.

What began as a steadying device no longer steadies.

My dear Sarah, I was wounded & abandoned in the Wilderness. When the army moved out of the Wilderness, they left me behind. I have no papers to prove it, as I wasn't formally discharged.

In the dream, Walt brings a bulging haversack & lays it on my bed. When he opens it, it's everything I'm missing: my uniform, intact; my forage cap; my weapon (though it's broken into many parts, I'm sure I can reassemble it); my canteen, which has a bullet hole in it; my red novel, my Dickens, given me by you; the base ball, given me by the chaplain, varnished & inscribed, 25 April 1864, Bachelors 24, Twighoppers 21; my shoes; & a packet of letters from you. I hadn't realized you'd written me so often. What happened to the letters I carried with me in the forest, I couldn't recall (nor can I recall it now). I am awakened by a man's crying out in pain, Casper, I think at first, but it turns out to be a nurse who has stubbed his toe on the iron leg of a bed. It's just dawn & I feel more clear-headed than I've felt for days. All this time I've been imagining my return to Brooklyn—humiliated, compromised in any number of ways . . . & now I see that fighting's my true fate, if only it can be managed. I long to be back with my friends, my comrades, Leggett & Billy Swift & Vesey & Rosamel & the others. I sense, even as I imagine this, that there's an insurmountable problem, though I cannot name it. I do understand I'll need to make sure my wounds have healed properly, which I believe they will. The whirring inside my ears will cease, I'm confident of that, for it has ceased before. My speech will return. I'll be all right. When the war is won, when victory comes, I'll be a part of it . . . & it will be part of me.

CASPER, who has developed two fresh abscesses on his left cheek, looks up at Anne, quite pathetically, and says, "I only asked him to bring me back some potatoes."

She has just finished rewetting his dressing with cold water and now dries her hands on her apron. She has taken to wearing her hair in curls, which, under Matron's watch, would never have been permitted. "Yes," she says to Casper, "and Mr. X, being the good fellow he is, brought you some. But, Casper, you're not allowed potatoes."

"I know I'm not," says Casper, looking straight ahead now, vacantly. "That's why I wanted them."

Hayes, who has pilfered from the dining room a small plate of boiled potatoes, puts it on the table and then sits on his own bed. He finds it difficult to look directly at Casper, for the boy's face has become a horror—the skin, splotched yellow and pink, sags and tugs down the lower eyelids, exposing the salmon-colored inner tissue, the abscesses, whose purplish aureoles overlap, peaked with pustules.

"I'm sorry, Casper," says Anne. "I can bring you some beef tea."

"I don't want no beef tea."

"What about a cup of milk?"

"I don't want no milk."

"Casper—"

He grabs her hand now and says, "What's the matter with everybody? Can nobody see I'm dying?"

Tears spring from his eyes, a remarkable sight as they arc toward the bedcovers and catch the orange light of sunset through the window. Anne turns and looks back at Hayes. She glances down the length of the ward, one way and the other, and then returns her eyes to Hayes, who reaches for the plate of potatoes and passes it into her free hand.

She places it in Casper's lap and whispers, "Eat them quickly then."

Which he does, using his fingers and making small squeaking noises.

Hayes watches for a moment, repulsed, a larger reaction than the thing deserves and having little to do with Casper's rapacious manners. Rather, it's Casper's begging that has offended him, the macabre and decisive argument of his dying, Anne's uneasy relenting, a plate of blandest cold potatoes made over as an offering of charity. He shuts his eyes and sees an image of Truman Leggett, forcing on him his sack of coffee mixed with sugar. He lowers his head, thinking, *Dearest Sarah, these will likely be the last words* . . . but then leaves off, recalling that this diversion no longer steadies him—no longer even diverts. Besides, when he has reviewed these fragmentary mental letters, he has found them wanting in both wit and wisdom. Among the several properties lost to his brief encounter with war, he supposes he must count his former modicum of ingenuity. Combat has dulled him, undoubtedly because combat's a dull business, befitting, after all, barbarians. This accounts, he thinks, for so much being made of military strategy and tactics, costume and matériel—they're meant to parade as warrantable, even noble, something that's fundamentally childish.

In the next moment, eyes still shut, a maddening whir inside his ears, he believes he has read similar sentiments expressed in newspaper editorials on the subject of grown men playing base ball. When he raises his head, he sees that Anne (holding an empty plate from the dining room) and Casper (licking the fingers of his one hand) each stare at him with a kind of wonderment.

Muttering, he thinks, *I have been muttering aloud.*

Anne sits next to him on the bed and starts to put her arm around his shoulders, but he pulls away, and she stands up again. His hands tremble madly, and so he squeezes them between his knees. He hears her say, "My dear Mr. X . . . don't you know by now I'm your friend?"

"'Friend,' ha, you're *sweet* on him!" cries Casper. "That's what makes him so scared. He pulled his pants down in front of the—"

"Oh, Casper, hush," says Anne and moves away quickly.

When Hayes raises his eyes, she is already gone.

Casper calls out, "Where's my punch? Where's my pill?" and then turns on Hayes a crushed-looking face.

He sighs, gives his stump a consoling pat, and shakes his head sadly. "I'll tell you one thing for sure," he says. "She's gonna be downright heartbroken when they cart you off to the booby hatch."

LEGGETT STANDS at the end of the bed, peering down at him through the mosquito curtain. The ward, bathed in amber light, is entirely quiet, but Hayes can hear the sound of a bell ringing somewhere outdoors, irregularly, as if blown by wind. Leggett stares at Hayes with his eyebrows arched and his mouth drawn into a straight line—as if he has just asked Hayes a question and awaits the answer. After a moment, he removes the canteen from his belt and takes a long drink, then offers it to Hayes.

A spiral of smoke rises from the opening in the canteen.

Hayes presses his hands over his eyes, and the moment he does so, he is filled with a longing for his father, as if it were his father's ghost at the end of the bed. He parts his fingers and sees that the specter has gone. He lowers his hands and turns onto his side.

Raugh, awake, looks at him wide-eyed and whispers, "Who was that?"

But Hayes pretends not to hear and closes his eyes again.

IN THE DREAM, he lies on his back somewhere warm and wet—he cannot tell where, for even though his eyes are wide open, he can see only absolute blackness. He hears a nearby crackle of fire, but whatever burns casts no light. Soon there's an increasing din of musketry, thundering artillery, and the maniacal rebel yell. What wakes him from the dream is not the noise but a startling awareness that he's bleeding from a wound at the middle of his spine and the warm wetness beneath him is his own blood.

A charred Billy Swift stands at the end of the bed, the whites of his eyes blazing in the ward's dark blue air. Billy has lost his cap. Wisps of smoke rise from the scorched fabric of his coat. He looks at Hayes with eyes like skewers, as if he means to read his mind or somehow see his future. At last his face softens, and he says, "It's a miracle, Hayes, a miracle," and then turns and limps away into a cluster of human-shaped shadows that appear to greet and envelop him.

HAYES FEELS a hand on his brow, and when he opens his eyes, he sees the face of Dr. Bliss, the hospital's surgeon in chief. "Wake up, son," says the major, "there's someone here who thinks he might know you."

The mosquito curtains have been drawn toward the rafters. Morning sunlight streams at a sharp angle through the windows on the opposite side of the ward. Hayes sits up partway and sees—standing at the end of the bed, precisely as Leggett and Swift had stood earlier—a uniformed surgeon, a large and strikingly handsome man, who smiles and narrows his gray eyes. "Yes," says the man, nodding, "though I might very well have missed him . . . his hair's grown long and he's terribly wasted."

"He's wasted because he doesn't eat," says Dr. Bliss. "And can't be persuaded to."

He turns back to Hayes and asks, "Do you know this gentleman? He says he met you at Brandy Station."

Naturally Hayes believes he's dreaming, but he gets to his feet anyway and salutes the man—who returns the salute, comes forward beaming and reeking of cigars, and pulls Hayes into a careful but firm embrace.

"You remember me," he whispers into his ear. "It's Speck, my boy . . . Dr. Speck."

He holds Hayes at arm's length, still smiling, and says, "Major Bliss, this young private was presumed dead by all who knew him."

"Oh, you know we're very good here," says Dr. Bliss. "He's not the first soldier we've managed to resurrect."

Dr. Speck laughs and says, "Well, I'm happy to report that this resurrected soldier is one of Brooklyn's finest young pitchers of the base ball . . . a member of the Eckford Club. Quite good at the bat as well and—"

Hayes's knees buckle and Dr. Speck catches him and settles him back onto the bed. He lifts Hayes's legs one at a time onto the mattress, and once he has got him arranged, he says, "Last week in Cold Harbor, I treated a certain Frenchman who revealed himself an acquaintance of yours."

He quickly confides to Dr. Bliss that a tree limb had fallen upon the Frenchman and fractured his shoulder. Then, to Hayes, he adds, "He told me the most extraordinary story about you."

Hayes recalls standing next to Leggett by a cooking fire and watching as Dr. Speck—who was assigned to a different regiment— walked away down a hillside; the doctor, whom Leggett called Major Sawbones, was suffering from the flux and turned abruptly and hurried toward the sinks. He recalls writing in a letter to Sarah that the surgeon who'd befriended him was named Speck, despite his being quite a large man.

Now Dr. Speck sits next to Hayes, leans down close, and peers into his eyes, as if he will mesmerize him. Softly he says, "You must start eating, my friend," and Hayes nods.

The doctor, never allowing his gaze to waver, says, "And you must speak to us, for there's no reason for you not to. Your voice still resides within you . . . you have only mislaid it."

Hayes turns his head to the side, but Dr. Speck rights him by the chin. "Look at me," he says. "I have absolute confidence in you. You might have walked through hell since I last saw you . . . I don't know . . . but you are still the exceptional young man who can hush the crowd at the Union Grounds . . . self-possessed as a man twice your age. I want you to take a deep breath, in and out, and then I want you to say my name aloud. Don't *try* to speak . . . Only speak."

Hayes inhales. He imagines himself running up to the line and releasing the ball inches from the ground, his knuckles nearly brushing the grass. He exhales and says, "Felix Rosamel."

He recognizes the voice as his own, though it sounds smaller than before, and dry, like Casper's.

Dr. Speck smiles and glances at Dr. Bliss. "That's the Frenchman with the fractured shoulder."

"Remarkable," says Dr. Bliss.

Hayes looks up at the surgeon in chief and says, "The attendant . . . the one named Babb . . . he steals money from the soldiers when they're sleeping."

"Is that so?" says Dr. Bliss.

Hayes, who can tell that the surgeon is more intrigued by his speaking than by what he has said, answers, "Yes . . . and he sells morphine to the ones in pain."

"Well—," starts the surgeon, but Raugh interrupts from the adjacent bed, surprising both Hayes and the two others.

"It's true," says Raugh in his deepest baritone. "He tried putting his hand under my pillow one night and got a good throttling for it."

———

"OF COURSE," says Walt with a dreamy look. "Your mother was a summer field and your father a haze . . . so naturally the happy product of their union would be a summer-field haze. Lovely."

Burroughs laughs and shakes his head, as if Walt has said something naughty. The three of them—Walt, Burroughs, and Hayes—sit at the end of a table in the dining room. It's the middle of the afternoon, and they are the only people left in the plain long room with its two rows of tables and one bare window.

"I believe I've heard of you," Walt says to Hayes. "I wonder if you've heard of me."

Hayes is thinking of Walt's remark about the summer field and the haze, and it has the effect of making him feel tired. At dinner, he made an effort to eat more than usual, and the fatigue revives his suspicions about the hospital food. He looks at Walt—who sits with his hands resting atop the silver handle of his cane—and notices, as if for the first time, the man's unusually high brow; also, there's a sunken quality to his cheeks Hayes has not seen before and a pained aspect to his eyes that never entirely goes away; his voice has grown so hoarse, he sounds now as if he's whispering everything he says.

"You're overwhelming him, Walt," says Burroughs. "Imagine how it must feel, to speak only a dozen words in all these weeks, and then be asked to—"

"Yes, yes, John, you're right, as usual," says Walt. "Where would I be without you to keep me in check? You tame me, and like a so-called lower animal, I end up loving you for it."

Burroughs bows his head in courtly fashion and says, "More than happy to oblige."

"You look splendid, my boy," says Walt to Hayes. "Freshly shaved and neat as a pin. Try not to be anxious. Remember, your supporters wildly outnumber any dandy self-seeking antagonists . . . and besides—"

"Besides," says Burroughs, "Walt won't allow anyone to bully you. You may be sure of it."

"That's right," says Walt, but Hayes observes a hint of self-doubt cross his face, even as he tries to veil it with a smile. Hayes has noticed variants of this symptom before: Walt's constant good nature is a cultivated thing, requiring preservation, and Hayes wonders if the always-pink rims of the man's eyes are not the mark of regular private weeping.

In truth, Hayes does not fear being bullied, not by the angry Captain Gracie or anyone else. He thinks perhaps he *should* fear it, but he has not been able quite to muster the feeling. He fears the hospital's catching fire. He fears being burned alive. He fears he might have actually already died in the Wilderness and that everything that has unfolded since (and unfolds still) is a sort of stagecraft, with none of the players being who they seem. He wants to believe that Dr. Speck's unexpected arrival in Washington is the miracle foretold just hours before it happened by Billy Swift's ghost. But he's afraid that at any moment what he perceives as Dr. Speck will change to a charred hull of the man, a kind of ashen gantry from which the soul has long departed. He wants to believe that now that he has found his mislaid voice, he might affect the course of his future for the better, but he fears, as he has feared all along, that finding it might work against him instead.

"I told you once, a while ago," says Walt, "and now I'll tell you again—"

But at that moment, the others—Captain Gracie and the two surgeons—enter the room. All three already at the table quickly stand, and Hayes notes that the room turns considerably darker. His salute seems to go unnoticed, and immediately, before Dr. Bliss can make any introductions, Captain Gracie says, "Why are these men here?"

"They are Private Hayes's friends," says Dr. Bliss.

"I see no need of them," says Captain Gracie. "What do we want here of infamous poets and poets' friends?"

"Well," says Dr. Bliss, smiling, "they're not here for you, Captain. I have given them permission to audit. Please, do try to proceed without needless insults. Walt, will you and Mr. Burroughs please take a seat over there?"

He indicates the opposite row of tables, to which Walt and Burroughs retreat. From Hayes's vantage, they are now only silhouettes, and Walt, possibly because of his being reduced to a silhouette, puts on his hat.

Dr. Bliss instructs Hayes to sit where he was sitting before, but the captain says, "I prefer the private to stand during questions."

"Private Hayes," says Dr. Bliss, with emphatic composure, "are you prepared to stand during the captain's questions?"

"Yes, sir," says Hayes, though his legs feel as if they might fold under him.

"Very well," says the surgeon. "But if the private is to stand, we'll all stand."

Dr. Speck, already seated opposite Hayes at the table and busy trimming a cigar, sighs and stands up again. Dr. Bliss draws a watch from his coat pocket and looks at it. "Since we find ourselves so inundated with new arrivals," he says, "and since that inundation is the cause for Dr. Speck's reassignment to us here, I'm eager to return him as quickly as—"

"Pardon me," calls out Walt from the other side of the room, "but should Mr. Burroughs and I stand as well?"

This provokes soft laughter from Dr. Speck, and Dr. Bliss says, "No, Walt, you should remain seated. Now, Captain Gracie, I was about to say—"

"If you wish to return Major Speck to the wards," says the captain, "you might let him go right now as far as it concerns me."

The surgeon in chief lowers his head for a moment, takes a breath, and then looks straight at the captain. "Sometimes, Captain, your lack of decorum tries my patience. As you know, I consider this interview unjustified, and I should think you might at the very least refrain from advising me, unbidden, in the process. Now, you have exactly five minutes."

"Thank you, sir, my apologies," says the captain. "I only meant that if the major would be more useful elsewhere, I don't want to be the cause of his detention."

Dr. Bliss looks down at his watch again, and at last the captain blinks his eyes, clears his throat, and turns to Hayes.

"Private Hayes," he says, "we've been told that following the battles in Virginia on the fourth, fifth, and sixth of May, you were deliberately abandoned in the field . . . by your commanding officers and by all other personnel . . . left to find your own way . . . purportedly to find your way back home. And this, without any sort of formal discharge."

"Yes, sir," says Hayes. "That is true."

"I wonder if you appreciate how such an improbable tale burdens our credulity?" asks the captain. "Abandoned on the battlefield by one's own comrades. And at a time when the army needs every possible—"

"Unfortunately, Captain," says Dr. Speck, "it's not so rare as you suggest. If it were, there wouldn't be a need for an order from the War Department stating—"

"Am I to have my five minutes?" says the captain to Dr. Bliss.

Dr. Bliss cautions Dr. Speck with a look.

Dr. Speck whispers, "Sorry," and returns his attention to lighting his cigar.

Hayes detects, beneath the floor, the gnawing and scratching of an animal trying to eat its way into the room. He thinks of Walt's saying *so-called lower animal* only minutes before. From the sash of the solitary window hangs a short piece of red ribbon, now and again stirred by a current of air, and outside, on the white clapboard wall of another building, sunlight blazes and then fades.

"At a time when the army needs every possible man," says the captain, "at a time when, for expediency sake, every kind of defect's overlooked . . . can you tell us why you would be cut loose?"

"No, sir," says Hayes. "I had temporarily lost my hearing. Despite my efforts to stay awake through the night, I fell asleep. The army was quitting the Wilderness. The bugles didn't wake me. When it was time to go, I wasn't ready. The officer said, 'Leave him. Take his weapon.'"

"What officer was that?"

"A sergeant, sir," says Hayes. "Unknown to me. I'd never seen him before."

"And to whom did he give these extraordinary orders?"

"To Private William Swift," says Hayes, "of my same regiment."

Across the table, Dr. Speck shakes his head.

"I have misremembered," says Hayes. "It was Felix Rosamel. Rosamel took my piece but secretly gave me his own bowie knife."

"Did he? And where is that knife now?"

Hayes has sometimes thought that Captain Gracie possesses the knife, but he doesn't say so now. He says, "I don't know, sir."

"And where exactly were you when this mysterious sergeant gave orders to someone named either Swift or Rosamel, who secretly gave you a bowie knife that has apparently vanished?"

"On the ground, sir."

"On the ground."

"Yes, sir."

"And why did you not get up from the ground?"

Hayes's right foot has gone numb. The noise beneath the floor grows ever louder, and he cannot think why someone doesn't do something about it. Now it sounds less like an animal's gnawing and more like the drone of an engine, the purr of turning wheels or gears— perhaps, he imagines, how an electrical motor might sound.

"And why did you not get up from the ground?" repeats the captain.

Hayes has lost the proper answer to this question, and finding it would require him to explore the Wilderness more painstakingly, which he would prefer to avoid. Impulsively, he says, "There was a horse."

"A horse?"

"Yes, sir. The sergeant rode a horse. He said, 'I've no time to be playing nursemaid.'"

Captain Gracie laughs and says, "Assuming these words were spoken by the sergeant and not by the horse, why did he think you in need of a nurse?"

"My shrapnel wounds were bleeding," says Hayes. "That's why I didn't get up from the ground."

"But Private Hayes," says the captain, "you didn't in fact have any shrapnel wounds, did you?"

Dr. Speck's tobacco smoke has virtually filled the room; a blue ring encircles the head of each of the three men near to Hayes. In the background, Walt and Burroughs appear to have dozed off, leaning upon each other. Hayes can tell exactly where the thing beneath the floor— animal or machine—will burst through, a spot under the table visible only to him and quite near his feet; the whirring has now become a hiss, within which voices intermittently communicate. Wholly distracted, Hayes says, "I'm sorry . . . would you repeat the question?"

The captain says, "I said that you were not in fact wounded, were you?"

It occurs to Hayes that the noise inhabits only the semicircular canals of his inner ear, and this explains why nobody else seems to mind it; it's but a new version of the saw's rasp already familiar to him. He recalls sitting on the ground in the Wilderness as the drunken sergeant peered down stoically from the saddle. He is struck anew by the man's resemblance to Captain Gracie, but he thinks this an observation best kept to himself. On the ground, he had removed both his coat and shirt in an effort to expose his wounds—he meant to see them, to assess their gravity—and his trousers were crumpled at his ankles, for one of the wounds burned at the back of his thigh. All about, the woods shuddered with the army's chaotic flight. The ground shook beneath him. He envisions himself as the drunken sergeant must have seen him, looking down from the saddle, and this view lends a new clarity. He recalls the remarkable silence of the ravaged forest: he remained on the ground and drew with a stick a circle around himself in the dirt; the entire army departed the Wilderness; and everything fell utterly still. He catches his breath now and speaks into the smoky dining room: "I *believed* that I was wounded, sir."

"Yes," says the captain, nodding and smiling sadly. "Evidently, Private Hayes, you *believed* a number of things."

Hayes interprets the captain's remark as an expression of sympathy. Surprised and encouraged, he says, "Yes, sir. I believed I would survive the battle . . . and I did. I believed I would be abandoned by my friends . . . and I was. I believed that war would make me a better man . . . but it has not."

"Is that why you chose to desert after only three days of battle?"

"Was it only three days?"

"Three days."

"It seemed much longer."

"No doubt," says the captain. "Tell me honestly, Private Hayes, were you not moved by a sense of duty to enlist but regretful once confronted with real fighting?"

This question strikes Hayes as a riddle, and he begins trying to parse it for the double entendre that might yield the right answer.

"Were you not, and are you not, eager to return to New York and get back to playing base ball?"

Hayes suspects the captain of laying a trap with these riddlelike questions, and he thinks he would do better to stand still than to step into it.

"I ask you," says the captain, "did you not in fact panic and run, and then later concoct a story to cover your tracks?"

In a certain book, Hayes has seen a drawing of the inner ear's labyrinth, which looked like something one might find in the wrackline at the seashore.

He hears himself say, softly, "I have wondered the same thing."

"Anyone can see the boy's unwell!" cries Dr. Speck. "You take advantage and purposely confuse him! How do you explain the fact that these same events were related to me by a man who witnessed them—a man who had nothing to gain by lying? And why is Private Hayes not reported by his company commander as having deserted?"

"I'm not a police detective," says the captain, "but I'm sure it could be worked out. In my judgment, it's a tale made of whole cloth . . . told by one of Private Hayes's good friends and brought to us by another."

"Now, see here—," starts Dr. Speck, but either stops himself or is stopped by the surgeon in chief.

"And isn't it too convenient," continues the captain, "that the officer alleged to have issued the unlikely orders was soon killed at Spotsylvania? I ask you again, Private Hayes, are you not a coward and a deserter?"

Hayes's palms burn with the precise sting that comes after fielding an especially hard-hit ball. The noise beneath the floor ceases abruptly. The numbness in his right foot abates. The air in the room seems to clear, and he can see the faces of the men before him. The fragment of red ribbon on the window sash swings forward into the room and then falls straight and still, the light on the clapboards outside now soft and unchanging. A small bell, like that on a shop door, jingles, there's the scent of pipe tobacco, and the wall lamps in the parlor at Hicks Street glow bright and then dim again. Mr. Hayes, in his funny embroidered slippers, rattles the newspaper and laughs warmly, infectiously, at something he has just read. He peers around the wing of the chair and smiles, his smoking cap crooked across his brow.

Hayes says, "I wonder . . . may I have permission to sit after all?"

"For heaven's sake, yes," says Dr. Bliss, "let's all sit," and though Hayes hears the scraping of chair legs, he cannot quite figure where to put himself. Somebody helps him—is it Walt? Burroughs?—and then he looks at the angry captain, who glares at him from across the table, his eyes wide, as if to say, *Well?*

Hayes says, "The smoke was so thick . . . sometimes we couldn't tell day from night."

He stops, for his thoughts charge and scatter in a thousand directions, but then he sees Dr. Speck, who offers a corroborating nod, his eyes suddenly watery. Hayes folds his hands—which do not shake—on the smooth oiled tabletop.

"We couldn't always tell our own men from theirs," he says. "Sometimes we couldn't tell the living from the dead . . . Sometimes we couldn't tell right from wrong. At night the woods caught fire. Wounded men lay between the lines where nobody could rescue them without being shot. We heard their shrieks and cries as they burned to death. I am not a deserter, Captain, and I am not insane. It's my hope to return to the front, where I might be of use."

The captain turns to Dr. Bliss and nods, rather triumphantly, which confounds Hayes; he fears he has somehow stepped into the captain's trap after all. He starts to say, "What I mean to say is—"

But he does not finish the sentence, for he senses he has already crossed a boundary he should not have crossed, said more than he should have. He closes his eyes and allows his mind to retire to a memory of sunshine and tree-bending breezes, the smell of new grass and baked earth, a scruffy foxhound charging across the sward with a ball in its maw, a chorus of cheering men, hats flying into the air.

Dr. Bliss calls him back to the room: "Private Hayes, you know that our commission has directed you to the Asylum for the Insane."

"But that was before I gained back my speech," says Hayes.

"Yes, that's right," says the doctor. "And it's a sign of progress, your gaining it back. But do you recall what happened when those gentlemen came to examine you?"

"They asked questions, sir," says Hayes. "And I couldn't answer because I couldn't make myself speak."

"That's right," says the doctor. "Do you recall anything else?"

Hayes casts his mind back to the day when a dozen or more very solemn uniformed men gathered around his bed, a mix of line officers and surgeons. They requested him to open his mouth, to stick out his tongue—nothing unusual in that—and asked him his name, where he had come from, and so on. They gave him pencil and paper and observed his humiliation at not being able to use them. They took his arms and bent them at the elbow; took his legs and bent them at the knee; peered into this mouth and throat and eyes and ears. They seemed, as a group, impatient, perhaps bored. A surgeon yawned, an officer sneered. One man—a colonel, Hayes believed, and the person in charge—said something that upset Hayes, or frightened him, he can't now recall what. The man had a bushy beard, like Walt's, but neater at the edges. Sunlight lit up the buttons on his coat, and—

"Do you recall anything else?" repeats Dr. Bliss.

Slowly, Hayes shakes his head and says, "Major, sir, I do not think I am insane."

"I didn't say you were," says Dr. Bliss.

"They put me through . . ."

"They put you through what, son?"

To Hayes's great regret, his hands have begun to shake, and he removes them from the tabletop and presses them flat into his lap, where no one can see them. His mouth has gone dry. "I *thought* there was a fire in the ward," he says at last, and tries to swallow. "It had happened before. I understand it wasn't actually . . . and I believe that's why they—"

"Do you recall tearing at your clothes?" asks the surgeon.

"Oh, yes, sir, I'd forgot that," says Hayes, happy to have a defect to pin on the commission. "Because of all their poking and prodding, my wounds started to bleed."

"Your shrapnel wounds."

"Yes, sir."

"Your shrapnel wounds that you know not to be real."

"Yes, sir," says Hayes. "I do know them not to be real, but I don't grasp how they sometimes sting and continue to bleed. How is it that blood—"

He stops, for now, to his surprise, he sees that it's Dr. Bliss who has laid the trap. Before he can hold his tongue, he says, "It's *you* then."

The surgeon looks at him for a long moment, until it appears he has understood what Hayes means. At last he says, "Give me your hand, son."

Reluctantly, Hayes lifts one hand from under the table and allows the surgeon to take it into his own. "We'll leave you alone now," he says. He releases Hayes's hand and stands up. "We'll leave you to your friends."

As all the others rise as well, the captain says quickly, "Even if he didn't desert, he should never have landed here . . . never been allowed to stay as long as he has and occupy a bed when—"

"Yes, yes, Captain Gracie," says Dr. Bliss, turning toward the door. "We thoroughly understand your feelings on the subject. Let's go to my office and continue there."

"Even if we cannot prove him a deserter or a malingerer," adds the captain, following the surgeon in chief to the door, "I will personally see him removed to the asylum, where he has already been directed."

"That will be most helpful, Captain," says Dr. Bliss.

"Maybe, there, he can toss some base balls—"

"That will do, Captain," says Dr. Bliss, "thank you."

On his way out of the room, Dr. Speck drops his cigar to the floor. He retrieves it and then turns back to Hayes. "We'll get you fixed up, my boy, if we possibly can. I've already written letters to the pertinent parties." He nods to Walt and Burroughs and adds, "We certainly will, if we can."

Once Dr. Speck has gone, Walt moves to the open window, sticks out his head, and lets loose with a fit of coughing so fierce Hayes imagines he has been repressing it for some time. Burroughs goes to Walt and lays a hand at the center of his back.

Before Walt's finished, Dr. Bliss reappears, holding open the door, but not coming through it. "Walt," he says, and Walt straightens up and covers his mouth with a handkerchief. The look the surgeon casts him seems to say all that needs to be said on the already belabored subject of Walt's failing health. After a moment, Dr. Bliss says, "Please come and find me today before you leave."

"With pleasure," says Walt.

Next Walt, aided by Burroughs, comes over (dragging his haversack across the floor by its straps) and sits down; he mops his whole face with the handkerchief, lifting his hat an inch to wipe beneath the brim. Burroughs takes the chair next to him, and they each gaze across the table at Hayes with a kindness so clear even Hayes cannot misconstrue it.

"I told you once," says Walt, "and now I'll tell you again: as your good friend, I mean to set you straight when you start to sell yourself short in your own mind. I won't let anyone persuade you that you've done anything wrong."

This makes Burroughs smile and nod, as if Walt has said something Burroughs already values and is delighted to hear repeated. Walt leans his cane against the edge of the table and bends to take from his bag a fan, which he opens with a downward snap.

"And as you know," he says, fanning himself, "I intended to do that even before I had any particulars about you."

He lets out an enormous sigh, places his free hand on the sloping plain of his belly, and adds, "Just imagine the girth and weight of my resolve now."

LATE INTO THE NIGHT, Hayes wakes to find Walt leaning over Casper, trying to hush him. Casper has Walt by the lapels. "Tell them," says Casper, his voice a rasp, "tell all of them . . . everyone."

"I will, I will," whispers Walt. "I'll tell them."

"I was good," says Casper. "I was brave. And I didn't get a bungtown copper for those damned shoes."

"Yes, yes," says Walt, freeing himself. "Rest now, Casper, rest."

Casper lies back on the pillow, mumbling, "Rest now . . . rest now," but immediately rears up again. "And tell that Millerite pa of mine we're *still waiting*!"

Walt gets him settled and strokes Casper's brow until he's calm and quiet. Casper falls asleep with his knees raised, and so Walt lowers them and carefully aligns the boy's legs, smoothing and tucking the covers even around his feet. He adjusts the small pillow under Casper's stump and places Casper's hand over his heart—exactly as if he's fixing him for death. When he's done, he lowers the mosquito curtain and sits in the chair between the two beds, his eyes full of tears. When Walt notices that Hayes is awake, he smiles and gently slides his chair closer. Hayes thinks some of the lowered lamps have gone out completely, for the ward is surprisingly cool and darker than usual. Walt reaches under the gauzy curtain and pats the back of Hayes's hand as a greeting. His own voice hoarse and dry, he says, "We must keep very quiet. The surgeon in chief has banished me from the hospital, and I don't wish to attract any attention."

Because he dreamed there was something alive and thrashing inside his mattress, Hayes is glad to be awake and glad for the ready distraction of Walt's company. Softly, he says, "What did Casper mean . . . What shoes?"

Walt shakes his head. "He hasn't *entirely* been making sense tonight."

"And what's a Millerite?" asks Hayes.

Obviously amused, Walt says, "A reference to William Miller, the man who predicted the Second Coming of Christ . . . back in the forties. The promised date came and went more than twenty years ago, but some stayed faithful one way or another. I gather Casper's father was a follower."

He pauses wearily to remove his hat and comb back his gray hair with his fingers. "It was once their practice," he continues, "always to greet each other with a kiss—sensible and very sweet if you ask me— but then they let that go."

He leans forward and taps the book on Hayes's table. "I would read to you, but as you can see I have practically no voice left."

"You might recite one of your poems," says Hayes.

"So you *do* know me in my other capacity," says Walt, clearly pleased.

"I'm afraid I've been slow to infer the obvious," says Hayes. "It was Captain Gracie's 'infamous poet' that finally woke me up."

"Yes," says Walt, with a sigh. "How peculiar life can be! I started out wanting fame and ended up with infamy. Who knew the love of the masses comes with such pockets of hatred? Very well, then, my friend, I'll recite a short one, but first . . . do you mind coming out from behind that mosquito curtain? This place is dreamy enough this time of night without my having to talk to you through a veil."

Hayes lifts the curtain over his head and drops it behind his shoulders.

"That's better," says Walt. "As it happens, I have the perfect lines for this very late and somber hour . . . but you mustn't be surprised if they make me cry."

He leans back in the chair, crosses his arms on his chest, and whispers the lines with a good amount of feeling. " 'Year that trembled and reeled beneath me . . . your summer wind was warm enough—yet the air I breathed froze me. / A thick gloom fell through the sunshine and darkened me. / Must I change my triumphant songs? said I to myself. / Must I indeed learn to chant the cold dirges of the baffled? / And sullen hymns of defeat?' "

Walt takes out his handkerchief, wipes his eyes, and blows his nose; he glances over at the sleeping Casper and chuckles softly. "I told you they might make me cry."

Hayes asks him to repeat the lines, but Walt, says, "Oh, no, I cannot . . . I'm weak and it makes me weaker."

"It's about the war," says Hayes.

Walt only looks at him and nods.

At last he folds the handkerchief and puts it away. "In truth," he says, "most of me's already back in Brooklyn. What's left of me here's only an echo of an earlier noise. You haven't finished the Dickens, have you?"

"This evening," says Hayes. "After supper."

"And what's your appraisal?"

"Very good, I think," says Hayes, though the book seems like something he only dreamed, his memory of it fragmentary and uncertain.

"Madame Defarge's pistol accidentally goes off," he adds. "The shock and the blast of it cause the governess to go deaf."

"Yes, of course . . . Miss Pross . . . you would make special note of that," says Walt. "Now, my friend, I have an idea: since I'm planning to stay the night, and since you're awake anyway, don't you think we might send off a letter to your folks? They must surely assume the worst by now. I can provide you with paper and pencil, stamps and envelopes, everything you need. I'll even take dictation if you like, though I don't believe you need me to."

"My parents are dead now three years," says Hayes, glad for his unexpected lack of emotion.

"How is that possible?" says Walt.

"I have a sister at home," says Hayes, dodging the question.

"Yes," says Walt, "the sister that gave you the Dickens. We must write to her straightaway."

"But I wouldn't know what to say to her," says Hayes.

"Well," says Walt, "I should think, to begin with, you might tell her you're still alive."

The prospect of composing a letter—one that's actually to be written down and mailed—feels insurmountable to Hayes. He imagines Walt is right—by now she has assumed him dead. He thinks it would be cruel to shock her with news of his being alive, only to shock her again later, if he returns to the front, with news of his being killed. And if he is in fact to be removed to the Asylum for the Insane, that would prompt her to travel to Washington City for a visit, which he would find unbearable.

"You *are*, you know," says Walt, "still alive."

"And in a hospital," says Hayes. "Though my wounds are not real. A gloom fell through the sunshine and darkened me."

Walt smiles. "Your wounds are not *visible* like other wounds," he says. "Which isn't quite the same thing as not real. I imagine your incautious desire to return to the battlefield is so you might get yourself some visible ones."

"I would prefer it, yes," says Hayes.

"Look at *him*," Walt says, indicating Casper. "Is that what you prefer?"

Hayes does not look at Casper but sees him in his mind's eye, a yellow cadaver.

"Or over there at Mr. Raugh," says Walt. "How would you like surviving but never being able to play base ball again? Would you prefer that? Perhaps you would enjoy being helped to the water closet for the rest of your life."

Again Hayes is silent—thinking of Walt's "hymns of defeat" and Raugh's "de-feeted"—and Walt, after a moment, says, with a sigh, "I'm sorry . . . forgive me . . . I don't mean to scold you."

Hayes says, "I wouldn't know what to write to my sister. How can I tell her what's to become of me when I don't know it myself?"

This question appears to enliven Walt—he sits up straight again and inches the chair even closer. "I can tell you this much," he says, "though I probably shouldn't. Dr. Bliss deems you unfit for service at this time . . . and, more to the point, believes the asylum will only further harm you. Once he has made up his mind about a thing, he can be a very effective wire-puller."

"Wire-puller?" says Hayes.

"Let me ask you," says Walt. "When did you last see the loathsome Mr. Babb?"

Hayes has not seen Babb since the morning Dr. Speck appeared at the hospital. Before he can answer, Walt nods, his eyebrows arched high, and says, "You see, the major has ways of making people vanish. Some mysteriously, never to be seen again . . . and others only temporarily, at exactly the right moment. Just when they're about to be collected, taken from the hospital, they simply can't be found."

"Is that it then?" says Hayes. "I'm to vanish?"

"Perhaps," says Walt. "We'll know more by tomorrow. There are still one or two hitches to be got over. Captain Gracie means to subvert us, and we've not yet devised a way to subvert him instead."

Hayes reaches into his trousers pocket and produces the oily scrap of paper Matron put under his pillow the night she left the hospital. As he passes it into Walt's hand, Walt says, "What's this?"

Hayes only shrugs his shoulders.

Walt looks up from reading it and says, "Where did you get this, my boy?"

"From Matron," says Hayes. "Her last night on the ward, she put it under my pillow . . . said it might be useful to me."

"Matron?" says Walt, shaking his head in awe.

"What does it mean?" asks Hayes.

"I can only surmise," says Walt. "But if it means what it appears to mean, we might not get the interference from Captain Gracie we've dreaded. I happen to know he has a very important wife and two young daughters back in Connecticut. May I keep this?"

Hayes nods, and Walt kisses the scrap of paper and slides it into his coat pocket. "Now," he says, "I suggest you write to your sister and tell her that you're alive—all safe, if not completely sound—and hoping to see her in Brooklyn ere long. It'll ease her mind, even without details. I'll write to her for you if you like."

Walt's writing on his behalf has a certain appeal to Hayes—it reminds him of the moment, some weeks before, when he gave himself over to being shaved by Walt, surrendering to all the possible outcomes, including a slit throat. "Yes, thank you," he says. "But if we'll know more by tomorrow, why not wait till then?"

Walt appears to think this proposal through. "Tomorrow then," he says, smiling in a way that seems to mark tomorrow's prospects as both happy and sad. "Tell me about her. She must be very intelligent, like you. And probably a bit older, I should think."

"By two years," says Hayes. "A schoolteacher."

"Yes, that fits," says Walt. "But not plain like my schoolteacher friend here in Washington. No sister of yours could ever be plain. Very beautiful, I imagine. And married, yes?"

Hayes shakes his head.

Walt, surprised, says, "Not married? Well, then you must have brothers . . . or at least . . ."

Hayes shakes his head again.

"But if . . . as you've told me," says Walt, "your parents are dead . . . what could possibly have prompted you to leave her alone?"

Hayes's face burns, and Walt, evidently sensing that he has flustered him, quickly says, "Do you know? I've just had a letter from my brother Jeff."

He bends and starts rooting inside the haversack on the floor by his feet. "He mentioned his good friend who's a principal at one of the Brooklyn schools. I wonder if you know him."

When he has found the letter, he pulls it from its envelope and begins scanning the page with his pointer finger, squinting in the dim light. "Here it is," he says. "Gilfinian, that's the name."

Of course Hayes recognizes the name, but hearing it spoken with a mock-Irish accent, and spoken in this peculiar setting, feels to Hayes as if it belongs to somebody he met long ago in his boyhood, rather than as recently as last Christmas. The memory of that day at his sister's school—the children's high spirits, the recitations and carols, the cakes and lemonade, the reticent boys, the girls giddy with the false rumor of his being Miss Hayes's fiancé—brings a sharp pain behind his eyes.

Walt continues studying the letter, paying him no mind, and says, "That's a very fishy name . . . has both a gill *and* a fin." Now he looks up rather suddenly. "Do you know him?"

Hayes feels his heart race and he wants nothing more than to be left alone. He thinks maybe his voice will desert him again, a liability about which he has mixed emotions. He takes a breath and says, "I believe I did meet him once."

"But not a friend?" asks Walt, already disappointed. "I was hoping you and Jeff might have a friend in common."

"No."

Walt folds the letter and puts it back into the envelope. As he's bent toward the floor and restoring the letter to the bag, he goes on: "Well . . . of no particular interest then . . . seems Mr. Gilfinian's got himself engaged to be married . . . one of his female teachers . . . a girl named Sarah . . . Jeff's not met her yet. You would like my brother Jeff . . . I love him more than anyone in the world. Good and kind and smart and . . . well, the best of us by far. We'd be quite lost without him. I can't wait to see him again."

When Walt sits up straight, Hayes, who has been watching him, averts his eyes. "Why, my dear boy," says Walt, alarmed, "you've gone all pale and peaked! What on earth's the matter?"

THE ROOF GROANS in the wind as if it might lift straight off the pavilion. The many flags coil and snap. The mosquito curtains, gathered
and suspended from the rafters, churn like tornadoes. The whitewashers have returned with their tall ladders, this time to paint the vaulted
ceiling above the rafters a watery blue. Casper has not yet awakened,
and from the looks of him, Hayes thinks he has not moved since Walt
tucked and fixed him in the bed the night before. Raugh lies flat and
inert as usual, either sleeping or awake, eyes shut. The stench of the
canal, stirred by the wind, is worse than ever. Now and again, Hayes
hears the strains of a brass band outdoors, now and again the explosive discharge of a steam locomotive and the banging of steel on steel.
A dozen or more new arrivals have wandered onto the ward, bloody
and bewildered, helped by comrades or attendants, and Hayes has
already witnessed no fewer than four corpses borne out on stretchers.

A black boy in short pants lurches and sways down the aisle, balancing a stack of folded cloths nearly his own height, making sport of
it. There are the usual card games and checkers and clouds of tobacco
smoke, but Hayes believes he hears more than the ordinary measure
of laughter on the ward. In his body—in his ears, behind his eyes,
and inside his chest—he feels calmer today, quieter. So far, he has
not suspected anyone of doing him harm or plotting against him. He
has seen no ghosts, no threatening flames out of the corner of his eye.
The pot of tea he brought back from the dining room earlier seems a
consoling luxury and for some reason makes him think of Dr. Speck,
which cheers him even more.

Anne, wearing a gray dress under her apron, stops by to check
on Casper. She tests the temperature of his brow and examines the
contents of the cup on the table. She seems to be avoiding Hayes altogether. At last, she looks at him and tries to smile but flushes instead.
The wind gusting through the nearby window rustles her hair; she
hooks a loose strand behind her ear.

"Quite a breeze," she says and then casts her gaze all about, the
length and breadth of the frenzied pavilion. A gold cross dangles on
a chain from her neck and rests askew at the top hem of her apron.
She puts both her hands into the apron pocket, as if she's screwing up
her courage for something, and then says, "I doubt you'll be moved

to write . . . but if you do find the time, I would welcome a word from you . . . how you're getting along and so forth."

"Am I going somewhere?" asks Hayes.

"I have heard that you are," she says. "I don't know when exactly it will be, and I didn't want you to leave without my telling you good-bye . . . without my saying . . . without saying I'm sorry to see you go."

"Thank you, Anne," says Hayes.

Now she smiles in earnest. "It's the first time you've spoken my name," she says.

"I guess it is," he says, "and you've never spoken mine . . . not to me at least . . . only 'Mr. X.'"

"I grew rather fond of 'Mr. X,'" she says.

"Me too. I think I'll miss it."

Hayes is aware—prompted by what he takes as *her* awareness—that he did not say, *I'll miss you.*

"And I shall miss you, too," he says quickly, surprised at how genuine it suddenly seems.

"Oh, I don't imagine so," she says, shaking her head. "All along, I've felt there was someone else who has your heart."

"Not true," he says, thinking what an odd and confusing expression, what an odd and confusing business, the business of heart-having. "And even if it were, I shall miss you anyway. You've been very kind . . . and taken very good care of me."

"Like a sister," she says, nodding.

"You still haven't said my name," he says.

"Mr. Hayes then," she says, shrugging. "Private Hayes. There, you see—not nearly so good as 'Mr. X.'"

"Why not call me Summerfield?"

"All right," she says, "but I really must go now."

She takes from the apron pocket a buff-colored envelope sealed with a white wafer and passes it to him. "I've taken the liberty of writing you a note, which includes my name and the address of the hospital. But I must ask you, as a favor, not to read it until after you've left."

He agrees to her terms and thanks her. As she turns away, he says, "I wonder if you've seen Walt."

"Not this morning," she answers.

"Do you think Casper's all right?"

She looks at him as if he has asked a foolish question, which he supposes he has.

"No," she says. "But I expect he'll be all right soon. I'm hoping . . . well, I may as well say it . . . I'm hoping dear Casper won't wake up. Good-bye, Summerfield."

As she moves hurriedly into the aisle, she nearly collides with a skeletal black-clad preacher who casts her a disapproving look— a look he turns on Hayes immediately afterward. Hayes at first wonders what the man might have observed that jogged such reproach, but then, as the preacher's unaltered gaze lights next on Casper, Raugh, and a brown dog that ambles by in the aisle, Hayes reckons it's a generic and permanent feature.

Soon the ward surgeon, Dr. Dinkle, approaches, making his rounds. To Hayes's surprise, he doesn't stop at Casper's bed but only gives Casper a quick glance. Hayes stands and salutes the corpulent surgeon, who says with a dissonant lack of irony, "Good morning, Private Hayes, and welcome back to the world of ceaseless blabbering."

"Thank you, sir," says Hayes.

"I've had a letter from Philadelphia, from Dr. Drum, who inquired about your health," says the ward surgeon—a flat statement of fact— and then moves on again.

The brown dog from the aisle eases alongside Casper's bed. A hound with floppy silken-looking ears and sagging jowls, the dog looks briefly at Hayes, its melancholy eyes blinking in the wind from the window. It turns to Casper and sniffs at the stump that rests on the small pillow. It gives the dressing a tentative exploratory lick, sniffs again, and then lowers its chin for a moment to the edge of the mattress. The dog, thinks Hayes, is giving poor Casper more attention and concern than any of the doctors.

With a sigh and a thud, the dog drops to the floor in the narrow space between the beds. When Hayes looks up, he sees, standing tattered and forlorn in the aisle, a soldier about his own age. At first, he thinks it's the ghost of Billy Swift, but then the soldier removes his cap and reveals an abundant shock of black hair. His right arm hangs in a blood- and mud-stained sling, and beneath his unbuttoned jacket, his middle is wrapped all round with dirty bandaging. Hayes gets off the bed and starts to go to the soldier, who appears transfixed by the hound on the floor. He allows Hayes to escort him to the bed—they move carefully, in half steps—and just as they reach the end of it and the soldier braces himself with a hand on the footrail, Captain Gracie appears and pauses next to them.

Hayes expects a reprimand—after all, the soldier is obviously a new arrival, and if Hayes means to help, he should be fetching a steward or a nurse—but the captain says nothing, only studies them coldly. Hayes would have thought the captain quite settled on all counts where he was concerned—there was nothing about Hayes still to be explored or debated—yet when at last he meets Hayes's eye, the usual glare of disdain is oddly complicated by traces of ambiguity. The captain seems as if he might speak but then thinks the better of it, turns, and strides away in a rush.

"Sit here," says Hayes to the soldier, as he helps him onto the edge of the mattress. "Did you lose your way? Are you in pain? What can I do for you?"

But the soldier, staring down at the hound, says only, "Is he yours?"

"No," answers Hayes, "I don't know whom it belongs to. Might be a stray who wandered in."

"Can I pet him?" asks the soldier.

Hayes sits beside the soldier and coaxes the dog up from the floor, snapping his fingers and whistling softly. The soldier reaches out his free hand, and without hesitation the hound lays its head in his lap. Hayes notices the soldier's fingernails—lined with grime and chewed down to the quick.

Grinning ear to ear and exposing a wide gap in the top row of his teeth, the soldier says, "I think he likes the way I smell." He cups the dog's muzzle in his palm for a moment and then gently scratches the forehead. "No," he says, "I didn't get lost. I just figured I'd take a little stroll . . . to collect myself. I'm supposed to be two wards over. I'm sorry to confess it, but I'm scared to death of doctors. After what we been through . . . what all we seen . . . it's doctors that scare me. Somebody told me—besides the saws and the knives—they got hypothermic styringes in this place. Needles . . . big as knitting needles . . .

they stick into you and pump you full of morphine and the like. Is that true?"

"I haven't seen anything like that on this ward," says Hayes. "Only pills and powders."

"I am very glad to hear it," says the soldier. "I ain't about to let nobody stick me with no needle, I don't care what. I took a bullet to my elbow and another one to my ribs . . . both of them just chipped me, though, one right after the other. The first hit my elbow, and I threw up my arm in the air, and the second scraped my ribs, just like that, *bang-bang*. I ought to be dead. Does that wind blow like that all the time?"

"No," says Hayes. "I've never seen it blow this hard."

"Does it always stink like that? Smells like a damn latrine."

"I'm afraid so."

The soldier lowers his voice and, indicating Casper, says, "What's wrong with him? He looks like he's already been dead a day or two."

"He's got a blood infection," says Hayes. "From the amputation wound."

"Did he get it here in the hospital?"

Hayes nods.

"I heard they kill about as many in these places as they help," says the soldier. "How'd you end up here? You look okay."

"A shell exploded right next to me," says Hayes. "I was . . ."

He stops, for he can't tell where the sentence might be going.

"I bet you went deaf for a while," says the soldier.

"For a while," says Hayes.

"I wonder how come it didn't kill you."

"What you mean?"

"You said it exploded right next to you. I wonder how come you didn't die. You didn't even . . . you still got all your limbs and everything."

A burst of wind blasts through the window, very loud, and Hayes flinches. A scent of gunpowder stings his nostrils. "I don't know," he says. "I don't know why I didn't die."

The soldier looks at him apologetically, and says, "Makes you feel kind of strange, don't it?"

"What?"

The soldier shrugs and turns his attention back to stroking the dog. Hayes says, "Oh, you mean surviving."

The soldier nods but doesn't look up. "Down in Piedmont," he says, "about three weeks ago . . . I was ten feet away from my best friend . . . watching him ram his piece . . . and the thing went off in his face. Burned him up good and blew off both his hands. Died the next day in the field hospital. Now he's dead and I'm not. I expect I could get used to it if I could stop dreaming about him most every night. I've about decided dreams is the worst part of war. Dreams and diarrhea . . . and *doctors*."

The wind howls down between the pavilions, whistles in the ridge vents, and then stops abruptly. The flags and mosquito curtains hang limp. Both Hayes and the soldier look up at the ceiling as each of the two whitewashers looks down from his wooden ladder, startled by the sudden change. A near silence falls over the ward.

Seconds later, the wind kicks back up and reinstates the former noisy commotion.

"Well," says the soldier. "I best be off before they start organizing a search party. I might not see you again. Looking at you, I figure you'll be heading back into the fray pretty soon."

"Pretty soon," says Hayes, surprised by the sheer readiness of the fib.

The soldier stands, puts on his cap, and gives the hound a last pat. He and Hayes wish each other good luck, and Hayes watches him thread along the aisle to the middle of the ward, where he leaves through the doors to the covered way.

"Pretty soon," whispers Hayes, and glimpses the shadow of his own future, a perseverance of things and sensations—horsecars and streetlamps, books and boat whistles, the scent of the ocean, the changing of seasons, mud and grass and ice, coals in the grate and Christmas boxes—but plagued by inquisitive men in black suits and sapped by a necessity for deceit. He'd gone to war and gone out of his senses, Orphan Hayes, a liar for being ashamed, further ashamed for being a liar.

Near the night watcher's table, a nurse drops a basin with a great clatter. Immediately the skinny clergyman with the permanent scowl slips in the spilled (and probably soapy) water and falls to the floor. The incident sets off an uproar of laughter, but evidently the preacher has hurt himself, for a steward and a visiting policeman assist him to the wardmaster's room.

The wind, if possible, increases. Hayes hears the staccato of grit driven against the outside walls of the pavilion. Soon the chaplain comes around with the mail, and to Hayes's astonishment he tosses onto the end of the bed an envelope—unsealed, no stamps, and the only address "Ward H, Bed #33."

Dear Comrade,

I will leave this for you with the chaplain—I don't trust it to stay where I might otherwise put it. I am pretty low this morning but up early in spite of it & have been very lively—So much to do & I must see my landlord, make a final appearance at my office, &c.

Sorry to have kept you awake last night & more sorry to have given you a start—I still wonder if I shouldn't have fetched the doctor—but the licorice you preferred did seem to restore your color & put you back to sleep—I regret you missed the moonrise . . . it came up over the roof of the next building, right inside your window—

I believe I have worked something out, dear son, abt your sister, who is undoubtedly named Sarah & to whom you are undoubtedly very close— If I am right, I saw in your face what my own face must have been when I first learned of my brother Jeff's marriage. We had been so close, Jeff & I . . . loved each other so dearly when we were younger—I would have stopped us in time (or stopped time in us) & foregone such inconvenient changes as marriage, babies, &c.

Burroughs will drop in for a visit later to-day & then I'll be along myself when I have accomplished all I must. We'll see you one way or another all safe back to Brooklyn, back to health, and back to base ball— in my opinion, the best & most romantic game our race has invented so far (unless of course you count democracy)—

Walt

———

HE RECOGNIZES his choosing compliance as an empty gesture, for what are the alternatives? Besides—and this is what he recognizes most acutely—he has stopped caring: Hicks Street, the Asylum for the Insane, the siege of Petersburg and Richmond . . . how do they differ? It strikes him as strange—when he himself is so detached—that his fate has been the cause of so much fuss. Earlier, Burroughs stopped by briefly, a large and bulging canvas bag over his shoulder, and said that he had a score of deliveries to make for Walt first, but then he would return as soon as humanly possible. He stood a pillow-sized package, wrapped in brown paper and tied with string, against a leg of Hayes's table and told him to keep a close eye on it. In a kind of cheerful frenzied state, and wearing a surprising red waistcoat, he spoke every-thing rapidly, in a stage whisper, and seemed to be executing a scheme designed earlier and elsewhere. Hayes observed a wave of relief cross Burroughs's face when he glanced at the sleeping Casper—Casper, at least, was one thing that didn't need to be seen to. Just before he rushed away, he admonished Hayes not to go anywhere, which Hayes thought rather enigmatic if not comical. High conspiracy was afoot, and Hayes decided the only sensible response was to play the role of an obedient soldier and to do as he was told.

The wind has ceased entirely, the ward very warm now and bathed in sunlight and shadows. The whitewashers, half finished with the ceiling, have quit and gone with their ladders. Hayes has read over Walt's letter several times. He imagines Walt pleased with himself for having worked out the matter of Sarah. (Most likely it didn't require clairvoyance, since all the blood left Hayes's face.) Of course Walt meant to express his characteristic empathy, but how could the love between Walt and his brother Jeff approximate the trou-bled waters of Hayes's love for Sarah? How could closeness between brothers ever run the risk of crossing the line Hayes's feelings had crossed? He was grateful for Walt's inapt analogy, grateful that the *real thing* would simply never occur to him. In any case, from the shock of the news, one truth has emerged immediate and undeniable: Hayes has himself to blame—she would never have got herself engaged to a man like Gilfinian, so obviously her inferior, had Hayes not left her bereft.

Bereft—a word no doubt prompted by egotism. True, she hadn't wanted him to leave, but was it because she loved him or because she didn't want to be left alone? It seems entirely possible that once he'd gone, she simply coped, and what better way to cope than to marry? It isn't likely that her connection to Gilfinian took root and bloomed into a betrothal in the span of a few months. Probably the thing was more than nascent already, and Hayes's leaving cleared the way. Surely there were signs, which he would have noticed had he not been so caught up in himself and his own feelings. Her spirit helped him through the Wilderness. The Wilderness did not push her from his mind. If anything has changed, it's that there is less room in his mind for her now. Less room, and if possible, even less clarity. It seems to him that his thinking on *all* subjects is now more akin to his thinking regarding her—a jumble, conflicted, confusing, wanting and not wanting—which accretes to a kind of brain-pressure . . . and which, if it persists, might conscript her into the ranks of the many things about which he is ceasing to care.

Two attendants arrive at Raugh's bed to wheel him to the sinks. Hayes watches the ordeal, noting Raugh's apparent passivity. He recalls a mind-trick he sometimes used to play on himself in base ball matches: when he had to face an especially dangerous batsman, he would adopt an attitude of indifference, convince himself he didn't care what happened. It helped him not to be afraid.

BURROUGHS, when he returns, is tuckered out and preoccupied—also worried about Walt's protracted failure to appear. He has taken out his watch three times since he sat in the chair by Hayes's bed. Now, looking at it for the fourth time, he says, simply, with a sigh, "Walt."

Hayes, bewilderingly composed amid what seems some kind of gathering storm, feels an urge to comfort him, maybe, if there were a way, with a dose of his own fresh-brewed indifference. Hayes, of course—spared the details of what Burroughs and Walt have cooked up—knows nothing of what's at stake and nothing of the consequences of Walt's tardiness; perhaps, he thinks, a privilege of being insane, even of being *perceived* as insane. He believes his composure has something to do with his recently acquiring (not through any effort of his own but rather the way one "acquires" an illness) a capacity to observe the curious antics of his mind, antics he has mistakenly taken far too seriously. Certainly he has learned the lesson of not believing everything he sees. Now, for example, and off and on throughout the day, he has felt sure that all fifty or sixty pairs of eyes on the ward are directed at him, but that's surely untrue. Even while it may be a strong-enough notion to keep him from idly wandering about, he understands that it's only a notion. He smiles at Burroughs and says, "Before I went to Virginia, I clerked for a while in a shipwrights' office . . . where I learned a new word. The men would say of a certain vessel that she was *walt* . . . poorly designed or poorly built . . . unable to bear her sails for standing too high in the water."

Burroughs laughs. "Did they have a word for a ship that perpetually arrives late to port?"

Mrs. Duffy enters the ward at that moment, carrying a guitar, and Burroughs groans and says, "All that was missing."

She has never before brought along a guitar, and Hayes is almost interested in this new development. He notices, too, that she is without a bonnet, her hair pinned up elaborately but messily, and that though she's past her prime and entirely unadorned, dressed in black, and has apparently set out to make herself as plain as possible, she has a lingering natural beauty; it shines through against all odds, rather like her occasional right notes, which always seem like accidents.

She sits near the stove, low to the floor, on what looks like a milking stool, the folds of her dress splayed around her. Happily, she does not sing, but only plays—plays very well, an air Hayes thinks might be from Mozart—and soon after she begins, a hush falls over the ward.

Suddenly Casper sits bolt upright in his bed, eyes shut, and says, "Oh . . . what a lovely breeze . . . I hear it singing . . ."

He pauses for a moment, as if to soak up the agreeable encounter.

He removes his cap, as if to let the breeze have at his red hair.

And then lies back down, immobile.

Burroughs stands and holds his flattened hand an inch above Casper's mouth and nose. He turns to Hayes, shakes his head, and says solemnly, "I'll fetch someone."

Mrs. Duffy goes on playing, and gradually people take up their conversations again and the usual chronic murmur comes back, though lowered.

A minute later, Burroughs returns with the ward surgeon and two attendants whom Hayes has never seen before.

Dr. Dinkle leans down close to Casper's face, lays his hand on Casper's shoulder, and jostles him. "Private Mallet," he says. "Wake up if you can."

Casper's eyes flutter open.

"Are you conscious that death is near, son?"

No sign of apprehension in Casper's face, though his eyes remain open.

"Have you accepted your death, son . . . are you at peace with what's happening to you?"

Still no response.

"Is there anything at all you want to say . . . either to your family or to God?"

Casper lies motionless, and at last Dr. Dinkle bends over and presses his ear to Casper's chest. After another moment, the doctor stands, closes Casper's eyes, and pulls the bedsheet over the boy's face.

He says to Burroughs, "I believe he heard me. I believe he was, at the very last, aware, though he could no longer speak."

He immediately takes his leave, nodding to the two attendants— dark-faced middle-aged convalescents, who go about their work in workmanlike fashion. They wrap Casper in the sheet that already covers him, lift him onto a stretcher, and, just like that, he's borne away by strangers to the deadhouse.

There is no alteration in the ward's constant lowered hum. Mrs. Duffy never misses a note in the air she plays.

Burroughs sits down in the chair and looks at his watch. He says to Hayes, "He was your friend."

"Even more Walt's," says Hayes.

"From what Walt's told me," says Burroughs, "I imagine he'll be relieved to arrive and find the empty bed. *If* he arrives."

The two are silent for a while, during which Mrs. Duffy plucks out "Jesus, Lover of My Soul."

Soon Raugh stretches his arm across the narrow space between the beds and offers his hand to Hayes, which Hayes takes. At first, it really does seem to Hayes that it's Abraham Lincoln who offers him solace. Raugh releases Hayes's hand and then, shaking his head, says, "'Jesus, . . . let me to thy bosom fly' . . . but please, if I must, let me fly there from home, and not from a place like this."

The sunlight leaves the ward in a wave from front to rear. The windows glare uniformly, bright silver.

Walt appears at last, looking red-faced and freshly bathed. He wears a tie with his wine-colored suit and a sprig of mint stuck into his lapel, the acorns on the cord of his felt hat newly polished. He kisses Burroughs on the cheek and then likewise Hayes. Clearly relying more heavily on his cane than usual, he sits on Casper's mattress without any apparent surprise. Hayes thinks Walt has aged ten years since his birthday scarcely more than three weeks ago.

"He was leaving as I was coming in," says Walt. "Please tell me he didn't go out raving."

"Quite the contrary, Walt," says Burroughs. "It only just happened, not more than five minutes ago. He slept all day, peacefully. And right before he died, he sat up and looked for all the world transported."

"'Transported'?" says Walt. "Good word."

"What was it he said?" Burroughs asks Hayes.

"'Oh, what a lovely breeze,'" answers Hayes. "'I hear it singing.'"

Walt stands and puts his arms around Hayes. As he squeezes him, he says, "You are a very fine young man. And John . . . I see you out of the corner of my eye, consulting your pocket watch."

Walt releases Hayes but, instead of sitting back down, turns to Burroughs and says, "Let me have your chair, please, John. I want to put my back to the window . . . the light hurts my eyes."

After they have rearranged themselves, Burroughs clears his throat and says to Walt, "So, tell us where we stand."

"I can tell you two things for absolute certain," says Walt. "First, Mrs. Duffy should definitely prefer this instrument to the one inside her neck. And second, I'm afraid I'm very ill and have procrastinated far too long. I can stay in Washington City not another day. I leave this very afternoon."

Hayes receives this news with a realization that his cultivated indifference does not extend to being left at the hospital without Walt.

Evidently Walt sees this in his face, for he says, "Don't worry, my friend. I'm not about to wave them around here, but I have in the pocket of my coat not one but two car tickets."

Captain Gracie passes by in the aisle accompanied by a member of the guard. He glances at the three of them as he goes, but only for a second and then looks quickly away—as if their sort doesn't merit even an iota of his consideration.

Burroughs says, "What about *him*?"

"All squared away," says Walt. "Deepening my respect for topsy-turvydom . . . Matron's scrap of paper has worked its magic. Abigail Cox, a female nurse in Ward K, turns out to be a very sweet but very brittle cookie . . . and crumbled quite readily. I felt sorry for the poor girl. I fully expect the captain to turn a blind eye. You might have noticed him just now in the aisle, practicing."

Hayes, a bit dizzy, says, "So I'm to leave with you . . . today?"

Walt smiles. "I told you already what Dr. Bliss feels about you. We're skirting officialism . . . and what's left are papers, forms, signatures, et cetera . . . which can catch up to you in Brooklyn as well as any other place. By the way, what happens today doesn't preclude your return to the front later, if that's still what you want. It's my earnest hope that the war will be over sooner than that."

Burroughs bends forward from Casper's bed and retrieves the parcel he left beneath Hayes's table.

Walt, observing, says, "Ah, yes, the all-important package."

Now Walt takes out *his* watch and looks at it. At that moment, Dr. Bliss enters the ward from one of the middle doors, coatless and wearing a bloodstained apron over his uniform. All the soldiers who are able, including Hayes, stand at attention, but Dr. Bliss strides down the aisle waving his arms like a bird in flight, encouraging the men to stay as they were.

The ward remains silent, and even Mrs. Duffy stops playing, mid-phrase. As Dr. Bliss is about to pass her milking stool, she bids him to stop. Gazing up, she says something to him, which appears to give him pause. His response to what she has said is a moment's hesitation, followed by a reluctant consent. He leans down and whispers something into her ear. She nods. He removes his apron, folds it, and holds it beneath one arm. He smiles round at the many wounded and sick soldiers, all of who seem to be in a state of suspense.

At last, Mrs. Duffy strikes a chord, and the surgeon in chief, in splendid voice, begins singing the first verse of "Woodman, Spare That Tree!"

At once, Walt whispers to Burroughs, "Go . . . go now."

Burroughs stands and reaches for Hayes's hand.

"Go with John," says Walt. "He'll tell you what you must do."

Hayes grabs from the table the Dickens novel, into which he has already placed the two letters, Walt's and Anne's, and then he and Burroughs walk quietly to the back of the ward. As they go, Hayes bravely glances at the other soldiers, who listen to the music with rapt attention ("In youth it sheltered me / And I'll protect it now . . ."), their eyes already glistening.

Burroughs opens the door to the bath-room, allowing Hayes to enter first, and then latches it from the inside. He places the package on the table, where rest a pitcher and basin, a towel, and a block of soap. He unties the string, and still facing away from Hayes, says, "Take off your clothes. Quickly as you can."

Hayes doesn't move but only looks around at the plain brown room, dimly lit by one small window—the two tin tubs hanging on hooks in the wall, the little round mirror the size of a base ball above the table.

Burroughs pours water into the basin and then turns to face him. "I'll put my back to you if you're modest," he says, "but we must work fast."

Hayes starts to undress, thinking that his short tenure in the army ridded him of modesty.

"Take off everything," says Burroughs, "even your drawers. I've brought fresh ones for you. The suit's exactly like mine and should be a good fit. Now come over here and wash up a bit."

The two men switch places, Hayes naked now, and for a second, Hayes worries about Burroughs seeing his shrapnel wounds. Then he recalls that he has none. It almost amuses him.

As Hayes sponges himself with the soapy water, Burroughs says, "Walt will be waiting for you by the front doors. I'll hang back here for a few minutes. You'll have to walk the entire length of the ward by yourself, but you'll do fine. Carry your book in your hand, that's a good touch. Don't stop for anything. Don't speak to anyone. Walk straight to where Walt's waiting. As you go out together, you might tell him the meaning of the word *walt*. He'll like that."

Hayes nods, and then Burroughs says something about his having seen Walt naked once, something about Walt's ruddy pink roundness, but Hayes is listening to the music he hears through the wall, Dr. Bliss's clear beautiful baritone:

> *"When but an idle boy*
> *I sought its grateful shade;*
> *In all their gushing joy*
> *Here too my sisters played.*
> *My mother kissed me here,*
> *My father pressed my hand—*
> *Forgive this foolish tear,*
> *But let that old oak stand!"*

SIX

Afloat

Early on the first day of July, a Friday, Summerfield takes his coffee into the garden, where he finds Jane pulling weeds from her tomato patch. The sun is well up, though it hasn't yet cleared the treetops at the riverbank, and he identifies the high misty glow in the air as sunlight reflected off the water. Since his return home a week ago, it has become his habit to dawdle about wearing his father's embroidered smoking cap and slippers—he reads the newspapers, naps when he can, sorts through the mail that accumulated in his absence—and he has the distinct impression that the three women of the house, each in her own way, labors to accommodate his new and lurking presence. Now he gazes down at Jane, on hands and knees among the tomatoes; she looks to him paler and thinner than ever, as if, in time, she'll simply fade away. He places his nearly empty cup on a nearby potting table. "I see the cabbages are coming along," he says idly. "What kind are they?"

Jane pauses, raises her head. "I used to know the name, but I've forgot it," she says, and returns to weeding.

He dodges a laundry pole and moves to the shed at the back of the garden, where vines, sagging with scores of young pods and small purple flowers, climb on strings against a wall. "Your beans are thriving, too," he says. "Do these have a name?"

"I expect they do," answers Jane, "but I don't know it. Mrs. Perkins gave 'em to me. They're long and green and get purple stripes when they're ready, and then you cook 'em, and the stripes disappear."

He returns to the tomato patch. "Have we always had tomatoes?" he asks. "I don't recall having tomatoes when I was a boy."

"Your mother was suspicious of tomatoes," says Jane.

"These fuzzy ones look as if they'll turn yellow," he says. "What are they called?"

"I call 'em yellow," says Jane with a sigh. "Yellow tomatoes. Mr. Foster gave me the seeds. That's all I know. I'm not one for names."

"I can see that," says Summerfield.

Jane gets up from the ground, wiping her hands on her apron. "Excuse me," she says, not looking at him. "I must go and wash."

An orange cat leaps onto the fence at the back of the garden, trots silently to the corner post, and disappears into the tall grasses on the other side. A warm breeze stirs the air, promising a scorching day. Summerfield puts his hands in his pockets and looks up at the blue and cloudless sky. He didn't sleep well last night (like most nights), his dreams full of thunder and voices and tall columns of fire. Since his return to Hicks Street, he has had an odd and ongoing feeling of suspension, as if he has been catapulted through the air and his feet haven't yet touched ground. He is back at home. He joined the army, saw three impossibly long days of battle, survived. For more than a month Sarah thought him dead. Everyone assumes he walked through hell, though certainly not without some measure of glory. But his memory of Virginia is blurry, insubstantial, indeterminate, as if he'd gone to touch what he thought to be a hard surface and his hand sank into it instead. He frequently suffers an urge to return, to touch the thing again, to confirm its nature and actuality. Increasingly, the stuff of his dreams mixes with the stuff of his waking hours, and when he sleeps, he often finds himself running, both *in* the dream and *from* it. Two recurring images stay with him during the day: a great wooden box (larger than a casket) and charred cylindrical shapes, tapered at the ends; he recognizes each of these as a sort of container but further recognizes that he can say nothing about their contents.

Sarah now steps into the garden, dressed gaily in a white frock with pink ribbons and carrying a straw bonnet in her hand. "Summerfield, darling," she says. "Won't you please change your mind . . . there's still time."

The "Summerfield, darling" is new, and he doesn't care for it, though he can't think exactly why—only that he has noticed before the irony that terms of endearment, spoken in a particular way, can put distance between people.

She comes to where he stands in the flagstone path and kisses him on the cheek. "Won't you change your mind?" she says again.

The public schools are to close today for the summer vacation, and she has entreated him to join her for the celebratory exercises at midday. In truth, he wouldn't mind going, save for having to greet Gilfinian—his greeting Gilfinian, he suspects, her primary purpose. "No," he says, "I won't change my mind."

"But why not?" she says. "What have you to do here? I understand your need for rest—I do—but it's been a full week. Don't you think you might benefit from a little outing?"

"I might actually," he says, "only I don't feel like going. I don't feel like people."

"You mean you don't feel like Thomas."

"Oh, Sarah, I'm barely out of bed," he says. "Must we talk about him this early in the day?"

"I suppose not," she says, "but we'll have to talk about him sometime."

Now she throws her arms around him and withdraws, laughing. She flattens her hands against his chest, patting him there three times for emphasis as she says, "I still can't believe you're here . . . alive . . . real!"

He feels an impulse to shrink from her touch but manages to contain it. He says nothing, though he thinks the three conditions she has named are exactly those he himself finds most mystifying.

Reaching up to touch his hair, she says, "You'll want to get this cut before you go to base ball practice. There's a new barber's saloon in Montague Street."

He only looks at her.

"Of *course* you'll go to practice," she says, abruptly serious. "Why do you look at me that way?"

"How am I looking at you?"

She shakes her head. "I don't know . . . as if you would run away again. It frightens me."

"I'm sorry," he says.

"Jane just now came inside and told me you were interrogating her in the garden."

"For heaven's sake," he says. "I only asked her what kind of tomatoes she was growing."

Sarah looks as if she doesn't believe him. "Summerfield," she says, "will you tell me . . . when you discover it yourself . . . how I might help you? I'm not so dull as to let my own relief at your return blind me to—"

"How *old* is he anyway?" he says suddenly.

Affronted, she pauses for a moment. "He's thirty-one."

"Thirty-one! That's nearly a decade—"

"Summerfield," she says, "first of all, Papa was six years older than—"

"I'm sure you know he could do very happily with much less than you," he says. "There'll be an awful lot of you squandered there."

She appears both astonished and hurt. "You exchanged a dozen words with him at a Christmas party last year," she says. "You can hardly claim to know him."

"Then look me in the eye and tell me you think I'm wrong."

"It's not like you to be arrogant, Summerfield," she says, lowering her head. "It's not your nature . . . I've always admired that about you."

"Then look me in the eye," he says. "Tell me you think I'm wrong."

She turns her face to one side. "I do think you're wrong," she says, "but even if I thought you right, it's not your place to say such things. It's horrid. What possible effect can it have but to make me unhappy?"

"I say it precisely in the interest of your happiness," he says. "*And* you haven't looked me in the eye."

"I won't be put to tests," she says. "I must say you've a very strange way of showing your interest in my happiness. For weeks, I thought you dead. I thought you'd accomplished what you set out to do . . . to leave me thoroughly alone. I can't imagine what you've been through, Summerfield, but you weren't here, were you . . . night after night, as I—"

Just then Thomas Gilfinian comes out the kitchen door, waving his hat and crying, "Hallo, hallo!"

Sarah moves hurriedly to the shed, putting her back to the house and situating Summerfield between herself and Gilfinian, who approaches the flagstone path, beaming. "Welcome home," he says, offering his hand, "welcome home, lad."

Summerfield thinks it odd to be welcomed to his own home by a visitor, but he supposes Gilfinian means it generally, *Welcome back to Brooklyn*. He doesn't much like being called lad either, and he finds the man's green plaid vest oddly familiar and a bit garish.

"What a day!" cries Gilfinian, and then calls out to Sarah, "Sarah, dear, are you all right?"

"Yes," she answers, turning and coming forward now. "I'd only got some dust in my eye."

"So, tell me what you think," says Gilfinian to Summerfield, smiling in a comradely fashion. "Will General Grant move against Petersburg again? I understand it hinges on the condition of the railroads."

Gilfinian refers to the question of how successfully the army has isolated General Lee from the support of his western reinforcements— but Summerfield refuses to be drawn into a jovial dialogue about troop movements, as if the war were a fascinating outdoor sport. He says, "I don't know," and then looks pointedly at Sarah.

His attention thus deflected, Gilfinian turns to her, takes the bonnet from her hand, and places it on her head, undertaking to tie the ribbons. "You best put this on," he says.

Summerfield sees with satisfaction that she blushes, embarrassed at being treated like a child. He smiles at her from over Gilfinian's shoulder, and she casts him a defiant look.

"There," says Gilfinian, ducking cheerfully beneath the brim of the straw bonnet to kiss her cheek.

Summerfield has never before seen his sister permit a kiss from anyone who was not a blood relative, and it appeared to him—though he can't entirely trust his own judgment—that she tolerated more than enjoyed it.

"Thomas," she says, "I've been trying to persuade Summerfield to come with us today."

"Oh, yes, you must," says Gilfinian. "You wouldn't want to miss our eloquent Mr. Hastings, our trustee, reading the Declaration of Independence."

Summerfield—who hadn't recalled Gilfinian's being quite so short, nor having such rosy, pudgy cheeks—smiles again, widening his eyes, and says, "'Let Facts be submitted to a candid world.'"

"What?" says Gilfinian. "What's that?"

"He's quoting from the Declaration," says Sarah quickly.

"Oh, yes, yes, of course," says Gilfinian. "And you don't want to miss the pupils' calisthenics . . . and 'On the Hill the Sunlight Playeth.' Do come with us, won't you?"

"Thank you," says Summerfield, "but I believe I'll stay indoors. I think it's going to be hot."

Gilfinian turns to Sarah and says, "I'm afraid he's immovable, my dear. And I can't very well argue that it won't be hot."

"But you've never minded hot weather," says Sarah. "You like hot weather."

Summerfield shrugs his shoulders. "Maybe I've changed," he says.

At that moment, as if to settle the matter, the sun clears the treetops and floods the garden with a blinding light. They each begin to move toward the house. Summerfield notices the pungent smell of the tomato vines, instantly awakened by the sun.

Just before going through the door, Sarah turns to him. "If you don't relish visiting the barbers," she says, "I'll do it for you this evening, after supper."

He holds back to retrieve his coffee cup. Then, once inside, he hears Gilfinian, already on the stairs, whispering, "He's awfully thin, isn't he?"

———

IN THE AFTERNOON, he sits at the writing desk in the library, lost in thought—or lost in something akin to thought, a somber composition with far fewer notes than rests and virtually no melody at all. He removes his father's smoking cap and touches a bald spot, about the size of a quarter, on the right side of the crown of his head, where, the previous night, he twined the hairs singly around a finger and absentmindedly pulled them from his scalp. For a moment, he hoped he'd only dreamed he'd done this stupid thing, and it's with a sense of shame that he accepts it now as fact. The last several minutes, he has been pondering an apparent paradox within himself—that having looked into the face of death, he sometimes feels fearless and at other times feels afraid of just about everything. He imagines himself swinging between two walls (another image of suspension, of not touching ground) and dimly recalls a passage from one of Emerson's famous essays—something about man, in pursuit of truth, being swung between walls, unmoored, submitting to "the inconvenience of suspense." Well, he thinks, it was nothing of his own doing—he can take no credit for it—but if Mr. Emerson would have him unmoored and afloat . . .

The face of death, he thinks suddenly, realizing he has no idea what it means or what it might look like, and just then Mrs. Bannister raps sharply against the library door and flings it open, marches into the room with a tray, and startles him so badly he nearly cries out. He quickly puts the smoking cap back on. She takes from the tray a tumbler of pale-green liquid and a single letter and sets them down on the desk.

He sighs, collecting himself, and says, "Mrs. B, do you think you might knock on the door gently and then wait for my reply before you enter?"

She pulls herself up straight and draws back her head, incredulous. "But I've brought you lemonade," she says. "And a new letter that's just arrived."

"Thank you," he says. "But still . . . do you think you might do as I ask . . . knock gently and wait for a reply?"

"I've never been asked to wait for any reply before entering the library or the parlor in this house," she says. "Not in my over twenty years here."

"But I'm asking you now," he says. "Do you think you might start?"

"I'm not sure I can," she answers.

"Well, I would be grateful if you would try," he says.

She looks at him sadly, turning down the corners of her mouth and wrinkling her forehead. "I don't suppose you've forgiven me for blabbing to Sarah last winter," she says. "About your plan to enlist."

"There was never anything to forgive," he says. "This has nothing to do with that. I only think it would be a lot more civilized than—"

"'More civilized'?" she says.

"More civilized than just barging in like that," he says.

She frowns at him again and turns to go. She stops at the door. "I wouldn't have guessed the Union army a place to pick up airs," she says. "Why, you make me out to be a herd of cattle."

He watches her as she closes the door with exaggerated, almost parodistic caution, so as not to make a sound. After another moment, he opens and reads the letter she brought, which is from Al Reach of the Eckford Club. Reach has heard that Hayes is back in town, recovering from an illness, and—assuming he's been mustered out—wants to encourage him, nay, *beseech* him, to rejoin the club as soon as possible. With only six of their principal players left, the ranks have never been in greater need. They've managed to acquire three new recruits, including an excellent catcher from Philadelphia and a young pitcher from the juniors, who shows promise but still wants a good bit of training. Hayes's return would be a godsend to the Eckfords—who, this late into the summer, have yet to play their first regular match. He eagerly awaits Hayes's prompt reply.

Summerfield refolds the letter and slips it inside the desk drawer, then goes to the low table between the wing chairs and collects three of the newspapers there. Back at the desk he begins tearing the paper into strips, about six inches wide and ten or twelve inches long. After he has accumulated a dozen of these, he rolls each into a narrow cylinder, moistening the seam with his tongue to make it stick, and flattening and gathering the ends to create a tapered effect. Meticulously he works, going mentally blank, and at last he brings out his mother's brass inkwell and dips the cigar-shaped things into it, an end at a time, to blacken them. One by one, he lays them on the remaining newspaper, side by side, to dry.

BROOKLYN WAS ONCE a noisy place—a cacophony of hammers and whistles, hooves and hooligans and stray pigs in the street. Now it seems curiously, objectionably quiet.

Also . . . overall . . . purposeless.

Where is the war now? Where does it still exist? Reading about it in the newspapers somehow makes it even less likely, less real—a burnt ship somewhere at the bottom of the globe, bereft of cargo and crew, adrift in a sea of ash.

EXPLOSIVE BURSTS OF STEAM, a ringing of wheels, an erratic, startling whistle. He recalls the ride home with Walt, back to Brooklyn, dreamlike, in and out of sleep. Through his own special channels, Walt had managed to obtain tickets for them on an army transport, and though their car had walls and doors, windows and seats, the journey was not unlike the earlier one that deposited him at the hospital, the mammoth world, beyond understanding. Darkness and light. A smell of wet wool. Warm night air. Even a pasture, dotted with white flowers.

Walt, ill, chronically flushed, coughed sporadically, but was otherwise unusually quiet; when he did speak, he was terse and appeared pained by the rough rocking of the car. In the hospital, Summerfield had envisioned himself in a railcar with Walt—he'd imagined Walt's patting him on the knee, saying, with his curious compound of maternal maleness, *Almost home, now,* and Walt did in fact say something to that effect. With his characteristic timing, he nodded and smiled and said, "You'll soon be among more familiar sights and sounds, my dear." The moment before, Summerfield had pondered the phantom shapes flying by outside the windows, indecipherable, unnameable; the quivering reflections on the inside of the glass; the curious silence of the men in the car, their apparent reluctance to converse; the play of eyes meeting, and quickly averted. Two worlds, signaled by attire: in Burroughs's civilian clothes, Summerfield had felt he properly belonged to neither of them.

Some of the uniformed men slept, pressed close against one another, swaying. Always the rattle of wheels below. *A raging world,* thought Summerfield, closing his eyes; *hurtling them through the night.*

A train.

And, *Not dead. Beyond understanding.*

VIGILANCE REWARDED: at irregular intervals, the library's tall lace curtains swing inward into the room a few inches—held there, suspended, by a current of air—then sway silently back into place. During the few seconds of suspension, he makes sure to hold his breath.

BASE BALL ONCE SEEMED to him the answer to an important inner question—pursuing it, playing it once settled some private confusion—but now he has lost any inkling of the original problem.

Since his mind has become such an intriguing and often-frightening organ, he has begun experimenting with telling himself lies—it's rather like tossing a trick ball at a batsman, just to see what will happen. He has, for example, told himself that the figures who stood at the end of his bed in the hospital were not ghosts at all, but angels.

DEEP-GOLD SUNLIGHT and the shadows of leaves fall over the topmost part of the library curtains, a pattern of lace upon lace—a layered effect, heavy and hot—that makes one long for the cold sharp blade of winter.

Now and again he takes two letters from his hip pocket—the two he brought with him from Washington, the one from Walt, the other from the nurse Anne—and passes his fingers over the paper, worn smooth and slack as cloth.

HE ARRANGES HIMSELF among the several pillows in the window seat and falls asleep. Soon a great pillar of fire, a towering pine, wavers and topples, crashing to the ground and shaking the earth; when first he opens his eyes, a mist of red sparks still wafts slowly down from the library ceiling.

He's sweating, and his head aches. As he sits up and touches his feet to the floor, he sees a face peering at him from around the wing of the farther chair—Sarah, barely visible in the dusky air. She smiles and says, "You're awake."

Strangely reassured, he says, "I suppose I am. How long have you been sitting there?"

She stands, moves across the room, and slides the small desk chair alongside him. She still wears her white dress from the school day. As she sits down, she says, "Nearly half an hour."

"Did Thomas not see you home?"

"He did," she says. "And was gravely disappointed by my not asking him to stay."

"I hope you didn't send him away on my account."

"Not exactly," she says.

"What do you mean?"

"I mean, not entirely . . . not entirely on your account. He wanted to celebrate the start of the summer vacation, naturally, a perfectly reasonable desire—to have supper together or something. But I only wanted to . . . I don't know what I wanted. I felt absurdly tired. When I found you asleep, I sat in Mommy's chair and watched the room grow dark. Somehow very restoring after a day of . . . *festivities*."

"Was it not what you expected?" he asks.

"Oh, yes," she answers. "Exactly what I expected, only much, much longer."

She takes a handkerchief from her sleeve and dabs it to her brow. "When I first came in," she says, "I asked Mrs. B if she'd brought you any tea. She only shook her head and seemed very peculiar about it."

"I'm afraid we had a few words," he says.

"What sort of words?"

"I only asked her if she might try to knock on the library door . . . rather than pound . . . and wait for my reply before entering."

"I see," she says. "I don't imagine that went over very well."

"No."

"It can't be easy," she says. "Managing us into maturity, and now being managed *by* us. Is it because you might not wish to be disturbed?"

"It's because I don't wish to be startled out of my chair," he says.

She appears a bit startled herself, but then, after a moment, nods thoughtfully. "You were whispering in your sleep," she says.

"What did I say?"

"I couldn't understand most of it, but several times you repeated, 'I can't . . . I can't.'"

It occurs to him to ask her not to sneak into rooms and spy on him when he's sleeping, but he restrains himself because he feels kindly toward her for sending Gilfinian away.

After a long pause—in which he might have spoken but didn't— she says, "Summerfield, you know you've told me almost nothing."

"There's almost nothing to tell," he says.

She considers this and then says, "I don't think that can be true. I'm sure it's not possible. Thomas suggested I should allow you to come out of your shell at your own speed."

"Is that how he put it? Do you think he meant to compare me to a snail or a tortoise? Or maybe to a clam?"

She sighs and looks into her lap. "You don't know the pains he took on my behalf to find you," she says. "To learn something about what had happened to you. His concern for you was steadfast . . . as it remains."

"Well, then I guess you'd better follow his advice," he says. "And allow me to come out of my shell at my own speed."

"Very well," she says, hopelessly, and stands up. Almost at once she touches the crown of his head and asks, "Oh, dear . . . what's hap-pened here?"

He recoils, casting about the window seat for the smoking cap, which he finds quickly and puts on his head. "Can you possibly leave me alone?" he says.

She looks down at him. The gray light through the lace curtains flattens her features, but he can see clearly that she is anxious.

"Of course," she says. "Why not?"

She drags the chair to its place at the writing desk. "But before I go," she says, her voice unsteady, "perhaps you'll tell me what these hideous black things are you've left on Mommy's desk."

He gets to his feet, goes to the desk, and begins gathering them up. She might have stepped back but instead moves closer, stands next to him, and lays a hand on his shoulder. "You made these," she says, obstinately kind. "Summerfield . . . darling . . . what are they?"

Now he drops them onto the desktop, where they land in a jumbled heap, and he experiences the pressure of his lifelong impulse to run. To his own surprise, he says, too sharply, "They're corpses."

Immediately remorseful, he sits in the chair, not looking at her. "At least that's what I think they are," he says. "I think they're corpses."

DESPITE HIMSELF—and despite how *shell* evokes artillery projectiles—he appreciates Gilfinian's suggestion for the good influence it has apparently had on Sarah's approach to the problem of his return, his having survived the war, his still being alive after all: she would allow him to proceed with his acclimation at his own speed. (Certainly none of her actions would be rash or wanting thought.) Since Friday in the library, she seems to have taken the idea to heart and has met each of his small flare-ups with patience and equanimity. Still, he has no intention of coming out of any shell. If it is possible to go farther *in*, he will do that instead.

Friday evening, after supper, Mrs. Bannister—having knocked gently on the parlor door and waited for Summerfield's reply—approached him and Sarah to ask if they might do without her and Jane for the next three days; they wanted to visit their cousins in Deerpark. It was not the first time the sisters had retreated to the country for the Glorious Fourth, on which occasion, in Mrs. B's opinion, far too many people get far too "glorious." And, as everyone knew, Jane detested all manner of fireworks—firecrackers especially made her nervous—and though they couldn't entirely escape them on Long

Island, they could, it seemed, get farther away from them. Naturally Sarah said yes, and at eight o'clock Saturday morning, the two women set off in the rain for the rail station.

On Sunday, Summerfield went with Sarah to Holy Trinity. He'd agreed to go only if they arrived five minutes late and left five minutes early, to avoid the risk of any socializing. Throughout the service, he kept his eyes either closed or fixed on the hymnal or prayer book. His thoughts repeatedly strayed and blurred, and he found the groined roof and the purples and ambers of the windows curiously oppressive. Dr. Littlejohn's sermon began with the words, "Tomorrow our great country turns eighty-eight . . ." and briskly ventured off onto the nature, causes, and costs of schism. Summerfield saw in his mind's eye a cloud of black smoke rising from behind the pulpit like an enormous flower, splaying its five petals and darkening the air of the chancel. At the Eucharist, he stayed in the pew, not because of any religious conflict but because of a deep irrational reluctance to enter the aisle, to take a place in line, to wait, to inch forward.

Now, as they walk the few streets home from the church, Sarah strikes him as unnaturally pensive—he imagines her silenced by Gilfinian's suggestion, treading cautiously, not asking questions she might otherwise ask. The day has turned cloudy, cool enough at this hour for her to leave her umbrella closed, and she repeatedly taps the tip of it on the pavement, a prickly noise that sets his teeth on edge. At last he says, "Do you think Mrs. B and Jane will be coming back to us?"

"Whatever do you mean?" she says.

"I fear they left because of my unexpected homecoming," he says. "And my starting to lay down new rules."

"Summerfield," she says, "Mrs. B and Jane—like everyone who knows you—are overjoyed by your homecoming."

Her tone is more pedagogical than he would like, but he knows she only means to put his mind at ease.

"They've gone to Deerpark before," she adds. "They've always come back."

"It seemed . . . I don't know . . . abrupt," he says.

She nods. "It did seem abrupt," she says, "but I wonder if they weren't undecided about leaving. I wonder if Mrs. B didn't think it too soon for them to go, scarcely more than a week after your arrival."

"Of course," he says. "And then our little blowup in the library settled the matter for her."

"Blowup?" says Sarah. "You didn't say you had a blowup."

"Our little spat then."

"That's even worse," she says. "I hate that word."

"Well, call it what you want," he says, "but I bet I'm right. Is that your Gilfinian sitting on our steps?"

She stops suddenly—they are about ten houses away—and Summerfield has the feeling, based almost entirely on instinct, that she might duck out of sight if she could. For no apparent reason she opens her umbrella.

"I believe it is," she says, disclosing no emotion, and then takes his arm and continues forward. "He must have walked over from church . . . from Clinton Avenue."

As they draw nearer, it appears to Summerfield that Gilfinian— seated on a lower step in his Sunday best and leaning against the railing—is sound asleep. "I think he might be napping," he whispers to Sarah.

"That's impossible," she says, stopping again.

A breeze stirs the limbs of a nearby locust tree and sheds down a few feathery leaves onto the pavement. "Oh, dear," she says. "He'll be terribly embarrassed if we surprise him."

"What do you propose? Would you like us to stand here until he wakes up?"

She releases his arm and closes the umbrella. "What I would like," she says, "is for you to be kind to him. There's no good reason why you shouldn't be friends."

Summerfield laughs—something about the prospect of any friend (not specifically Gilfinian) makes him uneasy—but then he sees the serious look on Sarah's face. He recalls her role, since the time of their parents' death, as his moral guide—how, prior to his going to war, he'd done well by trying not to disappoint her. Kindness to Gilfinian seems little enough to ask, easy enough to concede. He smiles and shrugs his shoulders. "Okay," he says. "Don't worry."

On the steps, a brown derby hat rests next to Gilfinian, who sleeps with his bare head against the railing and his hands pressed together in his lap. Next to the hat sits a large basket, covered with a blue-and-white checkered cloth.

Sarah leans toward him and says softly, "Thomas, dear . . ."

He blinks and immediately turns crimson. "Oh, my goodness," he says. "I dozed off."

"You're lucky you weren't eaten by a wild pig," says Summerfield, joking, but apparently frightening Gilfinian instead. Under his breath, he says to Sarah, "Sorry . . ." and then passes Gilfinian his hat, which the man puts on gingerly, as if he were trying it on for the first time.

GILFINIAN, having brought along a pic-nic dinner prepared by his mother, wanted to walk to a park and eat outdoors, but Sarah rejected the idea with a query for which he plainly had no answer: "Why is it men always want to eat outdoors?" she asked. And so they ate Mrs. Gilfinian's cold pork roast, potatoes, and applesauce in the dining room—"in the custom of Homo sapiens."

Afterward, Sarah retreated downstairs to the kitchen, telling Gilfinian that if he *had* to smoke, this would be a good time for it, during her absence. The two men moved into the parlor, where Gilfinian stood at the hearth and undertook to light his pipe. Summerfield— wanting more than anything to go upstairs to his room, shed his Sunday clothes, and lie down—sat at one end of the sofa and tried not to meet Gilfinian's gaze, which (he'd discovered over dinner) transmitted an unceasing desire to be liked.

Now, drawing at intervals on the pipe to get it started, Gilfinian says to him, "Sarah told me . . . that while you were . . . in camp . . . you became fond of backgammon."

An innocuous enough remark, it has the disagreeable effect of conjuring for Summerfield a mental tableau of Sarah's reading his letters to Gilfinian. "Yes," he says, yanking loose his tie.

"Backgammon was my father's game," says Gilfinian. "He called it tables. I'm afraid I have more enthusiasm for it than skill . . . but we must play sometime. And now that vacation's upon us, I'm determined to teach it to Sarah."

"I would rather you didn't," says Summerfield.

"Why not?" says Gilfinian, clearly taken aback.

"That is," says Summerfield, "if you don't mind . . . I've promised to teach her."

"Of course I don't mind," says Gilfinian. "I didn't mean to . . . well, I'll lend you my set if you like."

"Thank you," says Summerfield, "but I plan to buy us one of our own."

Gilfinian places his pipe (which appears to have gone out) onto Mr. Hayes's silver pipe rack on the mantel. He moves to the sofa and sits next to Summerfield, closer than necessary, and clears his throat.

"There's something I want to say to you," he says, looking earnest and perturbed. "I want you to know that I'm . . . by nature, I mean . . . I'm not an interloping sort. I don't fancy being the fellow who stole your sister from you. If you'll let me, I'd be an elder brother to you instead. You see, Sarah means for us to live together here, in Hicks Street, after we're married. I can't fault her for that—it's a great deal more comfortable than Mother's house . . . *and* less populated. But I'm well aware of its being your home, lad . . . yours and Sarah's, and . . . well, I want you to know you'll always be welcome here. We assume you'll go on living here with us . . . *hope* you will . . . for as long as it suits you."

Summerfield, overwhelmed by the quantity of information given here, can't think where to begin. There's Gilfinian's nature to consider, and his desire to be an elder brother, as well as their future living arrangements—none of which Summerfield has previously contemplated. To make matters worse, a fragment of Walt's lines (recited in the hospital) suddenly intrudes into his thoughts, "cold dirges of the baffled," and so he is most grateful when, after only a moment, Sarah appears at the dining room door and Gilfinian stands up, diverted and thoroughly absorbed by her entrance.

"Well," she says cheerfully, "what shall we do tomorrow?"

The question strikes Summerfield as oddly philosophical and far-reaching. He recalls the bellowed *Forward!* that flew down the long ragged gash of the earthworks at the Brock Road, its rapid repetition something like gunfire, and how the troops had poured out of the trenches, a blue-breaking ocean wave, and charged into the woods.

Gilfinian indicates for Sarah to take his seat on the sofa, and then he moves back to the mantel. He says, "I'm thinking of Coney Island and a saltwater bath."

"Oh, no," says Sarah, "that would mean a train ride. And loads of dust."

Gilfinian opens his mouth to speak but then only nods—of course he has foolishly forgotten about dust. "Well, there isn't to be a parade this year," he says, "but we'll have fireworks on Fort Greene."

"That might be fun," says Sarah, and looks at Summerfield.

"Not for me," says Summerfield. "But you two go."

"What, and leave you here all alone?" says Sarah.

"The aldermen have put everything into Fort Greene," says Gilfinian. "On account of a steep increase in the cost of fireworks . . . they'll pay as much for this one display as they used to pay for three."

"We wouldn't dream of leaving you alone," says Sarah, to Summerfield.

"Not even if it's what I prefer?"

"No," she says, "not even."

"I imagine it'll be quite grand," says Gilfinian. "I've read about some of the pieces . . . one of them starts as a horizontal wheel, then changes to a vertical globe, representing the motions of the earth. All sorts of colors and fires and stars . . . scarlets and greens and blues and so forth . . . and then it ends with the names of Grant, Meade, and McClellan."

Sarah casts a smile Gilfinian's way, and Summerfield thinks he detects too much benevolence in it, a smile she might cast an awkward, well-meaning child. He's offended by Gilfinian's easy recitation of the Union generals' names, as if they were his good friends; and there's a pain at the base of his skull, akin to the throbbing brain-pang he'd felt when he was lost in the forest.

Sarah says to him, "Tell us what *you* would like to do. What about a match of base ball? There must be oodles tomorrow."

Obviously, she means to question him at some length—tiresome for sure, but fortunately he has plenty of experience with questions. It now occurs to him that Gilfinian's speech about interloping and living arrangements was practiced between them, her withdrawal to the kitchen calculated to provide an opportunity.

"I would like to stay at home," Summerfield answers. "I think I would like to read a book."

"A book?" she says. "What book?"

"I don't know. Emerson maybe."

"Why Emerson?"

"Why not Emerson?"

"Oh," says Gilfinian, gazing distantly toward the windows. "Another's called the Jeweled Cross of the Legion of Honor. I wouldn't mind seeing that one."

"You could bring Emerson with you then," says Sarah. "We'll walk over early and spend the day."

She remains splintered into more than one person, he observes, just as she was during the weeks before he left for Virginia; now he understands this as Gilfinian's effect on her. He further observes that she wears their mother's gold locket, the carved octagonal pendant Mrs. Hayes had worn regularly and that enclosed strands of her children's hair. How maddening that Sarah should wear it—how could she possibly confound him more?—keeping close to her heart strands of their interwoven hair.

"Summerfield," she says. "I beg you . . . again . . . not to look at me that way. It's . . . it's . . . I don't know what it is, but—"

"I only noticed you're wearing Mommy's locket," he says.

She grasps it protectively, as if she thinks he would take it from her. "Yes," she says, "I am. Why do you call attention to it?"

"No reason," he says.

"Would you rather I didn't?"

"Why would I have an opinion one way or the other?" he says.

She appears to ponder the question for a moment—and to reach an idea she's unwilling to express.

"Well, then," she says at last, putting the subject aside and glancing at Gilfinian. "What about tomorrow?"

"I think it's got to be Fort Greene," says Gilfinian. "I've just recalled another of the advertised pieces . . . something with the intriguing title Gallopade of Serpents. We wouldn't want to miss something called Gallopade of Serpents, would we?"

Sarah casts Gilfinian that same indulgent smile again and then says to Summerfield, "What about it? You could bring your book along if you like."

Fatigued and inexplicably edgy, Summerfield stands and moves behind the sofa. "No," he says. "As I've already said . . . I prefer to stay at home. Please go without me."

"Well," she says, shaking her head. "I have to say that staying at home and reading a book doesn't seem a very fit way to celebrate—"

"To celebrate our independence?" he says. "Yes, I guess we should be very happy . . . very grateful we have our blessed independence."

He turns to Gilfinian. "Tell me," he says. "Do you suppose there'll be lots of Roman candles? Rocket sticks . . . golden lances?"

Gilfinian, unsure of where he's treading now, says, "Yes, lad . . . I expect there'll be a considerable—"

"Crystal fountains? Jets of fire?"

Gilfinian tries to smile. "Yes, I expect so," he says.

"Revolving suns? Perhaps a grand volute . . . a feu de joie?"

"Summerfield," says Sarah, "Thomas was only—"

"I wonder why there won't be a military parade?" says Summerfield. "I wonder if it's because there are no regiments wanting to march in one?"

He excuses himself and leaves the parlor abruptly. Once he has closed the door and stands alone in the hall, he lingers for a few seconds, thinking he'll hear their voices, their tone if not their actual words. But there's only silence, which makes him feel sorry and ashamed. The fanlight over the outer doors imparts a dismal glow to the hall, where the air is cool but alarmingly thin. As he starts to move toward the newel post and the stairs, he's aware, to his left and behind him, of the great mirror, whose frame was twined at Christmastime with festoons of holly. He's absolutely certain that if he turned and looked now, his would not be the only image reflected there.

————

As he walks down the wide aisle toward the wardmaster's room, he notices that he's wearing civilian clothes belonging to Burroughs, and he reminds himself he must return them before he leaves for Virginia. A steady wind blows throughout the ward, stirring the flags and mosquito curtains, and, most odd, everything is blue and wavy, as if he were looking down the chimney of an ink bottle. All of the beds are unoccupied, stripped of their linens, and he imagines everyone has died and gone to the deadhouse—there's nobody left to fight the war. President Lincoln, dressed in a frock coat and stovepipe hat, sits at the night watcher's table reading a picture magazine; next to him stands a tall wooden box. As Summerfield passes the table, the president looks up at him and smiles bravely, as if he's choking back tears, his lips encrusted with painful-looking fever blisters. Now he smells the odor of burnt hair and sees, some distance down the aisle, that one of the beds is in flames. Captain Gracie madly flails the mattress with a blanket, crying, "What have I done, what have I done?" A uniformed soldier lies in the bed, charred and weeping, but he cannot tell who it is. As he draws closer and is about to see the face, the poor fellow's cartridge belt detonates *pop pop pop pop pop* and he startles awake.

Of course it is a string of firecrackers going off somewhere nearby, and though he has shut his window, lowered the shade, and drawn the drapes, he can hear the myriad of explosions, near and far, small and not so small, all around Brooklyn. He sits up, on the edge of the bed, and covers his ears with his hands, thinking he has made a terrible mistake.

Against her great resistance, he persuaded her to go with Gilfinian to Fort Greene. She'd come and knocked softly on his door before he'd gotten out of bed. Already dressed for the day, she'd brought him a tray with coffee and toast and jam. She sat next to him and said she understood, of course she understood thoroughly, that he wouldn't feel like celebrating . . . celebrating *anything*, let alone the birth of the nation, now cleaved in two and destroying itself. "I've decided to stay at home with you," she said. "We'll pass the day quietly. We'll read together. We don't even have to talk."

But he'd begged her to go, claiming (truthfully) that he hadn't slept well, didn't feel well, and wanted nothing more than to loaf all day in bed. If she stayed at home on his account, it would only make him feel worse. He referenced one of Gilfinian's pyrotechnic "pieces," the Gallopade of Serpents, and said he wanted her to come home later and tell him all about it. Eventually, reluctantly, she gave in—the fireworks display on Fort Greene would be over by sunset, but she promised to be home even earlier—and not long after she left the house, he dozed off and dreamed he was back in the hospital.

Now, as he sits on the edge of the bed, hands covering his ears, flinching at every outdoor explosion, he regrets his own persuasive powers and wishes he were not alone. Then, immediately, he regrets having wished it, for something in the air suggests he might *not* be alone. He feels his heart inside his chest. On the floor before his window, a bit of light radiates from below the scalloped hem of the drapes. He fears that someone has stolen into the room while he slept and now conceals himself behind the drapes; he believes he sees, among the shadows there at the floor, the toes of a man's boots. He removes his hands from his ears and thinks he hears the man's breathing. Outdoors, quite near, there's another jangling salvo, and he stands, quickly walks to the window, and yanks open the drapes. No man hiding there, no intruder, no ghost. Only the flat blank canvas of the shade.

HE FORCES HIMSELF to bring up water and spend some time at the toilet-table. He bathes with a sponge and cleans his teeth and nails. He applies soap to his face with the brush and takes a razor from its case. He makes only one stroke and wipes the blade with a paper, but then abandons the shaving because each recurrent fusillade outdoors jolts him, and he cannot trust his hand. He wipes his face with a towel. He uses the dumbbells for ten minutes, after which he sponges himself all over again and gets dressed.

He goes downstairs to the library, finds the book of Mr. Emerson's essays, and takes it from the shelf. He sits in his father's wing chair but only holds the unopened book in his lap. He wears his father's embroidered slippers and smoking cap. He crosses one leg over the other and is suddenly overcome by a deep sense of fraudulence: aspiring to be a man, he has tried to behave as one, a charade so wanting in substance it has failed even to convince himself. What is it, then, that sits flinching and quailing in a chair, in a room of cold ash and half memories, in a house absent of both mother and father? Whatever it is, it lacks a rational essence, lacks even the narrow abandon of a boy. The constant crack-and-pop of the fireworks outdoors has renewed the ringing in his ears. For a minute or more, he feels pinned to the chair, eyes closed, unable to move, and then there's a sharp explosion somewhere downstairs. Hooligans have broken into the house and set off a firecracker indoors.

He lays the book aside and takes the poker from the hearth. He goes out onto the landing and creeps down the stairs. Careful to avoid the mirror in the hall, he inspects the living room and the dining room, both vacant. He continues down to the kitchen, also vacant. He checks the door to the garden, which is bolted. He leaves the poker there and covers his ears with his hands.

Going back up the stairs from the kitchen, he discovers that his leg has started to hurt, high on the back of his thigh, and this fills him with rage. In the hall again, enraged, he purposely confronts the mirror. Looking back at him there is the young man from the dream, the one on the bed engulfed in flames, only now the soldier is pressing his hands over his ears, as if to block out something he doesn't want to hear. Summerfield believes him to be someone he knows but can't put a name to him. Hatless, his face covered with soot, his eyes red with weeping, his charred sack coat releasing corkscrews of smoke, he casts Summerfield a pleading look.

Summerfield closes his eyes and backs away. When he bumps the wall behind him, he turns and starts up the stairs, just as a volley of detonations erupts out in the street. Again he thinks, *I have made a terrible mistake,* and as he passes the door to his parents' room he believes he hears someone speak his name. He opens the door, enters the room, and finds no one there, but most strangely the room is transformed, disarranged, stripped almost bare. The drapes have been taken down from the windows, as well as the bed curtains, and the rug rolled up. The wallpaper has been removed but not replaced, exposing a piebald plaster that resembles an enormous map of an unknown world. A variety of boxes and trunks are stacked opposite the windows. A visible layer of dust coats the tabletops. He wanders through the room in a state of awe and confusion, and then, all at once, he grasps the meaning of all this: having ridded the room of their parents' things, Sarah's readying it for herself and Gilfinian. In the next moment, he recalls the green plaid vest Gilfinian wore on Friday last, familiar and garish—it had belonged to Mr. Hayes! She must have given it to Gilfinian. Perhaps Gilfinian helped her sort through their parents' belongings and took whatever he liked.

He goes to the round-top table, now pushed against the footrail of the bed, and slides open its small drawer. *The Lover's Marriage Lighthouse,* the disquieting book he found there some months ago, is gone, but now the empty drawer emanates a sweet coppery odor once known to him but forgotten. Next, he moves around the left side of the bed and into his father's dressing room, where it seems that his vision contracts to a small circle enclosed by a starry darkness. He closes the door behind him, which has the happy effect of muting the sounds of the war outside. Drawn to his father's dressing table—for here the purging of the rooms has admitted an omission or two—he gazes down at his father's badger-hair brush and touches its soft bristles; he opens the case of razors, seven in all, one for each day of the week. Because it is Monday, he takes the second in the line. He looks into the little mirror, uncommonly moved by the recognizable image of his own face. As inside his head, a voice groans, *I beg you . . . I beg you . . . I beg you . . . ,* he holds the blade to his throat.

He hears the sound of rain beating on a roof.

He presses the blade harder and then hears Walt's voice: . . . *a riddle to be solved . . . a rose in the garden . . .*

His hand shakes. He mentally admonishes himself not to be such a coward, presses the blade yet harder, and then sees, reflected in the mirror to the right side of his own backward face, the box, the tall box, larger than a casket, that has recurred in his dreams: his father's elm-wood armoire.

He puts back the razor in its case, turns around, and opens the door to the armoire, which he finds vacant, emptied of every trace of his father's things. He puts his head inside, breathes in its clean woody aroma.

Once he has entered the armoire, in which he can stand without ducking, he lowers himself, sliding his back along one side, to the fabric-covered floor. Only mildly dismayed by the fact that both his old shrapnel wounds have begun to bleed again, he's calmer than he has been all morning. He pulls the door shut. Swaddled in darkness, he hears no gunfire, no voices, nothing but the sound of his own breathing.

Long afterward—very long afterward, he thinks, but he can't be sure—he again hears someone speak his name. He believes it's his sister's voice, muted by walls and doors, and with each repetition of his name, she seems to draw closer to where he is: inside his father's armoire, in darkness, all safe at last.

He must have dozed off. Independence Day. The chronic detonations of firecrackers outdoors, so like gunfire, unhinged him. Now he has slept, deeply, and awakened feeling much better, restored to himself. Quietly, he gets to his feet and pushes open the door to the armoire. Quietly, he steps out into the dimness of his father's dressing room. He no longer hears Sarah calling his name and assumes she has gone to search for him elsewhere. But when he opens the dressing room door, she stands at one of the bedroom windows, not looking out but looking down.

His sudden appearance gives her a start. She gasps, puts her hand to her heart. "You frightened me," she cries. "What on earth are you doing in there?"

From his vantage in the dressing room doorway, she is mostly a silhouette. Judging from the light behind her, it must be near sunset. Neither of them moves; they confront each other across a distance of several feet. She appears to hold something in her hand, a card of some sort.

"Where's Gilfinian?" he asks.

"I've sent him away again," she says. "You know, Summerfield . . . you might call him Thomas."

"I don't wish to call him Thomas," he says. "Why did you send him away?"

After a pause, she says, "Would you like for me to be frank?"

"Please."

"Because I don't feel I can trust you to be polite to him," she says.

"Have I been rude?"

"Not exactly," she says. "But you've been far from cordial."

"What's that in your hand?" he asks.

Now she comes forward and moves alongside him. "It's the photograph you sent to me in your letter," she says. "Here . . . see . . . very handsome despite the scraggy whiskers."

He can barely make out the image in the dusky light, and he doesn't much care to in any case. This close, he smells her perfume, a mix of rosemary and jasmine. Her pale-yellow dress appears almost white. "Why do you have it?" he asks. "Why were you looking at it just now?"

She faces him, still close, and then, after a moment, lowers her head. "I thought you were in your room," she says. "When I didn't find you there, I became worried. I *am* worried about you, Summerfield. I'm sure you heard me calling your name. Why did you not answer?"

"I fell asleep."

"You can't have fallen asleep in Papa's dressing room. Not unless you—"

"What have you done with their things?" he asks.

Now she looks at him a bit puzzled at first, but then with a kind of determination. "Mrs. B helped me sort through them," she says. "We've stored quite a lot. I gave a few things away. Of course I kept what I wanted of Mommy's. And everything of Papa's I thought you might want."

"Couldn't you have waited?" he says.

"Waited for what?"

"Until I came home."

"You seem to have forgot that for many weeks on end I had no word from you. You seem to have forgot that for some of those weeks I thought you dead."

"And besides," he says, "you needed to get it ready, didn't you?"

She puts her back to him and returns to the window, silent.

He moves closer and says, "You know, Sarah, if Mommy were alive, she wouldn't permit this."

She nods, three times, slowly, without turning. "And so now you get even with me," she says. "Though it's unfair of you to twist things that way. As if my marrying were the same as your going to war . . . which was entirely unnecessary. When I told you Mommy wouldn't let you go if she were alive, I was desperate."

"But *Gilfinian's* unnecessary," he says.

Now she turns and faces him again. "What do you mean?"

"I'm back now," he says. "I'm back."

"Summerfield," she says, "do you imagine that I—"

"Yes," he says, "I do imagine. You took up with him out of fear."

"First of all, I didn't 'take up with him,' and I wonder how it is you profess to know my mind so perfectly."

He goes to her, takes the photograph, tosses it to the floor, and grasps both her hands. "Don't I?" he says. "Don't I know your mind? I've seen you with him enough. You patiently abide about half of what he says and does. You gaily reject every one of his ideas and supplant it with one of your own. Is that the future you want? Is that the future you want for *him*?"

She pulls her hands free but doesn't otherwise withdraw. "So you know my mind better than I know it myself," she says. "You can see the future as well. What else, Summerfield? You've plainly come back altered, but I didn't know . . ."

She stops. Her eyes fill with tears and catch the reddening light from the windows.

"What's plain is your uncertainty," he says. "The only thing surprising is that *he* doesn't see it."

She bows her head.

"Or maybe he does," he adds. "And, like you, discounts it."

Without lifting her head, she says, "Do you know how many nights I wept myself to sleep? Of course you don't. How could you?"

"I'm sorry," he whispers, but she looks up at him skeptically.

"I still don't understand," she says, through tears, "why . . . if you were in a hospital . . . you couldn't have written to me. I don't understand how you could put me through such pointless and preventable grief. It was cruel of you. I felt . . . before you left last winter . . . that you meant somehow to punish me. I felt, while you were away, that you meant to punish me. Then, when I presumed you dead, I was convinced that you'd died . . . needlessly . . . to punish me. Now you're back . . . and despite my joy, Summerfield . . . I feel you mean to punish me still. And I can't for the life of me think how I've wronged you."

She looks at him fiercely, tears pouring forth and falling over her cheeks. "*Tell* me," she says.

With both arms he pulls her against himself and kisses her on the lips. Her body tightens, releases, tightens again, and then she pushes him away. She meets his eye, briefly—not with the question *Who are you* but with the answer *This is who you are*—and then she turns and rushes from the room.

From the floor near his right foot, within a white rectangular border, his own dim image, the likeness taken of a former self, stares up at him.

SEVEN

On Tiptoe

Six days later, on Sunday, he sits at the table by his window writing a letter and pauses for a minute, touching the end of the penholder to his lips. Through the glass, the visible patch of afternoon sky above the tree line glows white with a seamless cover of clouds. Jane—more pasty and insubstantial even than usual—enters the room to collect his dinner tray, and as she crosses the carpet toward the table, she fades away, apparently dissolving into the wallpaper and woodwork behind her. From the floor below, he hears his father's voice, deep and full of cheer, followed by the music of his mother's laughter; he has the feeling they're readying themselves for an outing. Next Sarah wanders in idly, wearing a pink dress and bent on prying; she positions herself next to him so that she can peer over his shoulder.

With his hands and forearms, he shields his work—two pages, the letter he's writing and the letter he's answering.

"Jane was just here and disappeared before my eyes," he says to Sarah. "Simply faded away into thin air."

"We always knew she would eventually," says Sarah. "I'll tell Papa—he'll know what to do. What's that you're writing?"

"If you must know," he says, "I'm writing a letter."

"A letter to whom?"

"Mind your own business," he says. "It's nobody you know."

"Oh, really," she says, and attempts to pull his hand from the tabletop.

"Go away," he says. "You're being rude."

"All right," she says, tugging playfully on his ear before she returns to the hallway. From the threshold, she leans again into the room, with one palm on each side of the doorframe. "But I don't see why you don't tell me," she says. "You know I'll find out sooner or later."

Shaking himself back to reality, Summerfield looks down at the letter he has started. He considers adding, *I have just had the most curious daydream.*

He continues staring vacantly at the page a moment longer, disappointed by his ungainly penmanship, his already crooked lines. He rereads the few words he has written so far:

Brooklyn July 10 1864

Dear Anne—

Please rest assured that you have not lessened yourself in my eyes with your kind note. On the contrary

He slides the other letter from beneath the page—which, dated with the address of the hospital, shows a legible, even beautiful hand:

My dear Mr. X,

My mother, whose regard for ladies' behavior manuals is surpassed only by her regard for Scripture, would be mortified if she knew of my writing this note. I proceed despite the clear sound of her voice, inside my head, reminding me that by initiating a correspondence with a gentleman not my relative I risk lessening myself in his eyes. I trust in your good will & in the certainty of your taking into account our uncommon times & circumstances. I have no doubt that I shall think of you after you are gone from here & I should very much like having a word from you, how you are getting along back in Brooklyn, &c. Whether you are moved to write or not, please know that I hope & pray for your safe journey home & happy reunion with your family.

Your friend,
Anne

Now there comes an actual knock at his door, Mrs. Bannister to collect his dinner tray. "I'm glad to see you dressed and out of bed," she says, crossing the carpet toward the table. "I should have known better than to go away and leave you children alone. I might have guessed something would happen."

"Happen?" he says, turning in his chair. "What is it you imagine has happened?"

She is already back at the doorway. Startled and self-defensive, she says, "Why, I only meant your and Sarah's taking ill. That's all I meant."

"Oh," he says.

Not long after she has gone, he believes he hears the bell downstairs, and he waits for a result, but none immediately comes. Yes, he thinks, we are like children again, sick in our rooms at the same time—though of course he would be hard-pressed to put a name to the illness. Evidently, like himself, Sarah has allowed Mrs. B to think what she likes, that their withdrawal to their rooms for six days in a row must mean they are ill. He has heard Sarah passing in the hallway, outside his door, but he is sure she has neither left the house (not even for church today) nor received any visitors. They seem to have reached a sort of bizarre and lamentable deadlock, and although he would very much like to break it, he has not been able to conceive of a way.

In yet another mode, he experiences himself swung between two walls. At times he feels himself prepared—even if he can see no clear path or scheme—to take up the part of life that is to happen on the latter side of the kiss. Whatever its unhappy effects on Sarah, the fact of it, its heated and awkward entry into their history, has somehow unburdened him. Just as she appeared minutes ago in his daydream, she exists for him now (he believes, even subconsciously) as a sister and only a sister; also (he has noted, without being able to explain it), he no longer seems to bear the obligation of not disappointing her. In short, the event was not at all as he had imagined it would be, and, in at least this singular incidence, the shame of desire turned out to be greater than the shame of commission.

Then, at other times, he suffers the worst kind of remorse about what he has done, what he has felt, who he is, and sees himself doomed to a life of perverse longings and unmerited losses—which quickly connects with the other thing, the larger thing, the Wilderness, the regret of having survived, the thunder and flames . . . beneath which hums the high-pitched whir, the rasp of the surgeon's saw, the plucked string growing tighter, the cries of the dying . . . beneath which simmers the smoke and the brilliant impenetrable silence, the speechlessness, the loss of meaning.

Following *On the contrary,* he writes:

> *it has provided me with some tangible proof of you—my time at the hospital seems most dreamlike*

No, he doesn't want to imply that she is like a dream to him, for it is both insulting and oddly suggestive. He scores *dreamlike* with the nib and tries to think of a suitable substitute. At last he writes:

> *uncertain and when I think of you I am glad to have*

Is it a too-direct expression of fact, to say that he thinks of her? Might it kindle an inflated—

He lays down the pen and holds his head in his hands, his elbows resting on the tabletop. Truthfully, he can think of no word for the terrible deep-rooted compunction that so often overtakes him, the sorrowful dereliction that makes his hands shake and his imaginary wounds sting and bleed, that sops him with the sense that no one can really be trusted, that he is alone, beyond forgiveness, less than human, and will forever dwell in a half world of rattling skulls, the stench of latrines and the sweet coppery stink of burning flesh, the sucking sound of the blade going in, the blade coming out—a kind of boiling syrup that pours over him and darkens the air, stills and steals the air, leaving an ash of bafflement and ugly, pointless vanity.

He has been reading Emerson, which strikes him, at turns, as incisive and as if it were crafted in code. He imagines that if Mr. Emerson examined him, the diagnosis would concern the condition of his soul. He thinks of the roses under Emerson's window, how—simple and pure in their existence—they make no reference to former or better roses; how there is no time to them; and how, by contrast, man "with reverted eye laments the past, or, heedless of the riches that surround him, stands on tiptoe to foresee the future."

Another knock comes at the door, Mrs. B again, this time to say that there are two gentlemen downstairs wishing to see him.

"I showed them into the parlor," she says. "I said they might wait there but that you are not well, and I could make them no promises."

"That's exactly right, Mrs. B," he says. "It's undoubtedly a delegation from the Eckford Club, come round to cajole me in person. Please tell them—"

"Oh, they don't look like ball players to me," she says.

"Well, they wouldn't necessarily . . . what name did they give?"

"The older one," she says, "the big, oddly dressed one with the bushy beard—he said only to tell you Walt had stopped for a visit."

WALT'S BROTHER JEFF—at least a decade younger, tall and slender, with a long face, long nose, and long mustaches—says immediately that he mustn't tarry, he has errands, but that he'd hoped to glimpse Gilfinian's betrothed if she were possibly at home. Summerfield, stumped, looks (probably hopelessly) to Walt, as if Walt might not only divine the problem but also offer a solution. Walt—in a respectable-looking blue suit, and still wearing his hat—smiles, apparently perceiving that *something* wants smoothing, and says, "My dear boy . . . I fear we've ambushed you."

"No," says Summerfield, "it's just . . . if you'll excuse me, I'll go and see . . ."

He turns toward the hall door, intending to find Mrs. B and ask her to approach Sarah. But when he opens it, Sarah herself stands in the hall, one hand still resting on the newel post. She says, "I believe I heard someone humming a tune down here only a few moments ago. Do we have company?"

It is the brittle shell he has met once before, some months earlier. Paradoxically, she wears his favorite blue-plaid dress.

Walt, who has heard her, comes toward the door, saying, "Oh, dear . . . I didn't know I was so loud as that!"

In the parlor, as Summerfield makes introductions, Sarah appears both in awe and at sea, almost as if she were in a trance. Of course Gilfinian has mentioned his friendship with the brother of the famous poet, but Summerfield has told her nothing of his own connection with Walt. To help her, he says, "Walt visited me regularly when I was in the hospital. More than anyone, he's responsible for seeing me home."

"You can't just now be telling her this," says Walt. "I believe I feel slighted."

"There's been surprisingly little time for—"

"I'm only teasing you, my boy," says Walt. "I'm sure you've had more important things to talk about. No doubt graver things as well."

Sarah narrows her eyes, and Summerfield wonders if Walt has reminded her of some graver thing. But she says, "Please . . . do tell me the name of that beautiful melody I heard you humming."

Walt turns to Jeff. "What was it, Jeff, do you know?"

Jeff rolls his eyes upward, as if Walt asks him this question a hundred times a day. "Donizetti," he says, flatly.

"Ah, yes," says Walt. "'Spirto Gentil,' that's it."

"Well, I found it haunting," says Sarah. "I've heard about your work in the hospitals. How admirable you are!"

"Thank you, dear," says Walt, "but I assure you, I've received much more than I've given."

"It's true," says Jeff. "He 'received' his near-death, for one thing. You should've seen him when he first got home."

"I only needed a rest," says Walt, to Sarah. "Jeff exaggerates . . . a family weakness."

Sarah casts her eyes about the room and says, "Has no one offered you any refreshment?"

Walt points to two empty glasses on the gaming table. "Your Mrs. Bannister brought us what we wanted most," he says. "Some of your delicious, pure clean water."

"If our water's delicious and pure clean," says Sarah, "I believe we have your brother to thank." Turning to Jeff, she adds, "Thomas has told me about your engineering . . . in the water office."

Jeff, obviously pleased, says, "Oh, not at all . . . my contributions are flimsy at best."

"There, you see it again," says Walt. "Exaggeration in the form of false modesty."

"In any case," says Sarah, "I thank you for our good water." To Walt, she adds, "And I thank you for helping my brother home . . . *and* for helping him recover from his own malaria. I'm fully aware that not everyone survives it."

"Malaria?" says Jeff, to Walt. "I thought you told me—"

"Your brother had some first-rate doctors," says Walt quickly, glancing first at Summerfield and then, differently, at Jeff.

A short silence occurs, and then Jeff, possibly sensing that he has somehow misspoken, says, "Well, I must be off. I've got my long list. Walt, I'll be back for you within the hour."

Sarah offers to help Jeff locate his hat and then sees him to the door.

Left alone with Walt, Summerfield finds in Walt's eyes a gaze of understanding that conjures the days of his own muteness—when meeting Walt's eye was everything. Walt comes forward and gives him a deeper embrace than he first did while Jeff was present. He kisses him briefly on the lips and says, "Darling boy, here you are."

They hear the sound of Sarah's laughter in the hallway, and Walt says, "I wonder if we might sit."

"Of course," says Summerfield. "I've kept you standing all this time."

He guides Walt to one end of the sofa and relieves him of his cane. He takes a seat at the opposite end of the sofa, where he places the silver handle of Walt's cane against his shoulder, like a firearm, and pretends to shoot at the parlor windows.

When Sarah returns to the room seconds later, Walt is still laughing. She sits on the ottoman near him and says, "Are you sure you wouldn't like some tea or lemonade or . . . more of our delicious water?"

Walt heaves a great sigh and removes his hat, laying it down beside him on the sofa. "No, thank you, my dear," he says. "I'm quite content."

He reaches for her hand, which she gives him, and he holds it in both his own. "This friend of Jeff's," he says, "this Gilfinian . . . he's a lucky man."

She withdraws her hand and says, with surprising seriousness, "Not nearly as lucky as you might assume."

As if she means to enlist his support, she looks—for the first time directly—at Summerfield, who cannot think what to say. In the next moment, he finds Walt looking at him, too, with a similar and bewildering expectation.

At last, he says, "Of course Gilfinian's lucky . . . very lucky. I would say lucky's exactly what he is."

He believes she almost smiles—subtly, fleetingly—and then she says, "I think Summerfield's been in his room reading Mr. Emerson the last several days. It's making him abstract."

"I hope that's all it makes him," says Walt. "It's the least of the dangers in reading Mr. Emerson."

"Yes, I agree," Sarah says.

Summerfield—who cannot discern the substance of what it is she agrees with, and who feels the slightest bit colluded against—says, "I'm afraid I don't know what either of you mean."

"Oh, don't worry," says Walt, waving a hand dismissively, "I don't know what I mean either." To Sarah he says, "Do you know what *you* mean?"

She laughs and says, "No, I don't, actually. I almost never do."

Bantering, thinks Summerfield, *silly flirtation.*

"It's a difficult business," says Walt. "Everything's so persistently illusive, don't you find?"

"Very," says Sarah, and they laugh together.

She turns to Summerfield and says, gaily, "Summerfield, darling . . . when you say or do a thing, do you always know exactly what you mean?"

He supposes it's his face—either serious or stony, he can't tell which—that causes her to fall so abruptly silent and to blush. Rashly, she has quit the brittle shell and taken up this clever giddy role, brimming with innuendo, and, in the process, fallen short of her own values. For his own part, Summerfield thinks perhaps he's simply losing his bearings, that after days of solitude, the motion of society is too much for him; he thinks of his father's ballroom polka, the music growing faster, the unknowable men (capable of anything) ending in a heap. He recalls how happy it made him when he first learned, only a few minutes before, that Walt had stopped by, and as if to steady himself, he says, "You look better than when I last saw you, Walt. How are you coming along?"

Walt's eyes cloud over with tears. "I was well enough today for my first outing in Jeff's cab," he says. "I'd hoped for some sunshine, but we may get some yet. You see . . . my very first outing, and I came to you, dear boy. How are *you* coming along?"

Summerfield can't think why he says what he says next, except that it's what occurred to him: "I met a man in the Wilderness who reminded me of my father."

Walt nods and then smiles sadly at Sarah, who returns the same sad smile and looks into her lap.

"Our father, I should say," says Summerfield, "mine and Sarah's . . . a man named Phipps . . . just about Papa's age . . . the age Papa would be now. Had his coloring, too, and a similar-sounding voice. When the rebels flanked us on two sides, broke us apart and beset us . . . I took cover with him in the limbs of a fallen tree. We waited there at the edge of a small clearing in the woods. A Confederate boy . . . about twelve or thirteen years old . . . soon walked into the clearing . . . and this man who reminded me of our father shot and killed him, asking God's forgiveness. Of course we were quickly discovered, and Mr. Phipps left me . . . took off running into the thicket. He knew he would likely be shot or captured, but he meant to draw the rebels away from me. He was willing to risk his own life to save mine . . . yet, only the moment before, he had shot and killed a young boy."

After a pause, Walt says, "This is what you meant at the hospital . . . when you told Captain Gracie that it was sometimes hard to tell right from wrong."

He's not at all sure that's what he meant then—nor can he clearly recall the interview with Captain Gracie—but now that Walt says it, it seems true, and so he nods.

"The whole war's like that, isn't it," says Walt. "Everything about it."

Summerfield nods again and says, "Our colonel told us he knew our side would win because he'd seen it portended in the heavens. He'd watched one afternoon, after a storm, as the gray clouds scattered and gave way to blue sky."

Sarah looks at him perplexed, so he says, "Because of the color of our uniforms . . . he took it as an omen."

Walt chuckles. "There was a bit of wisdom circulating around Washington recently, before we left," he says. "I heard it three different times, in three different places, from three different men: that in the war, God could not be on both sides at once. I never expressed my doubts on the subject, but I did wonder . . . maybe that's precisely who God is."

"If you're right in what you say," says Sarah, "then . . . just as we were taught in Sunday school . . . we're surely made in his likeness. I've certainly felt myself on two sides of a thing at once."

"Yes," says Walt, "but we say we're of 'two minds.' We say of ourselves that we are 'torn.' Maybe God's supremacy lies in his capacity to be thoroughly of one mind, entirely on both sides of a conflict at once, and not the least bit torn."

Now Walt leans forward and says, "Summerfield, my friend."

He waits for Summerfield to meet his eye.

"Summerfield, my friend," he repeats, a medium, summoning a reluctant spirit.

When Summerfield does meet his eye, he sees Walt as he first encountered him: a solicitous, gray-haired, gray-bearded old man;

perpetually flushed; pink around the eyes; sympathetic to the point of sometimes seeming telepathic; a sunny veneer cloaking a private sorrow.

"All of us have more than one side to us," says Walt. "And sometimes these sides oppose one another. There's no thoughtful person who doesn't find within himself both friends and enemies. I don't know if my saying this to you is a comfort or not. Please tell me what you have to say about it."

Summerfield is silent but soon finds himself shaking his head as he tries to ponder Walt's remarks. He believes they cut to the heart of the matter, but he cannot quite bring himself wholly into the room after having allowed himself to slip back into the Wilderness—a consequence his instincts have warned against.

After another moment, Sarah stands and says, "I'm going to fetch us some lemonade after all," and leaves hurriedly through the dining room.

Walt says, "She's so lovely . . . and I've upset her. I didn't mean to."

Summerfield still says nothing, and so, after another pause, Walt whispers, "You told her you had malaria."

Summerfield nods and then looks toward the gray windows. "I might take a stroll," he says. "Get some air."

"What, you mean now?"

"Only for a few minutes," he says. "To the river and back."

Walt looks puzzled, but then soon nods slowly. "I think I understand," he says. "You mean to leave me alone with her."

"If you don't mind," says Summerfield. "You see, I haven't been able to . . . of course I have my voice . . . but I haven't been able really to talk."

"And you want me to explain you to her," says Walt.

Summerfield gazes down at Walt's cane for a moment, which rests at an angle against the sofa cushion between them; keeping his head lowered, he reaches for the cane and passes it handle first to Walt. "If you don't mind," he repeats softly.

Walt plants the tip of the cane on the floor, puts both hands atop the handle, and rocks it in a little circle round and round. He knits his brow, exaggeratedly, and draws his mouth into a straight line, considering hard. At last—world-weary, a belle at a ball who has been too often asked to dance—he shrugs his shoulders and says, "I don't mind."

As Summerfield reaches the hall door, Walt adds, "But walk swiftly, will you? This won't take me very long."

AT THE FOOT of Remsen Street, he can see, looking southward, even above the trees of the private gardens, the tops of the grain silos at the Atlantic Docks. And before him spreads the panorama of the river and Buttermilk Channel, the stiff fringe of piers on Manhattan Island, the ribbonlike forests of ship masts on both shores (every kind of vessel docked), the tiers and casements of Fort Columbus and Castle Williams, and the blue-gray water, turbulent with currents, wind, crossings, and industry: clipper ships, whaleboats under oars, passenger ferries and wherries, lumps laden with anchors and chains, a handsome ketch in the foreground with a green star on its mizzen sail. In the distance, both north and south, a haze rises off the horizon, more violet than the water. On each side of the river, the tall chimneys of foundries and distilleries and the steeples of churches pierce the air, in which, near and far, seagulls inscribe their circles small and large, low and high, wings unmoving. An array of white parasols on the open stern deck of a ferryboat looks like flowers, a floating garden. All about, miniature people fish, boat, and swim; boys jump from and climb onto piers; antlike troops on Governors Island drill near a line of toy cannons; flags and pennants dot the spectacle with a variety of color; barges powered by a steam-tug slowly move their grain cargo toward the Narrows; a breeze rushes up the neat escarpment, carrying the scents of the river; and he thinks the scene is like a smart contraption with thousands of moving parts, enormous in size and complexity, and will continue long after he and everyone now alive has rotted back into the earth. He knows the bowels of Castle Williams hold Confederate prisoners, some of whom will die never having seen their loved ones again, others, luckier, exchanged for Union captives. This war will end, other wars will flare up to claim their own rosters of the dead, and the myriad of chimneys, like brick piles driven into and soaring out of concrete, will go on belching fumes, silver smoke, and soot into the skies of new centuries. Pilots will pilot now-unknown crafts driven by now-unknown sources of power. At the Navy Yard, faster, stronger, more lethal war vessels will be conceived, built, and repaired. Wheels, brighter and sharper, will turn at unimaginable new purposes, pipes pump unimaginable vapors into and out of the boroughs, ship hulls rock with unimaginable stuff, storehouses store unimaginable wares. How, he wonders, could such a vision—laid out in splendor, implying so certain a succession, so certain a permanence—appear so aimless, its players and purveyors damned to make old mistakes in new ways? The answer, he understands, resides in his wretched state of mind, but he cannot seem to dismiss the outward truth of it. Numerous couples and parties of family or friends arrive at the foot of the street, linger-ing for a while where he lingers, viewing with awe what he views, departing before he departs; he can hear them talking to one another, a frivolous-sounding murmur that signals the stupidity of everything they have to say. To his right and just behind him, a man sits on the lower steps of a stoop and has been watching him. Now, apparently, he has decided to approach, and Summerfield steels himself for what-ever bland or vexing business is in store. The man, small and drawn down by poor posture, comes and stands next to him; by way of intro-ducing himself into his company, he lights a cigar, and Summerfield only hopes, hopes and prays, he won't want to talk of the war.

"Have you heard?" the man soon says, touching his fingers to the brim of his hat. "Rebel troops moved into Maryland yesterday. They can't be far from the capital now, and most of the Federals who would otherwise defend Washington have already been sent down Rich-mond way."

Summerfield turns and looks into the man's face, a splotched, swol-len, weather-beaten visage, lined by too many years and too many brands of struggle; everything about him suggests that he's alone in the world and lonely, the fabric of his suit shiny and worn, his shirt collar soiled yellow, a smattering of gray in his whiskers—perhaps a farmer or mechanic in his Sunday clothes, come to the city for the sights, *these* sights, the spectacle, the sweep, the great dubious prospect. The man's news is exactly the wrong kind and awakens a vague fear inside Summerfield's belly. He returns his attention to the vista and notices high overhead a white disk behind the clouds, the sun on the brink of burning through. Something about the man's tone suggested that his report didn't spring from the usual vein of "war excitement" but that he wanted to relieve himself of a matter that really troubled him—and so Summerfield says, "Is there somebody . . . that is . . . do you have someone in harm's way?"

The man presses his lips together and looks down at his shoes. "Not anymore I don't," he says. "Already lost both my boys."

"I'm sorry," Summerfield says.

"I'm glad their mother didn't live to see it," he says. "I have to admit I wish the same for myself more days than I care to count."

After a pause, the man says, "Did you buy your way out?"

Because Summerfield doesn't answer at once, the man adds, "It's fine by me if you did. Believe me, I would've made no bones of it for my boys if I'd had the money."

Summerfield, who cannot think how to begin to explain his situation to the man, only continues to gaze at the busy sparkling channel below. How can he explore with a stranger this limbo of invisible wounds, a drunken discharge on the battlefield with no corroborative document, the influence of friends in influential positions? He is mustered out, to be sure, and has been assured there's nothing to worry about, but who knows how long he must wait for the proper forms and signatures? There is, after all, still a war to fight, a war to win.

"That's okay," says the man, evidently taking Summerfield's silence as consent. "I don't blame you a bit. My priest tells me I should be proud, and I guess I'm fairly up to the hub with pride . . . but I ask you . . . what's that next to the flesh and blood of your own living breathing sons, brought into the world and raised up on love? A pretty sorry swap, if you ask me."

"Yes, it is," says Summerfield, and the man says, "Damn right it is."

After a minute more, Summerfield apologizes and says he's expected at home and has already stayed too long. He shakes the man's hand and then takes his leave.

A few paces up Remsen Street he glances back: the man has moved alongside a nearby couple, is likely about to repeat the news of the rebel invasion of Maryland.

As he turns the corner, he can see, from a distance of two streets, a carriage in front of the house, Jeff already aboard, and Walt and Sarah standing at the top of the stoop. Jeff spots him from the same distance, points for the benefit of the two others, and then waves.

Just before Summerfield arrives at the steps, he sees Sarah kiss Walt on each cheek; she says good-bye and goes into the house, closing the door behind her.

"I'm sorry," says Summerfield. "I stayed gone too long."

Walt does not respond but makes his way, visibly fatigued, to the bottom step and onto the pavement. He tugs down the floppy brim of his hat, as if to make it tighter for the ride, and then, reaching into a side pocket of his coat, he says, "I've been keeping this for you."

He passes into Summerfield's hands an amber-colored base ball and adds, "Bachelors twenty-four, Twighoppers twenty-one."

Summerfield—moved by the sight of the ball, and moved by Walt's keeping and delivering it—thanks him. He brings it to his nose and smells a mix of grass, dirt, and horsehide. As he and Walt embrace, he whispers, "Walt . . . Walt, what am I to do?"

Walt releases him and smiles thoughtfully but only moves forward a few steps and gives Jeff's blood-bay horse a couple of pats on the neck. When he comes back to Summerfield's side, he says, "Give me a hand up, will you?"

Summerfield helps him aboard the carriage, which squeaks with the new weight. The horse lifts a front foot and clops it down again. Once settled next to Jeff, Walt leans toward Summerfield and says, "I'm not a doctor, only a poet and a soldier's missionary. But I'm confident the best of physicians would approve my prescription for you: go and play base ball, dear boy. It's what you were created to do. Go and play base ball."

Jeff tips his hat to Summerfield and then clucks with his tongue and calls, "Hup-hup!"

Summerfield watches the carriage roll down the street, scattering half a dozen panic-stricken chickens. The instant the carriage rounds the corner and disappears from view, the sun breaks through the clouds, casting shadows and blazing up the windows across the way.

Inside the house, Mrs. B's cooking aromas have pervaded the hall. He opens the parlor door, hoping to find Sarah, but the room is empty. He starts up the stairs, hugely let down that, after Walt's visit, she has only returned to her room, only returned to how things have been for the last six days. But on the landing, as he passes the library door, he hears her call out, "I'm in here."

She sits in the window seat amid the pillows and lacy bobbing shadows. "I didn't know you'd kept such illustrious company at the hospital," she says. "What an interesting and peculiar fellow! Is that a base ball in your hand?"

"From a match we had at Brandy Station," he answers. "When I landed at the hospital, it was about all I still had with me . . . it and the book you'd sent, the Dickens."

He puts the ball into his own coat pocket and then moves to his father's wing chair, which he turns toward Sarah, and sits down. From somewhere among the folds of her dress, she produces a fan and opens it, but only studies the painting on the silk skin—a painting of people by a lake playing music. He recognizes the fan as one of their mother's favorites and recalls his being fascinated by it as a boy: a woman in the painting also holds a fan, which has a painting of people by a lake playing music.

Sarah turns it toward him and says, "Remember this?"

He can see that whatever Walt said to her, she has been softened by it.

"I do," he says. "Tell me . . . what did you and Walt talk about?"

She closes the fan, lays it aside, takes a deep breath, and exhales. "He swore me to secrecy and told me his true feelings about Mr. Emerson," she says.

"Was that all?" he asks.

"No," she says, "he talked about Washington and the hospitals . . . Captain Gracie and Dr. Bliss."

She stands and goes to the little table behind Summerfield's chair. When he turns round, he sees that she has taken a newspaper from the table and is now unfolding the leaves and spreading them flat on the carpet next to the desk. As she does this, she says, "And he talked at some length about the curative effects of love. He said love's like truth, that no matter what form it takes, no matter how haplessly it's expressed, one must try to see to the heart of it and forgive any of the ugly bits."

She moves to the desk now and lifts the straight-backed chair, which she carries to the middle of the large square she has made on the floor with newspaper.

"Did he say anything specifically about me?" Summerfield asks.

She pauses, as if to think, still holding the chair up by the arms. "Oh, yes," she says. "He told me you'd lost your voice and then found it again. He said your temporary muteness was the most beautiful silence he'd ever heard."

She puts down the chair now. "And," she says, "he said I should cut your hair."

She turns again and takes from the desktop a scissors and a white-horn comb Summerfield recognizes from his father's dressing table. She waves these at him and says, "Come, sit, please, and no argument."

Once he's seated in the chair, facing the library windows, she begins to work, and he experiences the covert pleasure of yielding to her. He recalls coming home after base ball some years ago, a tender purple knot on his forehead where he'd got smacked by a wayward bat, and yielding then to her applications of a cold wet cloth.

After a minute, he says, "Sarah . . . about last Monday—"

But she hushes him.

"We don't have to talk about it," she says. "Of course you're right in what you've said about Thomas and me. I'm not sure what we'll do. Unfortunately, we don't have the advantage of a clean break . . . though I shouldn't be surprised if he asks me to find another school."

Summerfield brushes a shockingly long strand of hair from his lap.

"Are you very disappointed?" he asks.

"Yes," she answers, "I am. But I've learned a thing or two about disappointment, and I think I'll be all right. I might have been all right, too, if you hadn't come home and I'd spent my life married to Thomas. He's a decent man. We would have had some children, and when they grew old enough I would have told them about their wonderful uncle, whom they would never know. I would have told them about their sweet grandparents, whom they would never know. Thomas would make a good father . . . and I would do my very best not to harm any of them with my infinite sadness. But now . . . as things are . . . I must wait for something better. As you've mentioned, it's what Mommy would want me to do. And who knows what will happen? We can't foresee the future."

"No," he says. "But I wonder if the future can see us?"

She leans down to look into his face. "Whatever do you mean?"

He shrugs his shoulders. "I don't know what I mean," he says, and this makes her laugh.

She goes back to work with the comb and the scissors, and after another minute, she says, "But I'll always be your sister, my own Summerfield. And I don't intend ever to desert you."

The mystery of change progresses within him: having her for a sister, knowing she'll not desert him, seem more than enough. Careful not to move his head, he casts his eyes down to the newspaper on the floor, now strewn with long black tresses in the shape of sickles, C's, arches, X's, and U's. Near the middle of one column of print, he can read the bold words SPORTS AND PASTIMES.

"And I shall never desert you," he says. "Not ever again."

As HAYES GOES to the bat in the first inning and walks the short distance from the players' benches to the home base, the hundreds of spectators greet him with applause and cheers, an eager, amiable welcome-back. He sees, within the shade of the ball grounds' big wooden shed, a wild fluttering of ladies' handkerchiefs and a similar exuberant waving of arms and hats on the banks east and north outside the fences. It is a warm afternoon, late in July, and yesterday's storm has left a few soggy spots on the grounds. A steady but not overly stiff breeze keeps the Union flags fluttering above the roof of the shed and likewise the several long colorful pennants atop the pagoda deep in the center field. Something about the unceasing motion of the flags and pennants, in combination with the noise of the crowd, feels unexpectedly worrisome to Hayes, as if they originate from hidden causes. And there's an odd glow in the western sky—a gold glimmering inside the cavernous multitude of fair-weather clouds that have left only a few blue patches visible.

Naturally, Hayes thinks himself rusty, but as a few practices have shown over the past two weeks, he fits back into the club well enough—the Eckford's nine are altogether rusty. He is fifth in the order—the Eckford Club going first to the bat in the match against the Newarkers' pitcher Buckley—and comes to the home base with two runners on the bases and two outs in the inning. The Eckfords' second baseman, Wool (first in the order), made a good hit to the right field and gained the first base. Following him, the catcher, Manolt, went out on strikes after a frustrating time made tedious by umpire O'Brien's failure to observe the sixth rule, allowing Buckley extreme latitude and refusing to call balls on a profusion of unfair deliveries. Next came first baseman Reach, who sent a rocket into the center field left of the pagoda, gaining for himself the second base and giving Wool his third.

Fisher, the Eckfords' short stop, came to the bat next. The first pitch from Buckley was a passed ball, and Wool seized the opportunity to run in; but the Newarkers' catcher retrieved the stray quickly and, together with the third baseman, caught Wool between the bases; they exchanged the ball well, back and forth, narrowing the distance between themselves and closing in on Wool and, at last, colliding with the catcher and tumbling over him, Wool was put out. (Riotous noise from the crowds.) During this lively affair, Reach was able to gain the third base for himself. Then, with the scorers recording the second out in the inning, Fisher batted a ball on the ground to his Jersey counterpart at the short stop position, who threw it to his own catcher, preventing Reach from going in but also allowing Fisher to gain the first base.

Now, with Reach on the third base and Fisher on the first, Hayes braces the bat for a moment between his legs and adjusts the brim of his cap. He bends down and takes some dirt in one hand, rubs his palms together, and wipes the residue on his ball-suit trousers. He feels strong in his arms, the bat unusually light. He watches the first ball from Buckley, which rides up to the level of his chin. The second one comes in right where he wants it, and he strikes.

There's no doubt in his mind, no question of any kind. There's only striking the ball, less a thing done than a thing surrendered to, body and soul. He can tell in an instant, he's absolutely sure—from the location of the pitch, from how clearly he has seen it, from the ease and authority of his swing, from the deep resonant pop of the ball on the wood—that he has knocked it out of sight, that he has hit a home run, over the fence in left field.

An explosion of cheers from all directions confirms it, and he drops the bat and starts down the path toward the first base. As he rounds the corner and trots along the path between first and second, he sees Reach and Fisher each go in. Then that gold glimmering in the western sky catches his eye.

He has seen something like it before, but redder, and bound by darkness.

Carefully he'd slid from between Swift and Rosamel where they slept together on the ground; he'd gathered his gear and silently stolen into the woods to find his bunkmate, the slain Leggett. The ringing in his ears, the day's battle echo, had hardened to a yellow hiss. Some distance into the thicket, where a patch of ground still blazed, the flames suddenly leaped up a braid of vines and ignited the dead tree from which they dangled. The column of fire illumined the tangled forest, and at that same moment Hayes stumbled into a trench near a heap of dead soldiers. At the bottom of the heap a single pair of still-open eyes, rendered shiny by the flames, looked back at him. A rabbit darted into the trench and froze, trembling, and then scampered into the night. Hayes's hands began to shake as he crawled out of the trench and deeper into the thicket. Soon he climbed over a dead horse, cold the dew-damp coat, and down into a shallow ravine. He passed through bristling shrubs, strewn blankets, weapons, and soldiers, some asleep, others dead. He felt guided by instinct, as he'd felt guided all day, and presently he came to the spot where earlier (so long ago) he'd seen Leggett felled by a tempest of musket balls. One had caught him in the mouth and exited at the back of his neck. Jets of blood pulsed from the wound into the earth, and Hayes pressed his hand there, trying in vain to stanch the flow. He'd had no choice then but to leave Leggett and strive to outlast the day's battle. Now, finding the spot again, finding Leggett's body right where he'd left it, he gazed for a moment into the vacant eyes and then looked around for a blanket.

He brought two back to the body, spread one of them flat on the ground, rolled Leggett onto it, and covered him with the other, leaving only a portion of the blackened, mutilated face and one of Leggett's hands exposed. Again he gazed into the eyes, observing how nothing of the man abided there. He touched Leggett's hand, the lifeless cold of the flesh. A moderate breeze carried whiffs of campfires and burnt straw and a fragrance more raw, the scent of cooling night air. Soon he got to work with his own hands, digging a channel alongside Leggett's body. As he worked he heard a distant rumble of artillery from the direction of the Catharpin Road and saw that the sky in that region glowed red above and behind the trees. When the channel was long and deep enough, he moved around to Leggett's other side, where he sat on the ground.

He held his chin in his hands and the night passed like a dark and slow-turning wheel: the rumble of artillery faded, as did the glow in the western sky; stars advanced glacially overhead and disappeared from view as new ones rose at the canopy's eastern edge; and soon all was silent. He never spoke a word, nor whispered one. At first light, some minutes before the bugles sounded through the woods, he wrapped the blankets tight about Leggett, tucking them over the head and under the feet. Then, at last, he rolled his friend into the crude shoal grave, covered him with dirt and leaves and pine straw . . .

A world without time, of smoke and chaos, strange voids, the obliterative din of musketry, fountains of flame and blood. An errant shell rolled into a hollow and bumped silent against the trunk of a hazel bush. On the Orange Plank Road, a clatter of ambulance wagons, the neighing and snorting of horses and mules . . .

A butterfly landed next to a tiny pool of water in Billy Swift's palm as he slept naked on the boulder by the spring. He was underage, only sixteen; now that he'd had an ample taste of war, he knew it wasn't for him, he'd been rash to volunteer under false terms, made a bad mistake. He wanted to escape the Wilderness, get himself home to New York, and play ball, work to improve his batting and fielding— and Hayes had deterred him, persuaded him to see the folly of his muddled thinking. Bullied him back to walls of fire and rolling masses of pine-tar smoke and deafening artillery, slaughtered horses, clanging plunging swords and bayonets, muskets for cudgels, night for day, death-wails, and the sweet stench of burnt wool and human hair. In the charred slashing, Billy reached for Hayes, and when Hayes took the boy's hand, the flesh slipped off the bone. Swift's cartridge belt detonated, *pop pop pop pop pop* . . .

He begged Hayes to shoot him, and so Hayes did, in the side of the head, put a ball into his brain. The day before, Swift had proposed the North and South settle their differences with a good match of base ball.

Down near the third base, Hayes sees a colorfully clad organ-grinder, and Walt, giving the slight man alms—surely a trick of the mind, as when the dead soldiers on the Wilderness floor rose up in unison and crawled a few feet forward. He hears Sarah's voice—she says something about the streetlamps . . . she doesn't like them, how they make quivering shadows on the windows and ceiling. He strives to imagine a future for himself, a province of organ-grinders and alms, music and charity, streetlamps and quivering shadows, progress and misgivings—and it all seems utterly impossible. He's trying to peer too deeply, he thinks, and so he envisions himself as he might appear later this very day, after the match is over: he'll go and find a young boy named Valentine Swift, who resides somewhere in Kings County; he'll befriend the family and tell them what he knows of their lost son Billy; sparing them the horrors, he'll tell them Billy died bravely on the battlefield, a good death, conscious, accepting the inevitable end, and begging for the moment to come hurriedly, which indeed it did; he'll tell the young boy how Billy had spoken of him fondly and relayed his talent for base ball; he'll invite the boy to a match, to a practice, and, if he'll allow it, give him some lessons.

Valentine Swift, the proximate future, what he can see so far.

He turns the corner at the third base, gulping for air, as if his lungs have rejected their appointed task and mean to undo him. He can see his club mates, Reach and Fisher, who have waited at the home base all this very long time to greet him . . . but of course he's not quite who they think he is.

The noise of the crowd is like the sound of the ocean, storm-whetted swells breaking on rocks. When he gets all the way in, he drops to his hands and knees, humped over the base. Now, astonished, he recognizes the convulsions in his chest as weeping. The whole place (it seems to him, all of Williamsburgh) falls sharply silent—the ball players, the spectators, the ladies in the shed, even the rowdies on the banks outside the enclosure—and he recalls Dr. Speck's saying, at the hospital, ". . . you are still the exceptional young man who can hush the crowd at the Union Grounds."

He has hushed them, and hushed them good. The portly Mr. O'Brien—well known as maddeningly variable at the umpire's station—is first to come over, leaving his folding stool and taking off his top hat. He crouches next to Hayes and lays a hand on Hayes's back but says not a word. Next come Reach and Fisher, and next the Jersey catcher, and the pitcher, Buckley. Now, one by one, men from each club approach the home base and gather round him—those innermost stretching down a hand to touch him. Soon the cluster of ball players fully sheathes him, and he cannot seem to stop himself from weeping, though he's trying his best to do it quietly. He'd not wept when his parents failed to return from Ireland, for that would have been getting off on the wrong foot—if he and his sister were to go it alone, after all, without father or mother, he thought it best not to start in tears. Neither had he wept on the battlefield in Virginia, nor lost in the forest, nor wept in the hospital or at Hicks Street.

He's back too soon, says one man softly.

He's not ready, says another.

He'll be all right, says a third.

Through a watery film, he sees a single blade of grass growing from the dirt next to the base. A black ant climbs busily to the pointed tip of it and stands on four legs, evidently scouting what might be seen from such great height. As Hayes starts to get to his feet, blossoming open the huddle of men around him, he hears a mounting propulsive thunder overhead, a roar of turbines big as houses, that peaks and fades, crossing the sky at inconceivable speed, like some formidable airship, high above the clouds.

Acknowledgments

Fiction writers are often chagrined by how characters, given any kind of a decent chance, appear to evolve on their own terms; they refuse to bend to our will and turn out very different from how we conceived them. Never have I felt so controlled by a character as I did by Walt Whitman. Just as in real life he sought to manipulate his public image—writing and publishing celebrative reviews of his own work, becoming in his late years what a poet friend of mine calls "a caretaker of his past self"—his spirit, intent on being cast in the best possible light, seemed to elude my every effort to darken him. I cannot entirely account for this. I've concluded that Whitman, to the degree that his contemporaries misunderstood him, suffered the particular loneliness of artists who find themselves ahead of their times and the particular need to compensate for it.

When Whitman first began to think of himself as providing a national voice for that wonderful, comradely experiment, the United States of America, he probably couldn't have imagined anything like the Civil War. Probably nobody could—certainly nobody could imagine what the war eventually became. The longstanding and widely accepted estimate of Civil War deaths (620,000) represented about two percent of the American population—a rate that, if applied to today's population, would yield a loss of more than six million people.

A new study by historian David Hacker, as reported in *The New York Times* in April 2012, recommends increasing those former estimates by as much as 20 percent. It's believed that the three days of combat in Virginia's Wilderness, in May 1864, produced close to thirty thousand casualties. The battle, though considered a draw, marked a turning point in the war, the beginning of Grant's Overland Campaign. I urge readers wanting to learn more about this conflict to read Gordon C. Rhea's excellent book, *The Battle of the Wilderness.*

Because so much of the historical record is available nowadays on the World Wide Web, doing the research for a novel like *Nostalgia* is easier than it once was. But I expect that bringing any small portion of history to life through the devices of fiction is about as challenging as ever. I'm indebted to a number of other writers for their thoughtful works about Whitman, baseball, nineteenth-century medicine, the war, and what's known today as post-traumatic stress syndrome: George Worthington Adams, Louisa May Alcott, Ambrose Bierce, Robert Leigh Davis, Eric T. Dean, Drew Gilpin Faust, Frederick Clark Floyd, Shelby Foote, Justin Kaplan, Jonah Lehrer, Ilona Meagher, Peter Morris, Robert Morris, Gordon C. Rhea, Robert Roper, Francis Amasa Walker, and of course, Whitman himself. Any errors of history I may have committed are entirely my own and shouldn't be construed as a reflection of these fine writers.

I also owe thanks to many good people for their help with preparing the manuscript: Steven Alexander, Clarissa Atkinson, Susan Betz, Michael Downing, Ann Eggers, Lisa Fitzgerald, Kathleen Fridella, Nancy Hausman, Jeanne Heifetz, Gail Hochman, Juris Jurjevics, Rodger Kamenetz, Paul Magid, Gordon C. Rhea, Gordon Ritter, Marcia Scott, and Nancy Rubin Stuart.

Lastly, I extend my heartfelt gratitude to my wife, writer and poet Michelle Blake, who first suggested I include Whitman in this narrative; who for more than thirty years has read every word I write before anyone else does; and who, with her equally fierce powers of love and intelligence, improves most everything she touches, including me.

A NOTE ABOUT THE AUTHOR

DENNIS MCFARLAND is the best-selling author of six previous novels: *Letter from Point Clear*, *Prince Edward*, *Singing Boy*, *A Face at the Window*, *School for the Blind*, and *The Music Room*. His short fiction has appeared in *The American Scholar*, *The New Yorker*, *Prize Stories: The O. Henry Awards*, *Best American Short Stories*, and elsewhere. He has received a fellowship from the National Endowment for the Arts and the Wallace E. Stegner Fellowship from Stanford University, where he has also taught creative writing. He lives in rural Vermont with his wife, the writer and poet Michelle Blake.

A NOTE ABOUT THE TYPE

This book was set in a version of Monotype Baskerville, the ante-
cedent of which was a typeface designed by John Baskerville (1706–
1775). Baskerville, a writing master in Birmingham, England, began
experimenting around 1750 with type design and punch cutting. His
first book, published in 1757 and set throughout in his new types, was
a Virgil in royal quarto. It was followed by other famous editions
from his press. Baskerville's types, which are distinctive and elegant
in design, were a forerunner of what we know today as the "modern"
group of typefaces.

Typeset by Scribe,
Philadelphia, Pennsylvania

Printed and bound by Berryville Graphics,
Berryville, Virginia

Designed by Cassandra J. Pappas